ONE MAN'S SHADOW

One Man's Shadow

Brad Dennison

WHEELER PUBLISHING
A part of Gale, Cengage Learning

GALE
CENGAGE Learning·

Farmington Hills, Mich • San Francisco • New York • Waterville, Maine
Meriden, Conn • Mason, Ohio • Chicago

01137 1480

LIBRARY OF CONGRESS CATALOGING-IN-PUBLICATION DATA

Names: Dennison, Brad, author.
Title: One man's shadow / by Brad Dennison.
Description: Large print edition. | Waterville, Maine : Wheeler Publishing, 2016. | © 2013 | Series: Wheeler Publishing large print western
Identifiers: LCCN 2016004963| ISBN 9781410488527 (softcover) | ISBN 1410488527 (softcover)
Subjects: LCSH: Large type books. | GSAFD: Western stories
Classification: LCC PS3604.E5866 O54 2016 | DDC 813/.6—dc23
LC record available at http://lccn.loc.gov/2016004963

Published in 2016 by arrangement with Blue Cottage Agency

Printed in the United States of America
1 2 3 4 5 6 7 20 19 18 17 16

To Donna, as always.
And to Megan and Seth,
who I would be lost without.

A NOTE FROM THE AUTHOR

In my writing, I don't usually try to depict historical events. Instead I write fiction, but I set that fiction against a historical backdrop. Hence, the town of McCabe Gap is not a real town. The valley the McCabes live in is not really there, though there are valleys like theirs sprinkled throughout the Rockies from Colorado to the Canadian border. And the towns of Bozeman and Helena and Virginia City were, and still are, very real. The Bozeman trail, which in 1879 was the primary route from Wyoming to Bozeman, plays a prominent role in this story. War between the Army and the Sioux made travel along the trail kind of precarious in the mid-1870's — this was the war that gave us Custer's Last Stand. The war ended in 1877, and after that travel along the trail was a lot more frequent until the early 1880's, when the railroad built a line from Cheyenne north into Montana, and then travel along the trail began to dwindle again.

Likewise, I don't usually have real people in my novels. Jack McCabe, Darby Yates, Nina Harding, Harlan Carter and the others, regrettably, never existed. I did make one exception, though, with a cowboy working for the Zack Johnson spread. He was born Francisco Gomez, of Portuguese descent, the son of a wheat farmer and former merchant sea captain, and who became a cowboy by choice. He was called *Coyote* by his contemporaries. He was the real deal. He was one of the best there was with a rope and was known for his bronc busting and his tracking. He brought more than one herd from the southwest to the railheads of Kansas and Wyoming, and worked spreads from Oklahoma to Montana.

In the real world, Coyote Gomez was only 15 in the summer of 1879 and was just beginning his cowboy career. It would be a few more years before his travels would take him to Montana, but I played fast and loose with history in this case so I could include him in this story. You see, he was the father of the great New York Yankees pitcher Lefty Gomez, a player I greatly admire. My passion for the Old West and baseball intersect with the life of Coyote Gomez. Though he makes only a cameo appearance in this story, his presence is my way of tipping my cap to a great ballplayer.

I would like to offer a word of thanks to

Amazon for making this great opportunity for independent writers such as myself to find an audience. I also owe a lot to my father for encouraging me to write when it would have been too easy to allow discouragement to prevail.

I owe a great debt of thanks to Kay Jordan, copy editor extraordinaire.

I would also like to thank you, the reader, for buying this novel. It was a lot of fun to research and to write, and I hope you enjoy it. Please feel free to drop me an email at *braddennisonbooks@gmail.com.*

Brad Dennison
Buford, Georgia
July, 2013

A FEW COMMENTS ON
LIFE IN THE 1800's:

This story takes place in 1879, and people spoke much differently then than they do today. They tended to say the same kinds of things, because human nature doesn't really change, but people of the 19th century spoke in a lofty, verbose way that would outdo even today's politicians. The more words you used, and the bigger they were, the more educated you were perceived to be. People also tended to try to speak with a lot of stiff sounding formality, rather than in the more casual sort of way of people today. I tried to capture the feel of all of this in the dialogue of this story, but shied away from full 19th century talk as it might have made it kind of hard to follow what the characters were saying. And it would have been a pain to write.

The game of baseball is mentioned in this story. Professional baseball was played as early as 1869. But the game Jack McCabe and his friend Darby would have seen in Boston was much different than the one played today. Gloves were for the most part not yet used in 1879. Pitching was done as an underhand toss. To eliminate a base runner, the ball would actually be thrown right at him. Ballplayers didn't wear shoes with spikes on the soles, and a typical game would see players slip-sliding around the bases, ducking a ball as it's thrown at them, with the crowd roaring with laugher. Baseball back then was a hoot, more like a keystone cops event than today's elite, athletic game. And a ballgame was a drunken, rowdy affair. Beer flowed in the stands and gambling was rampant, and fans threw objects on the field if they disliked a player or a game situation. If they disagreed with an umpire's call, they might pelt him with empty beer bottles. Players smoked cigars on the field and openly engaged umpires in fist fights. It was the perfect atmosphere for a couple of college kids like Jack and Darby who liked their whiskey and could get a little rowdy themselves.

The team they watched, the Boston Red Stockings, played in a wooden ball park that seated 6,800. A far cry from today's super stadiums made of concrete and steel, and with jumbo screens set up behind the outfield and rock music filling the air between innings. The Boston park was grand for its time, though, with two steeple-type structures standing tall behind the stands. In photos, it has an almost elegant look.

The Red Stockings underwent a series of name changes and eventually changed cities a couple of times and became today's Atlanta Braves. Today's Boston Red Sox is a different franchise that first took the field in 1901.

The fast draw, in which a man whips a gun from his holster almost faster than the eye can follow and fans a couple of quick shots with pinpoint accuracy, is one of the most iconic aspects of the legend of the American West. Unfortunately, it is just that. Legend. None of my research indicates there was a fast draw executed until Hollywood got hold of the West. When gunmen of the real West talked about a fast draw, what they were actually referring to was a smooth, fluid draw. A draw in which the pistol was cocked in mid-motion and then the arm was brought out to full extension and the trigger pulled. One smooth, continuous motion. This is the type of fast draw I show in this and other stories.

Accuracy with a pistol was a precarious thing, because those old pistols actually used black powder, and the bores weren't made with the precision of today. Shooting at a target a couple hundred yards away was the equivalent of a football Hail Mary. Hitting a target at that distance would be more luck than anything, and the bullet would be so spent it wouldn't do much damage. If a gunman of 1879 was anticipating having to shoot at something more than even a hundred feet away, he often opted for a rifle.

In this novel and in others, I try to capture the views society had toward women and minorities. Views on both were different in the 1870's than they are today, but they were also much different on the frontier than in the more civilized regions. On the frontier, as politically incorrect as it might seem today, equality was seen as something earned. Simply being a white man gave no special favors, and being a minority was not seen as a detriment. Men of the frontier learned quickly that race was not really all that relevant. Regardless of race, men were often respected based on qualities like courage, honesty and work ethic. Some sources indicate one in four cowboys was African American, and they worked alongside their white counterparts with little or no grief. They all drank at the same saloons and slept in the same bunkhouses and frolicked in the same brothels.

Racial slurs were, unfortunately, an accepted part of society until recent decades. As such, I have a couple of characters use them in this story simply for the sake of historical accuracy. Please don't assume they in any way reflect my views.

Women were highly valued, almost revered. Violence against women was extremely rare because women themselves were rare. Especially women of marrying age. In some of the more remote frontier areas, men outnumbered women by as much as 10 to 1. Even an accusation of violence against a woman could get a man lynched, and did so on more than one occasion. Women were also seen as valuable contributors to the community, every bit as valuable as men and maybe even more so. Women were allowed to vote on local issues in some frontier communities as far back as the 1870's, although the federal government didn't get its act together and pass the Nineteenth Amendment until 1920.

Fashion was very different on the frontier from the view Hollywood has. The stetson with its brim curled at the sides is something perceived as common in the 1800's, but I have looked at many photographs of cowboys and gunmen from the time period and have never seen one hat like that. In the Southwest, brims tended to be straight and crowns rounded, and they were usually called *sombreros,* even though the hat was much different than the one we usually associate today with the word *sombrero.*

People kept away from the sun as much as possible. Men didn't roll up their sleeves to work, or take off their shirt entirely as is done sometimes today. Shirts stayed on and sleeves were worn to their full extension and buttoned at the wrists. If dirt got on the sleeves, well, that's what laundry was for. Women likewise wore dresses or blouses buttoned to the neck and had sleeves down to the wrists. Low-cut necklines and sleevelessness were things well-to-do women might go with at a ball, but you never saw that sort of thing among women on the frontier.

A woman's hair in the 1800's was worn extremely long, but on the frontier it seldom if ever fell loosely. It was tied up in a bun during the day and often worn under a bonnet, the reason being to keep dust and lice out of it. By night the hair was brushed out and tied into long braids.

■ ■ ■ ■

PART ONE:
THE TRAIL

■ ■ ■ ■

1

He pulled open a wooden drawer, and scooped out a load of folded socks and handkerchiefs and dropped them into a trunk lying open on the floor. He then grabbed a stack of union suits, also neatly folded like Aunt Ginny had taught him to keep them, and they joined the socks and handkerchiefs. In the trunk beside them was a hat box.

The final item in the drawer was a leather gunbelt. The belt was rolled up, the cartridge loops filled, and in the holster was a .44 caliber Colt Peacemaker. The holster had actually been designed for an older model Colt cap and ball revolver. But on a trip to New York he had seen the Peacemaker in a gunsmith shop, and after sampling it, found the balance too incredible to resist and coughed up the cash.

The money had been left over from what Aunt Ginny had provided him to purchase text books with. He doubted she would approve of him buying a gun with it, but the gun had almost called to him. He was, after all, the son of Johnny McCabe.

His name was Jackson, after his father's grandfather, and even though Aunt Ginny called him by his full first name, everyone else called him Jack.

He had been raised on the family ranch in Montana, and could ride a horse as well as most men walked. He was not the wizard with a gun his father was, but he could clear leather quickly enough, and shoot straight and hit his target most of the time.

His fellow college boys here at Harvard knew the name Johnny McCabe. It was being spoken on a level with Wild Bill Hickok and Wyatt Earp. There were even a couple of dime novels written about him. This brought Jack a sort of fame about campus. He found himself invited to fraternity parties that he would otherwise not have been.

When he had bought the Peacemaker, he traded in the older model the holster had been originally designed for. He had originally brought the older gun with him from Montana.

Aunt Ginny had said, "Jackson, I understand why a man needs a gun out here in the West. Your father has long convinced me of the practicality of a man walking about with a gun belted to his hip. But you are going to one of the finest Ivy League schools. You will hardly need that there."

She stood barely to his shoulder in height. Mid-fifties, with spectacles perched on her nose and speech that reflected her classical education.

"I suppose not," he said. "And yet, I would somehow feel incomplete without it at least nearby."

That statement disappointed her, he knew. She was generously paying for his education with a small fortune she inherited from her father, a shipping magnate in San Francisco. She saw his departure for college as leaving behind a world of leather and guns and branding irons, and embracing a future of books, classrooms and eventually, a career in medicine. And yet he was the son of Johnny McCabe, and that would always be with him no matter where he went.

His shoulders were wide and strong from working alongside his father in the years before college, and from belonging to the college boxing team and rowing team. His shoulders had once filled out a range shirt, and now as he stood in his room at Harvard, they filled out a gray blazer.

He stood with his trunk open before him and took a long look around him at his room. The room that would soon not be his anymore.

Summer break was upon him, and he was heading home for a visit, as he often did in the summer. He had told no one, but this time he would not be coming back.

"Hey, Jacko," a voice came from the doorway behind him.

Jack recognized it immediately. Darby Yates, his roommate for the past two years. A tangle of red wavy hair on top of his head, and with freckles decorating his nose and cheeks. Darby was always quick with a laugh, and even more so once he had downed a few mugs of beer. He held a paper bag in one hand.

"Darby," Jack said, without turning around.

"That gun is so radically impressive," Darby said. "You know, I've never actually seen you strap it on. Like a cowboy, you know?"

"And you never will." Jack set it gingerly into the trunk, not dropping it like the other items. He kept the gun loaded, even here at school.

Pa had said once an unloaded gun is of little use to you. You keep it loaded and treat it as though it is loaded. Never carelessly.

"Hey, Jacko, why so dour?"

Jack shrugged. "Got a lot on my mind."

Darby stepped in and placed a hand on Jack's shoulder.

Darby said, "My friend, I wish I was going with you. I'll be playing croquet and watching polo with the family back on their estate in New York, but you'll be out west, riding the range alongside your father. The legendary gunfighter."

Jack stood a little taller than Darby, with chestnut brown hair. He wore a white shirt under his gray jacket, but contrary to campus rules, he had yanked off his tie and it was folded and tucked into a jacket pocket.

"I so envy you," Darby said. "You'll have to tell us all about it in the fall. We'll have to hoist some mugs of beer and you can tell us all about your adventures in the west. Maybe you'll get to ride on a posse. Maybe get into a gunfight with outlaws."

Jack said, "Killing a man is never a thing to be taken lightly, Darby."

"Hey, Jacko." Darby gave a light punch to Jack's shoulder. "I'm just funning with you, my man. You need to lighten your mood. I mean, the semester's over. We're free for the summer. And I, for one, need the break. I think you do, too."

Jack nodded, and forced a half-smile. "That I do."

Jack closed the trunk and latched it shut. "Well, I'd best be going. My train leaves in an hour."

"I got you a little going-away present." Darby handed the package to Jack.

Jack reached into the paper bag and pulled out a pint of Kentucky bourbon. He couldn't help but smile.

Darby said, "I'm a Scotch man myself, but I know you have a taste for it."

"I'm sure I'll find some use for it." Jack opened the trunk and tucked the bottle into one corner.

He then extended a hand to Darby.

Darby grasped the hand, but his smile faded. Darby said, "Why is it I have the feeling that this is not just 'so long for the summer?' That it's somehow really good-bye?"

Jack shrugged. "You never know what the future holds."

"Now, that's cryptic."

Jack pulled a gray tweed flat cap on over his head. "Sorry. Don't mean it to be. Take care, old friend."

"Yeah, Jack. You too."

Jack gripped the trunk by one handle and slung it over his back. Darby was amazed at the strength Jack had, handling the trunk easily. Darby had boxed and rowed alongside Jack, but he couldn't match Jack for sheer bull strength. All those muscles built cowboying on that ranch in Montana, he supposed.

Darby watched as Jack turned a corner, and then disappeared down a stairwell.

Jack had been a great drinking buddy, and more than once a passport for Darby into a fraternity party. More importantly, Jack had been a friend. They had lain awake many a night, simply talking of dreams. Of future hopes. Of women.

And yet, there had always been something

somehow mysterious about Jack McCabe. There were times when Jack would just stand silently in the window, looking off toward the western sky.

Jack was gone, down the stairs and out to hail a carriage to take him to the train station. Then, he would be off for the wilds of Montana for a summer of sitting on a horse and cowboying, or, as he called it, punching cows. Then, in the fall, Darby would be seeing his old friend again. They were both signed up for one more year in this dormitory room.

Yet, for some reason, Darby had the feeling he was never going to see his friend again. There had been something somehow final in that handshake. Something intangible, but it spoke to Darby's gut. Somehow, he knew something had just ended.

Darby went to the window and looked down at the street below, and watched his old friend toss his trunk into the back of a carriage and then climb in. The carriage moved off, the shoes of the horse clattering along the cobble stones of the street.

2

Jack stepped off the train in Cheyenne.

This town had originally been a railhead —
a place where drovers brought herds up from
Texas to meet buyers who had come west
from Chicago. Brothels and saloons had
sprung up to help relieve the drovers of their
money. Some railheads closed up, but Cheyenne had hung on and a small town had
grown and become somewhat respectable.
However, when a herd arrived, that respect-
ability went out the window as the town
reverted to its railhead roots. The saloons and
brothels swung into full action, and the drovers ran wild and mothers kept their daughters
inside behind locked doors.

Some towns like this were little more than
a single street of single-floor wooden buildings slapped together, but Cheyenne actually
had numerous streets, and many of the buildings were beginning to take on a feeling of
permanency. Peaked roofs were numerous. A
bank was housed in a brick building. The

town actually had a fully functional train station.

Jack was now four days out of Harvard. There had been train stations where he could stop and stretch his legs, but much of the trip had meant sitting and watching the world go by out the window.

However, as he stood on the platform of this train station, his trunk over his shoulder and his tweed cap pulled down over his hair, he knew this would be the last one. This was as far north as the railroad went. The rest of the journey from here to the tiny town of McCabe Gap would be by stagecoach.

He stepped off the platform and crossed the tracks and made his way across the dirt street. The sign over one doorway read, TRAIN WHISTLE SALOON. He went no further.

He stepped into a dimly lit barroom. At the far wall was a mahogany bar, and behind it was a painting of a nude woman reclining in a bed of flowers. It was still early in the afternoon and the barroom was nearly empty. A bartender was milling about, waiting for business.

Jack crossed the floor and stopped at the bar and dropped the trunk onto the floor beside him.

The bartender was maybe forty, a thin man with thinning hair but a thick mustache, and an apron was tied about his middle.

He said, "What'll you have?"

"You have bourbon?"

The bartender shook his head. "Scotch."

"That'll do."

The bartender set a glass in front of him and poured a shot. Jack leaned one elbow on the bar, and downed the whiskey in one gulp.

He had experienced his first drink in a little saloon three miles from the ranch where he had grown up. The saloon was owned by an old friend of his father, name of Hunter. Biggest man Jack had ever seen, with an even bigger smile, and a huge, bushy beard. But Jack had learned to drink at Harvard, alongside Darby.

"Want a refill?" The bartender said.

"I wouldn't refuse."

This time, Jack took the whiskey a little more easily, letting the taste fill his mouth. As he did so, he decided he was going to take a break from his journey home. He had been traveling for four days, and had probably seven more in a bouncy stagecoach ahead of him. He decided he would stay in Cheyenne for a day. Maybe even rent a horse from the livery and ride about the countryside.

He could not allow himself more than a day in Cheyenne, though. The family would be expecting him. Most every summer, once school let out, he headed home. A few weeks in the little valley in the foothills of the Montana mountains. He had to admit, though, this year he was not feeling enthusiastic about returning home. In fact, had he not already promised Aunt Ginny in a letter that he would be spending his summer at the ranch, he probably wouldn't be returning at all.

As it was, he had delayed coming home by a full month. There were some projects a couple professors needed help with. He would be home for only about six weeks this summer. Part of the reason for the delay was to help the professors. And part of it was he just didn't really want to go home.

Jack knocked back the rest of the whiskey and set the glass on the table. The bartender glanced at him and Jack nodded. The bartender strolled over and filled the glass a third time.

Two men approached the bar. One bellied up, and the other stood sideways, leaning one elbow on the bar. They each ordered a glass of whiskey. The man leaning on his elbow was unshaven, with a shirt and vest that were covered with dust. But what caught Jack's attention was he wore his gun like he knew how to use it.

Before Jack had gone east to further his education, he had learned at the school of Johnny McCabe. The school house had been under the open sky, often involving riding through the wooded ridges surrounding the little valley where his family made their home. Sometimes he and his father camped for days in those ridges.

His father's lessons had been about survival. And one of the most important tools of survival was the skill of observation, primarily noting details that were out of place, such as the way this man at the bar wore his gun. Another skill was to adequately deduce what this meant.

In this case, the man was no cowhand looking for work. He was a gunhawk.

"Howdy, boy," the man said. "You look a little out of place, here. All dressed up in your fancy duds."

"I don't want any trouble," Jack said.

The man grinned. The man had a long face, with a long, blade-like nose. His grin showed no humor.

The man said, "Didn't say I wanted trouble, boy. What makes you think I want trouble?"

He thinks I am afraid, Jack thought. *He sees the jacket and the cap, and thinks I am a dude from the east. He doesn't know who I am.*

As if the bartender were reading Jack's thoughts, he cut in and said, "Mister, don't you know who that is?"

Jack hadn't introduced himself, but he had stopped in this town every time he returned home for a visit. Word got around as to who he was.

"I don't care who he is," the man said.

"That there is the son of Johnny McCabe."

The man blinked with surprise at the bartender, then gave Jack a longer look.

The bartender said, "I wouldn't want to do nothing that might give Johnny McCabe cause to come gunnin' for me."

The man said, "If I was you, I'd mind my own business. I ain't afraid of Johnny McCabe, and I sure ain't afraid of some dude like this, who's still wet behind the ears."

The man who had come in with him said, "I don't know, Cade. I mean, Johnny McCabe. Think about it."

"I don't have to think about nothing. It's time people got to know the name Lewis Cade. It's time people started thinking about not wanting to do anything that might cause *me* to come gunnin' for them."

Jack wasn't in a good mood, and he had his father's temper. Not the best mixture.

He should not egg this man on, he knew. But the man thought he was afraid, which grated on him a little, and Jack simply found he had no patience for this man's posturing.

"I know who you are, Cade," Jack said, turning away from him, and back toward the bar. "I've heard your name. Now, get away from me."

"What'd you say to me?"

The second man said, "Cade, don't start nothing."

"Why? You afraid of him? I don't see him wearing no gun."

31

Jack said, "I don't need a gun to deal with the likes of you, Cade. Back off."

Jack knew, however, Cade was not going to back off. Jack didn't really want him to.

"Listen, boy," Cade said. "You might think I'm afraid you because of who your daddy is, but I ain't."

"I don't blame you," Jack said. "If I were you, I would be afraid of me because of who *I* am."

Cade hesitated a moment, not sure what to say.

Jack set down his glass, then turned suddenly and shot a fist out, his knuckles bouncing off of Cade's cheekbone. Cade's head rocked back and he fell backwards and into his friend.

Jack stepped away from the bar calmly, shouldering out of his jacket and flipping his cap to the floor. Cade regained his footing, and sputtered a bit while he tried to shake off the punch.

Colleges were not simply places of learning, which this would-be gunfighter was going to learn the hard way, Jack thought. They had rowing teams. Cross-country running teams. Boxing teams. Wrestling teams. All of which Jack had partaken in. And before he had gone to school, he had been trained in the school of Johnny McCabe, which also involved boxing, and wrestling tricks he had learned from the Shoshone.

Cade, his balance fully regained, his vision now clear, pulled his gun.

Jack stepped into him, grabbing Cade by the wrist of his gun hand with a grip more firm than Cade was expecting, and shot a short hook punch into the side of Cade's head. He then took Cade's wrist with both hands and drove his knee up and into it as though he were breaking a stick over his knee, and the gun fell away.

Cade swung a fist at him, putting his weight into it. A mistake, Jack knew. Using skills his father had learned from the Shoshone, how to move efficiently and use an opponent's weight and momentum against himself, Jack grabbed the arm of the incoming punch, turned, and pulled Cade over his shoulder and slammed him down hard on the barroom floor.

The Shoshone had taught Pa how to fall. Pa had taught Jake and his brother Josh. Cade, however, didn't have this knowledge and took the brunt of the fall with his back. He remained where he had fallen on the beer-stained floorboards, gasping for breath.

Jack then turned to the man who had walked in with Cade. The man held up both hands in a stopping motion.

"Hold on," he said. "I ain't involved in this."

"Yeah, you are," Jack said, and shot a right cross into the man's face.

The man was driven backward and into the

bar. Jack stepped in, following the right cross with short, uppercutting punches to the man's midsection, then rocked a hook punch into the man's head, and the man's knees buckled and he slid to the floor.

Jack picked up Cade's pistol from the floor. He turned it upright, flipped open the loading gate and rotated the cylinder, letting the cartridges fall to the bar.

"A man like Cade can't be trusted with one of these," Jack said. "He might hurt himself."

The bartender, smiling broadly, filled Jack's whiskey glass to the rim. "I seen your old man in a fist fight, once. Cleaned out the saloon. You're a chip off the old block, all right."

"Maybe," Jack said.

There had been a time when Jack would have beamed with pride to be compared to his father. Not that his father wasn't a good man. It was just that Jack realized he had had enough of living in this man's shadow.

He took the glass and downed a mouthful of whiskey. Then he returned the cap to his head and slung the jacket over one shoulder and hefted his trunk over the other, and turned and walked out into the street.

3

The marshal of Cheyenne was a man named Kincaid. Tall, with black hair and a matching mustache. A badge the shape of a shield with the name *Cheyenne* imprinted on it was pinned to his shirt, and a gun was tied down low at his right side.

Jack stood behind the marshal. His jacket was once again in place. Though most men wore a tie and jacket when they traveled, Jack had removed his tie the day he left Harvard, and had not put one on since. He wore a tie every day of the year while at school, and enough was enough. He stood with his shirt collar open.

He knew disorderly conduct like fighting in public was against the city ordinances of Cheyenne, and he wanted no trouble that might delay his trip home, so he had gone to get the marshal himself.

"You done nothing wrong," Kincaid said to Jack, as he locked the cell door. Inside the cell were Cade and his partner, sitting on the bunk. "They had it coming. I wish I was there to see it, though."

The faces of Cade and his friend were cut up and bruised. Amazing what a fist can do to a man's face, Jack McCabe thought.

The marshal said, "I've seen your old man in action a couple of times. Not so much fast on the draw, as he is smooth. Fluid. And his aim is like nothing I've ever seen. Takes a lot of nerve to hold your hand steady when you're being shot at, but your old man — you would have thought he was just target practicing. And I've seen him with his fists. You're apparently a chip off the old block, all right."

"Marshal," Jack said, "all I really want is to be left alone."

Kincaid tossed the cell keys on his desk. "That's all the great ones really want. Hickok. Doc Holliday. Zack Johnson. Your father. They don't go looking for trouble. That's for small-time scum like Cade. Challenging the great ones, looking to build up his name. Cade's lucky you weren't carrying a gun, but I doubt he's smart enough to know that.

"But be careful, son. I can't hold him here forever, and my jurisdiction ends at the last building in town. Cade's not one to forgive and forget. You should watch your back. Friendly warning, that's all."

"Thanks. I'll keep that in mind."

Jack hefted his trunk onto his shoulder and

stepped out onto the boardwalk. What he wanted was to simply get a hotel room and maybe grab a little sleep.

No, he realized. What he really wanted was to change into his Levi's and a range shirt, and find a good horse.

There was nothing as relaxing, as cleansing to his mind, as sitting on the back of a running horse and feeling the wind strike him in the face. It was like the wind washed away his troubles.

And yet, the thought of one more whiskey was kind of appealing to him at the moment. He had downed a couple of them already, one really full, but that was a good two hours ago. With his cap in place, he strode toward the saloon down by the train station.

"Back for more?" the bartender said.

"One more."

"On the house," the bartender filled the glass, and Jack set his trunk on the floor.

"Excuse me," a man said from behind him.

Oh no, Jack thought. Not again. But as he turned, he saw the man was no gunfighter.

The man was fifty-ish, and about Jack's height. A thick mustache accentuated the thinness of his face. And where his left hand might have been was once an empty sleeve.

"Can I have a word with you?" the man asked.

He was not wearing a gun, Jack noticed quickly. He was wearing no vest, which meant he was not a horseman. If you rode a horse a lot, you wore a vest to carry your wallet, and your tobacco and rolling paper if you smoked. Maybe a pocket watch. Carrying such things in your trouser pockets could be a might uncomfortable as you rode.

The man's face was deeply tanned and lined, as though he spent much time out-doors. This, along with the fact that he was not a horseman, told Jack the man was prob-ably a farmer.

"What can I do for you?" Jack asked, impa-tiently.

"You're the son of Johnny McCabe, am I correct?"

"So they say."

"Well, if you are, then I have a job proposal for you."

"Not interested in work. Now, if you'll please excuse me . . ." Jack turned back to the bar.

"If you'll just give me five minutes of your time."

Jack didn't really have the patience for this, but he decided to listen to the man out of simple courtesy. And it was not as though he had anywhere he actually had to be.

They took a table. The man said, "Let me introduce myself. My name is Abel Brewster."

"Jack McCabe."

Brewster grinned as they shook hands. "I know who you are, sir."

"Mister Brewster, I don't mean to be rude. Really, I don't. But . . ."

"Yes, I'll get to the point. When you were coming into town on the noon train, you might have noticed three covered wagons just outside of town."

Jack had absently noticed them, but thought little of it. "Yes, I suppose I did."

"One belongs to me and my family, and there are two other families traveling with us. We are bound north."

"Looking to strike it rich in the gold fields?"

Brewster chuckled. "Oh, no, Mister Mc-Cabe. We're farmers. We have no delusions of riches. We seek only an honest living, from the earth God provided for us."

"Well, there's not much farming country north of here. Lots of open grassland. What they sometimes call the high plains. Good cattle country, but a little dry for farming."

"There is good farming country further west, though, in the foothills. Or so I've heard."

Jack nodded. The land in the valley where he was raised was fertile, and in the ridges surrounding the valley. "In places, yes. It's a long haul, though, and it's pretty remote country."

"Let me cut right to the point. The trains don't go that far north yet. The only way to go is by wagon. But we don't know anything about the territory. We're looking to hire a guide."

Jack shook his head. "I'm not looking for work. I'm heading out on the stage day after tomorrow."

"Is there any way you could be persuaded? Your reputation speaks for you. We don't have much money, but I'm sure we could put together a fee that would make it worth your while."

"You mean, my father's reputation speaks for itself." Jack felt his ire rising. "People look at me and they see him. They hear the name and they make assumptions they shouldn't make. You see, Mister Brewster, I am not my father. Never have been. And my services are not for hire."

"I didn't mean any offense, son. It's just that I have three families with me, and I'm real reluctant to head out with them over country I know nothing about."

"You should have thought about that before you headed west to begin with." Jack got to his feet. "Now if you'll excuse me, I really am not feeling very sociable."

Jack strode from the saloon, trunk held on one shoulder.

He walked down the street and to a small hotel he had stayed at before. He thought he would check in, then maybe head to the livery to rent a horse.

The man at the desk said, "Oh, yes sir, we

have a room for you, Mister McCabe. Absolutely."

Jack thought the man seemed almost giddy at having the son of Johnny McCabe under his roof. It might be a selling point he could use for future customers.

Jack dropped his trunk on the floor of his room and then stretched out on the bed. Not very comfortable. It couldn't compare to his bed in the room at Harvard he had shared with Darby Yates, or his bed at the ranch. But it sure beat being jostled about on a train.

The train was a marvel of modern science, reaching speeds previously unheard of in any other method of travel. And yet, all the jostling and bouncing about did not appeal to Jack. He found trains cramped and uncomfortable. His preferred method of travel was by horseback, moving at whatever speed best suited him and the horse. And to have the open range about him and the sky overhead.

His father, in his younger years, had traveled throughout Texas by horseback. He had spent a couple years with the Texas Rangers, then returned home to Pennsylvania in the saddle. Later on, he and his brothers had ridden clear to California on horseback. Even now, when Pa went on a business trip, he did so by saddling up and riding out. Trains and stagecoaches were not for him. He often rode overland, and took established trails only when they were convenient. He seldom

41

stayed in a hotel, preferring to camp under the open sky.

Jack got to his feet and looked out his window at the street below, and decided he had enough daylight hours left to take a ride.

He dug into his trunk and found a pair of Levi's and his riding boots. Not that he had much need for them at Harvard, but it felt good having them on hand. They were reminders of what he was coming to think of as his previous life on the ranch as a young cowhand and frontiersman, learning at his father's side.

He tossed aside his jacket, and then exchanged his trousers for the stiffer fabric of his Levi's, and pulled on the tattered, tight-fitting boots. A cowhand always wants his boots tight so his foot won't slip in the boot while the boot is in the stirrup.

Many frontiersman and cowboys wore their trouser legs tucked into their boots, but some were starting to pull the cuff down over the boot, which seemed to work better with Levi's. Jack did so, and then stood in his boots, appreciating the fit of the Levi's. Now he felt more like his old self.

Rolled up in the trunk was his gunbelt. He reached for it. Hello, old friend. He unrolled it, and then buckled it on. He pulled the pistol and checked the loads, and then slapped it back into its holster.

He then pulled out the hatbox, and lifted

the cover. In it was a brown sombrero. It had rounded crown, and a flat brim that had lost some of its stiffness. He pulled the sombrero down over his temples.

This felt right, he thought. He had gotten used to wearing a flat cap, but it had never really felt natural.

He decided he wouldn't need the hatbox anymore, because he had no plans to put the sombrero in storage again. He tossed the hatbox onto the small trash can beside the bed. The box was too big for the can and bounced off and landed on the floor.

He then grabbed the tweed flat cap he had set on an end table, and decided he would need this no more, either. He had worn it when he and Darby went into Boston looking to find some fun. It had been perched on his head as he and Darby hit taverns on Boston's waterfront and downed whiskey and sometimes got into fights with the locals. But it represented a life Jack was leaving behind. He tossed it into the trash can.

With his sombrero pulled down over his temples, he left his room and headed for the livery.

Word was spreading quickly. The son of Johnny McCabe was in town.

The hostler who ran the livery, an older man with a squeaky voice and thin, white hair, almost fell over himself finding just the right horse for the son of Johnny McCabe.

"Is it true?" the man asked. "About that gunbattle at your daddy's ranch a year ago? Word's spreading like wildfire. Fifty men rode on the ranch. Sam Patterson's men. And your daddy and his men just shot the stuffin' out of all of 'em."

Aunt Ginny had told Jack about it in her most recent letter.

"That's what they say," Jack said. "I wasn't there."

"His legend just grows and grows. Yessir."

"Seems to."

The man saddled a sorrel gelding for him, and when Jack asked the cost for an afternoon, the man said, "Oh, it's on the house, sir."

Jack shook his head with bewilderment, and stepped into the saddle.

The horse was long-legged and liked to run. At the edge of town, Jack let it have its head, and the horse broke into a mile-eating gallop, its mane fluttering in the wind. Jack leaned forward to provide less wind resistance, and the brim of his hat shook in the wind. Jack found he was smiling.

Two miles later, he reined up to let the horse blow, and he stepped out of saddle and loosened the cinch.

"That felt good, didn't it?" Jack said to the horse, as though the horse could understand him.

On either side of the trail were low, grassy

hills stretching away toward the horizon, with an occasional stunted tree attempting to hang on. In the far distance was a low line of gravely looking ridges.

Jack tightened the cinch and swung back into the saddle, and they were off at a spirited trot. Jack turned the horse from the trail and over one hill.

He eventually turned the horse so they would make a wide circle about town. He thought how much he would like to simply turn the horse north and make the rest of the journey on horseback, like his father. But he dismissed the thought as whimsical.

Aunt Ginny had sent him money for the train and the stagecoach, and the family would be waiting for him in McCabe Gap. The little town in a pass outside of the valley they called home. And yet, as he brought the horse to a stop atop a low grassy rise and looked off toward the sun that was now trailing low over the western horizon, the wind from the northwest catching him in the face, he found himself longing to forget the stage and simply ride on.

He dismissed this in the face of reality and turned his horse, and soon the buildings of Cheyenne were standing in front of him in the distance, maybe a half mile away.

Between him and the town were the three covered wagons he had seen earlier, belonging to Brewster and his party. The sun, now setting, was casting a soft, rosy light against the canvas of the wagons.

Campfires were being brought to life, and people were puttering about the wagons. Oxen were grazing lazily.

Jack suddenly felt a pang of guilt over the way he had talked to Brewster earlier in the day. He had been raised by Pa and Aunt Ginny to be courteous, and to assist people when he could. He had dismissed Brewster rudely.

He gave his horse's ribs a little nudge with the heels of his boots and started toward the wagons.

A man was kneeling before a fire and adding chunks of wood to it. He looked up at the sound of the approaching rider. He had a wide, floppy black hat, and a full, dark beard gave his face a fierce look. He glared at Jack, and when Jack nodded to him, the man simply returned his attention to his fire.

I guess I had that coming, Jack thought.

At the second fire, a woman had set up a pot with some sort of stew cooking, and a coffee kettle was heating. She had a round, matronly shape and her hair was hidden by a bonnet. She glanced toward Jack, and when he touched the tip of his that to her, she gave a polite smile and nodded.

A girl was there, walking up toward the woman. Maybe Jack's age, maybe a little younger. She stepped through the tall grass with a sort of lithe grace. She glanced toward Jack, her hair also hidden by a bonnet, but in the fading light of the day, he caught the light gray color of her eyes, and a face that was gently freckled.

He found himself smiling, and again touched his hat.

She glanced shyly away and continued toward the woman at the fire.

At a campfire before the third wagon was Brewster. He looked up. "Well, Mister McCabe. I assumed I would have seen the last of you."

Jack nodded. "I would have thought so, too. I was just taking a little ride through the hills. I saw the wagons."

"Yes. If you'll excuse me, I'm building a cook fire."

Brewster returned to what he was doing, dropping to one knee, and adding chunks of wood to a fire, much as the first man.

"What'll you use for wood, once you're on the trail?" Jack said. "There aren't a whole lot of trees between here and the foothills of Montana."

"I'm sure we'll manage."

"Used to be that settlers used buffalo droppings, but now that the buffalo are gone, there's little to be used."

A woman was stepping from behind the wagon. She said, "Buffalo droppings! Sounds quite dreadful."

47

"Mildred," Brewster said, "this is Mister McCabe. The man I attempted to hire as our guide."

Jack gave a touch to the brim of his hat, "Ma'am."

She gave a nod, curtly.

Following the woman was a boy of about twelve, and a girl closer to the age of the one at the other fire. She wore no bonnet, and long dark hair fell freely, catching the wind.

Jack touched his hat to her, also.

She gave him a smile that struck him as either teasing, or daring. She said, "So, you're Jack McCabe. The son of the famous gunfighter."

The woman said, "Hush, Jessica." Then, to Jack, "Forgive our daughter, Mister McCabe. She's too brazen, sometimes."

Jack shrugged. "It takes a lot to offend me, Mrs. Brewster."

Her husband said, "That wasn't the impression I gained when we talked earlier."

"Look, Mister Brewster, I owe you an apology. I really do. It was uncalled of for me to talk to you the way I did. I just, well, I had a lot on my mind. That's all."

Brewster looked up at him from the fire. "No harm done, I guess. But at the risk of being rude myself, we have to get on with our evening chores. We want to get an early start in the morning."

"I wish you all the best," Jack said. "You

know, there aren't many who travel so far overland by wagon, these days. Used to be there were long wagon trains that made their way overland from Missouri all the way to Oregon or California, but those days are gone."

"Thanks. But we'll fare the best we can." Jack nodded.

"Mister McCabe," Brewster's wife said, "if there are no trees, and as you said, the buffalo are gone, then what is used to start fires?"

He shrugged. "Most of the travel these days is either by train or stagecoach. The Army travels through in convoys, but they often bring firewood with them. Freight wagons make the trip too, and they often bring wood with them. I suppose," he was thinking quickly, wanting to offer these people some last minute advice, "some twist grass together, into little twists maybe the size of a small piece of firewood. But grass burns quickly and not very hot."

"Thank you, Mister McCabe," Brewster said dismissively.

"If you have an extra sheet of canvas, you can sling it under the wagon and use it to carry extra firewood. It's called a possum belly."

"We'll make do," Brewster said.

The girl, Jessica, threw a smile at Jack. "It was nice meeting you, Mister McCabe."

"Likewise, Miss." He touched the brim of

his hat, and turned his horse.

He returned the horse to the livery, and then after a steak dinner at Delmonico's, a restaurant a few doors down from the hotel, he returned to his room.

Still in his Levi's and boots, he stretched out on the bed, and attempted to sleep. However, he found sleep evasive, as it often had been since he received a letter from Aunt Ginny earlier in the year.

The letter was in his trunk. When he had first read it, he had thought of crumpling it and throwing it out, but then found himself folding it and putting it in his desk. When he was packing his trunk to leave, he again thought of throwing the letter into a waste paper basket by his desk, but instead it wound up in the trunk.

He now sat up and struck a match, and brought to life a lamp standing on a small table at the side of the bed. He then dug into his trunk and found the letter.

This was it. The letter that changed his life.

He thought of maybe unfolding it. Reading it again. He had read it maybe thirty times in the past few months. But instead, he tossed the letter back to the open trunk. He blew out the lamp and started for the door.

When he was troubled, he liked to move. To walk. Better still, to ride. But to ride through the barren countryside around town at night might be foolhardy. A horse could step into a gopher hole and break a leg. So he thought he would settle for walking.

He stepped out onto the boardwalk and began to stride along. The town was dark except for some lighted windows. At the Harvard campus, and the city of Boston where Jack and Darby sometimes went for drinks, the streets were lighted with gas lamps. But not here in a small cowtown like Cheyenne.

After a time, Jack found his wanderings had taken him toward the train station, and he saw the doorway to the Train Whistle was lighted, and he thought maybe he would cut his walk short. The whiskey here was a far cry from Kentucky whiskey, but it would suffice.

He leaned one elbow on the bar, taking the glass with his left hand keeping the right free. Something his father had taught him years earlier. Keep your gunhand free. At Harvard, such a thing wasn't necessary, but here in this frontier town, as he stood in his Levi's and riding boots, with his sombrero perched atop his head and his gun once again at his side, he found his father's old lessons returning to him.

The swinging doors were suddenly pushed open, and Jack tossed a glance back. To his surprise, stepping through the doorway were Brewster and the dark bearded man from the wagons.

"Mister McCabe," Brewster said. "Thank God."

Jack was about to make a comment about the two of them being out rather late, considering they were hoping to make an early start the following morning. But he thought better of it when he saw the urgency written on Brewster's face.

"What's wrong?" Jack asked.

"It's my daughter. Jessica. She's gone."

4

"Gone?" Jack said.

"I mean," Brewster said, trying to remain calm enough to get the words out, but obviously agitated, "she's not at the wagon. We said good-night to her, and she went into the tent. But a half hour ago, when we checked on her, she wasn't there."

"Could she have decided to take a walk, or something?"

The bearded man shook his head. He stood maybe four inches taller than Jack, and had a deep baritone voice and spoke in a tight-lipped way that made it seem like he was almost sneering. "There have been men from town milling about our camp. Uninvited. They've been trying to get the attention of our daughters."

Jack said, "I saw you earlier, when I was at the camp. Didn't have a chance to introduce myself."

"Carter Harding," the man said. He extended his hand but there was no smile.

Jack shook the hand. The man's grip was strong, his hand calloused.

"Did your daughters talk with these men?" Jack asked.

"Mine did not. You might have seen her when you were at the camp today. Nina. She's about the same age as Jessica Brewster."

You don't fail to notice two girls as fine looking as they both were, Jack thought, but such a thing shouldn't be voiced to their fathers.

Brewster said, "I'm afraid our Jessica has an adventurous streak in her. And it can only lead to trouble."

Jack said, "Tell me about these men."

"Three of them," Harding said. "They wear their guns like you do."

A polite way of saying they looked like gunfighters, Jack thought. He took no offense. His father had taught him how to shoot a gun and how to wear one, and he knew what his father was.

"This is a hard town," Jack said, "with hard men."

Harding said, "It's also the only town around, and if you want to buy supplies, there's no other choice."

Harding had said nothing wrong, but there was something in the tone of his voice that sounded to Jack like the man was forcing himself to be polite. And Jack was not really in the mood for politeness himself, so he decided to dispense with it.

"You don't like me much, do you, Harding?"

"I saw the way you were looking at my daughter this afternoon. And I see the way you wear your gun. In my eyes, you're no better than those men we're talking about. But it was Brewster, here, who thought we should find you. I was opposed, but it's his daughter who is missing."

"Well, at least we got that out in the open."

"Please," Brewster said. "I just want to find my daughter. Do you have any ideas?"

"The marshal," Jack said. "I'd start there, first."

Jack wanted to be left alone, so he could have his drink while the contents of his letter from Aunt Ginny replayed themselves over in his mind one more time. But these men needed help, and they obviously felt out of place here in this town.

"Come on," Jack said. "Let's go find the marshal."

He stepped out onto the boardwalk, Brewster and Harding behind him.

A woman stood with her back pressed against the saloon wall. Beside her was a man, leaning with one hand against the wall. She wore a dress lower cut than what the farmers walking with Jack might be accustomed to — she obviously worked at the saloon and was drumming up business — and the man wore his gun low, advertising he was no cowhand.

On the boardwalk across the wide street, another man stood. Jack couldn't see him clearly in the darkness, but he saw a wide hat, and this man also had a revolver riding low at his right side. In the darkness, the end of a cigar glowed a bright orange, then faded.

"This town is quiet right now," Jack said, as they walked along. "But when a herd arrives, with drovers who've been working hard and want to play hard, this town can light right up. Two or three herds come in at once, and there'll be chaos you can't imagine."

"You speaking from experience?" Harding asked.

"I've seen a railhead or two. But I'm not into drunken debauchery, despite what you might think."

Jack almost said it would probably surprise Harding to know that he had just completed his second year of medical school at Harvard, despite his young age, but decided to let it go. Impressing Harding was at the bottom of his list of things to do. He wanted to simply find Brewster's daughter, and then maybe he could be left alone to wallow in his own troubles.

He rapped on the door of the marshal's office, hoping the marshal, or at least a deputy, would be on duty.

After a moment, a pale glow filled a window as a kerosene lamp came to life, and a latch slid aside and the door was opened.

It was Kincaid himself, squinting as people do when just awakened.

"McCabe," he said.

"Sorry to bother you, Marshal, but these men need your help."

"Come on in."

Jack stepped aside to allow Harding and Brewster access to the doorway.

Jack said, "You won't need me any further. Marshal Kincaid will help you find Jessica."

And with that, Jack returned to the saloon.

The barkeep said, "I was thinking of closing down. There's a herd coming up from Texas, and it's expected sometime next week. We'll be open almost twenty-four hours a day while the drovers are here."

"Go ahead and close," Jack said. "Let me have the bottle."

The bottle was half empty, so the barkeep said, "Just go ahead and take it. Considering the money we'll make next week, we won't miss half a bottle of whiskey."

Jack stepped out onto the boardwalk, the bottle in his left hand so he could keep his gunhand free.

He shook his head, and found himself chuckling at himself. He was twenty years old and already a college graduate who had completed his second year of medical school. He had a family who loved him, and a promising career ahead of him as a surgeon in one of the finest hospitals in New York. And yet, here he was, standing on a board-walk in a railhead with a bottle of whiskey in his hand, feeling sorry for himself.

He had been raised on his father's ranch in Montana Territory. He and his brother Josh had been taught to ride almost as soon as they could walk. By age ten, Jack was riding into the mountains with his father and Josh. He learned to track an animal, to find water when none seemed readily available. By age thirteen, he was learning how to shoot a pistol.

However, Aunt Ginny had thought it impor-tant not to neglect what she called the more civilized education. The three R's. No school was available, so she taught Jack, Josh and their sister Bree herself.

It became apparent early on, however, that Jack's mind was sharper than most. He could think quickly, and had the ability to remem-ber almost everything he read. By age six he had a reading level better than most adults. And he handled mathematical concepts with ease.

By the time Jack was nine, Aunt Ginny felt she had no more to teach him, and that for him to reach his full potential, he needed to be sent back east for formal schooling.

Pa agreed, and even though Jack wanted nothing more in the world than to be like his father, he wanted even more for his father to be proud of him.

So, at age fifteen, Jack was sent east to boarding school. Philadelphia.

He was near enough to his grandmother and his Uncle Nathan, who still lived in the farming community in the western Pennsylvania hills where Pa had been raised, that he could visit during school breaks. And he often returned to the ranch for summers.

He graduated from high school after only one year at boarding school, and then entered Harvard, majoring in biology. Aunt Ginny had seemed to think either medicine or law would be the best way for Jack to reach what she felt was his full potential. Since studying law meant countless hours studying old, dusty law books, Jack decided to pursue medicine.

He quickly became a rising star in the college world, not only because of his age, but his grade-point-average. He had started college at age sixteen and flew through the courses with ease, and had completed his second year of medical school at an age when most were in their third year of college, and was at the top of his class.

And yet he wanted none of it. All he really wanted was to ride alongside his father and Josh. To work alongside them on the ranch. To stand with them against blizzards and droughts. He wanted to go into the mountains to catch wild horses and then break them using the method Pa had learned from the Shoshones. He should have been with Pa and Josh last year when the ranch was attacked by raiders.

He never quite knew how to tell Pa or Aunt Ginny any of this. They were so proud of him and what he was accomplishing at school. Aunt Ginny was generously paying for it all. And yet, he didn't really want to be a doctor. He wanted to raise cattle. He wanted branding season and roundups. He wanted to build a home for himself the way his father had.

And he wanted to find the right girl who could stand beside him and raise children with him. When the day was done, he wanted to stand by a roaring hearth made of stones he had placed himself, with his wife beside him and his children asleep in their beds.

Instead, he was looking at life in a major city, in a major hospital. Performing work he really felt no calling for.

He once voiced this to Darby, who said, "You're insane, Jack. To even think of preferring life on a rough frontier to the future waiting for you. Why, any one of us would jump at the chance to be you."

And so, Jack began to keep his feelings to himself.

He studied hard, occasionally got drunk with Darby, and tried to focus on his future as a surgeon and not the life he wanted.

And then, he got a letter from Aunt Ginny.

The letter in the trunk in his hotel room.

"Dear Jackson," it had begun, in her flowing hand. She always called him *Jackson*. His sister, called Bree by everyone else, was *Sabrina* to Aunt Ginny.

"Dear Jackson, I have the most wonderful and incredible news to relate to you, so let me begun without preamble."

Without preamble. She not only wrote like that, she actually used words like that when she spoke.

Jack remembered the first time he read the letter. Aunt Ginny, without preamble, went into a multi-page dissertation on an event that affected the entire family. Reshaping it. She seemed oblivious to the effect it would have on Jack, but then she had no idea what he really wanted in life. But he found he could no longer simply focus on medical school and the future everyone seemed to want for him.

And now, here he stood, on a boardwalk in Wyoming, a bottle of whiskey in one hand. He decided to go back to his room. It was getting a little chilly out here.

He ambled his way across the wide, muddy street. He inserted a key into the lock in his door, and then struck a match to light the lamp on the stand by the bed.

He dropped into the bed, not bothering to remove his boots. He took a swig from the bottle, and decided maybe he had had enough

61

whiskey.

Not that he wasn't in the mood for more, but this stuff was too far removed from the Kentucky corn whiskey he liked so much, it could barely even suffice as a substitute. Darby was the Scotch man. Jack stood the bottle by the lamp.

He reclined back on the bed, when there was a knock at the door.

"McCabe?" A man called from the other side of the door. "It's Marshal Kincaid."

With a sigh, Jack got to his feet and opened the door.

"McCabe, I need your help. That girl, Brewster's daughter, may have gone and gotten herself into some real trouble."

"How is it you expect me to help? I'm not my father. I'm starting to grow tired of people thinking I am."

"You're not your father, but you've got backbone and you can handle yourself in a fight. I've got a job to do and I'm going to need some help. This town doesn't have enough of a budget to allow me to hire deputies, except when a herd arrives."

Jack nodded. "All right. What can I do?"

"I need you to come with me. I think I've found the girl. There's a group of men who have been camping outside of town. They rode in maybe five days ago. I think the girl is there. And you might have a personal interest in this. One of the men, the one she might be

62

with, is Lewis Cade."

"Do you think she went with them willingly?"

"Let's go find out."

5

The night was alive with a bonfire that rose as tall as Jessica. She stood thirty feet from it but felt the warmth against her face. She had been wearing a bonnet but now had pulled it back and was letting it hang against her neck.

A small voice in the back of her mind, the voice of common sense, was telling her maybe she shouldn't be here. These were dangerous men. And yet, her sense of adventure was the stronger of the two. She found the danger somehow intriguing.

Four men were milling about the fire, lifting bottles and chugging whiskey as though it were water from a dipper. Each of these men wore his gun like he knew how to use it. Like the McCabe boy had, who had visited the wagons earlier in the day.

One of the men, the leader, spoke with a sense of sophistication, indicating he was a man of education. Yet, he was as dangerous as any of them, she sensed. Not just in the way he wore his gun, but by a look in his eye.

A hardness in the way he smiled.

Women from the saloon in town were also here at camp, and each of the men had paired off with one of the women. The leader, who seemed to answer to the name Vic, was sitting on a large rock and staring into the flames while the saloon woman of his choice stood behind him and worked her hands into his shoulders, kneading away tension. He had a glass in his hand, and a bottle was standing on the ground before him.

Cade was here, and he was eyeing Jessica hungrily.

"I'm glad you're here," he said, walking toward her. "I will admit, though, it kind of surprised me to see you."

"I came looking for you," she said. "Life at the wagons can get a little boring. And in the morning, we're heading out for parts-unknown. Some lonely stretch of land where we'll all be putting up cabins and putting in a crop."

A couple bruises decorated Cade's face — he had apparently been in a fight. "That's not the life for you?"

"I think life is something that should be tasted, savored. Explored." She was smiling as she did so, but attempting to smile not like a country girl but as one who was willing to explore the more dangerous sides of life.

He reached a hand to her neck, and untied the bonnet she had pulled off and let it drop to the earth behind her. He then let his fingers trail against the side of her neck. She found his touch frightening, and maybe because of this, exciting.

"I hope you know what you're in for, girl," Cade said, "because there aint no backin' out now."

She decided she was definitely afraid. And yet, somehow, she found herself feeling a sense of thrill at the danger.

"What if I want to leave?" she said. "After all, I'm just an innocent, little country girl."

"You came here of your own will, and you came here for a reason."

A voice spoke from out beyond the circle of firelight. "Back away from the girl, Cade."

Jessica recognized the voice as belonging to the McCabe boy.

Cade looked off into the night, following the direction of the voice, and Jessica followed his gaze. Jack McCabe stepped into the ring of firelight.

"What's he doing here?" she asked, more to herself than to Cade.

But he heard her and said, "I guess he wants to get himself killed."

Jack said, "I don't want to fight, Cade. But that girl is leaving here. Now."

"You're mighty demanding, considering it's just you against a whole passal of us."

The man called Vic rose from where he sat by the fire. "Cade, would you introduce your guest to the rest of us?"

Kincaid stepped into the ring of firelight, from the other side of the camp. In his hands was a double barrel scatter gun.

Kincaid said, "His name's Jack McCabe. And he's not alone."

All eyes turned toward the marshal, who stood with his boots planted three feet apart, the firelight glowing red against the badge pinned to his vest. He held his shotgun ready.

"Jubal Kincaid," Vic said. "I was wondering if I would get the pleasure of actually meeting you during our stay here in your fair town."

Kincaid stared at him a moment, tossing over the possibilities of who this man was. Finally, he said, "Vic Falcone."

"The one and only. I see you've heard of me."

"Your name is on reward posters from here all the way down to the Mexican border. And I see you've heard of me."

"Your reputation precedes you."

"So, what brings you and your little band of outlaws here, to this town? Our bank is a little small to get the attention of someone like you, I would think, and there are no payrolls for you to heist."

"Just passing through. Marshal, is it? Of course, you have worked on both sides of that badge."

"The past don't matter. What matters is

what side of the badge I'm on right now."

"Indeed it does. I must ask, Marshal, what the reason for this visit is. After all, it's not like we've broken any laws, per se. At least, not in this area."

"We've come for the girl. We're returning her to her family."

Falcone turned to face Cade. "Mister Cade, I was under the impression that the young lady was here of her own volition."

"Yes sir, that's right," Cade said.

Kincaid said, "The girl is sixteen, and we're taking her out of this camp."

Falcone suddenly turned to Jack. "McCabe, did you say?"

Jack said, "What about it?"

"You're the young man who gave Mister Cade such a severe beating at the saloon, earlier in the day."

"One and the same. He had it coming."

Falcone chuckled. "Oh, I'm sure he did. But it's the name that arouses my curiosity. Are you by any chance related to Johnny McCabe? The gunfighter?"

"That name precedes me as much as Marshal Kincaid's reputation precedes him, apparently."

Falcone outright laughed. "His son, then. And a man of education, apparently. A bit different than your brothers."

"How do you know my brothers?"

"I know one of them quite well, actually.

68

And even though I was never formally introduced to your father, we exchanged shots,
maybe a year ago."

"The gun battle at the ranch."

"Indeed."

Jack knew of the battle only from what he
had read in Aunt Ginny's letter. She hadn't
gone into great detail about the gun battle.
But from what Jack surmised, a year earlier, a
band of raiders, left-overs from the War
Between the States, had ridden into the
Montana foothills, scouting ranches to strike.
Outlaws on the run were forever in need of
horses and food. They struck the ranch, and
though they were driven back, Pa was criti-
cally wounded.

Pa survived, but Jack learned about it only
months later, when he opened a letter from
Aunt Ginny.

According to her, Josh and their new-found
brother Dusty had trailed the raiders all the
way back to their hideout and confronted
them, even killing a few of them. The leader,
however, escaped.

Jack said, "You were a bit grandiose in the
way you went about that. Not trying to make
your presence a secret. You give my father
time to prepare a defense, and you're asking
to get shot out of your saddle."

Falcone bowed his head graciously, conced-
ing the point. "I do tend, at times, to be a
little more theatrical than is good for me."

"Regardless of any of that, I'm not here for revenge, or any such thing. I'm here with Marshal Kincaid to take Jessica back to her parents. Nothing else."

"I know how good Mister Kincaid is in a gunfight. As I have said, his reputation precedes him. With that scattergun, he would take down two of us before we even got a shot off. And presuming you learned your skills with a gun from your father, you would get two more of us with your pistol."

Cade said, "Come on, Mister Falcone! We can't let them just walk into our camp like this and take the girl away."

"When one is in command, Mister Cade, one must weigh all factors. Such as, what can be gained must outweigh the potential losses. I'm not sure this is the case in this instance."

Jack said, "You don't sacrifice a bishop to save a pawn."

Falcone was delighted. "Precisely! A chess man, are you?"

Jack decided to ignore the question. "It's been nice chatting with you, Vic, but we have to be going. And Jessica is coming with us."

"Indeed. She may go. You have me not in checkmate, but shall we say a stalemate?"

Kincaid said, "Miss Brewster, step away from the outlaw and walk with Mister McCabe away from the fire."

She gave Cade a final glance and then turned and walked toward Jack.

70

Falcone said, "Mister McCabe, do you play poker, possibly? That is really more my game than chess."

Jack said, "I don't like to leave things to chance. I'll stay with chess."

Jessica took her place beside Jack, and Kincaid said, "Falcone, we're going to back our way away from the fire now. Anyone goes for their guns, and they'll be doing some dying."

Falcone said, "Rest assured, you are free to go. We will not be following you. Have a good evening, and I apologize for any trouble."

Jack and Jessica backed away from the fire, and Kincaid did the same from the other side of the camp and then doubled around and joined them.

Jack and Kincaid had left the horses at a small hollow less than a quarter mile from the camp so they could move in quietly on foot. Now, as they reached the horses, Jack swung into the saddle and then pulled Jessica up behind him.

"You ever ride a horse?" he asked.

"Not really."

"Just wrap your arms around me and hang on."

And they started away.

"That was a foolish thing you did," Jack said to Jessica as they rode. "And you worried your folks and everyone back there at the wagons. Your father was scared near to death."

71

"I was in no real danger," she said. "I just wanted a little adventure. I am so incredibly tired of the dreadful monotony of the day-to-day existence my family is trapped in."

"Begging your pardon, ma'am," Kincaid said as he rode along beside them, "but you were in real danger. More than you even realize, because you don't know those kind of men."

It was well past midnight when they rode into the Brewster camp, the canvas of the covered wagons taking on a pale glow in the moonlight.

"Hello, the camp," Kincaid called out.

A fire was still going, and Brewster was standing before it, a tin cup in his hand as the riders approached.

"Mildred," Brewster called out. "Riders coming. Looks like the marshal."

Brewster's wife stepped from a tent and Harding came running from his neighboring camp.

Jack reined up and lowered Jessica to the ground, and Brewster and his wife ran to her and took her in hugs.

Brewster said, "Girl, we were worried sick. What came over you?"

Mrs. Brewster said, "I am so glad you're safe."

"I'm so sorry, Momma," Jessica said. "I don't know what I was thinking."

Yes, you do, Jack thought. *Except you were*

72

in over your head and would have been in for a seriously rude awakening if he and the marshal hadn't shown up.

Brewster went to Kincaid, offering his hand which Kincaid reached down from the saddle to shake.

Brewster said, "Thank you, Marshal. I can never thank you enough."

It wasn't lost on Jack that Brewster was completely ignoring him, as though Jack wasn't there at all. As though it hadn't been on Jack's horse that Jessica returned to them.

Kincaid said, "Just doing my job. Nothing more, nothing less. I couldn't have done it without McCabe's help."

Mildred Brewster said, "Then, thank you too, Mister McCabe."

Brewster and Harding tossed a glance at Jack. Brewster turned his gaze back to the marshal and said, "Would you like to stay for some coffee? The wife just put on a fresh pot."

"Thanks, but no. I have a town to look after. But if you don't mind, I would like to leave Mister McCabe behind. Those riders probably won't cause any trouble, but I'd like a man here, just in case."

Jack gave him a pained look, as if to say, sarcastically, *thank you very much.*

Harding gave a cautious look toward Jack. "Well, if you think that's best, Marshal."

"I do. I'll ride back out at sunrise. See you then." And he turned his horse and started away, back toward town.

Jack stepped from the saddle and loosened the cinch. A rifle would be nice, he thought, but this was the saddle he had rented from the livery earlier in the day — it was loaned to Jack so he could accompany the marshal tonight — and there was no scabbard to hold a rifle. Not that Jack had packed one in his trunk, anyway.

He helped himself to a cup of coffee while Harding returned to his own camp, and Brewster saw his wife and daughter safely to the family tent.

When Brewster returned, he said, "I really don't think it's necessary for you to remain here. We should be all right."

"Begging your pardon, Mister Brewster, but you don't know the kind of men they are. Your daughter picked a bad lot to go running off to."

"It's just that I hate for us to be any more of a burden to you than is necessary. Come sunrise, we'll be moving on, and will be fully out of your hair."

Jack shook his head. "Not the best idea. None of you have gotten any rest tonight. Staying over one more day won't hurt anything. And when you do depart, you'll be doing so with me. I'm going to ride along as your guide."

"Because of those men?"

Jack shrugged. "Maybe. Though, I doubt

they'll be any trouble. The marshal and I hurt their pride a little tonight, and I did as much earlier in the day to one of them, but their leader is wise enough to pick his battles. Pursuing a band of farmers in covered wagons doesn't provide a lot of profit, and this man is motivated by profit.

"No, I'll be accompanying you because it's the right thing to do. Because I was rude to you earlier, and I'm sorry. And I won't take any money for it, because I'm doing it partly for me, too. It's something I need to do."

"You're a man of mystery, Mister McCabe."

"So it would seem."

Brewster returned to his fire, and Jack moved to the edge of the circle of firelight.

Come morning, the stage would be leaving for Bozeman, making a detour along the way to the small community known as McCabe Gap. However, it would be leaving without him.

This was not fair to Aunt Ginny, he knew. She had paid for his train ticket and given him the money for his stage ticket. But it was something he needed to do.

He thought he would take a ride into town come morning and write a quick letter to the family to tell them he would be later than expected. He figured there would be at least three weeks of travel ahead of him, moving at the pace these wagons would make.

He hoped there would be no trouble tonight. He didn't really expect any from Vic Falcone or his men. As much as Jack had stepped on Cade's pride, Jack figured Cade was essentially a bully, and most bullies are cowards at heart, and he wouldn't dare buck Falcone. But it would be best to be prepared.

Jack slept lightly by the fire, using the rough, woolen saddle blanket as a cover against the night air, and his saddle as a pillow.

When the eastern sky began to lighten, he added more wood to the fire, and the settlers began to come out of their tents to begin their morning chores. There were a couple cows that needed to be milked and breakfast to be prepared.

Jack decided to ride into town and see what the restaurant offered for breakfast. He didn't want to cut into the supplies the settlers had purchased for themselves, and figured he would be surviving the next few weeks on what he would shoot.

He pulled his wallet from his vest, and reached into it for the bills folded inside. All that was left of the money Aunt Ginny had sent him. He thought he might have enough to purchase a set of saddle bags, and maybe a sack of flour and of coffee, and some blankets to serve as a bedroll. And of course, he needed to purchase a horse and saddle.

He would also like to have a rifle along with him. A pistol made a poor tool for hunting. A

.44 was not very accurate beyond maybe twenty or thirty yards. Even his father, the best Jack had ever seen with a pistol, preferred a rifle whenever he needed to do any serious shooting.

Yet, Jack's funds were limited. He had enough for the saddlebags and supplies, but would have to make the ride north without a rifle.

He saddled his horse and was tightening the cinch when Jessica approached from behind.

"Good morning, Mister McCabe," she said.

He nodded. "Morning."

"You don't like me much, do you?"

He shrugged. "I wouldn't say that."

"You hardly said anything to me on the ride back from that camp, last night."

"Wasn't much to say."

"Are you expecting me to thank you for saving me?"

Jack turned to face her. He was in no mood for whatever game she was playing. "You went out there of your own free will. It's not like you were kidnapped. I really don't think you know what those men are like, or what kind of danger you were really in."

"What makes you think I couldn't handle myself?"

"Can you give me a straight answer to a question?"

She smiled. "I can try."

"I agreed to ride along with you and these families, to see that you all reach Montana safely. Can you promise me you won't cause any trouble? No more wandering off?"

"I can promise I won't cause any trouble on our way to Montana. Cross my heart," she said with a smirk, making a crossing motion with one hand at her chest.

"Why is it that doesn't make me feel any better?"

"Come on, Mister McCabe. Jack. Are you going to tell me you don't like a little adventure? I can tell you do. I can see it in your eyes. And you're agreeing to ride along, knowing Cade will probably follow us, because he wants me and he wants to kill you. You could just ride away on the stage and never look back. And once you reach Montana, your daddy's ranch, you know Cade will leave you alone. It would take a fool to ride onto the ranch of Johnny McCabe, looking to gun down his son.

"But admit it. You're riding along with us to make yourself a more tempting target for Cade. You want to face him, but you're not the kind who can just gun down a man. You have to let him make the first move."

"You don't know what you're talking about."

"Oh? Don't I?"

"I'm riding along partly because your father asked me to, and partly for my own reasons."

"Whatever you say, Jack. But let me tell you something." She took a step closer. "Adventure is a lot closer than you might think it is. If you want it to be."

"Jessica!" her father barked, striding toward her from the tent. "Come help your mother with breakfast."

"Yes, Daddy. We were just talking." She turned and walked away, the hem of her dress swishing through the knee-high grass.

She cast a backward glance toward Jack as she walked.

That girl is indeed going to be trouble, Jack thought. As dangerous as he thought Falcone and his men might be, the real danger to the settlers was right here in their camp.

6

Jack returned to his hotel room, finding his trunk undisturbed. He dug into and found a vest that belonged to a three-piece suit he often wore to class. He would be putting a lot of hours in the saddle over the next two or three weeks, and would need the vest.

He tucked Aunt Ginny's letter into a vest pocket, and then, with his trunk fastened shut and hefted onto one shoulder, he went downstairs to the front desk.

"I'm checking out," he said.

"Might I give you our card?"

"I really don't think I'll be back this way. At least, not for a long time."

With that explanation, which really was no explanation at all yet was no more than Jack cared to give, he stepped out onto the street holding his trunk on one shoulder.

He needed a place where this would be safe, he decided, while he made the purchases he needed.

The marshal's office, he thought. Kincaid

seemed like a stand-up sort of man. Like Pa often said about men he respected, Kincaid seemed like a man to ride the river with.

Jack crossed the street, which was dry and dusty in some places and muddy in others, and stepped into Kincaid's office.

Kincaid was seated behind his desk. He glanced up at Jack. "Good morning, Mc-Cabe."

"Morning, Marshal."

"Heading out? The stage isn't due for a few more hours."

Jack set the trunk down. "Heading out, yes. But I won't be taking the stage."

Jack accepted a cup of coffee, and took a wooden, wing-back chair across the desk from Kincaid. He explained he would be accompanying the wagons when they left in the morning. Serving as guide.

Kincaid sat back in his chair and put his feet up on the desk, crossing his ankles. His riding boots were worn and scuffed. They had seen a lot of miles.

"That takes care of one of my concerns," he said. "Those folks, out there alone, with possibly the likes of Cade dogging them."

He took a sip of his own coffee. "Many think folks from the east are unprepared for life out here. Tenderfoots, they call them. Green. But those folks are farmers. Brewster, Harding, and the other man. Ford. They've worked their lives trying to coax a living from

81

the land. There's nothing soft about 'em. They know how to use an axe, a shovel. They're strong, hardy men. Even Brewster, with just one hand. But when it comes to men like Cade and Falcone, they're out of their league."

"Well, I'll be along to keep them out of trouble."

"Trouble there may very well be, son."

"I don't think so. Cade is a coward. He wouldn't dare face me like a man. Not again. Not after I whupped him so solidly in the saloon yesterday. And Falcone wouldn't have any interest in robbing those folks. Men like him set their sights a might higher than that."

Interesting, Jack noted. Here he was, back in the west, in Levi's and riding boots and with a gun strapped to his side, and his college speech with polysyllabic words was sort of fading into talk that included things like *whupped,* and *a might higher.*

Yet, despite the fact that he was two years younger than the rest of his class in medical school, and yet was near the top of his class and viewed as some sort of a potential intellectual giant, he was from the west. This was where his heart was, and its ways were within him, never far from the surface.

"Normally, I would agree with you," Kincaid said. "Vic Falcone was Sam Patterson's right-hand-man for a long time. Word has it Patterson might be dead, and Falcone is now running his own gang. They hit stagecoaches, especially when there might be a payroll on board. And they hit trains and banks."

"As I recall, Sam Patterson usually confined his operations to Texas and New Mexico Territory."

Kincaid nodded. "Falcone is a might further north than might be expected, but he's not Patterson. He might have different ways, different ideas. He was far enough north to hit your father's ranch a year ago. Word is he shot up your Pa pretty bad."

Jack nodded. "The word is correct. My Pa is alive and well. Shot up bad, but he recovered."

"Word is also that your brothers rode after Falcone and his gang, and shot them up pretty bad."

"You know more about that than I do. I've been living back east. I've been out of touch."

"I have to admit, I never knew Johnny McCabe had more than two sons."

"I have to admit," Jack said darkly, staring into his coffee, "neither did I until a few months ago."

Kincaid nodded, studying the boy, deciding not to pursue it. "A man like Falcone might not have financial motivation to rob three covered wagons filled with farmers, but there is more than one kind of motivation. And Falcone is very human. Considering he attacked the McCabe Ranch last year and was driven back, a number of his men killed, and then your brothers rode after him. Sounds like he might have reason to have a beef with the McCabes. Revenge can be a stronger motive than money, sometimes. And then, there's the girl. For whatever reason, she has her hooks at least partly set into Falcone's man, Cade. Coward or not, he's not likely to forget her."

Jack nodded. He hadn't considered any of these ideas. "Well, Marshal, you've given me something to think about."

"I wish I could ride along with you, but I can't. I got me a job to do here."

"Any help would, of course, be appreciated, but I do understand. A man cannot be in two places at once." Jack took another sip of his coffee and set the cup down on the edge of the marshal's desk.

"How are you fixed for guns?"

Jack shrugged. "Aside from whatever squirrel guns those farmers might have with them, I have this Colt at my side. And that's about it. I wasn't expecting this kind of trouble."

Kincaid nodded, sitting in silence while he thought a moment.

He got to his feet and went to a rifle rack mounted on one wall. Standing in the rack were four Winchesters and the scatter gun he had taken with him the night before.

He pulled a Winchester and tossed it to Jack, who caught it with practiced hands.

"Take it," Kincaid said. "I have three others, all provided for me by the town. No one will miss one rifle."

"Much obliged," Jack said, working the action, chambering a round.

"I keep them all well oiled and in good working order."

"Apparently," Jack said, admiring the weapon. It was a 44-40, holding eighteen rounds. It would take the same cartridges his pistol did.

"I got a box of ammunition you can have, too. I would give you my scatter gun, but I need that for use here."

"The rifle will surely be a big help. Thank you."

"Watch your back trail, son. And at the same time, watch the trail ahead. Don't let your guard down. Not once."

7

Vic Falcone stretched out in on his bedroll blankets. The fire beside him had dwindled down to nothing more than charred cinders, with a trail of smoke drifting skyward.

It was morning, and he had finished a cup of coffee, which hadn't been enough to fully do away with the headache he had from the whiskey the night before.

Falcone had a black handlebar mustache, and a week's worth of coarse whiskers decorating his chin. He had been in his clothes for a week, and he knew he had easily three more days of riding before he could reach the little cabin in the mountains that served as his new hide-out.

Though, he preferred the word *sanctuary*. The men who rode with him used words like hide-out, but Falcone was a man of education. In what seemed like an earlier lifetime, he had stood before a classroom of eager students, expounding about things such as the Roman Empire and its rise and fall and all of the politics that occurred within that time.

Even now, he could launch into a lecture on the Empire and how its political philosophies had been the seeds from which the founding fathers of this country had put together the Constitution. He could still name the forty-one Roman emperors. In order.

And now, here he was, leading a band of outlaws on the frontier. Bedding saloon women when he was lonely, and drinking too much whiskey. And when he could, engaging in a game of poker.

Women, whiskey and gambling. About all life now had to offer. All because he had been on the losing effort in the late War Between the States. He had been a guerrilla raider, riding with Sam Patterson. Men like Wild Bill Hickok, who had been raiders but for the winning side, were hailed as heroes. But Falcone and Patterson had found themselves on the losing side.

Falcone had tried to return to his previous life. He had given it the old, proverbial college try. But his involvement as a raider during the war was well known and people now saw him as something different from what he had been. No parents wanted a man like Vic Falcone teaching their children. And he found he had killed too many men and been shot at too many times to allow himself to settle back into the sedate life in a private boy's school in Virginia.

Before long, he tendered his resignation and rode west and joined up with Patterson again. Patterson had formed a gang and was using guerrilla war tactics to procure a living from the robbing of banks and stagecoaches, and raiding ranches and farms. Falcone found he adapted to this lifestyle all too easily.

As these thoughts rolled their way through his head, as they often did when he woke up hurting from too much whiskey, he decided to sit up and maybe bring the fire back to life. More coffee, he decided, was what was needed.

A woman approached. She was wearing a saloon dress with cleavage pleasingly low. She was not from one of the local saloons, but generally traveled with Falcone and had spent the night with him, in his bedroll. She had been with him a couple of years, now. She had been with him at the previous sanctuary they had been forced to vacate after the incident with Dusty the previous summer.

She had gone to the creek to wash off the night's sleep. And she had covered herself with enough cheap-smelling perfume that he would have known she was approaching even with his eyes shut.

"I can't wait to get back to the cabin," she said, sitting on a rock at the other side of the fire. "I can't wait to have me a good, hot bath."

"Soon, Flossy. We shall be leaving here, soon."

"You never did tell me why you brought all of us this far south. I mean, it's not like there's a job, or anything."

Whenever he had a robbery in mind, hitting a bank or a stagecoach, or even raiding a ranch for supplies and horses as he had attempted with the McCabe Ranch the summer before, he referred to it as a job.

"No," he said, "there's no job. We're not here for a job."

"Well, then, what?"

He shot her an icy glance. "I didn't realize I was in the habit of explaining myself."

"I don't mean nothin' by it. It's just that some of the men are startin' to talk . . ."

"If they want to talk, tell them to talk to me directly. If any of them has the backbone for it."

Motion at the corner of his eye drew his attention. Cade and a man called White-Eye were approaching. White-Eye had been with him at the McCabe job the year before. A knife scar began at one cheekbone and extended upward across his eye to his brow, and the eye was a sightless milky white. Cade was new.

Falcone, Flossy and White-Eye were the only survivors after Dusty had infiltrated their

89

previous sanctuary. And the other girl, who had been there with Flossy. She had belonged to Loggins, who had been killed in the attack on their sanctuary by the McCabe men. The men Dusty had led to them. Falcone forgot her name. He never knew what had happened to her, but when he went back days later to survey the damage, she was not among the dead bodies.

"Mister Falcone," Cade said. "Pike's gone. Run off, I 'spect."

Pike was the man with Cade in town the day before, and who had shared the beating at the hands of Jack McCabe.

"Let him go," Falcone said. "I don't want a man here who's not loyal."

"Vic," White-Eye said. "I got me a question. Would you mind if me and Cade rode into town? Maybe hit the saloon? Had a drink? All the whiskey here is gone."

By *gone,* Falcone knew White-Eye meant it had been consumed the night before.

"Not today," Falcone said. "Not until those wagons are gone."

That drew a puzzled look from White-Eye.

Falcone continued, "I don't want any trouble with the McCabe boy. I doubt Cade, here, will be able to restrain himself, and I don't want him injured any more."

Cade reared back with offense. "I can handle him."

"You face off against him in a gunfight and

he'll put you in the ground. And you've already shown how you fare against him with your fists. It's written all over your face."

Cade had no reply, at least none he dared make. He looked away.

"I expect the wagons will be gone tomorrow, and the McCabe boy will be with them."

"How do you know he's going with them?"

"Because, let's just say I know the family. I know something of the way they think."

White-Eye nodded, and spit a load of brown tobacco juice to the grass. "That boy's Dusty's brother. I wouldn't mess with him."

Cade said, "Just who the hell is Dusty?"

White-Eye had been with Falcone back in the Patterson days. Before Patterson had ridden out never to be heard from again.

White-Eye said, "He's Johnny McCabe's son, and he was raised by Sam Patterson."

Falcone said, "I think you boys can manage a day away from whiskey without developing hallucinations and the shakes. Then, tomorrow, if the wagons are gone, you can go into town."

Cade and White-Eye walked away.

"I don't mean to pry," Flossy said, "but how much longer do you think we will have to be here?"

"We will be here," he said curtly, "until it is time to leave."

Falcone lounged the morning away. About

noon, he lit up a cigar and decided that he should probably send a man into town. He could go himself, but a leader sent others to do his bidding. The art of delegation. It reinforced that he was in command.

And yet, who to go? With Pike's desertion, he had only three men left. There was Lane, who had a thin mustache and always seemed to be sporting a few days' worth of stubble on his chin, who had a smile like a shark but still retained his Tennessee accent. White-Eye, who had been with him for years and seemed the most benign of the group. Of course, *benign* was relative — he could shoot you in the back if he was so motivated. And then there was Cade, who was probably the most efficient fighter among them, but he was two-dimensional in this thinking. When his minuscule mind got hold of an idea, no matter how idiotic it might be, he seemed unable to let it go.

Falcone could not send Cade into town, not as long as those wagons were still there. Cade would seek out the McCabe boy and probably get himself killed, and that would make Falcone two men short. Lane, the most blood-thirsty of the group, had his name on wanted posters throughout the west and Falcone did not doubt Jubal Kincaid would hesitate to throw Lane in his jail.

Falcone did not think it wise to do battle with Kincaid, right now. He would probably lose a couple men in the process. He had a big job planned and needed to be hiring men on, not getting them killed needlessly in a gunfight with Kincaid. You had to pick your battles, and a battle with Kincaid at the moment would simply not prove cost effective.

White-Eye was the man, he decided. He asked Flossy to fetch him.

White-Eye shuffled up to Falcone's campfire, a wad of chewing tobacco in one cheek. "You call, Boss?"

Falcone nodded. "I need you to do something for me. I need you to go into town and wait at the saloon."

"Sounds good to me, Boss. I'll leave right now."

"Don't you need to know what you will be waiting for?"

White-Eye shrugged. "Don't rightly care. I just want to get me a drink of whiskey."

"I want you to watch for a man. Tall, probably with long hair. Two fingers only on his right hand. Has a patch over one eye. Wears his guns like he knows how to use them. This man you won't mistake."

"What do I do if I see him?"

"Oh, it's not *if,* White-Eye. It's *when.* He's due in town any day, now. When you see him, tell him who you are and bring him out here to the camp."

White-Eye nodded with a shrug and shuffled off to the horses.

Flossy, who had been busying herself about the camp but remaining within earshot of Falcone, came up behind him and began to knead tension from his shoulders.

"I couldn't help but overhear," she said. "Sounds like you might have been describing Two-Finger Walker."

"Why, Flossy," Falcone removed the cigar from his teeth, closing his eyes as Flossy's fingers dug into his shoulders. "I do believe you're paying attention."

"Never met the man. Heard of him, though. I used to work a saloon down Texas way. Is that what we're here for? To meet up with him?"

Falcone nodded.

She said, "I've heard he's not a man you want to deal with."

"True. But then, he might be uniquely qualified for the job I have in mind. You see, my dear, he might be the only man alive who can handle Johnny McCabe in a fight to the death, and I know of no one else who is more motivated to kill McCabe than he is."

Flossy decided to pursue it no further. Vic Falcone was not a man who liked to answer questions.

Falcone sat in silence with his eyes shut as Flossy continued to work on his shoulders.

Jubal Kincaid stood outside his office leaning his back against the wall. In one hand was a hand-rolled cigarette. He watched a rider approaching from down the street.

The man rode down the center of the street, a black flat-brimmed hat covering his head. Long, stringy hair fell to his shoulders. He wore a long black jacket, which was held open on the right side by a pistol that was holstered at his belt, the handle of the gun facing out.

He sat tall, with wide shoulders. A black patch covered one eye, and he rode with a scatter gun lying across the front of his saddle.

The man gave the rein a slight tug and his horse came to a complete stop. With his one eye, the man looked to the marshal. "Jubal Kincaid?"

Kincaid nodded. "How do, Walker. Been a long time."

Walker's lips spread in a grimace that might have been a smile. "Not long enough. I see you're wearing a badge."

Kincaid nodded again, taking a draw from his cigarette. "A man's gotta work."

"So they say."

"What are you doing in town, Walker?"

"I ain't in the habit of answering questions."

"Fair enough. But I'm not in the habit of tolerating trouble."

"You threatening me?"

"Warning you. And you get one warning, only."

Walker sat in the saddle a moment, his one eye fixed on Kincaid, sizing up the man and the situation.

Then, he said, "I'm here to meet a man. That's all."

"Then, why don't you get to it?"

Walker nodded. "Good day. Marshal."

And he continued along.

Kincaid stood, watching as Two-Finger Walker continued along the wide street, keeping his horse to a walk.

He dismounted in front of the saloon and stepped in.

Another horse approached from down the street. Jack McCabe.

The boy swung out of the saddle. "Good afternoon, Marshal."

"You here to fetch that trunk?"

"Well, I was hoping to ask you for another favor."

Kincaid looked at him with a grin. "Let me guess. You want to store it in my office for a while."

"Well, it's just that none of the farmers have room for it in their wagons, and I really can't be prepared for trouble if I have a cumbersome trunk tied to the back of my saddle."

"*Cumbersome,* huh?" Kincaid was still grinning. "Ain't heard a ten-dollar word like that in a while."

Jack returned the grin. "That's what college will get you."

Kincaid let his gaze drift back to the saloon down the street, and the horse tethered outside.

"I'm thinking on spending the night out at the wagons," Jack said. "It might be easier to be right there come morning. We're planning on an early start."

Kincaid nodded. "Makes sense. Yeah, I'll keep that trunk for you. What's in it, anyhow?"

"Clothes. The kind of stuff you wear when you're sitting in lecture halls or libraries. Nothing I think I'll be needing again. If ever."

Kincaid grew silent, staring down toward the saloon. He took a final drag of the cigarette and tossed the stub out onto the dusty street.

"Actually," Jack said, pulling an envelope from his vest. "One more thing. A letter I was hoping maybe you could put on the next stage bound for McCabe Gap for me."

Kincaid took the letter and tucked it into his own vest. "Consider it done."

"Much obliged."

Kincaid returned his gaze to the far end of the street.

Jack said, "What're you watching?"

Before Kincaid could answer, Walker stepped out of the saloon with another man. They each mounted up and began riding away, each keeping his horse to a walk.

"That man," Kincaid said. "The one with

the long hair. His name's Walker. I never did know his first name, but they call him Two-Finger."

"Two-Finger Walker. Yeah, I think I've heard the name mentioned around a campfire or two."

"He got that name because, back in the day, down around the Texas border, he was a young gunhawk. They say he was good with a gun, but he was young and didn't have the common sense to pick his fights. A little liquored-up, he challenged another young gunhawk by the name of Johnny McCabe."

"Pa?" Jack knew his father had roamed the border country for a short time, before he met Ma.

"One and the same. Your Pa is about as good with a gun as I've ever seen. He actually shot the gun out of Walker's hand. Even though I think it was an accident, because no man is *that* good, your Pa had the presence of mind to say, without even hesitating, for Walker to consider himself lucky. Your Pa said the next one would be between the eyes."

Jack chuckled. "Pa has style."

"I was standing there on the boardwalk. Never actually met your Pa face-to-face, but we found ourselves in the same saloon a couple times back then. Walker stood there, hanging onto his wounded hand, blood dripping to the dirt, looking at your Pa with more hate than I thought it was possible for one man to muster. Your Pa's bullet shot that man's hand apart. He lost three fingers, blown right off as he stood there in the street. All he's got is a thumb and his first finger. That ended his days of being dangerous with a gun.

"But it didn't stop Walker from being dangerous. About six months later, he came across your Pa in another saloon. I wasn't there this time, but I heard about it. He pulled a knife on your Pa, and they fought hard. It ended with Walker catching his own knife in the eye.

"He's probably the only man who can say he fought your Pa to the death twice and lived to tell about it."

Jack had seen his father with his shirt off more than once, and Pa had a scar across his chest, and another thin line of a scar across his shoulder. He asked his Pa one time what they were from, thinking they looked like knife wounds. Pa simply said, "Oh, just reminders of when I was young and foolish."

Jack wondered now if those scars came from the knife of Two-Finger Walker.

"So," Jack said. "What do you suppose he's doing here in town?"

"There might not be any man alive who hates your father as much as Two-Finger. And that man he just rode away with, he rides for Falcone. His name's White-Eye. Had his name on a reward poster in New Mexico Territory, at one time. Son, I think you might be in even more trouble than we thought."

8

Jack awoke with the sky still dark. Stars silently flickered overhead, but the eastern sky was beginning to show a faint light. Predawn, his Pa called it.

His horse stood fifty feet to one side, its head hanging lazily in the unique way a horse had of resting, almost sleeping, while it was on its feet.

Jack had learned horseflesh from Pa, and this horse had sand. It was the same horse he had borrowed from the livery. The afternoon before he had bought it and the saddle from the livery attendant. The old man had included a scabbard that was now tied to the saddle, and in it was the Winchester Marshal Kincaid had given him.

He had also bought a few supplies from the general store, including the blankets he was now wrapped in. He climbed out of the blankets and reached for his boots. He held each upside down and gave it a good shake to dislodge anything that might have crawled in during the night, then pulled them on snugly over his feet.

He stacked some kindling and wood to build a small fire, and then filled a kettle from a canteen. A little morning coffee to start the day.

He buckled his gunbelt about his hips and tied the gun down to his leg, and then stood before the fire, enjoying the wind in his hair. The ever-present wind of the plains.

Symbolically, he felt like this day was somehow a new beginning. Like yesterday had been the last day of something old, and now he was starting something new. A new direction. A new life, even.

He had studied symbolism in school. Shakespeare's writing, the old Greek plays. Enough poetry to choke the proverbial horse. He thought it was all little more than nonsense, trying to find something profound in a play or a poem so you could feel scholarly.

And yet, he thought of the trunk he had left at Kincaid's office. It was filled with clothes he had worn at school. Jackets and trousers of finely milled wood or tweed. White shirts with stiff collars. Various ties. The trappings of a university man. A man of letters. A man who had gotten a classical education and was beginning medical school.

Now, as he stood in his boots and his Levi's, with a Colt strapped down to his right leg, standing not in a lecture hall but on the open grasslands with a campfire before him and a pot of coffee beginning to boil, he was leaving behind the university man. He was once again a man of the west.

And though he didn't know how he would ever break this to Aunt Ginny and he dreaded the look of disappointment in Pa's eye, Harvard was behind him.

He took a deep breath of the crisp, fresh air.

Some would think him a fool, he was sure. He had the intellectual capacity to excel at studies to the point that he had finished his second year of medical school when most young men his age were still working on their undergraduate degrees. But they simply didn't understand. Apparently even Pa and Aunt Ginny didn't fully understand. But as he stood by the fire, the wind in his hair, he felt like he was truly where he belonged.

Soon, the farmers were awake. Starting cook fires and fixing breakfast. Rolling tents and packing them into wagons. Harnassing teams of oxen.

As the sun slowly made its way over the eastern horizon, teams were hitched to wagons and Jack was saddling his horse.

Jubal Kincaid rode out to see them off.

"Marshal," Jack said, stepping into the saddle.

"I just wanted to say good-bye. And good luck."

"If a man is careful and good at what he does, he doesn't need luck."

Kincaid grinned. "You've had a good teacher. One of the best."

Jack nudged his horse over to Kincaid's, and extended a hand which Kincaid shook.

"Thanks for everything," Jack said.

With his hat pulled down tightly over his temples, the winds of the grasslands now fully in his face, Jack looked down to Brewster. The man was standing beside his team of oxen. His wife and Jessica were sitting on the front seat. The Brewsters had two wagons, and Brewster's son was standing by the second team.

"Well, Mister Brewster," Jack said, "I suppose we should be on our way."

Kincaid watched as Brewster urged his team forward and the wagon lurched into motion. Brewster's son did the same, and his wagon fell into place behind his father's. The Harding wagon came next, and then the fourth wagon, Kincaid believed their name was Ford, took its place behind the Hardings. Ford, with a drooping gray hat and an equally drooping mustache, threw a wave at Kincaid, who returned it.

Kincaid sat and watched a moment, then turned his horse back toward town.

Kincaid regretted that he couldn't do more to help young Jack McCabe. The boy seemed to have spine and integrity. Yet, to simply ride along and desert this town was not an option. The townspeople had hired him to do a job and they needed the job done.

He dismounted in front of his office, leaving his horse tethered to a hitching rail. He would take the horse to the livery later.

With his scatter gun cradled in one arm, he began to walk his rounds, which meant strolling about the town, up one boardwalk and down another. Stopping in sporadically at various businesses to sort of make his presence felt. Folks simply felt safer knowing the law was easily accessible.

He stopped in at the saloon, chatted with the bartender for a few minutes. Then, he stepped into the general store and visited with the proprietor, a man who had been a farmer in Ohio but whose father had once operated a feed and grain store. The man had come west to start a new life, and was doing so not behind a plow but as his father had, but behind a counter.

As Kincaid walked along, a stagecoach rolled onto the town's main street, its horses lathered from a long haul. The passengers would deboard and take a meal at the restaurant while the hostler replaced the team with a fresh one.

"Okay, folks," the stage driver said. "You got about an hour, then we'll be continuing on."

Kincaid was about to pull out of his vest

pocket the letter Jack had given him, but then he got an idea.

He walked up to the stage. The driver was a man he knew as Ned, with a deeply lined face and a thick graying beard, and a floppy hat the color of dirt.

"Morning, Ned," Kincaid called out.

"Marshal," Ned said, dropping down from his seat atop the front of the stage to the dusty earth of the street.

"Ned, I have a question for you. Do you pass directly through McCabe Gap?"

"Nope. Not me, at least. I'll take the passengers as far as Bozeman. There is a stage that goes through there once a week, though."

"If I write you a letter, addressed to someone in McCabe Gap, can you make sure it gets delivered?"

"Well," he shrugged, "we ain't the mail service, but I don't see why we can't. Is it official business?"

"Sort of. There'll be two letters, actually. And I'd consider it a personal favor."

Kincaid went to his office and pulled open a desk drawer where he kept a bottle of ink and a quill pen.

Kincaid knew how to read and write, though he had met many who could not. He was hoping the man he was about to address this letter to was literate, or at the very least, there was someone in his life who could read. Since Jack's letter was addressed to the very same man, Kincaid figured there was a good chance there was.

Kincaid wrote his letter using the back of an old reward poster for stationary. His office was an extremely low-budget operation. Then, he stuffed the letter into an envelope, and across the front, wrote, *Johnny McCabe. McCabe Gap, Montana.*

Outside, he found the stage with a fresh team hitched. Ned was once again atop, checking some luggage he had tied down.

"Ned," Kincaid said. "Here they are."

Ned took the envelopes and tucked them into a vest pocket. "I know the gent who'll be running the route that goes through McCabe Gap. I'll see that it's delivered."

Kincaid nodded. He only hoped it wouldn't arrive too late.

9

Jack McCabe and the covered wagons were following the main trail that led out of town, and north. The trail that was identified on most maps as the Bozeman Trail.

These grassy flat lands were not as flat as they appeared from the window of a train. The land was actually a series of countless low, rolling hills. At the crest of one of these hills, you could see for miles in any direction, but some of the depressions between hills were deceptively deep. A rider could be hidden from view at the lowest point between some of them.

The grass, Jack knew, would become a dry brown as the summer wore on. But at the moment it was a luxuriant green. The ever-present winds of the plains passed along, causing the grass to ripple like a sea of green.

Wild flowers grew sporadically, bobbing their heads in the wind as though they were bowing to the settlers passing by.

The noon stage, the one that would have

been carrying Jack had he held to his original plans, approached from behind.

Unlike in dime novels, in which stages charged along with their horses moving at a full gallop, this team was kept to a light trot. After all, there were a lot of miles to cover and a galloping team would quickly become exhausted.

The farmers pulled their wagons aside to let the stage pass. The driver nodded to Jack, who nodded back, and then the stage was gone.

Jack sat in his saddle, watching the stage move along.

Brewster urged his team of oxen along, to get the wagon moving once again. He saw Jack sitting in the saddle, staring toward the stage.

"What are you thinking, McCabe?" Brewster asked, walking alongside the oxen.

Jack said, "I'm thinking that I feel like a sitting duck, out here in the open like this."

"You think those men back there are coming for us, don't you?"

"I have a bad feeling, that's all."

They pushed the wagons along, moving until the sun drooped low in the sky. Jack recommended stopping while there was still enough daylight to gather wood and set up tents.

On three sides of their camp was open grassland stretching in long, low hills into the distance. However, on the fourth was a small creek, with some oak and willow.

Green wood, of course, won't burn well, but they found some deadfalls and a few dead branches lying on the ground. Axes and hatchets were put to use, and the settlers had enough wood for three small cook fires. Each wagon had a small load of firewood tucked in a corner, but Jack had recommended they save that wood until they really needed it.

Jack sat by the Brewster fire and chewed on some jerky he had purchased in town. And then, with the sun fully set and the sky overhead now a canopy of stars, he pulled his rifle from his saddle.

"I'm going to scout about a bit," he said to Brewster, and stepped away from the firelight and into the night.

Brewster stood watching, amazed at how well the boy seemed to handle moving about in the darkness. With his rifle held ready in both hands, he seemed to simply step away into the darkness and blend into it. Like an Indian, Brewster thought. Not that he knew much about how an Indian moved in the night.

Brewster poured a cup of coffee.

Mildred said, "You drink too much of that and you won't sleep. And you need your sleep. We'll be wanting an early start in the morning."

Brewster smiled. "I'll be all right. Young McCabe has gone off to scout, and I'm going to wait up for him."

"This time of night?"

Brewster shrugged.

Mildred returned to their tent, and Brewster sat on a barrel he had fetched from the wagon to serve as an impromptu chair.

Harding approached. Tall and seeming to always be brooding, he was one of these men who was thin and yet somehow surprisingly strong.

"I saw your fire still going," Harding said.

Brewster nodded. "McCabe has gone out to do some scouting. I'm not sure what's going on, but I want to talk to him. I'm going to wait up until he's back."

"You don't much like that boy, do you?" Harding spoke through tight lips.

"It's not that I don't like him, exactly. It's that I don't quite understand him. He's like a bit of one thing and a bit of another, all kind of rolled into one. On one hand he speaks like a highly educated young man. And you can see in his manner that he has some refinement. And yet the way he wears his gun, and the look in his eye — a times he seems not much different from the men we rescued Jessica from."

Harding said, "I don't like him at all. Not one bit. I think it's a bad idea to have him along."

"Well, Ford seems to like him well enough. Said he feels a lot better going off into new territory now that he has someone along who knows the way. Especially with men like that Cade out there."

"You're caught betwixt and between."

"I guess that about sums it up."

"I'll sit up with you. Got another cup?"

And so they waited, Brewster sitting on a barrel, and Harding pacing about.

Nina Harding felt a little uncomfortable, stepping past her sleeping mother and out through the tent flap to the darkness beyond. After all, this was just the kind of thing Jessica Brewster would do. And while Jessica was not quite a harlot, she seemed to have aspirations in that direction.

And yet, Nina found she couldn't sleep. Her back hurt from sitting on the wagon seat all day. Her body was desperately tired, but sometimes it was possible to simply be too tired to sleep.

She thought she might walk about the camp a bit. With her father and Mister Brewster still awake — she could hear their voices coming from the Brewster camp — she felt she would be safe enough.

The wagons were spaced apart in a rough line with the creek on one side. The tents were set up each beside a wagon. As Nina stepped from the Harding tent, she could see her father pacing about the Brewster fire.

A woman spoke from the darkness behind her. "Lovely night, isn't it?"

Nina jumped at the sound of the voice. She then saw, in the light of the crescent moon, a form sitting on something to one side.

It was Jessica Brewster.

"Jessica," Nina said, in a loud whisper. "You nearly scared me to death."

Nina walked over to Jessica, who was sitting on a small stool.

"What are you doing out here?" Nina asked.

"I could ask the same of you."

"Haven't you gotten into enough trouble?"

"Is that what you're looking for?" Jessica asked playfully. "Trouble?"

"No. I just couldn't sleep, is all."

Jessica leaned forward, placing her elbows on her knees and resting her chin in her hands. "I just feel like I'm going crazy inside. It's like I have all these wants and desires, and they're all bottled up inside me and I feel like I'm about to burst wide open."

"I think you're insane. Running off to that campfire, the way you did. With those men."

"Those men aren't why I did it."

"No? I saw the way that one called Cade was looking at you. And you can say different, but I know you liked it."

"I liked being looked at like that, sure. But not from him specifically. It's just . . . I don't know . . . don't you sometimes wonder if what you have will ever be enough? I mean — the life of a farmer. Working from sun-up to sundown, doing the same work, day after day for the rest of your life?"

"It's the life I've always known. I haven't thought about it much."

"Well, I have. Sitting on a farm for all of my days is just not enough. Life is something that has to be sought after, that has to be grabbed. So much is out there, and I want to experience it. I want to taste life. To savor it. When I'm old and gray and looking back, I want to know I've lived."

"I think maybe it's that you don't know what you want."

"Are you really going to tell me what you have is enough for you?"

Their fathers' voices suddenly got a little louder.

Brewster said, "You're back. Is everything all right?"

And there was the voice of Jack McCabe. "Seems to be."

Jessica shot to her feet. "Jack's back."

"I wonder where he was off to?"

Jessica shot her a wicked smile. "Let's go find out. Come on."

"They'll hear us."

"Not if we're quiet. Come on."

Jessica crept closer to the Brewster fire, stopping behind the wagon and then peered around the corner of a wagon. Nina joined her, wanting to say that they were being foolish, that they would be caught eavesdropping. But she dared not even venture a whisper this near to the Brewsters' camp.

Jessica's father was saying, "You really think we might be in danger, don't you?"

Jack hesitated a moment. He held his rifle in one hand, and in the other was a tin cup filled with coffee. He said, "Yes, sir. I don't want to scare anyone, but I believe we could be in trouble."

He told them about his conversation with Marshal Kincaid. He told them about Two-Finger Walker, and how Walker acquired the name and that he was apparently in town to see Vic Falcone.

"I was against this from the start," Harding said to Brewster. "I told you there would be trouble, that we would be better off just trusting to our own judgment. We got this far without any help."

Jack said, "Yes, it might be partly my fault. It might be my partly presence that is putting us all in danger. Both Falcone and Walker have a beef with my family. But these men have do have reason to follow you, even if I wasn't here."

"Jessica," Brewster said.

"Yes. Women out here are rare. Young women of marrying age, even moreso. A young woman who is not a saloon whore, even moreso again."

"You think that man, what's his name? Cade? You think he has set his sights on Jessica?"

Jack nodded and took a sip of coffee. "Most likely. The marshal certainly thinks so."

Brewster said, "So, what did you find when you went out scouting?"

"A campfire. Maybe five miles back."

"That isn't necessarily those outlaws," Harding said. "It could be anyone back there. This trail is traveled a lot. It's the only trail between Cheyenne and Bozeman."

"It could be. But my gut feeling says it isn't. Besides, when dealing with men like this, it's best to err on the side of caution."

Harding finished his coffee, then excused himself and headed back to his own tent.

Jessica, growing bored with the situation, and maybe wanting to get back to the family tent before her father discovered her missing, mouthed a *good night* to Nina and hurried away into the darkness.

Nina was about to leave, also. After all, her father, though not a cruel man, was strict and would not approve of his daughter wandering about the camp alone at this late hour.

However, she paused a moment, allowing herself one last look at Jack McCabe.

He stood by the fire, his tin coffee cup in one hand, looking off into the night.

He was not overly tall, but he carried

himself in a tall way. Not arrogant, but confident. He seemed strong, not in a burly blacksmith sort of way, but in a lithe way. Like a horse, more than a bear.

Her father saw him as somehow evil. He had used the word *gunhawk,* spitting it out as though it were somehow vulgar.

And yet, as Jack stood in the night, the firelight dancing about his face and with his gun strapped to his side and his rifle in one hand, he struck her as a latter day knight.

She tore her gaze from him and made her way back to her family's tent before her father could realize she was missing and begin bellowing out her name.

10

The days passed. The settlers moved along at a walking pace, the oxen pulling the wagon slowly along. The trail was sometimes little more than two ruts cut into the sod, and other times was more of a stretch of gravel that ran along into the distance. The days were hot, the countryside about them dry and gravely, sometimes with outcroppings of bedrock. Sage and small bushes dotted the landscape, and the grass grew in some places thick and tall, and in others thin and sparse. There were ridges that would rise up, usually to the west. Some were a dark green with pine, but most were rocky and gravely with only sparse growth.

Jack would sometimes ride with the wagons, but other times ride along their back trail, searching for any signs of pursuit. Sometimes at night, he would see a campfire in the distance, but other times all he would see behind them was the empty blackness of night.

On their eighth morning since leaving Cheyenne, Jack hung back a mile or so behind the wagons, watching for any sign of riders in the distance behind them. He turned his horse away from the trail and rode to the crest of a low hill maybe a mile in the distance. There, he swung out of the saddle and loosened the cinch to let his horse rest a moment while he surveyed their back trail.

From the crest of the hill, he could see five miles into any direction. The day was three hours old, and the wagons had been moving at a pace of maybe three miles per hour. With their slow-moving teams of oxen, that was about the best that could be expected. This would put their previous night's camp approximately nine miles behind them, and the campfire Jack had seen in the distance the night before, closer to fourteen.

He could wait here, he thought. He would prefer to find a good spot with adequate cover, but this was open grassland and there wasn't a tree within miles.

While he waited, he tossed over in his mind all he knew about Falcone and the men with him. When he and Kincaid had taken Jessica from Falcone's camp a few nights earlier, he had taken a quick count of the men present. Jack had seen three other than Falcone himself. He decided he was going to assume Two-Finger Walker was with them until he learned otherwise. Better to be prepared, Pa had said more than once. And Walker was probably better with a gun than anyone else in Falcone's camp.

Jack decided if it came to a gun battle, he would make sure his first bullet found Walker. This man had fought Pa twice, intending to kill him both times, and though the battles had cost an eye and three fingers, he was still alive. A man who could survive a toe-to-toe fight with Pa was not one to be taken lightly.

Jack pulled his canteen from his saddle horn and took a swig of water while he waited. He looked about him — miles of arid land in any direction. Gravel underfoot, with strands of grass sprouting. Good enough to feed a longhorn, and Jack's horse was grazing contentedly, and maybe someday with proper irrigation it could be farmed. But the science of irrigation was still developing, and he figured it would be awhile before this land was turned into cornfields. If ever.

He squatted on his heels and idly pulled a blade of grass to chew on, and he kept his eye on the back trail.

The sun grew warm while he waited. Further ahead on the trail, the wagons made their way along slowly. At this distance, it looked like they weren't moving at all.

Jack chewed on some jerky and he checked the loads in his pistol. Of course, he had checked them this morning, as well as the night before, but you could never be too careful. There were five cartridges in the cylinder, with one chamber empty. He gave the cylinder a quick spin to make sure it could spin unencumbered, that there was no dust that might have worked its way into the mechanism. Then he realigned the cylinder so the empty chamber would be in front of the firing pin, so the gun wouldn't fire if accidentally jostled, and he slapped the gun back into his holster.

It became apparent to him the riders following them were hanging back. They had camped five miles behind the wagons and they should have come into view long ago if they were indeed following the wagons.

He tightened the cinch and swung back into the saddle, and took one more long look toward the back trail. Nothing was moving, other than a hawk circling about in the distant sky. Jack turned his horse back to the trial.

The trail was little more than two wheel ruts with a hump of grass running down the middle, and from this point on the trail the wagons were no longer in sight. At the rate the wagons were going, they had made maybe three miles since Jack had last seen them. His horse liked to run, but he held it to a shambling trot as he didn't want the animal to wear itself out. Within a half hour he caught up with them.

The fourth wagon in line belonged to the

Fords. Ford's wife was in the wagon seat, a baby in her arms. Jack had little experience with babies, and as such wouldn't venture a guess as to the child's age, but it was not yet walking.

Ford was fifty-ish, but his wife was not much older than Jack. A boy of twelve or thirteen was helping Ford with the oxen. Jack was not about to ask questions, as that was not the way on the frontier, but even though Ford referred to the boy as his son, the boy was too old to be the child of Ford's wife.

Ford looked up as Jack rode up alongside the wagon and slowed his horse to a walk.

"How do?" Ford said.

"Well enough, I suppose," Jack said. "Been scouting the back trail."

"Any sign of anyone?" Even tough Ford had not been at the campfire the night before, the details had apparently been related to him by Brewster or Harding.

"No visible pursuit, if that's what you mean. How have things been here?"

"Harding has a bad axle. Got a crack running half the length of it. But he's been able to keep moving."

Jack touched his heels to the ribs of his horse and it quickened its gait and brought him to the Harding wagon.

Jack said, "I'm told you have a bad axle."

Harding was leading along his team of

oxen. "I'll take care of it. None of your concern."

"Begging your pardon, Mister Harding. Maybe I was a little rude to all of you at first, but I offered my apologies for that. There are some things going on in my life and they had me in a foul mood. But we're all out here on this trail together. It seems to me a bad axle on a wagon is a concern for all of us."

Harding shot a dark glance at Jack. "I don't object to any rudeness. I object to who you are. I never wanted you along. You see, McCabe, I don't look at you as being all that much different than those men you think might be following us. But I got voted down by Brewster and Ford. As far as I'm concerned, you scout for them, not me."

"And what are we supposed to do if that axle fully breaks out here? Just ride on and leave you behind?"

"I don't really care what you do, as long as you leave me and mine alone."

With exasperation, Jack clicked his horse ahead.

Nina and Jessica were out walking a little ways ahead of the wagons. Jack reined up beside them.

"Good afternoon, ladies," he said.

Nina glanced up at him and for a moment he saw a smile forming, then she shyly shot her gaze down and away. Jessica, however, looked him in the eye with a beaming smile.

Jessica said, "Good afternoon, Mister McCabe. Where have you been all day?"

"Scouting the back trail. And please, both of you, call me Jack."

"Keeping us safe from outlaws?" Jessica asked with a smile that was flirtatious and bold, and struck Jack was maybe a little taunting.

"Those men were much more dangerous than you realize. We've talked about this before, Miss Brewster."

Jessica's smile disappeared, replaced by a flash of anger. "And I think you and the marshal maybe were more worried than you need to be. You have as much faith in my ability to take care of myself as my father has."

He shook his head. "Your attitude is going to be the death of you."

As he spoke, he could see up ahead a wooden sign nailed to a post.

Jessica said, "You sound like an old man. Like my father. You're not much older than I am. Don't you know how to have a little fun?"

"It's just that when I was being raised, I saw more than one man like them. I know what they're capable of."

Jessica shook her head. "You were raised among gunfighters, but that doesn't give you the right to dictate what's best for me. When you pulled me out of that camp, you treated me like a child. And for that I can't forgive you."

Jack found his temper heating up. "I was rescuing you, and if you weren't acting like a child you'd realize it. I pulled you out of that camp like a child because that's the way you were acting."

Jessica said to Nina, "The company out here has suddenly got a little stuffy and haughty. I'm going back to the wagons. Are you coming?"

Nina shrugged. "I might walk a while."

"Whatever. Suit yourself." Jessica turned and strode back to the wagons.

"I'm sorry," Nina said, looking up to Jack but not fully meeting his gaze. As though she didn't quite dare to. "She had no right to talk to you that way."

"That's all right. You have no need to apologize for her. Besides, I've done my share of being rude, lately. I suppose I had it coming."

"Even still, there's no excuse."

"Would you mind if I walked along with you for a while? I mean, to rest my horse a bit?"

"That would be nice."

He swung out of the saddle and fell into place at Nina's side, leading his horse behind him.

He said, "I don't think your father likes me much."

She gave a quick chuckle. "Don't feel bad. He doesn't like anyone."

Jack glanced to the sign post that was now within reading distance. *Bozeman. 150 Mi.*

He said, "I'm kind of concerned about the axle in your family's wagon. According to Mister Ford, there's a deep crack in it."

"My father doesn't seem to be worried about it. Besides, maybe he can find a replacement along the way. A stage passed by today, and the driver said there's a way station twenty-five miles ahead."

"I don't know. Twenty-five miles is a long haul with a bad axle. If it should break out here, we'll lose more than a day trying to get a new one."

"My father can be a little pig-headed sometimes, but he means well."

"I didn't mean to imply that he didn't, miss."

She smiled. And for the first time, she looked him in the eye. "I'm sure you didn't. And it's not *miss*. It's Nina."

"Fine. Nina." He returned the smile.

At his smile, her gaze darted downward again. "Is it true what they say? I mean, if I may be so bold?"

"Is what true? What do they say?"

"That you attended school in the east?"

He nodded. "It is indeed true. Harvard Medical School."

"Harvard? Medical school?" She looked at him again, clearly astonished. "But you're so young."

"I graduated from high school at sixteen."

And he found himself explaining how he had been raised on a ranch in Montana, but at an early age had shown unusual aptitude for things scholastic and was sent to boarding school in the east where he could gain a classical education.

"That sounds so exciting."

He shrugged. "My father wants the best for me. For all of his children. And my Aunt Ginny wants it, too. She helped my father raise us after our mother died."

"I'm sorry about your mother."

"Thanks. It was a long time ago. I don't really remember her, but I feel I know her because Pa and Aunt Ginny kept her memory alive."

"And now, what? You're returning to the ranch for the summer?"

He shrugged again, noncommittally. "I suppose."

"So, medical school is what your father and your aunt wanted for you?"

"Either that or law."

She was silent a moment, then said, "Mister McCabe — Jack — you speak of what your father wants. Again, if I may be so bold, what is it that *you* want?"

His gaze met hers. "You know, I think you're the first person who ever asked me that."

It was then that Nina's father called to her

from the wagon. "Nina!"

"I'd best get back," she said.

He touched the brim of his hat. "Thanks for the pleasant conversation."

She flashed him a smile and turned to walk back to her family's wagon.

It was late in the afternoon when Jack told Brewster he was going to scout their back trail again.

"We'll be stopping to make camp in a couple of hours," Brewster said. "And whether Harding likes it or not, I'm going to crawl under the wagon and have a look at his axle."

Jack rode away along the trail, heading back in the direction they had come. Soon he found what he was looking for. A hill with a crest that was not too far from the trail, but high enough that he could have a good look at their back trail.

His horse made easy work of the long grassy slope. From the crest of the hill he had a view that was even better than the one he had found earlier in the day. Maybe seven miles, he guessed. And it was truly a guess because with landscapes like this, with a countryside made up of long low hills but no trees for points of reference, distances could be deceiving.

Movement to his left caught his eye. The low hill he was sitting on stretched down and away in a gradually descending slope, and then beyond it another hill began. Climbing this hill was an elk.

Its coat was the color of light buckskin, a color which blended into most backgrounds, and if the elk had been standing motionless Jack might have missed it entirely.

Elk would be a welcome improvement from the jerky and canned beans he was expecting for be his dinner. He would offer some to the settlers so they could make their own supplies last a little longer. Some fresh elk might also serve as a little peace offering with Nina's father.

Nina Harding. He hadn't given her much thought the day he first rode into the settler's camp outside of Cheyenne. She seemed to be a girl who tried not to draw attention to herself. And yet, she had a quiet sort of natural beauty. The more Jack looked, the more he found he wanted to look.

He pulled his Winchester from the saddle boot, jacked the action to chamber a round and brought the rifle to his shoulder.

The elk was moving along leisurely. The way the wind was blowing, it hadn't caught the scent of Jack or his horse. It was approaching the summit of the hill. Jack sighted in on a spot at the base of the elk's skull and squeezed the trigger and the rifle roared and bucked against his shoulder. The elk pitched forward and came to a sliding stop in the grass. It flopped onto its side and kicked a couple of times, and was dead.

Jack rode to where the elk lay dead. With his Winchester returned to the scabbard, he stepped down to the grass and pulled a pocket knife from his vest. Though the blade was only three inches long, he kept it sharp to split a hair. He gutted the animal, then tied the carcass over the back of his saddle.

With the animal in place, Jack thought he would abandon his vigil of the back trail and return to the wagons. The added weight of the elk onto the horse would slow him down, and Jack wanted to be at camp before sundown.

He decided to take one last quick look at the back trail, and as he topped the hill from which he had shot the elk, visible in the distance maybe two miles away was a dust cloud. Riders. They must have been stopped when he rode out here, because he had a view of nearly seven miles and never saw them approaching. They must have been sitting and waiting. Maybe letting their horses rest a bit. Then they heard the rifle shot and were now coming.

Judging by the size of the dust cloud, Jack figured they weren't riding hard, but they weren't walking their animals either. At this speed they could cover two miles in less than twenty minutes. With the carcass tied to the back of his horse, there was no way Jack would be able to make it back to the wagons before the riders could overtake him. He would have to cut the elk free and leave it behind.

He hated the idea of leaving those men free food. He had essentially shot their supper for them. But he saw no alternative.

Then he looked closer and realized he might have been wrong in his first estimation of the cloud. The way the dust was being generated, he now thought it might have been created by wheels as much as by horse hooves. It was a wagon. Possibly a stage coach. He couldn't imagine what other kind of wagon would be out here and moving that fast.

He cursed himself for his inexperience. He had retained all of the knowledge Pa had given him, but much of it was academic. He didn't have the experience necessary to put that knowledge to practical use. He doubted Pa or Josh would have made that mistake in evaluating a dust cloud.

Jack rode down to the side of the trail to wait for the wagon. He dismounted and loosened the cinch to let his horse breathe a bit before he began the long ride back to the wagons.

After a time, a stage came into view. The horses were being held to a trot, but even still, the hooves and the iron rims of the stage's wheels kicked up a fair amount of dust. There was little rain in this land, and even though grass grew, the dirt could be loose and dry.

Jack held up his hand and the stage drive pulled the team to a halt.

"Howdy," Jack called to the driver.

"Howdy, stranger." The driver was maybe ten years older than Jack, with a face already weathered from years of riding into the sun and wind. Beside him on the seat was another man cradling a shot gun. The driver said, "Your horse pull up lame?"

"No, he's fine. I'm with a small group of wagons that are camping a few miles up the road."

The driver nodded with recognition. "Johnny McCabe's son. I heard about you back in Cheyenne. They're still talking about the way you beat up two of those gunhawks, and the way you and the marshal rescued that girl from their camp."

"Those gunhawks — were they still in town?"

The driver shook his head and spat a wad of tobacco juice. "Nope. From what I heard, they pulled out about a week ago."

Not good news, Jack thought.

The driver said, "Look, pilgrim, I'd like to stay and palaver all day but I got me a schedule to keep."

"I understand. One more question, though. One of the wagons has a cracked axle. Is there any chance we could find a new one at that way station ahead?"

The driver shook his head. "Maybe. That's where we're headed now. He keeps stuff like that on hand, in case a stage breaks down. Axles and wheels. Extra harnesses."

"I won't hold you up any longer, then."

"Nice meetin' you, McCabe," and the driver *giddyapped* his team and off they went.

Good news, Jack thought, as he tightened the cinch and stepped into the saddle. The way station would be, according from what Nina had they were told earlier in the day, maybe twenty miles further down the road. The teams of oxen couldn't match the speed of the stage coach, but Jack thought they should be able to reach the place within a couple of days, should Harding's axle hold up.

Before he started along the trail, he cast one more glance back. There, in the distance, a narrow finger of white smoke was beginning to rise toward the sky. Out here, it was most likely a campfire.

From the trail, he had visibility of only maybe two miles, and the smoke was from further away than that, but just how far was hard to guess. From the positioning of it, he estimated it to be a mile or more away from the trail. Someone traveling overland but keeping away from the trail.

Jack had no way of knowing for sure who

the campfire belonged to. But he had a good guess.

He kicked his horse into a shambling trot, and began his way back to the wagons.

11

Cook fires had started, but dinners were not yet being prepared when Jack rode into camp.

"You been huntin'," Ford said, his eyes lighting with a smile at the elk draped across the back of Jack's saddle.

"That I have. Elk meat for everyone tonight."

Elk was divided between the three families and roasted over the fires. As the sky darkened and stars began to show, Jack sat cross-legged in the grass in front of the Brewster fire with a plate of elk in front of him. Brewster was on a stool with a small wooden table in front of him. He held a fork in his one hand and was spearing a chunk of meat.

Brewster said, "This was such a welcome surprise."

Jessica was in a small wooden chair, a plate of elk balancing on her lap. She said, "This might go a long way with mending fences with Mister Harding, since you seem to have set your sights on Nina."

Jack was suddenly uncomfortable at the direction the conversation was taking. "What makes you think I've set my sights on anyone?"

"I can tell by the way you look at her."

"Jessica," her mother said. "That's not talk for a lady."

Jessica gave Jack a wicked smile. "Who says I'm a lady?"

Not me, Jack almost said.

"Jessica," Brewster said. "That's enough."

She shrugged and went back to her plate, cutting another piece of elk and chewing into it.

Once he was done eating, Jack got his rifle. He said to Brewster, "I'm going to go do some scouting."

Brewster nodded. "Be safe."

Jack went on foot, as he did the night before. He was able to step down on the grass silently, but his smooth bootsoles were a little slippery. Pa usually carried a pair of deerskin boots in his saddlebags, in case he needed to move silently, and Jack found himself wishing he had a pair with him. Pa had made him some a couple years ago for Christmas, but he had left them in his room at the ranch. You don't normally need deerskin boots at Harvard.

He had put maybe a quarter mile between himself and the camp when he saw a point of light in the distance. It was shimmering and flickering. A campfire. Most likely the one the smoke he had seen earlier belonged to.

He returned to camp and the Brewster's fire and took a cup of coffee, draining what was left in the pot. The camp was quiet as everyone had turned in, and the fires were burning down.

Brewster stepped from his tent. He had removed his hat and jacket, and stood in a white shirt and suspenders. His sleeve was folded over the remains of his forearm, and looked to be somehow fastened. A button, maybe.

"They're out there, aren't they?" Brewster said. "You saw their campfire."

Jack nodded. "I saw it."

"And you're sure it's them?"

"I'm not really sure of anything. But the stage driver I talked to said those men had pulled out the day after we had, and it's good to never take chances with men like that."

"It seems like the prudent thing would be to post a guard, but no one here is qualified for anything like that, except you. Ford's a good man, and Harding carry's himself in a strong way, but they've never served in the Army. I can't imagine either of them out there in the dark with a squirrel gun."

"What about you?"

"I was in the Army once, back in the war. A long time ago. Back when I still had both hands. I can't really use a rifle anymore."

"How about a pistol?"

Brewster looked at him curiously, like he hadn't considered that option.

Jack drew his revolver and flipped it over in his hand so he could hand it butt-first to Brewster.

"This is one of them Peacemakers," Brewster said, holding it up before his eyes in the firelight.

"Forty-four caliber. Loaded with only five rounds. I keep the chamber in front of the hammer empty so it won't fire accidentally when I'm riding. You hang onto that for the night. I'll take the first guard and wake you up in a few hours and you can spell me, and we can switch off like that until morning."

"No need to even worry Harding or Ford, I suppose."

"Tell me about Harding. What's his problem? He seems like he has a deep anger smoldering inside him."

"Poetically put."

"I'd hate to think all those years at school went to waste."

Brewster chuckled. "I've known Carter Harding for years. We lived outside the same town in Vermont."

It seemed to Jack like there was more Brewster wanted to say, but didn't.

Jack said, "What about Ford?"

"A good man. He lived there, also. But all

he knows is farming. That's all either of them know."

"Except for you. You went off to the war."

Brewster nodded. "Lost my hand at Gettysburg. Took a Confederate musket ball right through the wrist. Most men shot that bad died of infection within a week, but I was spared."

Brewster tucked the pistol into the front of his belt. "Harding has his own ideas, and is stubborn to a fault. It's hard for him to accept help and I don't know if I've ever heard him admit he was wrong. But he's a hard worker and pulls his own weight, and he might be a good man to have your back in a fight."

"He won't be pulling his own weight if that axle breaks before we get to the way station."

Brewster nodded and chuckled. "I don't think he sees it that way."

"He sure hates me."

"He doesn't understand you."

"And you do?"

Brewster shrugged. "Maybe not entirely. But I met some hard men during the war. Met some good ones, and some bad ones. You kind of straddle the fence in some ways. You seem like a good man. An educated man. And yet, you move like a gunman."

"I suppose you're right on all accounts. I hope I'm a good man. And I have enough education to choke a horse. But I suppose I wear the gunhawk label honestly. It's part of where I'm from. My Pa rode a dangerous trail. I suppose he still does. He taught me all he could."

"He sent you off to school in the east. Maybe he wanted something better for you."

Jack shrugged. "Maybe. Though I don't know if I'm meant to ride that trail."

Brewster hesitated a moment, then said, "Is it true what my daughter said? About you and Harding's daughter?"

"She seems like a nice girl. But I don't know if it would be fair to get too close to her. I don't really know what lies ahead of me."

"You're not going back to school?"

Jack shook his head. "No. I don't think so. But I don't know where I will be going. The future's like a blank page."

"It is for us all, son. Just most of us don't realize it. We plug along in a certain direction, but we never really know what the good Lord has planned for us."

"Well, you might as well turn in. I think the wagons should be moving as soon as possible in the morning. Make that way station as fast as we can. With any luck, Harding's axle will hold out until then."

"Do you think we'll be safe from those men there?"

"For a time. I really don't think they'll try anything while we're there. They won't want

140

any witnesses."

"What is their beef with you? I understand they might be a little miffed because of the way you and the marshal pulled Jessica out of their camp. But to follow us like this strikes me as a little obsessive."

"It seems Falcone, their leader, feels there is some sort of unfinished business between himself and my brothers, and Marshal Kincaid thinks he might want to take it out on me. Or try to strike at my brothers through me.

"There's also a gunfighter who might be with them. By the name of Two-Finger Walker. He's an old enemy of my father. They don't come much worse than Walker.

"There's also Cade, one of his men. He challenged me back in town and came out the worse for it. He might want another try at me. And Cade has taken a liking to your daughter."

"Harding might blame you for our troubles, but I wonder if this Cade would have been coming for Jessica, anyway."

Jack said, "Especially since she went willingly to their camp. Out here in this land, Mister Brewster, with women of marrying age so rare, a woman is seldom abused. She will often be safe even in the company of ruthless men. Even though we have two women of marrying age in our party, Falcone and his men would likely have never tried to take them by force."

"Marrying age?" Brewster said. "Jessica is only sixteen."

"Marrying age out here might be considerably younger than what it is in Vermont. If a girl is old enough to bear a child, she's of marrying age."

"And," Brewster said, "Jessica went with them willingly."

Jack nodded. "She opened a door when she did that. She voluntarily entered their world. There were women at their camp, but they were all saloon women. Jessica is not one of them, and is presumably untouched. A treasure, in their eyes, who would normally be beyond reach. But she went to them willingly, and I doubt they are going to let it go."

"But she's just a child. She didn't know what she was getting herself into."

"My father told me once one of the most difficult aspects of being a parent is trying to remember how old your child is becoming. He said he would see me in his mind's eye as being five or six, when in reality I was ten. By the time he got used to the idea that I was ten, I was fifteen. You need to take a strong look at your daughter, Mister Brewster. She is young, yes, and maybe less schooled in the ways of the world than she realizes. But she is no child."

Brewster was silent a moment, looking off into the night. Then he said, "You are wise beyond your years, my friend."

"Get some rest. I'll take first watch. I'll come get you in four hours."

Brewster clapped his hand onto Jack's shoulder and ambled off to his family's tent.

Jack had gotten off to a bad start with Brewster — admittedly his own fault — but that was now apparently behind them. Brewster seemed to be warming up to him, and Ford had liked him from the start. Now, if only Jack could break through the icy exterior of Carter Harding.

Not that Jack needed people to like him to feel good about himself. Pa had taught him it's not so important what people think of you, because they will think what they want no matter what you do. The truly important thing is what you think of yourself.

Except, things were not quite so simple with Harding. It so happened the stubborn, tight-lipped farmer, with his narrow mind and unbending opinions, was also the father of a girl Jack was finding himself growing fond of.

It was not simply her looks that appealed to Jack, though she was quite breathtaking in a subtle sort of way. It was her heart, her mind, the way she moved, the look in her eye when she glanced at him. The way her smile seemed to light him up inside.

One thing about college life in Massachussetts — unlike the west, there was no shortage of marrying-age women. Especially for college men. Jack had known a few. Sure, he had gotten more intimate with them than Aunt Ginny would have approved of. But none caught his attention quite like Nina Harding.

Jack took a sip of coffee from his tin cup, looking off into the darkness as he did so. He kept his gaze away from the dwindling fire because he wanted his eyes fully adjusted to the night. His holster was now empty as he had given his revolver to Brewster. He thought about unbuckling his gunbelt and tossing it onto his bedroll, then decided against it. There were twenty cartridge loops in his belt, every one of them filled. Cartridges that fit his pistol would also fit his rifle.

He took a final gulp of coffee, emptying his tin cup when he heard the heard a sound of motion behind him. A boot or shoe sole scuffing ever so slightly against the gravel underfoot. He turned quickly, tossing away his cup and grabbing the rifle with both hands, his finger on the trigger.

It was Nina. She gasped and took a step backward at the sudden motion. "Jack. It's me."

Jack stood down. "Nina. You could get yourself shot, sneaking around out here like that."

"I just wanted to say hi," she said, a little

sheepishly.

He smiled. He was glad she did. He fetched his cup from the grass, and snatched the kettle for a refill of coffee. "Does your father know you're out here?"

"Of course not. I'm forbidden to speak with you."

"I really don't want you in trouble with him."

"Do you want me to go away?"

"No," he found himself saying. "That's one thing I truly do not want.

She smiled, and stepped toward the fire. She held her hands out to the heat. "It's a little chilly tonight."

"In all honesty, I was just thinking about you."

"Nothing bad, I hope."

"Just the opposite."

He found her a place to sit, on an upended wooden basket that came from Brewster's camp.

He said, "Would you like some coffee?"

"No, thanks. It would keep me up all night. And from what I heard of you and Mister Brewster talking, we will be up and moving quite early."

"You were back there listening."

She nodded. "Yes, I was. I couldn't hear everything you said. I wasn't trying to eavesdrop, really. I was just waiting for Mister Brewster to leave so we could maybe talk for a might. I know you must think me brazen. Approaching a man alone at night is more like something Jessica would do."

"No, not at all. I could never think badly of you."

She smiled again. She was not looking away shyly now.

"Coffee helps me think, sometimes," he said, "At school, I would often pour a cup and sit outside on the steps at night and look up at the night sky."

"And what would you think about on those nights?"

"Where I wanted to be."

"And where did you want to be?"

Jack looked upward at the stars overhead. "In a place like this. With a campfire burning, and a cup of trail coffee in my hand. A gun at my side."

She looked down at his holster, seeing it was empty. "Where's your gun now?"

"I gave it to Mister Brewster for the night, for when it's his turn to stand guard."

"Do you really think we're in danger from those men?"

"I hope not. But my father always said in a situation like this, prepare for the worst. I'd rather be prepared and have those men leave us alone, than not be expecting them and be taken by surprise." He took a sip of his coffee.

"You and Mister Brewster were talking

about unfinished business their leader has with your brothers. I heard that much. But I also overheard Father and Mister Brewster talking, back when we were camped outside of town. They spoke of what they had heard of your father. Apparently he's something of a living legend."

He shrugged. "So it would seem. They talk about him sometimes around campfires, or in cattle camps or saloons. He's done some pretty incredible things, and those things tend to grow with the retelling. A writer from New York approached him three or four years ago to write a dime novel about him. Pa refused, but the man wrote one anyway. Now he's written a second. Though, the Johnny McCabe in those novels has little to do with the real man."

"They said that your family has a ranch in Montana Territory, and they spoke of a sister. They only spoke of one brother."

Jack looked away from her, to the darkness beyond the edge of camp. "Didn't know I had second one myself, till about six months ago."

"Really? I'm sorry. I don't mean to pry."

"No. It's all right. Really." He wasn't simply being polite. He found this girl made him want to share himself. To tell her things he had never even shared with Darby, back at school.

He took a drink of coffee and said, "Six

147

months ago, I got a letter. A long one from my Aunt Ginny, catching me up to date on some of the goings-on with the family. I hadn't returned home last summer, because I was helping some professors with some projects for extra credit. One of them is writing a book and needed help with some research."

"That sounds exciting."

"It was interesting. And I was focused on doing the best I possibly could. Push my grade-point average as far upward as it could possibly go. I had graduated high school two years earlier than most. I finished undergraduate school in two and a half years, where most students need four. And I wanted to excel at medical school the same way. Then, with that letter, it all came crashing down."

She was silent, waiting for him. As though she sensed there are times you just need to be still and let someone continue at their own pace.

"I never really wanted medical school. I always just wanted to do what my father had done. To build a home for myself out here. To build a cabin in the mountains. Run some cattle. Maybe raise a family. But I ignored all of that. I pushed it away from my center and focused only on excelling academically. I knew Pa wanted what was best for me, and what he believed was best was school back east. Medical school or law school. And I wanted his respect so badly, I guess just pushed myself and what I wanted aside to try to be everything he wanted."

She said, "And then, you got that letter."

He nodded. "And then I got that letter."

The letter had told him of the attack on the ranch by raiders the summer before. How his father had been shot and nearly killed.

As he spoke, he knelt by the coffee pot, which was now nearly empty. He tossed out the remains, and then began scooping in coffee grounds.

She didn't mean to interrupt, but she had to say something about what he was doing. "Pardon my saying, but that's an awful lot of coffee for that pot."

"This is what we call trail coffee. Pa says it can take the rust off a nail, and he's probably right. The very thought of it makes Aunt Ginny cringe. I developed a taste for it over the years, on my visits home. The coffee has to boil over three times, then it's ready."

"But what about the grounds? Mother drops an egg in to collect them."

He chuckled. "We just spit 'em out."

She sort of grimaced. "I think I agree with your Aunt Ginny."

He started laughing. Within a few moments, she was too. She said, "I suppose any wife of yours will have to learn to make this trail coffee."

He found himself smiling at her. "Yeah. I suppose she would."

"So, you were telling me about the attack on your family's ranch last summer. The whole thing sounds dreadful."

"Yeah. Pa was shot bad, but he survived. He's doing well. Fully recovered. But it turns out apparently some of the men following us might have been involved."

"There's more," she said. It was not a question. "I can see it in your eyes. There's something troubling you. And it's more than the attack on your home, and it's more than just whether or not you want to go back to medical school."

She was perceptive. Such a thing would be annoying if it was anyone else other than Nina.

"Yeah," he said. "There's more."

At that moment, the coffee kettle began to hiss and roar, and the brownish water boiled up and out of it, hissing into the fire. With a bandanna wrapped around his hand, he grabbed the kettle by the handle and lifted it from the heat.

"So, that's one," she said. "It has to boil over three times?"

"Three times," he said. He held the kettle out to let it cool until the roaring from inside the pot had stopped, then he put it back on the fire.

He then stood up to stretch his legs a little

while he waited for the coffee to boil a second time.

"In that letter from home," he said, "I found out I have a brother. A second one. Just like that. In a letter."

"That strikes me as a rather abrupt way to learn something so important and personal."

"Apparently they all found out just as abruptly. He just rode in and announced who he was, according to Aunt Ginny's letter. Pa never knew about him. None of us did. Pa's life was kind of complicated when he was younger."

"So I see."

"Turns out this boy, just about the age of my brother Josh, which makes him a year older than I am, is called Dusty."

The pot began to make noise like it was about to boil. He waited a moment, and then the coffee came slurping up and over and hissed into the fire. Jack removed the kettle so the contents could again settle down.

"So, did she tell you much about Dusty in the letter?"

Jack nodded. "Aunt Ginny should have been a writer. She expresses herself on paper in such vivid detail. It seems Dusty is the spitting image of Pa, except Dusty's eyes are darker. His Indian heritage, she presumes.

"She said that watching Dusty is like looking into the past. She said Dusty walks like Pa. Wears his gun the same way. Sits a horse the same way. She said watching him walk across the parlor floor in the evening, when the only light is from the fireplace, you would think it was Pa."

The pot boiled a third time. Jack lifted the kettle from the fire. "Sure you don't want some?"

She gave a facial expression that Jack could only describe as a smiling grimace. "No thanks. I'll keep it in mind, though, the next time I need to take rust off a nail."

Jack refilled his tin cup. "I'm going to be standing guard a while. I might need this to keep me awake."

"Oh?" she said playfully. "Am I boring you?"

He smiled at her. "Hardly. At the risk of being inappropriate, you are the least boring person I have ever met."

It might have been the firelight dancing on her face, but he thought he saw a little blush.

She said, "So, your brother Dusty looks like a younger version of your father, right down to the way he moves."

Jack nodded.

Nina said, "And yet, Mister McCabe, something tells me the root of all of this lies even deeper than that."

He sighed, taking a long look out into the darkness. "How is it you can see me so clearly, when others who have known me so much longer don't? My own father, my brother and sister, Aunt Ginny. Even Darby. I've roomed with him for two years, now. You could say he's my closest friend there, which probably makes him my closest friend anywhere. And yet, he looks but doesn't really see me. But you, a girl I've known not even a week, and you seem to see me so clearly."

"Maybe it's because I'm taking the time to really look. Of course, it may not be necessarily that the others haven't, but sometimes, I think, when you raise a child it's easy to get notions of who that child is and what's best for him. Then as the child grows it might go in a different direction than anyone figured on, but you're blinded by preconceived notions.

"Even your friend from school might be a little blinded. You swagger in there, the dashing man from the west with a famous father, and already an image forms in the mind before they really get to know you."

He grinned. "So, I swagger?"

She shrugged and returned the grin. "I plead the fifth."

"So, how is it you're so wise for someone so young?"

"It's not that I'm all that wise. It's just that, from the first time I saw you, I found myself wanting to know absolutely everything about you."

"What would you like to know?"

"Oh, I don't know. Your favorite color. Your

favorite holiday. Your favorite piece of music."

He walked over to her. "Blue, like the sky. Christmas. *Swing Low, Sweet Chariot.*"

She cocked her head a little. "I'm not familiar with that one."

"It's a Negro spiritual. You haven't lived until you've heard it sung by Henry Freeman. He's a former slave who does a lot of the blacksmith work for the ranch. Got an incredibly rich baritone. He said he picked up the song in Texas, where he and his family lived for a little while before they went to Montana."

"You are a fascinating, multi-layered man."

"That's me."

"So, Mister McCabe."

"Jack."

She smiled. "Jack. Despite your incredible accomplishments at school, what you really want is to live out here. Build a cabin. Raise children and cattle."

"Actually," he said, kneeling beside her and setting his coffee cup on the ground, "what I really want at the moment is this."

He touched her cheek gently, his fingers sliding to her chin. Then he drew her closer and their lips met.

"You see," he said, "from the first time I've seen you, I've been watching you, too. Wondering about you. Hoping to get to know you."

They kissed again. Longer. His hand

touched hers and she gripped his tightly. He realized his rifle was lying in the grass beside him. He didn't remember letting it go, it simply was there.

They suddenly heard a woman's voice, from one of the other wagons. "Nina?"

Nina jumped to her feet. "That's mother. I have to go."

"Good night," he said. "Thanks for the company."

She gave him a quick smile, and hurried away to the Harding camp. Jake snatched his rifle and followed along. A gentleman didn't let a lady wander around alone at night.

Nina's mother was in a robe. Her hair was tied into a long, graying braid.

"Nina," she said. "Where have you been?"

"I couldn't sleep, so I took a walk. I was at Mister McCabe's fire, talking to him."

Jack said, coming up behind her, "It may not be safe to wander around out here alone. Not if those riders are out there."

Mrs. Harding said to Nina, "Get in the tent before your father wakes up and finds out you were out here."

"Yes'm." Nina started for the tent but threw a glance over her shoulder at Jack. "Good night, Jack."

Jack tipped his hat to her. "Good night."

The Harding woman looked at Jack, a moment, then turned and followed her daughter into the tent.

Jack decided it might be best for him to finish his coffee and then take another wander out into the night and see if that campfire was still burning off in the distance.

As he grabbed his coffee from where he had set it down in the grass beside the upended bucket Nina had been sitting on, he found his gaze drifting back in the direction of the Harding tent. And it was not the campfire off in the distance that he was thinking about.

12

Brewster took the final guard, and as the eastern sky was beginning to lighten with pre-dawn, he woke Jack up and handed him back his pistol.

Jack climbed out of his bedroll and reached for his boots. He then pulled the trigger of his pistol and eased the hammer back a bit so he could freely spin the cylinder, and gave the loads a quick check. Force of habit. Then he returned the gun to his holster.

Jack's face was scruffy as he hadn't shaved since the day before they left Cheyenne. He had slept in his clothes every night since they had been on the trail. Not much of a chance for a bath out here.

He joined the Brewsters at their cook fire for a plate of hot cakes and a cup of coffee. Every so often, trying to be as casual as he could, he would steal a glance toward the Harding camp. He would see Nina milling about, helping her mother prepare their breakfast. A couple of times she glanced toward Jack and gave him a little smile.

One time Jack stood, plate in hand, and looked about like he was surveying the situation. Like a good scout should. But he let his gaze linger on the Harding camp for a few moments.

Jessica was sitting on a small wooden stool, her plate in her lap. She rolled her eyes at Jack and shook her head. She said, "Could you be more obvious?"

He looked at her, trying to muster up the most questioning look he could find. As if to say, *but whatever do you mean?*

She said, "We all know you were out here talking to Nina for all hours of the night."

Mildred Brewster said, "Jessica. A lady does not pry into the affairs of others."

"Mother," she rolled her eyes again, as only a teen-aged girl can. "Everyone knows they were out here. Everyone except old man Harding himself."

Mildred said, "*Mister* Harding to you."

She got up to go join her husband. He was at the oxen, getting ready to hitch them up. Their son was with him. Jack thought Brewster did well for a man with one hand, but sometimes you just needed a second hand to hitch up a team.

Jessica was still on the stool, finishing her last hot cake. Jack was really coming to dislike Jessica, and saw an opportunity to get in a dig at her. He said, "Besides, whoever said you were a lady?"

She shot him a wicked grin. "Touché, cowboy."

The wagons were in motion at sunrise. Brewster's son was leading the team. He stood almost to Jack's shoulder, and wore a white shirt and dark pants and suspenders over his shoulders. He wore a floppy felt hat. They all called him A.J., which Jack figured probably was short for Abel Junior. They often called him *Age,* a sort of abbreviated version of A.J.

At Jack's suggestion, the women walked. It would give the oxen a little less weight to pull. Brewster was leading one of the teams, and his wife was walking alongside him. Jessica and Nina were off a couple hundred yards, strolling through hip-high grass. Occasionally they would come across a patch of wild flowers, and at one point Nina picked a tall pinkish flower and was holding it in one hand as she walked. Jack was not one to know the names of flowers. Aunt Ginny knew chrysanthemums and peonies from jonquils. All Jack knew was the flower Nina had picked was pink.

He decided as scout he should check on everyone, so he rode out to the girls.

"Good morning, ladies," he said.

Jessica rolled her eyes at him again. "Good morning, cowboy."

Nina gave him a shy smile. "Hello."

"I just thought I'd check on you both. As the scout, I also have to recommend that you don't wander too far from the wagons."

Jessica said, "I'm sure if you thought we were in trouble, you'd come rescue us, whether we wanted to be rescued or not."

Jack decided the best course of action would be to ignore her.

Nina said, looking at Jack playfully, "Could there be wild Indians out here?"

He raised his brows and shook his head. "You never know. Or big scary grizzly bears."

Jessica said, "How much more of this do I have to listen to?"

"I'd best be going," Jack said. "I'm thinking of scouting the back trail a little."

"Be careful," Nina said.

"Always. You know, tonight, I'll be out by the fire a while, after everyone's asleep. Standing guard. You know, hypothetically speaking, if a girl, say, was having trouble sleeping and wanted to come out by the fire, I would sure appreciate the company. Hypothetically."

Nina gave him a sly smile. "Well, if this hypothetical girl has trouble sleeping, maybe she'll wander out your way."

Jack tipped his hat to them both. "Ladies."

He turned his horse and started away toward their back trail.

He heard Jessica saying, "Why don't you just jump on him and kiss him tonight? I know that's what you want to do."

Nina said, "Jessica. You are shameless."

"You can bet your life on that."

And then he was out of earshot, but he smiled as he rode along.

Jack rode over to the Brewsters. Their wagons were first in line this morning. They usually were.

"I'm thinking of riding back and scouting the back trail again for a bit."

Mildred Brewster said, "What are you looking for back there?"

"Any sign of movement. This land is so dry, a group of riders moving along will stir up a small dust cloud that can be visible from a distance. Even in the grass. Not much of a dust cloud, but enough that you can notice it if you're looking carefully."

The Harding wagon was number three in line. Carter Harding was moving the oxen along. He glanced at Jack for a moment, but then turned his eyes to the wagon ahead of him, and the trail beyond.

"How's the axle holding up?" Jack said.

"Fair enough."

Jack knew Harding must have seen him talking to the girls, which might account for a little extra coarse attitude from him.

Jack said, "I cautioned the girls about not wandering too far from the wagons."

"I'm sure they'll be all right."

There was a lot Jack wanted to say. He

161

didn't take to being treated rudely. He had his father's temper, just like his brother Josh did. You shove any one of them, and they'll shove back twice as hard. But Jack also knew something of diplomacy, and decided this was the better option for the moment. And the diplomatic thing to do at the moment was simply to remain silent.

Jack turned his horse away.

Behind the Harding wagon were the Fords. Mister Ford was moving the oxen along, and his wife was sitting in the wagon seat with their young child.

Ford looked up at him. "How are things?"

Jack nodded. "Fine. No sign of trouble at all. I'm going to go scout the back trail a bit, though. Just to be sure."

Ford smiled. "You happen to see another elk, it would be mighty welcome at dinner."

Jack returned the smile. "If I see one, you'll get first choice of the cut."

Jack's glance drifted to the wagon seat, and Ford's young wife. Jack had suggested that everyone walk, but the Fords were apparently not following his advice. He wanted to ask why, but again thought of diplomacy. Ford might not take kindly to being instructed by a man young enough to be his son.

What Jack said was, "Is Missus Ford okay?"

"Oh, she's fine. Just a little tired this morning."

Jack nodded. "I'll see you all in a few hours."

The country was still wide-open, as it had been outside of Cheyenne. Grass in all directions, and not a tree in sight. But the hills seemed to rise a little more sharply now. They weren't quite so long and stretched out. In the far distance, off to the left of the trail, was a long, low ridge that looked to be rocky and arid.

Jack turned his horse away from the trail and climbed one of the low hills. At the top, he stepped out of the saddle so he wouldn't be as visible from a distance. Again, Pa's teaching. Don't skyline yourself.

Jack loosened the cinch so the horse could breathe a little more comfortably, and while the horse grazed he stood with the wind in his face, rattling the brim of his sombrero, and he searched the horizon with his eyes.

Pa had said in desert country, riders will kick up such a dust cloud you could see it for miles. You could even guess the number of riders by the size of the cloud. But here where there was grass, any dust kicked up by riders would be minimal. Riders keeping to the trail where the grass was worn down, like with the stage yesterday, would create a dust cloud. But if they were going overland, staying away from the trails and not riding too hard, there would be very little dust.

Jack thought he saw a sort of smudge near

the horizon. Maybe four or five miles off. Might be dust, he thought. Hard to tell.

He realized he was getting hungry. Maybe he would ride about and see if he could find another elk. Ford's idea had been a good one. Now that elk had been mentioned, he found himself hankering for another taste of it.

He tightened the cinch and swung into the saddle, and turned his horse north and east. He would cut a wide circle around the wagons, seeing what he could scare up for game as he went. But all the time, he kept an eye on their back trail.

13

That night, they camped by a small creek. The grass was worn away in places where wild animals had come to graze, and in a few places sections of bedrock were exposed. Some alders grew and provided dead branches. The men attacked a deadfall with saws, and there was firewood for the night.

Jack returned with a white-tailed buck draped across the back of his saddle, and the mood at the camp became festive. Even Harding cracked a smile and shared in a laugh with Ford and Brewster. Jack found a piece of bedrock rose high enough to make a convenient stool, and sat with a plate of venison and enjoyed the lighter mood around camp.

When the meal was done and the fires burning low, and everyone turned in for the night, Jack gave his pistol to Brewster again and again volunteered for the first watch.

Jack had dropped in another piece of alder into the Brewster's fire, and then poured himself a cup of coffee. He fetched some water from the creek and started a second pot of coffee boiling. His saddle and bedroll were in the grass, a few yards from the fire. His horse grazed contentedly off at the edge of the firelight.

After a time, Nina emerged from the tent. She was stepping lightly, and cast a glance over her shoulder toward her family's tent as she made her way over to the Brewsters' fire.

"So," she said with a smile. "This hypothetical girl had a little trouble sleeping and thought she'd take a walk."

"I put a pot of coffee on," he said. "I made it the civilized way."

She raised her brows. "Oh? I didn't realize you knew how to make civilized coffee."

He smiled. "I learned from my Aunt Ginny. I even cracked an egg into it. Just in anticipation of a hypothetical girl who couldn't sleep."

She brought her arms about her as a chill struck her. "It's so much colder out here at night than I would have thought. In Vermont, we were further north than we are now, but it's almost summer. Back home, it would be quite warm in the evening this time of year."

Jack went to his bedroll and pulled out a jacket. It was a waist-length and made of deerskin, sewn together with strips of rawhide.

"My father made this for me a couple years ago," he said. "It's not lined, but it's surprisingly warm."

He draped it about her shoulders. She gave him the kind of smile a girl gives a man she likes when he does something like that.

"I don't want you cold," she said.

"I'm fine. Really."

She said, "I think we made really good time with the wagons, today."

He nodded. "I think we should be at the way station by early tomorrow afternoon."

He knelt to stir the fire a little. "I hope being out here doesn't cause problems with your father."

"Mother knows I'm here. She was awake when I left the tent. She whispered to me not to be long."

"Will your father be angry if he finds out?"

"He'll put on a show of anger, yes. But deep down, I think he knows how I feel about you. Father's a complicated man, and you have to know how to play your cards around him. He's deep feeling and cares greatly for his family, but it's all buried beneath this exterior of gruffness."

"Why is he like that?"

She shrugged. "Mother always deflects the question, but I've heard things over the years. His father was rough on him. Used a belt on him more than once."

"There are those who believe the only way to raise a boy is with a firm hand. I never remember Pa striking Josh or me, though.

Our respect for him is so great a simple firm word was all it took. And Aunt Ginny . . ." He shook his head with a smile. "She can glare at you in a way that can almost cut you in half. I've seen many a man a lot tougher than I am shake in his boots when she did that to him."

She gave a little laugh. "I would like to meet your family some day."

"Well, we'll be in the area. Brewster's talking about settling in the Montana foothills. There's no better farming land than right there outside the town of McCabe Gap."

"McCabe Gap? Is it named after your family?"

He nodded. "It's not really a town, though. It's just a few buildings gathered together in a pass that leads into the little valley we call home. It's very sparsely populated, but what the place has to offer is land. Thousands and thousands of acres. The center of the valley is mostly unsettled, and there's enough water there to make farming very possible."

"And what about you? Have you ever thought about farming?"

He smiled and shook his head. "Oh no, ma'am. No self-respecting cowboy would ever be caught working afoot."

She looked at him curiously.

He said, "That's cattleman humor. You'll see when you get there."

The coffee was ready, so he poured her a

cup. A wooden chair Jessica had used during dinner was still out, so he held it for Nina as she gently lowered herself into it. He then handed her the cup.

Aunt Ginny had said once you can tell a lot about a person by the way they sit. If they just plop down in a chair, or if they lower themselves gracefully. Nina had done the second. She was classy, but not like it was an affectation, but something natural. Like it was just part of who she was.

He poured himself a cup. This stuff was much too thin for his liking, but this pot of coffee wasn't about taste. It was about who he was sharing it with.

She said, "My father is a little like you, in a way. According to Mother, he never wanted to be a farmer."

"What did he want to do?"

"She said he has the soul of a poet."

That got a look of surprise from Jack. If he had just taken a mouthful of coffee, he was sure it would have sprayed everywhere. How could a man as ornery as Carter Harding have the soul of a poet?

Nina continued, "No, really. He can be quite gentle, sometimes. But he was taught by his father that such things are a sign of weakness. And publishing poetry is a thing for the wealthy. Father was the son of a farmer and they couldn't afford the schooling needed. Father has a natural gift with working with the land, coaxing it to grow things. He has a natural gift with livestock, too."

Jack nodded. He could see where she was going with this. "I suppose I do know a thing or two about being shackled by your own gift. With me, the gift pertains to things academic."

"You're highly intelligent."

He shook his head with a smile. "No. That's what everyone thinks, but it's just an illusion. The gift is that I can remember almost everything I read. Excelling at school is easy for me because I don't have to study. I just have to read something once and I can test on it. I graduated high school at the head of my class, and I did so without even really trying. Not that I mean to boast, because I surely don't. It's just this confounded memory of mine. I can read a page out of a book, and then even months later, quote it almost verbatim.

"For instance . . ." He searched his memory for a moment. " 'And the Lord said unto Gideon, The people that are with thee are too many for me to give the Midianites into their hands, lest Israel vaunt themselves against me, saying, Mine own hand hath saved me.'

"Old Testament. Judges, chapter seven. Verse two, or three. I forget which. I read that passage once, for a course I took in Biblical literature, my freshman year in college. It was all about how the Bible as literature affected the literature of western Europe and this country. And even the politics, and to a large extent, the European and American mindset."

"Did you get an A in the course?"

He nodded. "I just fed the teacher back the stuff he was feeding us, as though I agreed with it, and got an A."

"You disagreed with him?"

"It's not so much that I disagreed with him, it's that I don't really care. I don't have any interest in debating that sort of thing. I want to ride the mountains. Raise cattle."

She smiled. "And raise children."

He returned the smile. "With the right woman."

"Do another one," she said. "Recite from another book."

He had to think a moment. "Well, there was one by Dickens."

"Who?"

"Charles Dickens. A writer out of England."

"Is he any good?"

Jack shrugged. "A matter of opinion, I suppose. He wrote one called *Dombey and Son*. It starts something like this . . .

"*Dombey sat in the corner of the darkened room in the great arm-chair by the bedside, and Son lay tucked up warm in a little basket bedstead, carefully disposed on a low settee*

*immediately in front of the fire and close to it,
as if his constitution were analogous to that of
a muffin.* Or, something like that. It was kind
of a stupid book, really. I don't really like
Dickens. Now Mark Twain — he can write."

"So, how will you know the right woman
when you meet her?"

"It could be possible I've already met her.
Only the future can tell. And the future is an
open book. A tapestry not yet woven."

She raised her brows. "My. You're getting
poetic."

He nodded. "I took a class in that, too. The
analysis of poetry. Got an A."

"But let me guess. You don't like poetry
much, either."

"Well, at least not the kind written on paper
by intellectual stuffed shirts."

"What kind of poetry do you like?" She
took a sip of coffee. "This is very good, by
the way."

He glanced upward, to a scattering of stars
above them and a crescent moon hugging the
horizon. "There. Above us."

She followed his gaze. "It's a beautiful sky."

"You've never experienced anything until
you've stood on a mountainside at night and
looked up at those stars. They seem so close,
somehow. It almost takes your breath away."

"And you never told anyone that you don't
like reading poetry? Your father or your aunt,
or any of your professors?"

He shook his head. "Never. They all just assumed because of this so-called gift, my supposedly high level of intelligence, that I would just naturally like that kind of thing. I wanted so badly to make Pa proud of me, I just went along with all of it.

"I've been schooled in Mozart and Beethoven. I've never told anyone, but I don't like that, either. To me, music is a harmonica being played by a campfire. Or a banjo or a fiddle. That's music."

"Or *Swing Low, Sweet Chariot* being sung by a rich baritone."

He smiled. "Indeed."

He took another sip of coffee. She did the same.

He said, "I've come to think education is really little more than a glorified parlor trick. All these university professors who are held in such high esteem are really doing is repeating things they've read, as though it's all their own idea. I learned to play that game early. Since I have this strange ability to remember so thoroughly what I read, I found I could play the game easily.

"Did you know I don't even like to read?"

She shook her head. "I can't imagine. I love to read."

"I've read all of Hawthorne's works. All of Shakespeare's. I have a couple shelves filled with volumes of their work, back at the school. Aunt Ginny has given me a couple novels by a British author named Dickens. She loves to sit and read in the evening. She assumes I do, too. I really don't care if I ever read another book."

"What do you like to do to relax?"

He shrugged. "I can play a harmonica. Not very well, but I play. I like to go to Gap Town. And I like baseball."

This got a surprised chuckle from her. "Baseball?"

He nodded. "My friend Darby and I would go into Boston for games. There's a professional league set up."

"You mean, they get paid for playing baseball?"

He nodded again. "The National League. The local team is called the Boston Red Stockings. It can be a rowdy time. Fights break out and the beer flows. The highbrow professors at Harvard look down on it, and it's no place you'd take a lady, but a bunch of us would sneak off to games. It can be a rollicking good time."

"So, life at school wasn't all bad."

He shook his head. "No. There were some good times. And I met some good people."

"And then you got that letter."

He grew a little somber, his smile fading. "Then I got that letter. This brother I never knew even existed simply rode in, and took his place beside Pa. The place I always wanted, but was denied."

She nodded. "That's the crux of it."

"Indeed. I suppose it is. My brother Dusty has everything I always wanted, and he has it so easily. He doesn't have to aspire toward it. He simply is it. Josh too, really, but I've learned to accept it with Josh. But Dusty is even more than that. He's the spitting image of Pa. From what Aunt Ginny says, he's almost a younger version of Pa."

"Josh doesn't look like your father?"

"No. He looks more like Ma. He has kind of a wiry build, and hair that's really light colored. Bree and me, we look sort of like a blend of Ma and Pa."

"So, where do you go from here?"

"I don't really know. I suppose, after we get these wagons to Montana, I'll have to finally meet my brother. One thing I do know, though. I'm not going back to school."

"Would it be brazen of me to say if my family is going to settle near this McCabe Gap of yours and build a farm, that I hope you're there too?"

He looked at her silently for a moment. Such a feeling of warmth flooded through him. He had never felt like this before.

He said, "I don't think I could ever think you brazen."

"What does cowboy etiquette say about a cattleman courting a farm girl? Or is that allowed?"

"I have found I have little interest in what

people think."

"You daringly break the rules."

He nodded with a smile. "Sort of a family tradition, I guess."

He finished his coffee and then reached for her hand. "Come. It's late. I should walk you back to your tent."

She took his hand and rose to her feet. "You said something about finding the right girl and raising a family. Will you know this girl when you see her?"

He smiled. "I'll know because she'll be able to look at me and really see me."

And they kissed again. Like the night before, but a little longer. A little deeper.

He took her hand in his and they started for the Harding tent.

They stepped beyond the Brewsters' wagon and away from the flickering light of the fire. The moonlight touched the canvas of the Hardings' tent, giving it a pale glow.

And then a man then spoke from the darkness to one side. A voice low and gravely. "Don't make a move, boy."

And Jack heard the unmistakable click of a gun's hammer being hauled back.

14

Jack did make a move, however. He released Nina's hand and stepped between her and the man in the shadows, to use himself as a shield should bullets start flying.

The man casually walked into the firelight. Long hair fell to his shoulders from beneath a dark, wide brimmed hat. A patch covered one eye. In his left hand was a revolver, cocked and aimed toward Jack.

"Two-finger," Jack said.

"That's been my name for a lot of years now, thanks to your daddy."

"And so, you figure shooting me down will bring back your fingers? Or your eye?"

"Maybe not, but it'll sure make me feel better."

"Why not holster that gun and then we can square off man-to-man? But you can't do that because you might get beaten by the son of the man who beat you. You don't dare face me man-to-man, so you have to sneak up on me."

"I'd be quiet, boy."

"Truth hurts, doesn't it? Admit it. You're afraid to face me."

"I ain't afraid of nothin'. But I have my orders. As long as I'm bein' paid, I do what the man says."

There was motion behind Two-Finger, and Cade stepped into view, followed by Jessica Brewster.

"Jessica!" Nina said.

"Throw down your gun," Cade said with a smile. "You're coming with us. The girls, too."

"I'm sorry," Jessica said, "but you better do as they say."

It suddenly dawned on Nina. "You're not their prisoner. You're with them."

"Yes. I'm going with them. I'm sure not going to rot away as a farmer's wife in some remote, God-forsaken patch of wilderness. I'm sorry, Nina. I didn't mean for any of this to involve you."

Cade said to Jack, "It was sure easy to sneak up on you, boy. You with your eyes on the girl. You made this too easy."

"That's enough talk," Two-Finger said. "Boy, drop that rifle to the ground, or I'll shoot you where you stand."

Jack released the grip on his rifle and let it fall to the grass.

Jack said, "If I go with you, Nina stays here."

"No deals. Her being with us will keep you

honest. Now, unbuckle that gunbelt."

It occurred to Jack that they hadn't realized his gunbelt was empty. He had given his pistol to Brewster.

That was when things suddenly began happening fast.

Brewster stepped out from behind the family wagon, maybe thirty feet from where they stood, and he fired. The bullet missed, but both Walker and Cade turned in that direction. Two-Finger fired, his bullet missing Brewster by inches and tearing into the wood of the wagon box. Cade was drawing his gun.

Jack dove for his rifle, grabbing it as he hit the ground and rolled, coming up to knees. Jack worked the lever action and fired form his hip One shot and then another. His first bullet went off somewhere into the night but his second caught Cade and sent him staggering back.

Two-Finger Walker turned toward Jack and fired. Jack was spun around by the impact of the bullet, and landed in the grass. The rifle slid away from his grasp.

"Jack!" Nina screamed.

The flap to the Harding tent opened, and Harding charged out, shotgun in hand.

Two-Finger ran toward Nina and pushed his revolver into her temple.

He yelled, "Don't nobody move or I'll blow her head clean off'n her shoulders!"

Harding stopped to stand still, shotgun in

hand. "You harm a hair on her head and I'll hunt you down and skin you alive."

Walker blinked with surprise. "You don't talk like no farmer I've ever met."

"Don't hurt her," Emily Harding said, from behind her husband.

"Tell your husband not to make me have to."

Brewster stepped out from behind his wagon, holding the pistol high to indicate surrender. Jack was lying in the grass not moving.

"Jack," Nina said, her eyes on him.

Cade was on still on his feet. He was holding onto the side of his ribs.

Two-Finger said, "Now, I want you two farmers to drop them shootin' irons. Right now."

Brewster let Jack's pistol drop to the grass. Harding gave Walker a long glare, but then eased the shotgun's hammer off, and dropped the weapon. Two-Finger said, "Now, we're leaving, and we're taking both girls. Anyone tries to stop us, they'll wind up as dead as the hero, there."

Cade said, "Falcone is gonna be r'iled. He wanted the McCabe boy, too."

"Well, we had to kill him. No choice. Come on. Let's get goin' "

"I'm sorry," Jessica said, looking to her father.

Two-Finger grabbed Nina by one arm.

"Come on."

She walked along with him, but she was looking over her shoulder at Jack's lifeless form lying in the grass.

Brewster and Harding stood helplessly while the two outlaws slipped away into the night with their daughters.

15

Elizabeth Ford knelt in the grass by the side of Jack McCabe. She had a kerchief tied lightly about her hair. She looked up at her husband and said, "He's breathing. He's still alive."

Harding snatched his shotgun from where he had dropped it to the ground. "I don't care. A lot of good it did us having him along."

Ford had a shotgun in his hands. He and his wife had come running at the sound of gunfire, but had gotten there just moments after the outlaws had left.

"They took both girls?" Ford said.

Harding nodded. "I'm gonna go get 'em back."

Brewster retrieved the pistol from the grass. He said to Ford, "I'll go with you."

Mildred grasped her husband by the arm "You'll only get yourselves killed."

"We have to do something," Harding said.

Elizabeth said, "Someone fetch me a lantern."

"I'll get one," Age Brewster said, and ran to his tent and brought one back.

With the lantern standing on the ground, Elizabeth Ford could see Jack's sleeve torn at the left shoulder. She could see where the bullet had caught his shoulder and torn into the skin and he was bleeding, but she didn't think the furrow was very deep.

"I don't understand why he's not awake," she said.

"Look," Age said. By Jack's head was a stone. It looked like a small piece of bedrock that emerged from ground.

Ford walked over. "His head hit that when he got spun around by the bullet."

His wife pulled a kerchief from her head and began tying it around the side of Jack's shoulder. "Doesn't look like the bullet's in there. And I don't think it hit any muscle."

Brewster walked over to where Ford stood by Harding. Brewster said, "Do you really think we can catch them?"

"We got no choice," Harding said. "They have our daughters. I'm going, even if no one goes with me."

"You'll not go alone," Ford said. "We'll all go."

Jack looked up at them, a little groggy but conscious. "No. None of you is going. They'll just shoot you down before you even get close

183

to their camp."

Harding said, "I don't see as how you have a say in this at all. Despite your reputation as a big, bad gunfighter, you proved completely useless. Those men wouldn't even have been here at all if not for you. I was against having you along from the start."

Mildred Brewster had drifted over to help Elizabeth. She said to Jack, "You have to lie still so we can get control of that bleeding."

But Jack shrugged both women off and pushed himself to sit up, despite the pounding in his head. "Useless is right. I let myself get distracted. I wasn't paying attention. They shouldn't have been able to come into our camp like that. But none of you is going after them. Getting yourselves killed won't help the girls, or anyone here."

"What do you have in mind?" Brewster said.

"I'll be the one going. It's what I'm here for. It's why I came along." He pushed himself to his feet, staggered a bit and then got his balance.

"Look at you," Harding said. "You can hardly stand."

Age grabbed Jack's rifle and handed it to him.

Jack looked down at his torn sleeve, and the kerchief tied about the side of his shoulder. It was already soaking with blood. He said to the women, "Can you wrap this any tighter?"

Elizabeth nodded. "I can tear up a bed sheet for a bandage."

She got to her feet.

Mildred said, "I'll help." Both women hurried off to the Ford tent.

Ford said to Jack, "What'll you do? How will you even find them? You're just one man alone. And you're wounded."

"I'll find them. And I'll bring them back, or die trying."

Harding said, "You'd better. If you don't come back with the girls, don't come back at all."

His wife said, "Carter."

Mildred and Elizabeth came scurrying back. Elizabeth had a white bedsheet balled up in her arms.

"Sit," Mildred said.

Jack nodded. He sat in the grass, setting the rifle beside him.

Age held the lantern high while his mother tore away more of the sleeve. She removed the kerchief that was now sopping with blood.

Mildred said, "You lose much more blood, you won't be of any good to anyone."

Jack said, "Can you patch me up? At least so I can ride?"

She nodded. "I worked as a nurse during the war. It's how Abel and I met. I've worked with worse than this. The only problem is infection could set in."

"It won't set in yet. I'll be able to get the

girls back first," Jack said. "Besides. There's a way to handle infection."

"No, there's really not. Modern medicine has no way to stop one, once it sets in. All we can do is clean the wound thoroughly and wrap it up and hope for the best."

Jack said, "I don't mean to be rude, ma'am. Really, I don't. But there is a treatment. My father taught it to me. Have your son go to my saddle bags. Inside is a bottle of whiskey."

"Mister McCabe," she said.

"I'll show you a new use for it."

The boy ran to Jack's saddle bags.

"Does the arm hurt?" Mildred said.

Actually, Jack thought, the arm didn't hurt at all, which he knew could be a bad sign. The more severe the wound, Pa had said, the less the immediate pain. But there would be in a few minutes, Jack knew. As soon as Age returned with the bottle.

"Found it!" the boy called out.

The boy ran back to Jack and handed the bottle to him.

Jack said, "Kentucky whiskey.

Mildred Brewster said, "You can drink some of that to numb your pain, but then you won't be in any condition to go after the girls."

Harding said, "Enough of this nonsense. The longer we wait, the further away those men will be taking our girls. We need to get moving."

186

"Hold on," Brewster said, looking to Jack.

Jack said to Mildred, "I want you to pour this directly into the wound."

"Gracious, no," she said.

"My father has found this actually prevents infection. He learned it when rode with the Texas Rangers. He saw a friend take an arrowhead in the leg, and kept the leg because of this."

"But to pour it directly into the wound? I can't imagine the pain."

"It'll hurt like hell, but do it. We don't have time to waste. Those men already have too much of a head start."

"I can't believe you want me to do this. This goes against all of the medical training I've had."

"With all due respect, ma'am, I've had two years of medical school, and it goes against all I've learned, too. But it works. I've seen it. My father has seen it. It's what they did to him when he was shot up so bad last summer, and he's still alive."

"How much? How much should I pour?"

"A couple ounces. Wash the wound out really well."

She pulled the cork from the bottle. The last thought he had before she poured it was he doubted this was the use Darby had intended when he gave him the bottle.

The whiskey went into the wound with blinding pain. But he refused to cry out. If nothing else, he would not give Carter Harding the satisfaction. There had been no pain from the wound at first, but now it was like a hot branding iron was being pushed into it. He had balled both hands into fists, and realized he was shuddering. But he would not cry out.

He could not afford to pass out from the pain, he thought. He had to remain conscious. As soon as Mrs. Brewster was finished washing the wound with whiskey and wrapping it, he needed to be going after the girls.

It was a few moments before he realized she had stopped pouring the whiskey. The fire in his wound began to subside a little.

"I will say one thing," she said. "The bleeding has stopped."

Jack looked to Age and said, his voice a little shaky, "Do you know how to saddle a horse?"

The boy nodded. "Yes, sir."

"Then, go have at it."

The boy looked to his father, who nodded.

The boy said, "Yes sir," and ran to where Jack's horse was picketed.

Mildred fetched her sewing kit from her tent, and said, "The thread I have is not ideal for stitching a wound shut, but it'll have to do. I want to get this done before the bleeding starts up again."

While she was working on his shoulder, Jack watched Age saddling his horse. The boy knew what he was doing. The saddle was

188

heavy, but he heaved it up onto the horse's back. He then reached under the horse to grab the cinch. The horse stood, chomping on some grass and looking bored.

Elizabeth Ford tore the bedsheet into long strips. Once Mildred was finished with the thread, she wrapped one strip of cloth over the shoulder and under Jack's arm, then followed with another and then a third.

"You gotta keep dirt out of this," she said.

"Believe me. I don't want to do anything to make it necessary to wash it out again."

That got a small grin from her.

Jack got to his feet, and snatched up his rifle.

"How are you going to track them in this darkness?" Harding said.

"I'm not. I have an idea where their camp is. They're going to have a campfire just like we have here. It'll be visible from a distance. They might not be inclined to be worried about that because they think I'm dead, and they don't think any of you to be really a threat. No offense."

Brewster said, "I'm really sorry. I can't believe Jessica went along with them willingly. I feel somehow responsible for this."

"You should be," Harding said.

His wife said, "Carter."

Jack put a hand on Brewster's shoulder. "I'll get them both back."

The horse was ready, and Jack pushed the

rifle into the saddle boot. He buckled on his gunbelt, and Brewster handed him the pistol.

Brewster said, "What do you want us to do?"

"Sit tight. Don't anyone come after me. Come morning, if I'm not back, make for the way station as fast as you can."

"Good luck to you, son."

Harding stepped forward. "You said you'd either bring them back or die trying."

"Yes sir," Jack said and swung into the saddle.

"If you can't bring them back, make sure you die trying."

Jack gave him a long look. Nina had said this man had a kind heart beneath his angry exterior. Jack thought if this was true, his heart was apparently buried deep.

Jack's horse shifted its hooves restlessly. Despite having been ridden all day, it wanted to run.

"Mister Harding," he said, "we can continue this after I bring your daughter back."

And he turned his horse away from them and was off into the night.

16

Nina sat in the saddle ahead of the one called Two-Finger. The horse rode hard into the night, the hooves pounding the earth.

Nina had never ridden a horse before and was jarred so severely she was trembling by the time Two-Finger reined up at the camp.

A fire was blazing and a man stood by the fire. He carried himself in an upright, almost regal way.

He said, "Where's the McCabe boy?"

"There was trouble," Two-Finger said, sliding from the back of the horse. "He took a shot at us and I had to kill him. He hit Cade and he would've killed both of us."

He grabbed Nina with a hand at each side of the ribs and pulled her from the saddle. She landed in the grass on all fours, trying to catch her breath.

Jack, she thought. *Dead.* She could not believe this was happening. And yet, she could not afford to allow herself tears. She had to keep her mind focused if she was to survive.

Jack was gone, and none of the men back at the camp would be able to help. Of that she had no doubt. If any of them even approached this camp, she had no hope they could survive a gunfight with these men. She was on her own.

She didn't know what they had planned for her, but she could imagine. If she had any hope of escape, she would be able to depend only on herself. And she didn't feel she could trust Jessica at all.

The regal man's attention was now on Cade, who had ridden with Jessica behind him in the saddle. A man with a scar across his face and a horrible white eye was helping Jessica slide from the horse. Cade was sitting slumped over a little, his arm folded over one side of his ribs.

"How bad is it?" their leader said. Nina thought she remembered Jack saying to Mister Brewster the man's name was Falcone.

"Bad enough," Cade said.

He swung out of the saddle. Falcone and White-Eye were ready to catch him, but he managed to step down to the ground himself.

"Come on over to the fire," Falcone said. "We'll have a look at it. Between White-Eye and myself, we've seen enough gunshot wounds."

"I don't wanna die," Cade said.

Two-Finger said, "You should'a thought of that before you got into this business. Men like us, we live on the edge of life and death all the time."

Falcone looked at him curiously. "Poetry, Walker?"

"Reality."

Falcone nodded. He turned toward the fire, and Cade and White-Eye followed him over.

Nina got to her feet a little weakly. The ride had knocked a lot of strength from her.

Falcone said, "Bring the girls to the fire."

Two-Finger grabbed Nina roughly by one arm and half pulled, half dragged her over to the fire. Jessica walked behind her.

Walker said to a tall, spindly built man with a thin mustache, "Lane, go take care of the horses."

"Why do I have to do it?"

"Because I told you to."

Lane turned away sulkily and went to the horses.

Falcone told Cade to sit. Cade dropped onto a small hump of earth that allowed him to sit as though he were on a low stool. Falcone opened the man's shirt. A woman was there, too. Jessica remembered her from the camp outside of Cheyenne.

"Hello, Jessica," she said.

Jessica said, "Flossy."

Flossy said to Falcone, "How bad's he hit?"

"I think I'm dyin'," Cade said. "I don't

wanna die."

"I think we've all figured that out," Falcone said. "Now if you'll be still a moment, I'll determine just how badly you're hurt."

Flossy assisted him in getting the shirt open. Nina thought Cade looked dirty, like he had been in the same clothes for perhaps weeks. How Jessica could cavort with men like this was beyond her.

Falcone poked a bit at Cade's ribs. Cade howled in pain.

"I need whiskey!" he called out.

Walker said, "I could put him out of his pain right now."

"I'm tempted," Falcone said. "But we'll need all the guns we have for the job I have planned."

Flossy was now on her knees, peering at the wound. "I don't think the bullet went all the way in. Looks like it hit his ribs and bounced away. Maybe cracked 'em, and he's losing some blood. But he's gonna be all right."

Cade looked at her and Falcone curiously. "You mean, I ain't gonna die?"

Falcone said, "Disappointed, Cade?"

Two-Finger smirked. "I know I am."

It was then that Falcone looked at Nina. "Why did you bring the second girl?"

"Those was the orders," Two-Finger said. "You said to bring both her and the McCabe boy. McCabe shot at us and I had to kill him."

Cade said, "We was just doin' like we was told, Vic."

Falcone, clearly exasperated, looked off into the night a moment to hold his composure. He drew a deep breath, then looked to Cade.

Falcone said, "I told you both the plan. I clearly explained it to you. We needed Jack McCabe as bait. We needed the girl to keep him in line. As long as a gun is pointed at her, he would be more easy to manage."

Cade glanced with puzzlement to Two-Finger, then back to Falcone. "McCabe had a rifle in his hand and was shooting. He hit me. Two-Finger had to kill him. It couldn't be helped. McCabe would've killed both of us. But we still brought the girl."

"And why do we need the girl?"

"To keep McCabe in line. Oh. I see."

Two-Finger said, "After I had to kill McCabe, we should'a left the girl behind."

Falcone nodded. Now they were seeing it. He said, "Tell me about how McCabe was killed."

Two-Finger shrugged and walked over to a pot of coffee. He grabbed a tin cup and filled it. "Just about the way Cade said it. He grabbed his rifle and shot Cade and I had to put a bullet in him."

"How exactly did he die? *Details,* Walker."

Jessica stepped forward. "Mister Walker shot Jack, and Jack spun around and landed on the ground. He didn't get up."

195

"Did any of you go over and confirm he was dead?"

Cade shrugged and looked at Walker. Cade said, "He looked dead from where we was standing. I'd been shot. We had to get out of there."

"So, you left the body there but didn't confirm that he's dead."

"That's about the size of it," Walker said, standing by the fire with the tin cup in one hand. "Didn't see the point. I aimed for his heart and I ain't in the habit of missing."

Falcone sighed wearily. Why did nothing ever go easily? He said, "Do any of you know what a knight is?"

Cade glanced about the darkness in confusion. "The night?"

"A *knight,* Cade. The McCabes are knights. They always do the noble thing."

"If you say so, Boss."

"They will always do the noble thing, right down to their dying breath. If Jack McCabe's wounded but not dead, then what do you think he's going to do?"

Cade shrugged. "Come after us?"

"Very good, Cade."

Jessica said, "Mister Falcone, could you let Nina go? With Jack dead, you don't really need her."

Cade said, "She's got a point, Boss. She'll just slow us down."

"It's obvious I don't pay you to think,"

196

Falcone said. "You don't know the McCabes. Until we have a body, I'm going to presume Jack McCabe is not dead. We might need her to use against him if he comes for us."

Nina was standing the furthest from the fire. All had their backs to her, as their attention was focused on their leader. His gaze was at one moment on the ground, and then looking off into the darkness philosophically. It was clear to her he liked to pontificate and he had an audience.

Now, Nina thought. While they were paying no attention to her. Now was her chance, possibly the only one she would get.

She turned and bolted away into the darkness.

Behind her, Jessica called out. "Nina! No!"

Falcone said, "Stop her!"

Nina had always been able to run fast and long. As a child in school, she always outpaced the boys. Whenever they had a foot race, she always won.

As she charged away from the fire, she broke into a long stride. She cursed the cumbersome skirt and petticoats which slowed her down, and the smooth soles of her shoes slipped against the grass. The terrain was a little uneven, and she had to make sure she didn't step into a low area in the darkness and twist an ankle.

She heard shouts behind her. They were pursuing her. Men who were tougher and stronger. If they caught her, she would never be able to fight her way free. Her only hope was to outrun them. These were men who spent much time in the saddle and might be a little out of their element trying to run. And running was one thing she could do.

She didn't know where she was running to. She wasn't even exactly sure of the direction she was heading in. She knew only that she had to put as much distance as possible between herself and them. Once she was free of them, once she had run far enough that they might give up on her, she would try to find her way back to her family.

She felt a hand from behind suddenly clamp onto her shoulder, and that was when the earth fell away before her in a low dip and she stumbled forward.

The man grabbing her from behind hadn't seen the dip either because of the darkness and he fell with her.

She landed hard on her face, and the man's knee was driven into her back as his momentum propelled him over her head.

She couldn't move. Couldn't breathe. The wind had been knocked from her. But she knew she couldn't afford the luxury of lying here trying to determine how badly she was hurt.

She pushed herself to her hands and knees, gasping for air. Her forehead and one cheek burned from landing face first and sliding a bit in the grass, and she tasted blood. Yet she knew the sudden fall was all that kept her from being overpowered by the man.

In the light of the crescent moon, she could see the man sitting up. It was the one called Lane. With one hand, he was tightly gripping his other wrist.

"You little fool!" he shouted at her. "You done broke my wrist!"

She could hear voices nearby. The rest of them were approaching. She pushed herself to her feet.

"Hey, Missy," Lane said. "Don't you go nowhere. It'll just make it harder on yourself. You don't want to go makin' Vic mad."

She was now fully able to breathe again, but her back hurt from where his knee had crunched into her. It was just off to one side of her backbone. She hoped she hadn't broken a rib. But she had no intention of waiting around for Vic and the others.

She took off in a sprint. Lane, sitting up, lunged at her with one hand but she was past his reach and charging away.

"Hey, Vic!" Lane called out. "Hey! She's over here!"

She ran blindly into the night. She tried to control her panic, because when you panic you can't breathe and if you can't breathe you can't run.

She had to think strategically. The one called Lane had been the first to reach her, which meant he was their best runner. He was now out of commission with a broken wrist. Cade was probably not among them, because of his bullet wound. This left just Falcone and the one called Two-Finger and the one with the white eye. Probably the three most dangerous among them, but apparently not in her class when it came to running. She thought her chances were reasonably good, as long as she didn't run out of wind.

When she was twelve, she had run the entire four miles from the school to her family's farmhouse in half an hour, and it had barely left her winded. But she had been running along a dirt trail, not over uneven ground in the darkness with killers chasing her and possibly a broken rib in her back.

She fell again, but not as severely this time. A finger got somehow jammed when she landed. She said a word she never thought she would hear herself say, but pushed herself to her feet ignoring the pain, and continued on.

She didn't see him until she was almost on top of him. He had been kneeling and suddenly stood, seeming to rise out of the darkness right in front of her. He grabbed her arm with one hand, spinning her around.

"Nina! It's me." It was Jack.

"Oh, Jack!" she squealed and wrapped her arms about him. He was somehow alive, and had been coming for her. But she dared not allow herself the luxury of feeling safe with him. "Jack, they're right behind me."

"Get in back of me," he said.

She did so, and Jack drew his pistol.

Within seconds, they were approaching. Two-Finger in a stumbling run. Vic Falcone was with them. Lane was there, too, holding onto one wrist as he ran.

All three came to a sliding stop in the grass when they saw Jack. Lane lost his balance and had to reach down to keep from falling. Within seconds, White-Eye came huffing out of the darkness to join them.

"My turn," Jack said. "Make a move and you're dead."

Two-Finger was staring at him with a cross between shock and outrage. "I shot you dead."

Falcone said, "Apparently not. Like I said, you should have checked to see if he was breathing."

Jack's gun was pointing at Two-Finger. Jack said, "Now, why don't you make this easy and go for your gun?"

"Nope. I ain't that stupid."

"Boss," Lane said, holding his broken wrist. "There's four of us. Only one of him."

"No," Falcone said. "You have broken your gunhand, and won't be much good. It's just Walker, White-Eye and me, and I have no doubt Mister McCabe will get all three of us."

"No man is that good."

Two-Finger said, "You don't know his father."

Falcone said, "Both of you, stand down."

Jack said, "Now that we're all out here, tell me. Just what do you want from me? Revenge of some sort?"

Falcone said, "Not against you personally. The goal was to use you as a hostage, to give me an edge on a man I have a grudge against."

"My brother. And let me guess — you were going to use Nina as insurance against me."

"Such go the best laid schemes of mice and men."

Two-Finger turned to look at Falcone, as if to say *what are you possibly talking about?* Lane was looking at him curiously, too. Lane said,

Jack said, "Robert Burns."

Falcone nodded his head. "It's so indeed a pleasure to meet another literate man."

"And I was supposed to be the mouse, I suppose."

Falcone shrugged. "I was hoping."

Jessica called out from somewhere in the darkness, in the direction of the camp. She was calling Nina's name, her voice dwarfed by distance.

Jack said to Falcone, "You remind me of a literature professor I had a couple years ago."

"How so?"

"He was a pompous fool, too."

Falcone smirked. "I concede the point to you. After all, you have the gun."

"And now it's time for you three to drop yours to the ground. Don't think for a second I won't shoot you where you stand if you don't."

In the moonlight, they could see Jessica approaching. "There you are," she called to them. "Have you found Nina?"

"It would seem so," Falcone called back to her. "And her knight has found us."

Jessica walked up. "He's alive."

"Sorry to disappoint," Jack said.

"Not disappointed, cowboy. Just a little amazed."

"Now," Jack looked to Falcone. "How about dropping those guns? Last chance"

Falcone shrugged. "You're the one in command at the moment."

He unbuckled his gunbelt and let it drop to the ground. Lane did the same.

As Two-Finger was unbuckling his gunbelt, he said to Jack, "Don't think this is over, boy. Now I got a beef with you, too."

"I'm shaking in my shoes," Jack said.

Jack looked to Falcone. "You boys start walking in that direction toward your camp. I'm leaving with the girls and going in the opposite direction. Let's hope we don't meet again."

Falcone said, "This is the mistake with all

of you noble types. There's nothing to keep us from coming back and snatching our guns and coming after you. Or retrieving rifles from the camp and coming after you."

"That'll be your funeral. You're down to only two reliable gunhands, now. That one with the broken wrist is not going to be any good to anyone, and I notice my old friend Cade isn't with you at all. Must be too shot up."

Two-Finger said, "I don't need no help in bringing you down."

"You're not doing so well proving that tonight. Now, start walking."

"Come on," Falcone said. "This battle is lost."

He turned and began away. Lane did the same. Two-Finger did his best to give a menacing gaze at Jack, then followed the other two.

Jessica said, "Look, Jack. I'm glad you're not dead. Really. When Two-Finger shot you, I thought you were gone. I don't want anyone killed. Believe me. But I'm not going back. I would die a slow death as a wife to some sodbuster, off in the woods of Montana. No offense, Nina, because I know that's the life you want. But it's just not for me."

Jack said, "I promised your father I would bring both of you back."

Falcone was still within hearing distance. He turned to them and said, "Now, Mister

McCabe. I know you apparently fancy yourself a noble latter-day knight, but I do believe the lady has spoken. It's her desire to stay with us."

"All right," Jack said, looking to Jessica. "If this is truly what you want."

"It is," she said.

He shrugged. He looked at Nina, who grasped his arm. She gave the sort of multi-layered look only a woman can do. She was concerned about Jessica, but she also believed Jessica should be free to make up her own mind. She was concerned about the reception Jack would get back at camp for not bringing back both girls. And she was afraid that sooner or later a fight between Jack and Two-Finger would be unavoidable. She believed they had not seen the last of Two-Finger or Falcone. Jack agreed with her on that one.

Jessica said, "I'm sorry. Tell my family I love them."

And she turned to follow the outlaws. Lane, White-Eye and Two-Finger were now almost lost in the darkness. Falcone, however, stood and waited for her. Then the two walked off together.

"What do we do now?" Nina said.

"Give them a few minutes. Make sure none of them get the idea to try and double back on us. We take those guns, too. It wouldn't hurt for your father and Brewster and Ford to be a little better armed."

"Stealing?"

He shook his head with a smile. "Spoils of war."

They waited a few minutes, then Jack said, "I think we should be safe, now. I left my horse about a quarter-mile back. Are you up to walking?"

She nodded. "After that run, I would be more than pleased just to walk for a little while."

Jack buckled one gunbelt and slung it over his good shoulder. He handed the other two to her.

She looked at the torn sleeve on his left side. "That's where the bullet got you."

He nodded. "Mildred Brewster and Elizabeth Ford doctored me up as well as they could. It looks worse than it is."

They found his horse where he had left it. Ground hitched and waiting. Normally, Jack had noticed, a horse won't graze at night, but this one was chewing away at the grass in the moonlight. They slung the gunbelts over the saddle horn, then Jack climbed into the saddle and reached one hand down to pull Nina up. She had to do this on the right side of the horse, because his left shoulder was now so sore he could barely move the arm. Many horses are a bit skittish about having a rider mount from the right side, but this one seemed not to mind.

Nina settled into place behind him, wrapping her arms around his ribs.

She said, "Jessica was wrong about one thing."

"And what might that be?" he asked as he touched his heels lightly to the sides of the horse, and the horse started forward at a spirited walk.

"She said I wanted to be a farmer's wife. If may be so bold, now I don't think I could ever settle for anything less than a cattleman's wife."

Jack smiled. "I'm finding I kind of like boldness."

17

The settlers heard the sound of the horse approaching before they could clearly see the riders in the faint moonlight. As such, Jack and Nina were met with three shotguns aimed at them as they rode into camp.

Nina's mother and father rushed to the horse and Harding pulled Nina from the saddle and both he and his wife wrapped their arms around her.

Abel Brewster walked over to the horse. He looked up at Jack, questions in his eyes, though he knew the answers couldn't be good.

"She wouldn't come," Jack said.

"She's not being held prisoner," Brewster said. It was more of a statement than a question.

"No. She's staying of her own free will. I'm so sorry."

Jack swung wearily out of the saddle.

Mildred approached her husband and he took her in a long, sad hug. Then Mildred drew a deep breath to sort of shore up her strength, and said to Jack, "Come. Let's have a look at that arm."

The wound was holding together well and had stopped bleeding. Mildred washed the surface of it, using water this time and not Jack's whiskey. She then wrapped it in a fresh linen bandage. Jack then pulled on a fresh range shirt from his saddle bags. He hated to put on a clean shirt when he was covered with a few days' worth of sweat and trail dust, but the shirt he had been in was torn at the shoulder and streaked with dirt.

Ford walked over while Jack was buttoning his shirt. Jack moved carefully because his shoulder was now so stiff it hurt to bend his arm. According to his father, when you dump raw whiskey into a wound, the pain can cause stiffening like that. Also, a bullet doesn't just tear into you, it can bruise you up. His father had said a shot of whiskey can sometimes ease off the pain, but Jack thought it might not be the best idea for these farmers to see him tipping a bottle.

Ford said, "I just wanted to check on you. You've been through a lot tonight. Taking a bullet like that, you should be in bed, not gallivanting around the countryside. Even though it couldn't be helped."

Jack said, "Sunrise is still a couple of hours away, but I think we should hitch the teams now and get moving. They let us go without a fight because I had the drop on them. But that doesn't mean they won't change their minds."

Ford nodded. "I'll go spread the word."

Jack began to roll up his bedding, but found it slow going with his left arm. He then tucked his coffee kettle into his saddle bags, and found Age had returned the bottle. He decided maybe he would take his father's advice. He glanced around quickly. There was movement over at the Brewster's wagon. Brewster and Age were hitching the team. They each had their back to him. Mildred was milling about somewhere out of sight.

He pulled out the cork and took a quick gulp. It burned gloriously all the way down. Kentucky whiskey. He allowed himself a moment to appreciate the lingering taste, then he pushed the cork back in and tucked the bottle into in his saddle bags. Then with the saddle bags draped gingerly over his bad shoulder and his bedroll tucked under his good arm, he walked to where his horse was picketed.

The horse was still saddled, but Jack had loosened the cinch. The rifle was still in its place in the scabbard.

Motion caught his peripheral vision, and he looked over to see Carter Harding approaching. *What now,* Jack wondered.

Harding said, "I suppose a word of thanks

is in order for what you did. But don't think you're going to be getting one. If not for you, Nina would never have been taken by those men in the first place. I want you to stay away from my daughter or I'll shoot you myself."

He turned to walk away, but then glanced back over his shoulder. "It appears you're not a man of your word. You're here, alive, but the Brewster girl is still with them."

Jack was weary and his shoulder hurt, and he found his patience nearly gone. He had the thought that if not for Nina, he would beat the hell out of Harding.

Brewster came up behind Jack and laid a hand on his shoulder.

Brewster said, "Don't let it bother you. You did what you could."

Jack nodded. "Thank you, sir."

"I know it would be easier just to ignore his comments and his attitude if you didn't care for his daughter. But she complicates things. Women always do."

"Is it that obvious? How I feel about her?"

Brewster nodded. "It couldn't be more obvious if you were carrying around a sign announcing it."

Jack gave a little chuckle. Here he thought he was discreet.

Brewster said, "You and Nina Harding look at each other the way Mildred and I do."

"It's precisely because he is Nina's father that he gets away with talking to me like that.

I wonder if he knows that?"

"Back home, he talked to everyone in town that way, one time or another."

"How is it he never got the tar whupped out of him. Where I'm from, he wouldn't have lasted three days. And since where I'm from is where we're all going, he's going to have to learn to water down his attitude. There are men I know of in the mountains who would take a man's scalp for less."

"Harding has a lot of good points, too."

"I have yet to see any."

Brewster grinned. "Maybe it takes a while for them to show. But he can be loyal. Once he believes in you, he will stand by you, no matter what. And he's not afraid of hard work. He's capable of pulling his own weight and then some. Whenever there was a barnraising, he was always one of the first ones there, and one of the last to quit work at the end of the day. If word gets around that someone needs help, he's there without even being asked. He's a good man to have in a community. You just have to be a little thick skinned around him."

Jack nodded. He said nothing. There was really nothing more to say.

Brewster said, "We have the team hitched. Ford's almost ready. We should be ready to get underway in maybe fifteen minutes or so."

Jack nodded. "Good. I'm going to ride ahead a little. See what's ahead of us."

Brewster clapped Jack on the shoulder again. "Don't worry about the Harding situation. You and Nina. Things will work out the way they are intended to."

Brewster seemed so sure, but Jack wasn't. He tightened the cinch and then swung wearily into the saddle. He reined up beside the first Brewster wagon. Brewster had returned to his wagon and was helping Mildred up and into the wagon seat. Jack noticed Brewster had buckled on Two-Finger's gunbelt. The revolver was a Peacemaker, and could be loaded one-handed.

Jack said, "I won't be gone long. But stay alert, just in case."

Mrs. Brewster said from the wagon seat, "You don't think we're out of trouble yet, do you?"

"No, ma'am. Not by a long shot."

He clicked his horse on up ahead, past the little creek they had camped by. Nina stood in the tall grass by her family's wagon, watching him ride away into the night.

18

They had two hours and maybe five miles behind them when the sun began to show itself over the eastern horizon. Jack had scouted ahead and behind, and was now dismounted and walking alongside Abel Brewster to give his horse a rest. The animal had covered many miles the previous day and then again during the night, and had gotten no sleep. Like a human, an animal could be driven to exhaustion. Jack had even heard of a horse being ridden to death, to the point it would actually drop to the ground, rider and all, and simply die.

Jack walked with the horse's rein in his right hand. His left arm was stiff and sore, and he let it hang to his side. Though he had to admit, the shot of whiskey had broken up some of the stiffness in his shoulder. A sling would be ideal, he thought, because every time the arm moved, even a few inches, he felt it in his bullet wound. But he didn't want to be hampered. If he was correct and Falcone decided not to give up on them, then he wanted both hands free should he need to fight or use his rifle.

Once they got to McCabe Gap, he would let Granny Tate have a look at the shoulder. She was Henry Freeman's mother, and what they called in the southern hill country a granny doctor. She had never attended medical school. As far as Jack knew, she had no formal education of any kind. She could read and write, but had picked it up somewhere along the way. Her entire knowledge of medicine was folk knowledge, and had been handed down to her by a granny doctor she apprenticed with when she was a young girl. But her knowledge was in some ways more thorough than that of modern doctors.

As Jack walked, Mildred Brewster called him over to the wagon and stuck a thermometer into his mouth. She was surprised to find no sign of fever.

"Fever is a sign of infection," she said. "I had never heard of pouring raw whiskey into a wound to prevent infection. I don't see how it could possibly work. The pain it causes seems inhumane, and doctors take an oath against that sort of thing."

"It seems barbaric," Jack said. "but it works. Granny Tate, back home, swears by it. As does Pa."

"Granny Tate?"

Jack explained about granny doctors.

"I would like to meet her."

"I'll surely see that you do."

Age was leading the oxen at the second wagon, which at this point required little more than to tap lightly at them with a bull whip from time to time. His father walked beside the first wagon, nudging the oxen every so often. Jack let himself drift away from Mildred and fall back into place at Brewster's side.

"The day looks clear," Brewster said. "And already it's getting warmer. Going to be a scorcher. But the weather is so different out here. The heat is easier to take. Somehow the humidity isn't as strong as it is back east."

Jack nodded. "Eighty-five degrees on a summer day in Massachussetts can seem as hot as one hundred out here."

"I could stand a little rain. Our water supply is getting low. We refilled at the creek back there, but that creek was rather small. It didn't offer a lot."

"Rain would only slow us down, though. I want to make that way station as fast as we can. By mid-afternoon, if possible."

Brewster's gaze had been ahead, but now he turned his eyes to Jack. "You think those men will leave us alone there?"

Jack nodded. "A way station can be a busy place. Stages coming and going. Stages have shotgun riders. Generally, the keeper of a way station is no lightweight, either. Men out here are often seasoned fighters. Many are veterans of the war, like yourself. I've seen communities where even boys as young as Age carry a gun and know how to use it."

"Sounds like a violent land. I'm wondering if I made the right decision to bring my family out here."

"There's very little law. But men like Falcone aren't very prominent. They're the exception, not the rule. Most everyone carries a gun out here, but as such very few ever have to use one. A man like Falcone will only strike if he feels he can get away unharmed. He's not looking for a contest. Back there last night, once it was clear he couldn't take Nina without getting shot, he backed down. The idea is to take as much as he can while sustaining as little harm as possible."

Brewster snickered. "In a perverse sort of way, it's almost like business. You could say he wants to keep his cost of doing business low."

Jack nodded with a silent laugh. "Except in his case, his cost of doing business is not in the form of money, but of blood lost."

Brewster said, "I'll admit, after our first meeting, I had changed my mind about wanting to hire you. But you've convinced me you're a good man. I like the way you think. I'd like to meet your father. A school can give you education, but it's often your parents who teach you how to think."

Jack had the fleeting thought that his life would be a whole lot easier if this man was Nina's father. He said, "I'm sure my Pa would like to meet you, too."

They walked in silence a moment, then Jack said, "I wonder how old Harding's axle is holding out. I'm sure not riding back to ask him. No need for there to be some sort of confrontation in front of Nina."

Brewster said, "I've seen situations where a father refuses to accept a man his daughter has her sights set on. It happens more often than you might think. It can tear a family apart."

"A similar thing happened in my mother's family. They refused to accept Pa. He was about my age when they met, and he was a ramrod of a local cattle outfit."

"Ramrod?"

Jack nodded. "The head man. The foreman. My mother's father was the doctor in town and a man of education, and my Pa was a cattleman, and even though the bulk of his gunfighter years was behind him by then, he still wore his gun like a gunfighter. Even to this day, many people see gunfighter when they look at him."

Brewster was looking at him with amusement.

Jack said, "Like father like son, I suppose."

"You know how to use your fists, and you wear your gun like you know how to use it.

People tend to figure if you are good at fighting, there must be a reason for it. And a fight with a gun is usually one to the death."

"My mother's parents refused to get to know him, to find out if there was something more beneath that gunhawk exterior. They wouldn't even go to the wedding. Ma died before I turned five, and I don't think she had seen her parents since before the wedding. I've seen my grandparents only twice, and that was on visits to California, where they live. They want little to do with my brother or sister or me, because they see our father in us. They blame him for my mother's death, too, which just makes the rift even worse."

"I don't mean to be out of line, but your father is quite well known. Legend has it that your mother took a bullet meant for him."

"That's how the story goes. The truth is, though, it's never been proven. She was shot, yes, and died in my father's arms. The shooter was on a hillside just beyond the house, back when they lived in California. They had a small ranch there. The killer used a high caliber rifle, like a Sharps. He was never caught, so we never had any way of knowing for sure whether he was shooting at Pa and missed, or tried to hit Ma. We can assume he was trying to hit Pa because at one time he had a price on his head. The assumption was it was a bounty hunter, maybe not realizing the reward money on my father had been rescinded, and shot at him but missed and hit Ma. But there's no way of knowing for sure.

"Stories are spun about it and told in cattle camps and saloons, and they seem to grow with the telling. The same with some of my father's exploits. The legend of my father creates a shadow that's awfully easy to become lost in."

"The way you took off after those men last night, with a bullet wound in your shoulder no less, and brought Nina Harding back safely, is itself the stuff of legend. I don't think it'll be long before they're talking about you in those saloons."

"Tell that to Nina's father. I think he would get along well with my grandparents."

After a time, Jack stepped back into the saddle. He wanted to scout the back trail a little and look for any possible sign of pursuit.

"Stay alert," he said.

"I have this pistol belted on, just like a real desperado," Brewster said, and laughed. "I also have a shotgun right up there on the wagon seat. Even with one hand, I can cradle it with my other arm and still do some damage. You don't have to be a crack shot to use a shotgun."

As Jack rode back along the small line of three wagons, Nina tossed him a smile from the wagon seat. He returned it, and touched the brim of his hat to her.

Harding was prodding along the team, and didn't miss the silent exchange. He glared at Jack.

Jack decided he would be remiss in his duties as scout if he didn't stop and check on a family with a questionable axle. Especially if it gave him the chance to pester Harding a little. Such a way was not usually Jack's — he was his father's son and preferred outright confrontation to subterfuge, but he had Nina to think of. If Harding and Jack got into a shouting match, or even worse began swinging fists at each other, she would be the one caught in the middle.

It occurred to Jack that even if Harding didn't realize this, he did. It would be up to him to take the high ground, but he wasn't going to miss the opportunity to dig at Harding a little.

He gave the reins of his horse a little tug, and the horse stopped. He said, "You folks doing all right?"

"Just fine, young man," Emily Harding said. She was walking beside her husband, taking Jack's advice and not riding in the wagon.

Well, Jack thought, at least she apparently didn't share her husband's sentiments.

To Nina he said, "You took a hard fall last night, miss. I hope you're feeling all right."

Nina couldn't help but smile at the sudden mock formality. She knew it was for her

221

father's sake. "I'm a bit bruised up, but I'm on the mend. Mrs. Brewster doesn't think I broke any ribs."

He touched the brim of his hat once again, and gave her a smile and a wink. She returned the smile, nodding her head in acknowledgment of him tipping his hat to her, and he rode on.

"I have to admit," Emily Harding said to her daughter, "I do like him."

Nina's father said to her, "I believe I said I do not want you associating with that boy."

Emily said, "Do as your father says, dear."

Harding turned away from them and focused his attention on the team.

Emily said to Nina, "At least for now."

Harding said, "I heard that."

Jack passed Ford, tossing a nod his way. Ford was leading his oxen, and returned the nod. He held a shotgun in one hand, and a gunbelt was now buckled about his waist.

Jack thought the gunbelt looked a little comical on Ford. The belt was buckled tightly and the gun rode high on his hip and a little to the front. He wore it like a man who had no idea how to use it, which essentially he was. But he had a shotgun, and Mister Brewster had been right. You don't have to be a crack shot to be deadly with one of those. The question was, would Ford be able to actually fire the gun at another human being?

Jack hoped it would not come to that. He estimated they would reach the way station within three or four hours, if they could maintain a steady pace. And if Harding's axle held up.

Jack rode to the crest of a long, low hill. He didn't know what he really expected to see, because the day before Falcone and his men had apparently hung back enough so there were no clear signs of pursuit, then approached the camp after dark. The cook fires probably acted like beacons, visible from miles away.

What he did see was a dust cloud further back on the trail. A stage, maybe? But no, the shape of the cloud told him it was being made by individual riders. No more than five, he thought. Maybe he was wrong. He had been wrong about the stage two days ago.

Even if it was riders, he had no way of knowing if it was Vic Falcone and his men, but until he knew differently he would assume it was them. That they were coming for him.

He rode back to the wagons and told Brewster what he had seen. Harding and Ford stopped their teams and walked forward to hear.

"What do you think would be best?" Brewster said. "To continue on, or try to make some sort of stand here?"

"His opinion doesn't matter," Harding said.

"We're going to wait here for them. We can't hardly circle four wagons but we can back them together into a sort of a square shape."

Jack said, "Do you think you could actually kill a man? Could you actually look down the barrel of a gun, looking him in the eye, and pull the trigger? Because unless you're absolutely sure, fortifying here would be a waste of time and get everyone here killed."

Brewster said, looking at Harding and Ford, "It's harder than you might think. Killing a man."

Brewster was speaking as a war veteran.

Harding met Brewster's gaze firmly. "I am absolutely sure."

Jack didn't know if Harding was serious, or just full of hot air in his cryptic way. He decided to ignore him.

Ford said, "I was in the war."

Brewster was surprised. "You were?"

Ford nodded. "Fought for the twenty-sixth Michigan."

Brewster said to Jack, "Ford only moved to our little town in Vermont maybe fifteen years ago. I didn't know he was in the war."

Ford said, "I don't talk about it much."

Well, Jack thought. This answered any questions he had about how well Ford would hold up in a fight.

The wagons were brought about to form the roughly square configuration Harding had suggested, the teams unhitched and led away.

Harding said, "After we're done dealing with these men, we can round up the stock again."

When all was ready, the families within the fortified triangle of wagon, Jack climbed into the saddle.

"Where are you going?" Ford said.

Harding said, "Don't matter where he's going. We don't need him. He's proven himself unreliable."

Jack replied to Ford's question, "I'm riding back along the trail, maybe half a mile. If it's me they want, maybe they'll leave you folks alone."

"No, Jack," Brewster said. "We're in this together. All of us."

But Harding said, "I say let him go. He's done us no good at all. He's actually brought trouble to us. If he's the one those outlaws want, let them have him."

Ford said to Harding, "You've been a good friend over the years. But it's time you shut your mouth."

"If it comes to a shooting match," Jack said, ignoring Harding, "the one you need to take out first is the tall one. Long hair, a patch over his eye. He has only two fingers on his gun hand. Take him down first. He's the most dangerous. Then focus on Falcone himself. He's their leader."

And with that, Jack turned his horse and started back along the trail.

His horse was showing exhaustion as he rode away. Normally this animal stepped along at a spirited clip, but now its steps were a little sluggish and it was starting to hang its head. Twice over a mile ride, Jack stepped out of the saddle and loosened the cinch so the horse could simply rest.

Jack had been thinking maybe he would lead Falcone and his men on a chase, away from the settlers. But with his horse hanging its head from fatigue, jack knew this was going to be out of the question.

After he had put a mile of grassland between himself and the settlers, he stepped out of the saddle and let the horse graze. If there was going to be a gunbattle, this spot was as good as any.

Actually, he thought, it was a terrible location. His father had taught him to think tactically, and this hill was low and grassy, wide open without a single tree or rock for cover. But it would have to do.

His arm was aching. Also, his head was aching from striking a piece of open bedrock when he went down. A lump had risen just above his ear, and his hat set gingerly on his head.

What he would have liked, he thought, was to simply lie down. Maybe sleep for a while. But such a luxury was not to be his.

His Winchester was waiting for him in his saddle. He decided to leave it there because he could see so far into the distance he would have more than enough time to grab the rifle if he saw riders coming.

He drew his pistol and checked the loads. Only five cartridges were in the cylinder. He pulled one more cartridge from his belt and thumbed it in, then gave the cylinder a spin and slapped the pistol back into the holster.

He looked about him. To the south, the land fell away in an arid flat stretch. To the west, there was grass that was largely green with spring, and maybe two miles in the distance was a ridge that was dark and hazy.

At the base of the low hill he stood on, the trail began and sort of wound its way along south, disappearing into the distance. He estimated he could see maybe five miles. His brother Josh saw breathtaking vistas all the time and to him they were common place, and they were once to Jack, also. But now, living in the east and coming home for only a few months most every summer, he had learned not to take views like this for granted.

And yet, it was hard to fully appreciate this, as he stood with an ache in his head from not only the collision with the rock the night before but also a lack of sleep, and a shoulder that felt bruised and sore.

If I live to make it back to the ranch, I'm going to sleep for a week. He laughed to himself over the maudlin direction his mind was taking.

After a time, he saw motion in the distance along the trail. A little dust was being kicked up, too. Four riders, he thought. They seemed to be moving along at a leisurely pace.

He stood and watched as they gradually drew closer. He wished he had thought to bring along a pair of binoculars. At the general store in Cheyenne he had seen a scratched-up set of Army binoculars, but had left them there. Not good strategic thinking. It was clear to him that even though he had learned all he could from his father, he still lacked experience. *Good Lord, I'm a greenhorn. A tenderfoot.* He had never considered himself that way before. The thought didn't settle well.

The riders drew closer, and he realized none of them were Vic Falcone or Two-Finger Walker. Each of the four wore wide sombreros and shotgun chaps. Drovers, Jack thought. From Texas, maybe. If so, they were a long way from home.

Jack swung into the saddle and rode down to the trail at the bottom of the hill to meet to meet them.

They reined up.

"Howdy," one of them said. A long willowy man about Jack's age. He was a little bent in the shoulders, but in a relaxed way. Despite his build, there was a way of strength in his movements. "The name's Barrow."

"Jack McCabe."

"Look like you've seen some trouble."

"We had a run-in with some riders last night. I'm scouting for a small wagon train that's a few miles north of here."

"Wagon train?" Barrow shook his head. "You don't see many of those, anymore."

"It's a small one. Only four wagons. Three families of farmers trying to make to make their way north to the Montana hills."

Another man spoke. Shorter than Barrow. Stockier. Dark whiskers covered his jaw and matched his sombrero in color. "We came across a camp. Must'a been them riders you spoke of. They left a couple whiskey bottles on the ground. Such a thing can start a fire out here. Grass like this."

Jack said, "If you see them, stay clear of them."

"I doubt we'll see them," Barrow said. "From their tracks, it looks like they headed west."

"We're drovers," the stockier man said. "Just up from Texas. We delivered a herd to some buyers at Dodge City, and thought we might have a look around before we headed back."

A large Mexican said, "Good country. Good grass. A man could run cattle, here. It would sure beat working as a drover."

Jack nodded. "You're near enough the

railroad so you wouldn't have to hire drovers to get your cattle to market, either. More profits for you. There was a time when the Sioux and Cheyenne made ranching here next to impossible, but those days are pretty much behind us, I think."

Barrow said, "You from these parts?'

"Further north. Montana. That's why I hired on to scout for the settlers I spoke of."

"You say your name is McCabe? Any relation to Johnny McCabe? They say he has a ranch up in Montana somewheres."

Jack nodded. "I'm his son."

Jack said he was going to be returning to the wagons, and appreciated the news that the outlaws he had spoken of had swung west.

Barrow said, "you're welcome to ride along with us, if'n you'd like."

They found the wagons where Jack had left them. Harding and Brewster and Ford all stepped forward when they saw the riders coming.

Barrow said, "You weren't kidding about trouble, were you? These wagons all fortified up like that. These folks are expecting trouble."

Jack said, "One of these men has a daughter who was kidnapped by those riders. I rode half the night getting her back."

Barrow looked at him with surprise. "You don't say. You almost never hear of that sort of thing."

The Mexican said, "Comancheros, maybe. But we're too far north for them."

"They're not Comancheros," Jack said. "But a couple of 'em might be almost a dangerous."

Jack introduced the drovers to the settlers. Jack told them what Barrow and the others had said about Falcone and his men heading west.

"Is that good news?" Brewster asked.

Jack said, "It could be. The trail we're on continues north for a little while more. If they continue riding due west, it means they might have given up on us."

Brewster shook his head and looked away into the distance. He said, "Jessica."

Jack said, "I'm so sorry. If there was anything I could do . . ."

"I know. Doesn't make it any easier, though."

Jack decided sometimes the best thing to say is nothing. He dropped a hand onto Brewster's shoulder, then turned and found Nina hurrying up to him.

"Jack," she said. "I was so worried."

"I'm all right," he said.

Harding glared at his daughter, but she ignored him. He took a step toward her and Jack like he was about to say something, but then backed off and walked away.

"Is it true?" Nina asked. "Those men are gone?"

He shrugged, and noticed the motion hurt his shoulder a little. "There's no guarantee. But we can hope."

The men rounded up the oxen so they could get the wagons moving.

Jack said to Barrow, "We've been told there's a way station just a few miles down the trail. One of our wagons has a cracked axle. We're hoping to make the way station within a few hours."

"Maybe we'll ride along with you," Barrow said. "Just to make sure you get there all right. This business of them riders trying to kidnap a woman just don't set well with us. I'm sure you're a good enough scout, and you wear that gun like you know how to use it. But you look like you've been rode hard and hung up wet, so maybe we'll ride along to make sure you all get to that way station safe."

"Much obliged," Jack said, trying to mask the outright relief he felt at the idea of having four Texas boys riding along with them. Not that any of them looked like gunhawks, but he had never met a Texas cowhand who couldn't hold his own in a fight. And now that four more capable men were with them, Falcone and his crew were outnumbered.

"That girl you was talking to. She the one they tried to kidnap?"

Jack nodded.

Barrow smiled and shook his head. "I saw

the way she was looking at you. I'd hang onto her and never let go, if'n I was you."

19

The way station was a long cabin made of large upright planks. The barn had walls made of sod stacked like bricks, and a peaked wooden roof. In a corral attached to the barn eight large horses stood about, ripping grass from the earth with their teeth and munching contentedly.

A man with a bushy white beard came to the door when Jack knocked.

"I was told by a stage that came through a couple days ago to be expecting some wagons," he said.

"One of our wagons has a cracked axle. I was hoping you might be able to help us with that."

"I'll see what I can do."

The man's name was Malden, and he opened the way station's facilities, such as they were, to the settlers. There was a large steel tub, not built for comfort, but the water was hot.

After Jack had a fresh bath and a shave,

Mildred Brewster tied a sling around his neck.

She said, "Keep your arm in there. It'll be best for your shoulder not to have to support weight."

"Thank you, ma'am."

Jack saw little of Nina. She and the other women were busy taking advantage of the fact that there was a well with plentiful water, and doing laundry and taking their turns in the tub. They had managed some light bathing in their tents, but there was nothing like a tub of hot water.

At one point in the afternoon, Jack was standing on the rickety front porch with a cup of coffee in his hand, and Nina suddenly was at his side.

"I only have a moment," she said.

"You don't want to anger your father."

"That, and I'm trying to help Mother. Mister Brewster wants to be on the trail again by tomorrow morning."

He couldn't help but smile. He said, "Even a moment with you is like a treasure."

That brought a light blush for a moment.

She said, "I hope you don't mind I took the liberty of doing your laundry. I got the blood out of your shirt and I sewed up the sleeve. It's still a sight because I'm not a master with a needle and thread, and there's not much you can do with a rip like that, anyway."

"I don't mind at all. In fact, I'm greatly pleased."

She beamed a smile at him. "I'd best be getting back to Mother."

He nodded. "It's great seeing you."

She scurried back into the cabin.

Barrow and the other three drovers decided to stay on for the night, but would sleep outside.

Malden said, "I don't really have a lot of accommodations, and I have to keep the rooms for stage passengers, but you're more than welcome to the kitchen floor."

"Thanks," Barrow said, "but we'll sleep outside. We haven't slept under a roof in longer than we can remember and don't want to start now."

The fourth cowhand said, "It'd make us outright nervous to act like civilized folk."

He was a black man of maybe twenty with a toothy smile but eyes that said he had already seen a world of pain in his short life.

They unrolled their bedding a hundred yards from the cabin, and in a section of clear open dirt they built a fire. They sat about the fire as the sun set and the sky overhead darkened, and they invited Jack to join them.

Knowing how hard drovers worked, and that they tended to play as hard as they worked, he was not surprised to find a whiskey bottle being handed back and forth. And this was why he brought something to share with them.

He took a place on the ground by the fire and then pulled from his sling his pint bottle.

He said, "Any of you boys have a taste for Kentucky whiskey?"

Barrow's face spread into a broad smile. "I'm from Kentucky. Ain't had a taste of it since I don't remember when."

Jack handed it to him and he pulled the cork and knocked back a mouthful. He sat in silence, enjoying the taste and the feeling of it burning its way down.

"Now that's whiskey," he said.

"Help yourself," Jack said. "All of you."

They sat, three of the men taking pulls from the bottle that was already there, which Jack figured was probably some sort of rotgut they picked up in a saloon somewhere along the trail, and Barrow and Jack drinking the bourbon.

Barrow said, "They're talking about you, you know. Back in Cheyenne. The son of Johnny McCabe. About how you fought a couple gunfighters, beating 'em both with nothing but your bare hands. Tore up the saloon in the process."

"We didn't really tear up the saloon. It wasn't much, really. Hardly worth anyone talking about."

"The thing is, it's because of who your father is. It creates interest. People want to hear about anything you do like that. The bartender actually has the section of bar you were standing at marked off in chalk. He says, 'This here is where Johnny McCabe's son stood right before he whupped the tar out of them two gunhawks.' "

Jack shook his head with disbelief. "Well, one of them is one of the riders I mentioned. That's how I got on their bad side."

Barrow said, "According to the scuttlebutt around Cheyenne, Vic Falcone was camped outside of town a few days. He rode with Sam Patterson. And Two-Finger Walker was there. Sam Patterson and Two-Finger Walker are names well known to Texas boys."

From what Barrow and the others said, news about the attack Falcone had made on the McCabe ranch the year before was being talked about in saloons all the way to Texas. And they were talking about how Johnny McCabe's sons rode after the outlaws to their hideout and killed most of them in a massive shoot out.

"Was one of 'em you?" Barrow said.

Jack shook his head. "No, that was my brothers. I was east at the time."

Jack took a mouthful of whiskey and handed the bottle back to Barrow. Jack said, "You know, I never really wanted any of this. For my name to be known like this. My father — he's been a living legend in the making for as far back as I can remember. But me, I just want to make my way in the world. To make my own name. I have absolutely no interest of being talked about in saloons like that."

"Well, sometimes we don't have any choice in how we're talked about. Them settlers, Brewster and Ford, they're talking in the cabin about how you went after the Harding girl alone and brought her back safe, and did it with a bullet in your shoulder."

"It was just a graze."

"Don't matter. You don't think that hostler Malden is going to keep that to himself? Working a way station can be a lonely business, and I never did meet a hostler who could keep his mouth shut once folks arrived. He'll be telling the story to every stage passenger he sees. And you can bet the story is gonna grow with the retelling. Jack McCabe, you're on your way to being a legend, yourself."

Jack sighed. "God help me."

The following sunrise, the drovers stepped into the cabin for a cup of coffee and then were on their way. Jack stood on the porch, a tin cup filled with coffee in his hand, as he watched them ride off along the trail.

Harding and Brewster and Age drifted out of the cabin onto the porch. The air was filled with the smell of bacon. The old hostler could surely cook. The farmers had filled themselves with breakfast.

Jack figured the men were about to go hitch

the teams, but Brewster said, "We've decided to stay and rest one more day. The teams need it. *We* need it."

Jack nodded his head. "That might be wise. I know I could use the rest."

Harding said, "I disagree."

Brewster rolled his eyes. "No surprise there."

Harding shot him a look, then said, "I think we should get going as soon as possible. We still have many miles to cover."

"And we will cover them, with freshly rested oxen."

Harding looked away. "I was outvoted two-to-one."

Malden had a couple axles stored in his barn for stage coach repair, but they were too wide for Harding's wagon. However, Malden had a buckboard beside the barn, and agreed to a swap. The buckboard was a little narrower than the wagon, but longer. There would be no arches for a canvas canopy, but Harding could drape a tarp over the cargo. It had not been a straight-up swap, though, because of the broken axle. Malden would need to purchase an axle and have one shipped in.

Harding was saying to Brewster, "We didn't bring much cash with us, and after the cost of that wagon, we're going to have very little even for supplies once we get to where we're going."

Jack wasn't really part of the conversation, but he said, "I wouldn't worry about buying supplies. I know the owner of the general store in McCabe Gap. A man named Franklin. I'll put in a word for you."

Harding glared at him. "I want no help from you. None. Do you understand?"

Jack shrugged. "Suit yourself."

Harding said to Brewster, "Why don't we all just stop right here? There's miles of open land all around us."

"What about water, Harding?" Brewster said, a little impatiently.

"We can dig. I've never been afraid of a little work. The well here's got good water."

"We'll need more than one well if we're going to try to put in a crop."

Jack said, "There's plenty of water in the valley where my home is. And even outside the valley, in the foothills to the east, there are plenty of streams. The land is rich and fertile."

Harding said, "We don't want nothing from you."

"It won't be from me. It's open land. Thousands of acres available for homesteading."

"If it's so great, why are those acres still available?"

"It's kind of remote. There's a stage that comes through only once a week or so. But people are moving west. The little town is going to grow. The land around the town was just made for both ranching and farming. And there is timber. I wouldn't even dare to venture a guess as to the board feet available. Probably millions. And they're finding gold in Montana. It won't be long before someone has homesteaded the acres I speak of. It might as well be you folks."

Harding said to Brewster, "I say we consider it."

The cabin door was opening and Ford was stepping out. He said, "Consider what?"

"Homesteading right here."

Jack said, "Out here, you can dig for days and not hit water. The land I'm speaking of has mountain streams. And there are trees. Timber. The hills and ridges are covered with pine. You'll be able to put your family in a cabin. Out here, the best you're looking at would be a sod house until you're able to afford lumber."

Brewster said, "You can do what you like, Harding. But I'm come morning I'm moving on. I'm going to check out this valley Jack's talking about."

Jack said, "And I'm going to go in and refresh this coffee."

He stepped in and closed the door behind him, and then just stood for a moment, drawing a breath and trying to let the exasperation he felt toward Nina's father wash away.

Through the door, he could hear Ford say,

"Why do you have to be so stubborn, Carter? Sometimes you are stubborn to an absolute fault. Why turn away from the land McCabe is talking about?"

"Do you really think we're going to find land that's as good as he says?"

"What do you really have against him?"

They were silent for a moment, then Brewster said, "I know what you have against him, Harding. You might not think he's a good man, but . . ."

Harding cut him off. "I think he's little better than the men your Jessica ran off with."

Bastard, Jack thought. To say something like that to Abel Brewster, considering the hurt and worry he and his wife were living with.

Brewster said, "It's precisely because of Jessica that I'm telling you to ease off on the boy. I know what it feels like to lose a daughter. We all know how Nina looks at him. You've seen it."

"I can control my daughter."

"Can you? Can you really? She's of marrying age, Harding. She'll make up her own mind."

"Don't talk to me about my daughter."

"I found out the hard way that a man can't control his daughter. Don't be so stubborn that you have to find out the hard way, too."

There was silence, then.

Jack walked over to the stove. The morning was a little cool outside, but the stove made the kitchen nearly sweltering. The kitchen was large, and the table long so it could accommodate a full stage worth of passengers. The walls were simply the reverse side of the planks visible from the outside, with a small wooden pantry that looked like it had been slapped together.

Jack filled his cup from the kettle on the stove and then stepped outside again.

He found the porch now deserted. He stood and took in the cool morning air, and took a sip of Malden's coffee. Not quite as strong as the trail coffee he liked, but it would do.

His head felt a little better this morning. He had slept on the kitchen floor rolled in his blankets, but he had been so tired he didn't even notice any discomfort from the stiff floorboards. Sleep was what he needed, and the whiskey he had consumed with Barrow and the boys had worked like a sedative. His shoulder was still sore, and he now felt a solid bruise on one side of his head, but he was in much better shape than he had been the morning before.

The door opened and Nina stepped out, glancing about quickly before fully stepping onto the porch.

"Well, you're looking better," she said.

"Nothing a good night's sleep couldn't cure."

"Is Father with the wagons?"

Jack nodded. "I would hate to get you into any trouble with him. In fact, I really don't want to come between a father and his daughter."

She shook her head. "It's not your fault, really. If it hadn't been this, it would have been something else. Every time I disagree with him, or Mother does, he refuses to bend."

"I'm sure he wants what he feels is best for his family."

"Maybe. I hope so. But sometimes I think what he's actually doing is trying to reshape the world to the way he wants it to be, by his own force of will."

Jack didn't know what to say to that.

She said, changing the subject, "I'm glad Missus Brewster asked me to come out and ask how you were feeling. I was looking for an excuse."

He stepped closer, and touched the side of her face where there was a scrape from when she pitched headfirst into the grass two nights earlier.

He said, "Does this hurt much?"

"Not much. I must look a dreadful sight."

He shook his head with a smile. "Not at all. Is it even possible for you to look dreadful?"

She laughed. "Oh, yes."

"I don't believe it. It would take more than a bruise and a scrape to make you look anything less than beautiful."

245

"Why, Mister McCabe," she said with a playful smile. "I do believe you're being quite forward."

"I believe you're right."

He kissed her. Lightly at first, and then more deeply.

One arm was in a sling, but with the other he pulled her to him, and her arms were about his shoulders and behind his neck.

She then said, "I had better get inside. I could justify to Father coming out here because Missus Brewster wanted to know how you were feeling, but this is going a little beyond."

"You're just trying to make Missus Brewster's patient more comfortable, that's all. You have a fantastic bedside manner."

She was smiling. "I don't think that would hold up in court."

She stepped back into the house, but not before flashing him one final smile.

After a dinner that cut even further into the meager cash supply of the three families, Mildred Brewster cleaned and redressed Jack's wound.

She found it healing nicely. There was no bleeding and no sign of infection.

She said, "Once we reach that valley of yours, I want to look up this mountain doctor you speak of."

"She knows things my professors told me

couldn't possibly work, but I have seen them work with my own eyes."

There were three bedrooms to be used by stage passengers. Since there was no stage due this night, Malden let the settlers have the rooms free of charge. Jack slept on the floor in the kitchen again, fully dressed and wrapped in his bedroll. Malden found an extra pillow, so Jack didn't have to go out to the barn and haul in his saddle for use as a pillow.

Jack slept lightly, despite his fatigue. Though the drovers had seen the tracks of Falcone and his men heading west, Jack was not about to let his guard down. Hope for the best, but prepare for the worst. Words of his father.

Finally, he climbed out of the blankets and pulled his boots on. With his gunbelt buckled into place, he went to the stove to add some wood and put on some coffee.

A bedroom door opened, its hinges squeaking a little, and Harding stepped out.

He said, "I thought I heard you stirring about out here."

Great, Jack thought, sarcastically. But he said, "It might be a good idea for us not to let our guard down too soon. Just in case."

"I want to talk to you alone. I figure this might be a good time. We'll be leaving at sun up, and you don't get much chance to talk privately on the trail."

"Mister Harding, I know you don't like me.

But . . ."

Harding cut him off. "It's not that I don't like you. Not really. I hardly know you. What I don't like is what you represent."

"And what do I represent?"

"You're a gunfighter."

Jack chuckled. "Is that what I am? Until just recently, I was a medical student. You have been listening to stories about my father's exploits. I assure you, they're exaggerations. Some are complete falsehoods."

Harding held his hands out to the warmth of the stove. The night had turned off chilly. It was the second week of June and at this altitude, even though the sun could warm the day, the nights could cool off considerably.

"I've heard the stories," Harding said. "But I don't take them seriously. I know enough about such things to know what part of a story is likely being stretched. Like shooting five Indians who were charging at him with five shots."

"No, that one's actually true."

"But it's not those stories that concern me. Not really."

Jack was openly perplexed. "Then I guess you have me confused."

"Look at the way you wear that gun. You might be lately of Harvard, but you wear that gun like it's a part of you. And," he glanced to where Jack had left his Winchester, leaning against a wall not far from his blankets, "Your rifle is nearby so you can grab it if need be."

"Just being cautious."

He shook his head. "It's more than that. Even if those riders weren't out there. Even if they had never threatened us, or kidnapped Nina, your rifle would still be within reach. Guns are a part of you. Death walks with you, and you with it. It'll always be a part of you.

"This is why I didn't want you riding along with us. Many glorify the gunfighter, as though he is somehow a hero. And with two young women with us, I didn't want either of them, especially my daughter, becoming infatuated with a man she would see as a romantic hero.

"Death walks with you, McCabe. I've known your kind before. Death walks with you and sooner or later it'll either come to you, or you'll bring it to those around you. I don't want my daughter caught up in all that."

Jack was about to ask how Harding knew anything about gunfighters. The man spoke as though he was more than simply speculating.

But before Jack could speak, a dog outside suddenly barked.

Jack and Harding both grew silent and listened. The dog barked again. Malden had said he kept the dog and let it roam outside at night for just this purpose. He said if something was out there that shouldn't be, the dog would let him know.

Malden climbed down from the loft over the kitchen which he used as a bedroom. He had a double-barrel shotgun in one hand. Jack thought it looked bigger than a twelve gauge. Possibly a ten gauge. It would cut a man in half at close range.

"Something's out there," Malden said. "Maybe them outlaws that gave you trouble."

Jack then heard it — the sound of hooves, muffled a bit by the sod. Sounded like two horses.

He drew his pistol. Harding was wearing one of the gunbelts Jack had taken from the outlaws. He drew the pistol and gave the cylinder a quick spin, checking the loads. Jack thought he looked a lot more familiar with a revolver than he would have expected with a farmer from back east.

The only light in the room was provided by a lamp standing on the table. Malden blew it out. Jack pulled the sling from his left arm and tossed it away, and then turned the door handle and let the door hang ajar.

A man called from outside. "Hello, the house!"

Jack smiled. He knew the voice. He holstered his pistol and called out, "Come on in!"

"You know these men?" Harding said.

"Like it or not, Mister Harding, you're

about to meet the legendary Johnny McCabe, himself."

20

The sound of a man hailing the cabin from outside and Jack calling back to him awakened the household. Brewster and Ford came running from their bedrooms. Ford had a shotgun in his hands, and Brewster was gripping his revolver. They were followed by the women. Nina, her long hair tied into braids, was tying a robe shut over her nightgown. Her mother and Mildred Brewster were doing likewise. Age Brewster was in his pants with suspenders up and over his union suit. He and Ford's son were staring wide-eyed, not knowing if gunplay was going to erupt.

"Carter," Mrs. Harding said to her husband. "What's happening?"

"Riders, approaching the house. But I think it's all right."

Harding slid his revolver back into its holster. Pa had taught Jack to be aware of the little details. Sometimes they tell more of a story than you would think. Jack noticed how Harding didn't look downward to find his holster, the way Ford and Brewster did when they were holstering their guns. He just slid it back into its resting place without even looking at it. This Vermont farmer seemed awfully comfortable with a gun.

Jack swung the door wide and stepped back, and in came a man maybe an inch taller than he was. A brown sombrero with a wide brim was pulled down over his temples, and long graying hair fell from behind his head to his shoulders. His jaw as firm and square, and his face lined from years of riding into the sun and wind.

The legs of his Levi's were tucked into tall, black riding boots, and he wore a deerskin jacket that fell to his belt.

Riding low at each leg was a Remington, tied down for easy access and a quick draw.

"Son," the man said with a smile, and held out his hand.

"Pa," Jack said, also breaking into a smile. They shook hands, and then Pa pulled Jack in for a hug.

Jack said, "It's mighty good to see you. I have to admit, though, I'm somewhat at a loss. I didn't expect you to be down this way."

"I got a letter from the marshal of Cheyenne. Jubal Kincaid. Said my help might be needed. Your brother and I rode twelve hours a day and brought spare mounts with us so we could just change the saddle and keep riding."

"Jubal Kincaid." Jack shook his head with amazement. "He's a good man."

"Thinks highly of you, apparently."

"So, Josh is with you?"

Johnny shook his head. "Not Josh."

That was when he walked in, almost as if on cue. He needed no introduction. Aunt Ginny had said in her letter that the boy uncannily resembled a younger version of Pa. She was right.

According to Aunt Ginny's letter, he was four months younger than Josh, which made him about a full year older than Jack.

He wore a tattered hat with a chin strap hanging to his chest. His hair was dark and fell to his shoulders. Long, like Pa wore his. Pa had done so ever since he wintered with a band of Shoshone, before he married Ma.

The boy's cheekbones were maybe a little more pronounced than Pa's, but even still, the resemblance was strong. The set of his shoulders was the same, and the way he walked.

The boy wore a buckskin shirt and Levi's, and riding low on his right side was a Colt Peacemaker.

Jack extended his hand. "I'm Jack."

The boy, smiling broadly, shook Josh's hand. "I'm Dusty. It's so great to finally meet you."

Jack said, "I've been looking forward to it ever since Aunt Ginny wrote about you in a letter, last winter."

And yet, he asked himself, did he really? This boy was everything Jack had always wanted to be. He was so much like Pa, he even looked like him. And he did it without even trying.

Pa clasped a hand to Jack's shoulder, and the other to Dusty's, and broke into a broad smile. Dusty was also smiling, and seemed genuinely glad to be meeting his brother. Jack forced a smile in return.

Everyone in the room was gathering around, all wanting to meet the legendary Johnny McCabe, about whom such tall tales were spun.

All except Carter Harding, who held back.

Jack realized Nina had very inconspicuously made her way to his side, and slipped her hand into his.

She glanced at him, and their eyes met. In a subtle way that can only be done when you have an intimate understanding of someone, she asked with her eyes if he was all right. As a reply, he simply gave his shoulders a little shrug. He really didn't know. She gave his hand a little squeeze.

It was at that moment, despite the fact that he felt like an outsider in the presence of his own father and brother, that he knew he was going to marry this girl. They were going to have children. And he wasn't going to do it as a mathematics professor at some Ivy

League school. He was going to do it on his own terms.

Jack began introducing his father and Dusty to everyone in the room. Hands were shaken. Everyone was pleased to meet the legend. Age was staring at him like he was a god descended from on high. A Greek god in buckskin and smelling of gun oil, Jack thought.

As the introductions continued, it became Nina's turn. She extended her hand to Johnny, who grasped it the way a gentleman should grasp a lady's hand. But her other hand remained in Jack's. Johnny caught this, and gave a quick smiling glance to Jack. "Pleased to meet you, Miss Harding."

"Please, call me Nina."

"Only if you'll call me Johnny."

Then came the introduction Jack knew was coming, to the man across the room.

"Pa," Jack said, "this is Nina's father. Carter Harding."

Harding made his way through the small crowd, and Pa clasped the man's hand firmly. Harding said, "I've heard much about you."

"I assure you, most of it isn't true. And that which is, I wish wasn't."

Everyone laughed. Even Harding cracked a little smile and a snicker.

The settlers began to excuse themselves to return to bed. Morning was going to come early and they had a lot of miles ahead of them.

Nina gave Jack's hand a final squeeze, and said to Pa, "It was really great to meet you, Mister McCabe. And you, Dusty."

"Likewise," Johnny said.

Jack noticed even though Pa had said to call him by his first name, she had not. He wondered what it meant. Maybe a sort of subtle gesture of not letting him get too close, as a sort of defensive stance toward Jack. Because no one in the room, not even Pa himself, understood Jack like she did, or understood that Jack felt like an outsider when in the presence of this man.

Malden, however, did not climb back into his loft. He said, "It's not too often I have a man of your stature here, Mister McCabe. Do you like a taste of whiskey?"

Johnny said, "I've met very few who don't."

Malden smiled. "I'd be honored if you and your boys would share a drink with me."

Malden got out a ceramic jug, and they sat at the table and began handing it back and forth.

"So," Johnny said, "tell us about your past two weeks on the trail."

Jack decided now was not the time to explain his decision not to return to school. Instead he began with the saloon fight with Cade back in Cheyenne, and then the forcible rescue of Jessica Brewster from Vic

Falcone and his men. He told of Falcone hiring Two-Finger Walker, and then how they kidnapped Nina and shot Jack, and Jack rescued her from them.

Jack told them about how he got Mrs. Brewster to clean the wound, by washing it with a couple of ounces of bourbon. Pa's old trick, and it worked. There was no sign of infection in the wound.

Malden said, "They're gonna be talking about this for a long time. He's a chip off the old block, Mister McCabe."

"Vic Falcone," Dusty said, shaking his head. "Last summer we should've trailed him and finished him off. I had Josh with me, and Hunter and Zack Johnson."

Johnny said, "And now Two-Finger Walker's with them. I haven't thought about him in a long time."

Jack's turn with the bottle. He took a pull from it. "So, Dusty. What's your connection to Vic Falcone?"

"Apparently Aunt Ginny didn't cover that if her letter to you."

Jack shook his head.

And so, Dusty told of how he had been raised by the outlaw Sam Patterson. Falcone had been Patterson's right hand man during Dusty's final years with them. And they talked of the raid Falcone and his men had made on the ranch the summer before.

"I wish I could have been with all of you

258

last summer," Jack said.

Pa handed him the jug. "I'm glad you weren't. You being at school, using your God-given gift, is too important. The best thing many a man can ever truly give back to the world is to want the best for his children. For them to make the most of their lives. And it was bad enough having Aunt Ginny and Bree there, in danger. And Josh and Dusty in the line of fire. At least one of my children was safe."

"With all due respect," Jack said, "it doesn't make me feel any better about not being there."

Dusty looked at Jack and nodded. Jack thought he understood. Pa did too, apparently, because he clasped a hand to Jack's shoulder. Pa said, "You wouldn't be my son if you felt any different."

Malden invited Pa and Dusty to spend the night, and then he and Dusty went out to take care of the horses.

"So," Johnny said to Jack. "That man Harding doesn't say much."

Jack chuckled. "He doesn't have much use for me, that's for sure."

"I think I've seen him before." Pa pushed the cork back in the jug and set it on the table.

Jack looked at his father, waiting for him to continue.

Pa said, "And his name's not Harding."

21

Though Johnny McCabe had only a few hours of sleep, when Jack awoke he found his father already on his feet, building a fire in the kitchen stove. The eastern sky was still dark.

Johnny said, "We've got an hour to go before sunrise. I'd like us to be already moving by then. Even though Falcone and his men are probably long gone by now, I still don't want to take any chances. Especially with women and children with us."

Dusty had stretched out his bedroll on the floor by one wall, but Jack noticed that section of floor was now empty, and Dusty's blankets were gone.

He said, "Where's Dusty?"

"He's already ridden out, scouting ahead. I wanted him to be already out there by sunrise."

Malden stepped from his bedroom, and once the stove was heated, he brewed up a pot of coffee and began bringing some hotcakes to life. Pa went out to saddle his horse and Jack's, and when he returned, the settlers were stirring to life.

"Mister McCabe," Mildred Brewster said, "what kind of danger do you think we will be in?"

"None, really, now that Dusty and I are here. With us and Jack, the three of us, those men will be less likely to want to attack. Also, from what we understand, they rode off west of here. Hopefully they're gone"

"Men like that are cowards," Harding said.

"Well, I've fought Two-Finger Walker, and he's not afraid of anything. That says something about him. A normal person is afraid of *something*. To be afraid of nothing at all means he's not quite right in the head. Which makes him even more of a problem."

Harding nodded. "A man who knows no fear has no boundaries."

Johnny nodded in agreement. Jack was now sitting at the table with his left arm once again in a sling, and a cup of coffee in front of him. Again he was struck by the fact that Harding spoke not out of speculation, but as one who knew.

Mildred Brewster said, "Do you believe it is fear that creates the boundaries of civilization?"

Jack rolled his eyes and shook his head. Here we go. You get Pa talking philosophically, and he could go on for hours. Jack sighed and took a sip of coffee.

Pa said, "Among the civilized, no. But among the uncivilized, it's a way of keeping them in line. They have no understanding of civic responsibility. Fear of prison, even fear of hanging, is what keeps them at bay. But a man like Two-Finger Walker, who knows no fear and is about as uncivilized as you can get, won't have any reason to acknowledge boundaries at all."

Please don't ask him about religion, Jack thought. Jack had once asked Pa if he thought the Shoshones and the Baptists worshipped the same god. This led to a talk that lasted well into the evening, when really it was just a yes or *no* question.

Pa had a cup of coffee in hand. His gunbelt was buckled on, as it usually was except when he was asleep. He said, "Now, as for Vic Falcone, would I call him a coward?" Pa glanced to Harding. "Maybe. He's never been known to actually face a man in a fight. But he's also a businessman, and I believe he has to understand that to attack us will cost him some men."

Brewster said, "From what you have said, he wasn't afraid to attack your ranch head-on, last summer."

Jack said, "He miscalculated, and it cost him half of his men."

Pa said, "Not only that, his only reason for attacking us now would be revenge. He has to realize none of you is carrying large amounts of cash, and your supplies wouldn't benefit him all that much. I can't believe he would be willing to take the risk, especially with Two-Finger Walker along. A gunhand of that sort must be costing him some money."

As Pa talked with Brewster and Harding, Nina sort of inconspicuously slid into a chair at the table across from Jack. Jack gave her a smile, which she returned. Somehow, the freckles that sort of spread from one cheek to the other across her nose seemed more noticeable when she smiled.

"Morning," he said to her.

"Morning."

"You sleep well?"

She nodded. "You?"

He shrugged. "As well as can be expected."

Pa said, "A man like Two-Finger is going to expect to be paid. Outlaw raiders don't generally run with a large cash reserve. They tend to make a big haul somewhere, hitting a bank or robbing a payroll, then they live off that until its gone. Then they have to rob again. It's going to be hard for Falcone to convince Two-Finger to attack these wagons when there's no money to be gained."

Mrs. Harding said, "I'm starting to wish we had never made the move west."

Her husband said, through tight lips, "Not like we had much choice."

■ ■ ■ ■

With clouds in the eastern sky back lit with crimson, but the morning sun not yet into view, the wagons began their journey toward the mountains the McCabes called home.

The Brewster wagon being driven by Age was in the lead, followed by the one driven by his father. Then came the buckboard that had replaced Harding's wagon. The Ford wagon was bringing up the rear.

Johnny McCabe rode over to the Harding wagon. Carter Harding was prodding his oxen along.

Johnny said to Harding, "Keep your shotgun near, and don't be afraid to use it."

Harding said, "What makes you think I know how to use one, or that I could shoot a man? I'm just a simple farmer."

"Not saying you're anything but." Johnny rode on.

Nina was up front, walking alongside Age to keep him company. Her father had said he didn't see any problem with that. Of course, the actual reason was it would be easier for Jack to ride alongside and they could chat without any grief from her father.

All about them were hills covered with grass and junipers, but they now rose higher than the hills that had been surrounding them since they left Cheyenne. At one point they came to a flat stretch, and the terrain became gravely with bushes and sage that stretched off to a distant rocky cliff. Then they came to more hills.

Johnny rode back to Harding. Partly to check on the wagon, and partly because he was trying to figure out who this man actually was. He had struck Johnny as familiar the first time he had seen him but he was having trouble placing just when and where he had seen him before. He thought the more he talked with him, the more it might jar his memory.

"How's that wagon handling?"

Harding shrugged. "We're managing."

Jack watched his father ride back, but made no effort to follow along. Until Pa arrived, Jack had been the scout for these families, and he would have felt it was his duty to check on everyone. But Pa seemed to naturally fall into a role of leadership. It gave Jack more of an opportunity to spend time with Nina. He rode over to the first wagon and swung out of the saddle to walk beside her.

She said, "I haven't seen your brother all day."

Jack looked on to some grassy hills ahead, and a low ridge dotted with juniper. "He's out there. Somewhere. If he's as good as Aunt Ginny said he was in her letter, then we won't see him until he wants us to."

"Are you holding up all right?"

He shrugged. "It's sort of a mixed thing, I suppose. I'm glad to see my father. Of course I am. And yet, it means I can no longer hide from the issues I have to face."

She nodded. "If there's anything I can do . . ."

He smiled. "You do so much already. I don't think you even realize."

Age was looking at them curiously. He wasn't sure what they were talking about at first, but he knew the direction this was going in.

He said, "If you two are gonna get all kissy, can you do it somewhere else?"

Nina and Jack both laughed.

After a time, some ridges came into view in the distance ahead of them. They were a few miles away and looked dark and hazy, but Jack knew they looked dark because they were covered with pines.

The day had turned off warm, but the breeze was strong and the air clean.

Nina said, "It's breathtaking — the views out here."

Jack nodded. "I never get tired of it. And you haven't seen anything until you've seen some of the views from the valley. From the front porch of the house, you can see the low mountains and ridges that ring the valley, but you can also see a snow-capped peak off in the far distance. Josh and Pa, they live there and see that sort of view every day and I suppose it's become commonplace for them. But when I'm visiting, I sometimes just stand on the porch and stare."

Jack's left arm was once again in a sling. His pistol was at his right side within reach, and his Winchester was tucked into his saddle. Not that he would be able to use a rifle adequately until his shoulder healed.

After a time, Pa rode up beside them and said, "I'm going to ride ahead a bit. See if I can find Dusty."

Jack said, "I'll keep an eye on things."

Johnny reached down and clasped a hand to Jack's shoulder with a smile. That sort of gesture from a father to his son said a lot. In spoke of pride and approval. And then Johnny turned and clicked his horse into a trot and was away up the trail.

Approval, Jack thought. What every son wants from his father. And yet, Jack felt somehow dishonest. He wondered how much his father would approve if he knew how Jack had felt about going away to school all those years, and that he had no intention of going back?

Beside the trail, a hill rose long and low, but at its summit he thought he would find a view of the terrain around them.

He said to Nina, "I'm going to ride up there for a look around."

She smiled. "I'll be here when you get back."

That struck him somehow as one of the nicest things anyone had ever said to him. Simple and yet loaded with meaning. He found himself looking at her, and realized he was smiling. She was returning the smile, the freckles on her nose and cheeks coming to life.

Jack mounted up and rode away from the trail and climbed the hill. The slope was dotted with an occasional juniper but was mostly grass, supple and green and standing as high as his stirrups. Yellow and red wildflowers bobbed their heads in the ever present wind.

At the crest of the long hill, Jack looked about for any sign of riders. Further ahead of the wagons was a single rider. His father, now over half a mile away. But there were no others.

On the trail below him the wagons were working their way along. From this distance he couldn't really make out the people, but he could see the canvas of the first wagon billowing in the wind. The wagon Nina was walking near. The very thought of her made his heart feel full and warm, and yet aching with a longing. A longing that was more than simple physical desire. He had experienced desire with a couple different girls back at Harvard. Three, actually, if he remembered correctly. Local girls trying to nab a college boy. But it was nothing like what he felt when he looked at Nina, or even thought about her.

Two wagons back was the buckboard, which was now the Harding wagon. He knew it was Carter Harding leading the team. Except his name was not Carter Harding.

The night before, Pa said he didn't know who Carter Harding was, but he knew Harding was not his real name.

This caught Jack's interest. Suddenly he wasn't so tired anymore.

Jack said, "You know him?"

"I don't know him personally, but I think I know of him. Might have met him once. There was a man during the War whose name was mentioned a few times. A couple men I knew had met him, and gave a good description. His name was Harlan Carter, and he rode with the Red Legs."

Jack had heard his father talk about them before. "A group of guerrilla raiders riding for the Union."

"That's right. They're not talked about much now, because they fought for the winning side. All we hear about now are names like Quantrill or the James brothers or Sam Patterson. But in their time, the Red Legs were every bit as bad.

"It's said that Harlan Carter was one of the worst. One of the most vicious. That he really enjoyed the killing, and that the war effort was secondary. After the war ended, he and a few others formed their own outlaw gang and robbed a few banks and such in the Missouri area, and then Carter just disappeared. Sort of fell off the map."

"So, you think Carter Harding is really this Harlan Carter?"

Pa shrugged. "I don't know. Just a feeling. He was a tall man, with dark eyes and a distinctive way of moving. They say the look in his eye was something between an undertaker, a preacher and an executioner. And there's something in Harding's eye you don't normally see in a farmer. I've seen it in many a gunfighter over the years. Whoever he is, that man has killed before."

This gave Jack more to consider. Could Carter Harding be more than he appeared? And yet, what would take a former guerrilla raider back east, to take up the life of a farmer? Not that Jack meant to disparage farming. But it was a rather tranquil life for an outlaw raider to settle into.

Jack returned to the wagons. For a time, he rode up front, chatting a bit with Brewster about trail conditions. Brewster asked him about rainfall in the mountains where they were heading.

"It's not like back east," Jack said. "In Massachussetts, it seems like it rains almost half the time. I've seen four straight days of drizzle."

Brewster nodded. "The same in Vermont."

"But in the Montana mountains, you don't see that kind of rain very often. There are dry spells. There's a lot of snow in the winter most often, and that creates a lot of spring run-off. There's a stream that cuts through our valley, and in the spring the stream is deep enough to paddle a canoe from one end of the valley to the other. Toward the center of the valley is a large pond that can be easily two feet deeper in May than it is in August. And there's a good supply of ground water, if you know where to dig."

Jack then urged his horse ahead a bit, until he was again riding beside the second Brewster wagon.

Nina said, "I missed you."

Age rolled his eyes and shook his head.

She said, "How did things look?"

"I didn't see any riders, other than Pa up ahead."

"Do you really think they've gone away?"

Jack shrugged. "I hope so."

"The sooner we get to those mountains of yours, the happier I'll be."

"Yeah. Me too."

A little after noon, Jack rode ahead of the wagons. There was a hill off to one side, a little sharper climb than the one he had ridden up earlier, but he wanted another look at the land around them. The hill was mostly grass but gravely in some places. Once he was at the top, he swung out of the saddle to let his horse breathe a bit. He lifted the canteen from his saddle horn and pulled the cork and took a drink. The water was warm, but at least it was wet. The wind was strong, rattling the brim of his sombrero and making the mane of his horse flutter wildly.

From the top of the hill, he estimated he was maybe a half mile from the wagons. They had stopped and were resting the teams. Further ahead on the trail he saw two riders, maybe a couple miles from the wagons. He lost sight of them as they passed behind a low, grassy hill, then they emerged into view again. Pa and Dusty. They were coming back.

Jack climbed into the saddle again and descended the hill, and rode on to the trail to meet them.

Dusty had a deer tied across the back of his saddle. It was a white-tail, and Jack estimated it to be maybe a hundred and forty pounds. Large enough that everyone would have a little venison to eat tonight.

"I come across it at sunrise," Dusty said. "Four of 'em, grazin'. They hadn't seen me and the wind was in my favor, so I pulled on my moccasins and grabbed my rifle and approached 'em on foot. I figured some deer meat might help the farmers save some on their supplies."

They brought the deer back to the wagon. By sunset, the teams were unhitched and grazing, and tents were set up. Venison was roasting over the cookfires, creating a smell that set Jack's mouth to watering.

Pa and Dusty had built a fire and improvised a roasting spit. Pa had stepped back
and was letting Dusty work on their dinner.
Dusty had a natural way with food. According to Aunt Ginny's letter, he had worked at
Hunter's Saloon for a while cooking steak
dinners and preparing breakfasts for stage
travelers. He still filled in there once in a
while.

Despite how great the roasting meat
smelled, Jack found what he really wanted
was distance. He went to the fire to fill his tin
cup with coffee, and made some quick polite
chat with Dusty, then stepped away beyond
the edge of the firelight.

He removed the sling from his arm, because
it was made from a white bedsheet and
picked up the glow from the fires. He didn't
want to be seen, partly because he was sort
of informally standing guard. Pa hadn't as-
signed him the duty, he just felt maybe
someone should be out here, in case Falcone
and Walker take it into their heads to get
sneaky. After all, Walker had entered camp
under the cover of darkness once before. But
the main reason was that Jack simply felt like
being alone.

He took a sip of coffee. He could hear the
chatter of various conversations going on at
once. Abel and Mildred Brewster at their fire.
Age had wandered over to Pa and Dusty. Pa

was saying something funny, and Dusty and Age were laughing. Pa had a knack for taking some of his old adventures and putting a comical spin on them. Jack remembered many an evening years ago when he, Josh and Bree would sit by the stone hearth at the ranch house and Pa would regale them with his stories. Jack remembered the laughter ripping through him until his stomach muscles hurt. Even Aunt Ginny would crack a begrudging grin.

Jack shifted the cup to his left hand, and found he could bring the cup to his mouth without his shoulder hurting too much. This allowed his gunhand to be free. He reached down to his holster and let his hand brush the gun. He gave it a gentle tug to make sure it was not tucked too tightly into the holster. Things Pa did all the time, almost without even thinking about it.

The breeze was cool. Refreshing from the heat of the day. Crickets chirped from somewhere out in the darkness.

As he stood, he became aware of someone approaching. In the dim light that made its way out here from the fire, he could see it was a woman. Her long dress swished its way through the tall grass. Though he could see only a dark silhouette, he recognized the way of moving. Graceful and easy, with just a hint of a sway to her head and shoulders. Almost like there was a dance going on inside her that only she could hear. Nina.

"Good evening," he said.

"I hope I'm not intruding," she said. "You looked a little bit like you wanted to be alone."

He found himself smiling, though he knew she could not see the smile in the darkness. How easily she read him. She who had known him only a couple weeks. And yet those who had known him for years didn't really seem to know him at all.

He said, "You are never an intrusion."

She sort of glided her way to his side. "Dusty's roasting up some venison at your fire. He's been offering advice on the best way to roast it over an open fire. Brewster and Ford are grateful, but of course, Father resents it."

Jack chuckled. "I'm sure."

"Are you all right?"

Jack shrugged. "I feel so torn inside. Conflicted. Am I just feeling petty jealousy? Is that what it is? Because my brother can so easily walk in shoes I don't think I'll ever fill?"

"Do you really want to fill your father's shoes? Or do you want to be your own man?"

"Sometimes it's one, I guess, and sometimes it's the other. I so hate feelings of uncertainty, but that's what I'm filled with. My professors back at school taught me to be a rational thinker. That's what a scholar does. He thinks rationally. But I'm such a jumbled mess inside."

"I don't think you're really a scholar."

His brows arched a little out of surprise. "Hmm?"

"Really. I mean, you're a man of intellect. You have much more than I. But a scholar is one who is drawn to a life of education. Books and classrooms. He yearns to study and write papers and give lectures and attend lectures. You were just thrust into that world without ever really wanting it. Just because, as you say, you have this gift of remembering everything you read."

"A curse, is more like it."

"You're a student, sure. But a student of the world around you. I don't think you're feeling jealousy at all. I think what you are is a man who wants to find his own way, without anyone trying to steer him based on their notions. And sometimes your father and his great reputation and his grand ways make you feel sort of restrained, like you're somehow lost when in his presence. It makes you feel almost insignificant. And no one likes to feel that way. I'm sure he doesn't mean it that way, and would be truly grieved if he knew the truth. But truth it is."

He was shaking his head with amazement. "How is it you know me so well?"

"Maybe because I look at you without any preconceived notions."

"I really think you are no slouch in the

276

intellect department."

She smiled and looked down with embarrassment. "Me? I'm just a farm girl."

He gently took her chin with one hand. "You, Nina, are not *just* anything."

He gave her a light kiss, and then she took wrapped her arms around his right arm and rested her head on his shoulder.

After a time, Jack said, "Pa said after he's done eating he's going to ride out and scout about. Look for any campfires in the distance. Like I usually do. He volunteered to go because I should stay back and get some rest."

"He's probably right. You were shot only a few days ago."

"I suppose."

He took another sip of coffee, and found it was starting to grow cold. He decided he could put his free hand to better use than holding a cup of cold coffee. He dropped the cup to the grass, then reached to her arms, which were wrapped around his right, and began to gently caress her along the shoulder and down the length of one arm.

She said, "It bothers you staying back at camp. You aren't accustomed to being idle for long, are you?"

"Makes me feel useless."

"Oh, Jack. You are anything but useless."

"You know, I have to wonder how I ever got along all these years without you."

She snickered. "I do have to wonder, my-self."

They then stood in silence. The ever-present wind had died down a little, the way it seemed to do at night. The sky was cloud-less, and a canopy of stars stretched above them.

After a time, she said, "The stars seem so big out here."

"It's the elevation. We've been climbing steadily since leaving Cheyenne. In fact, it's really all uphill after Missouri. The grasslands east of the mountains I speak of are close to four thousand feet above sea level. That's higher than some of the mountains in the Appalachian range. That's why the air is a little thinner out here, and even though the days can be hot, there's very little humidity."

She let herself digest that thought. "Four thousand feet? That's almost pushing a mile."

He nodded. "Kind of staggering, when you think about it. We still have a ways to go, but we're probably at close to three thousand feet now."

They stood in silence again for a few mo-ments, then a thought occurred to him. "Hey, does your father know you're out here with me?"

"Mother does. It'll be all right. Father's bark is worse than his bite. Once he gets to know you, he'll lighten up toward you. Mother and I are sure."

The night breeze lightly touched the side of Jack's face. Nina's hair was tied back in a bun. Jack reached to the back of the hear head and found a pin in the bun, holding it together. He slid the pin free and worked his fingers into the bun and her hair came free. She gave her head heard a light shake and her hair fell down over her shoulders.

Jack thought that a woman's hair was often much longer than he would have guessed from a bun, and he always wondered how long, full hair like Nina had could be compacted into such a tight bun. But it was a fleeting thought, only. He was mostly focused on how beautiful she was in the moonlight, and how her hair hanging freely gave her a look of sensuality. The wind caught her hair and caused it to sift and stir.

As Jack looked into her eyes, with his peripheral vision he caught a hint of motion from somewhere off to the side. At first he paid it little mind. Nina had a way of mesmerizing him, never less so than right now. But then he forced himself to remember that there was at least a potential for danger out here. Falcone and his men were out and about, and revenge was on their minds.

He glanced off to the side, where he thought he had seen the motion. It was now gone.

"What is it?" Nina said.

"Nothing, I guess. I thought I saw something."

He then became aware that the crickets had stopped chirping. All was silent about them. Not a good sign. Then there was then a slight snapping sound, like something or someone trying to walk quietly had stepped on a small stick.

He looked at her again, but this time it was to try a trick his father had told him about. Your straight-on vision can pick up detail better, but your side-vision is better at detecting motion. At night, Pa would often turn his head so he could scan the darkness around their camp with his side-vision. This is what Jack was doing now. Looking at Nina while he tried to focus his attention onto his side vision.

He saw it again. Off to the side, in the darkness. Hard to tell how far away. Thirty feet. Fifty, maybe.

He brought his fingers to Nina's lips in a gesture to encourage silence. He then brought her in for a hug, and said quietly in her ear, "Something's out there."

"We should go get your father and brother," she said, her voice little more than a whisper. "If it is those men, it would be better to have three guns instead of one."

"True. But if we suddenly head back to camp, it might let whoever is out there know we're aware of them."

He moved her around to a place behind him, and then he drew his pistol. He had only five shots, but the sound of loading in a sixth might carry in the night.

He glanced back toward the wagons. Brewster and his wife were at their fire, tending to their roasting venison. One of the Brewster's wagons blocked his view of the Harding wagon, but he could occasionally catch the foghorn voice of Nina's father. Beyond them would be the Ford's wagon. He could also see Dusty and Pa, at their own fire. Dusty was turning the haunch of venison on the spit over the flames.

Jack waited, while it came closer. He could see the shape, now. To his relief, it was not a man. It was walking low, on all fours.

This far out from the camp, the light cast by the cook fires was meager, but enough that Jack could see it looked like a large dog. But it wasn't a dog.

"What is it?" Nina said, looking over his shoulder.

"It's a wolf."

It continued to approach, walking toward Nina and Jack. When it was ten feet away, Jack cocked his pistol. It stopped at the sound.

Then it showed its teeth, looking a dull orange in the dim light from camp. And it growled low and throaty.

It looked like it was getting ready to charge at them. Unusual for a wolf. Despite the fear most people seemed to instinctively have for a wolf, Jack had never heard of one attacking a human. But here it was, advancing toward them.

Jack knew he would have time for one shot only. And he dared not miss.

The wolf suddenly charged and leaped. Nina let out a scream that cut through the silence of the night, and Jack's gun went off.

22

Pa stood over the wolf carcass. Brewster was beside him, holding a lantern. Harding and Ford were there, each with a shotgun in their hands.

"The thing about wolves," Brewster said, "they run in packs. Where there's one, there's bound to be more."

Harding said, in his close-mouthed deep rumbling voice, "Never heard of a wolf attacking a man before."

Nina stood by Jack, as close as she could possibly get. She wasn't about to step away if there could be more wolves out there.

Dusty had disappeared into the night to scout, a Winchester in his hands.

Johnny said, "This wolf is rabid."

That sent a chill throughout everyone there.

Harding said, "That would explain it, then."

Johnny nodded. "A wolf is normally as afraid of people as people are of it. And they're afraid of fire. A real hungry wolf might hang near a camp beyond the firelight, and wait for any scraps that might be left behind. They can sneak into a camp after everyone's asleep and the fires are burning low."

Jack said, "I've seen a rabid wolf before. They kind of sway when they walk. This one was walking steady, and charged right at us."

"I remember that wolf you're talking about. Back when you were maybe ten."

Jack could remember it vividly. Pa had taken Josh and him on an overnight camping venture into the ridges that surround their valley. Bree was only six and had stayed behind with Aunt Ginny. They had happened upon a wolf, in broad daylight, staggering about and making a sort of wailing sound that sounded like no wolf Jack had ever heard. Foamy saliva had been dripping from its mouth.

"You put a bullet in it," Jack said.

Pa nodded. "This wolf wasn't as far along. But probably would have been within a few days."

"What should we do with the carcass?" Brewster said.

"Nothing. Leave it right here. Nobody even touch it."

Dusty materialized from the darkness off to one side. He said, "There don't seem to be any others. Is this one rabid?"

Pa nodded. "I don't expect there will be another wolf within miles. They know enough

284

to avoid a rabid animal."

They returned to the camp. Mildred poured a cup of coffee for Johnny and Abel. Dusty had left his venison unattended when he heard Jack's gunshot, so he went to the spit and gave the chunk of meat a turn.

Mildred said to Johnny, "A rabid wolf."

He nodded. "Men like Victor Falcone aren't the only dangers out here."

Harding was standing nearby, near enough to hear what was said. He shook his head. "We shouldn't have come out here. I should've known better."

His wife was at his side. "Carter," she said, keeping her voice low, "we had no choice. Remember that."

He nodded gravely. They started back for the campfire.

Jack had taken Nina's hand as they walked back to camp. He had retrieved his tin coffee cup from the grass where he had dropped it.

Jack said to her, "I guess life with me is always an adventure, isn't it?"

She smiled. "I would have it no other way. I'm so glad you shot that wolf, though. Rabid." She shuddered. "I hate to think what would have happened had you missed."

He found himself returning her smile. "Good thing I didn't, then, isn't it?"

Harding called out to her, his voice breaking the silence of the night like a loud tuba sounding off. "Nina!"

"I believe you're being hailed," Jack said to her with a smile.

"Good night."

"I'm sorry if being with me tonight causes you grief with your father."

She smiled again. She seemed to smile a lot when she was with Jack. "I'll be all right. I promise. He's really a good man."

If you say so, Jack thought. But what he said was, "Good night."

He watched her walk away, toward her family's camp. Her hair was still down, falling in full dark waves almost to her hips.

"Mister McCabe," Mildred Brewster called out. It took a moment for Jack to realize she was talking to him. "Would you like some coffee?"

Pa was standing by their fire. He had a cup in his hand, and Abel Brewster had a cup in his one hand. Jack strolled over and held his cup while Mrs. Brewster filled it.

"Much obliged," he said. "But I've asked you to call me Jack."

She put the pot down, and then gave the venison a prod with a stick. "I believe our dinner is about ready."

Pa said, "And I'm sure ours is, too. This is our cue to excuse ourselves. Thanks again for the coffee."

The McCabes returned to their own fire. Dusty had removed the haunch of deer meat from the spit and was slicing off steaks with his bowie knife. Not the technique of the finer chefs in Boston, Jack thought with a smile, but there was something more earnest about frontier cooking.

The steak was served up on tin plates. Jack sat in the grass and set his cup of coffee beside him. He sat cross-legged, what he called *Indian style,* and balanced the plate on his lap. Pa was doing the same. Pa's coffee cup was also tin, and was battered and scratched up. It had been with him many years.

Jack cut into his steak with his own knife, and then brought a chunk to his mouth to chew it off the knife point. Aunt Ginny would have shuddered at the thought of it.

There was something about venison roasted over a camp fire under God's open sky. Jack had eaten at some of the finer restaurants in Boston, but none of those gourmet meals could compare to the supper he was having now.

When they were finished eating, Jack took a sip of coffee. Pa said, "Let's try something a little stronger than coffee."

He went to his saddle bags and produced a tin flask.

"For medicinal purposes," he said with a grin. "Every bit as useful as Granny Tate's corn whiskey at keeping infection away, but a lot better tasting."

He tossed it to Jack, who unscrewed the

cap and took a swing. Not quite Kentucky bourbon — few things were — but it served the purpose.

Jack handed it to Dusty who took a pull, and handed it to Pa.

Once the flask had made a couple rounds, Pa left the fire to saddle up and do the scouting he had talked about.

Jack's stomach was full of venison, and the whiskey was bringing on a relaxed feeling. He lounged back against his saddle, and stretched his legs out before him. Dusty had braced his bedroll against a large clump of grass and was sitting against it.

The whiskey flask was in his hand. He took a deep pull from it, then capped the flask so none of the whiskey would spill in flight, and tossed it to Jack. Jack caught it nimbly.

"Good catch," Dusty said.

"I played some baseball once in a while at school." He unscrewed the cap and also took a deep mouthful. He paused while he enjoyed the burning all the way down.

"Baseball, huh? Men our age playing a kid's game?"

Jack shrugged. "It's catching on. They actually have leagues where you get paid just for playing ball."

Dusty gave him a squinty-eyed look. Like he wasn't sure if Jack was funning him.

With the cap once again firmly in place, Jack launched the flask through the air and back to Dusty.

"I'm mighty glad to finally get the chance to meet you, you know," Dusty said. "I've heard a lot about you. There's always the feeling of an empty place at the table. Now that you're gonna be back home for the summer, the family will be complete."

Jack said, "I spend so much time away, I have to confess, sometimes when I'm at the house it feels more like I'm visiting than coming home."

He hadn't really intended to say that, but the whiskey was sort of loosening his tongue.

He kept on talking. "Not that I would ever say that to Pa or Aunt Ginny. But for the past two years, my home has been a small twelve-by-eight room that I share with a fellow student named Darby."

"Do you think of that as home now?"

Jack shrugged. "Not really. It's just a place. I don't really miss it when I'm away.

"You know," he said, dropping back a bit against his saddle and looking up at the breathtaking Wyoming sky. "It's just occurred to me that I don't really think of any place as home. The school is where I go to study. The ranch is where I go to visit the family."

Dusty sat with the whiskey flask in his hand, sort of staring into space. "That's how I felt. All my life. Until last summer and I found the family. Now I have a home. A place to belong."

Jack nodded and almost said, *must be nice,* but he held that back. He was still sorting out his feelings about the whole situation. He didn't want to say anything he might not truly mean, and he surely didn't want to say anything that might hurt Pa or Aunt Ginny, should it get back to them. He didn't know if he would ever be able to explain things to them, but he surely didn't want to try until he had all of the jumbled feelings inside him figured out.

Interesting, he thought, how easily Nina seemed to understand him. He didn't have to struggle to quantify his feelings or put things into words around her. She seemed to be able to figure him out just by the look in his eye. The way he moved. The tone of his voice. She so incredibly perceptive.

The flask came flying back toward him and he snagged it out of the air. He took a mouthful from the flask. It had been half-empty when Pa first took it from his saddlebags, and now there wasn't much left at all.

He had to admit, the whiskey was warming him considerably from the inside out, and he felt mellow and calm. And he found his shoulder felt much better.

He tossed the flask back to Dusty. He shook it to measure the contents, and said, "There won't be any left for Pa when he gets back."

"Life can be hard."

Dusty cracked a grin, and took another swig.

Dusty said, "Y'know, I envy you."

This caught Jack a little by surprise. *"You envy me?"*

"At that school, with all that learning there for you. A whole library full of books. You can be anything you want. If you decide medicine isn't for you, then there's always law. Or you can be an architect. Or you can teach. The world's just open to you, waiting for you to decide your place in it.

"Me, I can read and write, but not all that good. I never had a book in my life. Never read one until I moved in at the ranch. Aunt Ginny has some and I read one cover-to-cover over the past winter. First time I'd ever done that. I labored with it, but I got through it."

"What did you read?"

"A Christmas Carol, by Dickens."

Jack nodded. He knew the book.

Dusty said, "Pa says it's all foolishness. Ghosts showing up to show you your past. But Aunt Ginny says the purpose of literature is to expand your mind beyond your everyday life."

Jack said, "That's the purpose of it, I guess."

"Now me, I'll always just be a cowhand. And a gunhawk. A gunhawk who prefers to be a cowhand, I guess. Not that I'm complaining because I like my life. But you've got a future ahead of you that's sort of like an open book. All you have to do is reach out and grab it."

Pa returned to the fire. "It's probably best that we turn in. Sunrise is gonna come mighty early. We should take turns standing watch, maybe two-hour shifts."

Dusty said, "Shouldn't at least two of us stand watch?"

"No. I think one should be enough. There's no sign at all that there's anyone behind us on the trail."

"I'll take the first shift," Jack said, pushing to his feet. Despite the effects of the whiskey, he wasn't ready to sleep. Too much was rolling over in his mind.

Pa and Dusty stretched out their bedrolls and pulled their boots off. Pa placed his gun-belt at his side so his gun would be within easy reach. His gun was always within reach. Jack had wondered about this more than once. Aunt Ginny had said once that Pa seemed to always live in a state of war. Zack Johnson, a friend of the family Pa had met back in his Texas Ranger days, had said it came from Pa having been shot at once too much.

Jack brought a pot of coffee to life, and with a fresh cup of trail coffee in one hand and a sixth cartridge now loaded into his pistol, he stepped away from the circle of firelight.

Jack said, "Dusty, I'll come get you in a

couple hours."

"Sounds good," Dusty said. A jacket was rolled up under his head and his eyes were shut.

Jack decided to take a stroll about the camp as he drank his coffee, then maybe he would go out into the darkness beyond the camp and walk the perimeter.

Funny, he thought, how often he put things in military terms. Things like *walk the perimeter.* It came from being raised by a man who was forever in a state of war, he supposed.

Another funny thing, he thought, as his conversation with Dusty replayed itself in his mind. Dusty envied him, and yet Dusty currently had all Jack had ever wanted. Simply to be a cowhand, and enough of a gunhawk to ride alongside their father. To work alongside him at the ranch. Being an active member of the family, not simply a guest who visited occasionally.

Jack knew he should feel grateful for the opportunities. Not only his ability to easily comprehend what he read, but to retain it so easily. As such, he had done much reading and had gotten so he could read words on a page with even more ease than Pa could read tracks in the dirt.

Jack had also read the book by Dickens, but he hadn't labored over it. He had read it on a Sunday afternoon, sitting on his bed with a glass of Kentucky bourbon beside him.

He had found the book relatively easy reading. Admittedly, Dickens could be a little poetic in his phrasings, but Jack had found the entire thing to be little more than an intellectual exercise.

Jack had little interest in literature. Something that, until he had confessed this to Nina, he had told no one but Darby. Would Dickens one day take his place among the literary giants, or simply be forgotten as a hack? Jack didn't know, and neither did he care.

And yet, knowing he had Dusty's envy did nothing to resolve the restlessness in his own heart.

The Brewster's camp was quiet. They were in the tent and the fire was burning low. Jack added some wood to the fire. Best to keep the fire burning. Kept coyotes and wolves away, though he doubted any would be near because of that rabid carcass lying out there in the darkness.

He took a sip of coffee and moseyed on to the Harding camp, where he found Nina's father still awake. He was kneeling by the fire, adding a chunk of wood.

Jack said, "It's getting late. We'll be starting early in the morning."

"I'll be ready," Harding said, not looking up at him.

Jack decided to reach out a little. After all, he recognized the sign of troubled thoughts that can keep you awake. He had enough of them himself over the years. Many a time at school he would lie awake, thinking of the life he wanted but was somehow being denied him.

Jack said, "Trouble sleeping?"

Harding looked up at him with annoyance. "I thought I asked you to stay away from my daughter. She snuck out to be with you tonight. She might've gotten away with it if it hadn't been for that wolf."

"Look, Mister Harding. I mean no disrespect. I really don't. But isn't she at an age when she should be making her own decisions?"

"Not when it comes to the likes of you. You and your kind. She has no experience with the likes of you. And if you had any of decency, you would leave her alone."

Jack couldn't help but chuckle. "Most people who look at me and see a scholar. They see Harvard. But not you."

Harding rose to his feet. He was indeed tall. Jack rose not much higher than his shoulder.

He said, "You speak well. The fact that you're educated is obvious. But when I look at you, I see the gun at your side, and that you wear it as though you were born to it. On the surface you might seem like a well mannered college boy. But I can tell the way you carry that gun, and the look in your eye, that beneath the surface you're your father's son."

Harding had meant it as an insult, but ironically Jack thought it was one of the greatest compliments he had ever been given. Not that it excused Harding's belligerence.

Jack decided to change tactics. Sometimes the best defense is a strong offense.

He said, "Ever hear of Harlan Carter?"

This caught Harding by surprise. He simply stood and stared at Jack, trying to hide his surprise but failing to do so.

"Good night," Jack said, and walked on.

23

The following day the small wagon train continued along. The oxen pulled against their loads, and the men walked beside them, urging them along. The land now rose and fell in great hills, and pine covered ridges rose up at either side of the trail. Pa figured they were now only maybe three days out of McCabe Gap.

Duty pulled in another deer while he was scouting ahead, and once again the settlers set up camp and began roasting venison for their evening meal.

Once they had eaten, Dusty grabbed his rifle and headed out into the darkness to stand guard for a while. Just in case. It had been days since Jack's encounter with Vic Falcone and his men, and there had been no sign of them being followed.

"I'll be back in a while," Dusty said, and disappeared into the night.

Johnny knew he would see Dusty when he saw him. Could be half an hour. Could be hours. Dusty would roam about and satisfy himself they weren't being followed, and all was right out there.

Jack then said, a little too innocently, "I'm gonna go stretch my legs a bit. Been a long day in the saddle."

Johnny figured Jack was probably going to rendezvous somewhere out there with Nina Harding. Not that he blamed him. Nina was a fetching young girl. Had Johnny been Jack's age, she probably would have had his attention. And something about the way she and Jack looked at each other sort of set him to mind of himself and Lura, years ago. That kind of love doesn't come along often. When you do see it, it kind of stands out.

Johnny slapped his pipe to the palm of his hand to knock burnt tobacco out, then stuffed the pipe into a vest pocket. He knelt by the fire and added a couple more pieces. A stand of aspen grew not far from here, and they had been able to take enough for the night's fires. This far along the trail, finding wood for fires was no longer a problem.

About him, all was dark. The ridges that stood tall at either side of the trail were now lost to the blackness of night. The air was cool and crisp. From somewhere off in the night, a coyote howled. Johnny smiled. It was the sound of the mountains at night. He was home.

He saw motion from off by the wagons, and

298

saw a man stirring about. No, he was walking. Toward Johnny's fire. It was too dark to see who he was, but he was long and narrow and sort of loped along when he walked. Only one man like that among the settlers.

"Evening, Harding," Johnny said as the man approached. Johnny rose back to his feet.

Harding stepped into the firelight, and with his deep baritone he mumbled an, "Evenin'."

Harding was not wearing a hat. He was in a gray shirt and suspenders. His pistol was buckled about his waist. One of the gunbelts Jack had taken from Falcone and his men. Harding didn't wear it hanging low or tied down. He wore it high on his hip. But this didn't mean he was a stranger to using one. Johnny had seen more than one gunhawk wear his pistol like this. John Selman, for one.

"Where are your boys?" Harding said.

"Out and about." Johnny wasn't going to tell Harding that Jack was probably meeting secretly with Nina. Though, he wondered how much of a secret it could be when the entire camp knew how Jack and Nina felt about each other.

Johnny said, "We're almost at the end of the trail. I figure at this rate, day after tomorrow we'll be swinging north, off of this trail. Following a stage route that will take us into the little town they're naming after my family."

"Lookin' forward to it. Seems like we been

299

traveling forever. Left Vermont nigh onto four months ago. Been livin' out of a wagon since."

They stood in awkward silence for a moment. Then Harding said, "I figure you know who I am."

"Out here, we go by whatever name a man gives."

"Last night, your boy Jack asked me if I knew the name Harlan Carter."

Johnny chuckled. Jack had told Johnny and Dusty about that conversation. He said, "Comes right to the point, doesn't he? That's always been his way. Doesn't waste much time on subtleties or small talk."

"Harlan Carter died a long time ago, along with everything he was."

Johnny drew a breath of the clear night air. He could smell the grass that was becoming wet with dew, and there was a hint of balsam on the breeze. "I don't put a lot of thought into who a man was. I'm more interested in who he is, now."

"I had a price on my head. My name was on reward posters. If I was to have any kind of life, Harlan Carter had to stop existing. But I wondered, what kind of life could a man like me have?"

Johnny decided not to be polite, but to get right down to the brass tacks. "They say you killed because you liked killing."

He drew a breath and was silent a moment. "That wasn't why I killed. I killed because I needed to, to stay alive. Bounty hunters. Law-men. I never shot a man in cold blood. And I never shot a man what didn't need killing, either. Not really. Some of them lawmen were little better than gunhawks themselves."

Johnny nodded. "Often the case."

"But I liked it. God, I liked it. When the bullets were flying. That was the only time I really felt alive. What kind of life can a man like that make for himself?"

Johnny looked off into the night. This was something he didn't like to talk about. "I know what you mean. When the gunfire starts, some men find their legs just turn to rubber. But for some of us, we come really alive. I know the feeling. I felt bad about kill-ing, but never at the time it was happening. But it was always a sort of after-the-fact thing. When the guns are going off and it's either kill or be killed, I always found I could just pull the trigger without hesitating."

"I forced myself to turn away from it. I walked away. I just up and rode out. I had a small group of men. We were hiding in a small cabin in a canyon down in west Texas. I said I was riding out to do some hunting, and I just kept going. Changed my name."

"Why Vermont?"

"Why not Vermont?"

Johnny shrugged.

Harding said, "I had never been to that part of the world. I come from a small farm in the

Michigan woods. I had nothing left in Michigan, so I headed east, going almost as far as I could go. Staked out a section of woods no one had claimed. Started farming it. I was maybe twenty miles from the nearest town. Never planned on having a family, but then I met Emily."

"She knows who you are."

Harding nodded. "She knows everything."

"But then you decided to leave Vermont and come west again?"

"Someone there figured out who I might be. I have no idea how. It was Emily's idea to pack up and head west. I figured it maybe had been enough years. We could maybe find some remote place and settle in and farm."

"Not a bad plan."

Harding looked at him curiously. "You didn't give it up. The lifestyle. You know it's wrong to kill, and you feel bad when you have to. But you kept your name and you still wear a gun."

Johnny nodded. "We each made different decisions. Maybe it was easier for me. I never actually robbed anyone."

"I seen a reward poster for you and your brothers, years ago. For murder and theft."

Johnny nodded. "We did steal that one time, yes. A general store, in Missouri. We hadn't eaten in almost two days, and the marshal ran us out of town. We were there trying to find a job. We went back that night to take some canned goods from the general store. A cousin of ours was riding with us. Thaddeus, his name was. He shot and killed the marshal. It wasn't necessary, either. He just did it almost for the thrill of it. I thought I knew Thad. We had grown up together. But I hadn't seen him in three years, and when I did, he was in a lot of ways like a stranger. The reward poster was for all of us.

"But we got our names cleared of that killing. And we paid back every cent to the owner of that store."

"You never hit a stagecoach or a train? Or a bank?"

Johnny shook his head. Harding raised his brows and looked away. He hadn't been expecting that answer. Then he said, "Well, maybe you don't have as much to run from as I did. The kind of things I was running from can eat away at you after a time."

"It's been my experience that you can't run from yourself. You can try. You hid behind a plow for a number of years. But eventually the part of you you're running from sort of catches up with you."

Harding shuffled his feet and looked off into the night. Johnny was sure it was hard for Harding to hear this, but it was Harding who had opened this particular can of worms.

Harding said, "Nina doesn't know. We never told her. I don't want her to ever know."

Johnny looked down at the fire. The two

chunks of wood he had tossed on were catching. Another chunk he had put on earlier was nearly burned through and had broken in two, and one of the fresh pieces slid down a bit.

Johnny said, "My son Jack and your daughter have taken a liking to each other. He's a good boy. All three of my sons are."

Harding turned his gaze from the darkness beyond the firelight back to Johnny. Harding's eyes were like two lumps of coal beneath a heavy brow.

Harding said, "You chose to raise your boys in the path you're walking. Taught them to survive out here. How to shoot. How to kill a man. A good thing for them to know, considering the trouble having your name will bring them."

Johnny hadn't raised Dusty, but if he had, he wouldn't want Dusty to be any different than he was.

Harding said, "But me, I chose to raise my daughter away from what I am. What I was. I kept her safe, removed from the life your boys lead."

"I respect that decision."

"She has never heard the name Harlan Carter, and if I have my say, she never will. She had never seen one man shoot at another until we came west, and that was because of your son. He brings that life, the life of a gunfighter, right to her. I can't keep her shielded from it with Jack in her life."

"We're not bad people, Harding. We're law-abiding citizens. We run a cattle ranch. Sort of like farming, but we have to tend the livestock from the back of a horse."

"And yet you have a past. And a name that goes with that past. You never know when some young gunhawk might hunt you down, wanting to make a name for himself. And look at the trouble with Vic Falcone. I know who he is. Never met him, but I know the name. Just like I'm sure he knows mine. If your boy hadn't been with us, we wouldn't have had any trouble with them. But he has a grudge against your family. Jack being here brought Falcone down on us, and now Brewster's daughter is gone."

Harding drew a breath. "And then, there's your wife."

Johnny felt a stab of anger. Like a red hot branding iron pushing into an old wound. But he said nothing, letting Harding continue.

Harding said, "The story is she died taking a bullet meant for you. I don't want that for my daughter. I want her to marry a respectable man. Maybe a farmer or a shopkeeper. Not a man who wears death buckled around his hips. I want her to raise children and grow old happy, surrounded by grandchildren. I don't want her in a grave because of a bullet meant for someone else. Or to be carried off

305

by men like Falcone, the way Jessica Brewster was."

Johnny wanted to reply, but found he could not.

Harding said, "I want you to keep your boy away. Both of them, for that matter. Keep them away from my daughter."

"My boys are grown. They make up their own minds."

"I'm not making a request. Keep them away from me and mine, or they'll meet Harlan Carter. And they won't like it. Do you catch my meaning?"

"I don't take kindly to threats, Carter."

"I ain't making one. I'm just saying it like it is. I'm not someone you want to tangle with."

"I hope you know the same could be said about me."

"I came here to speak my piece."

"Sounds like you done that. It'd be best for everyone here if you walked away."

Harding nodded. "I'll walk away. This time. But keep those boys away from my daughter."

Harding backed away a few steps. Johnny was reminded of an animal in the wild, not wanting to turn its back on an adversary. Almost as though Harding might have suspected Johnny was going to go for his gun on the spot. Johnny thought this told him a lot about Harding. It told him Harding might have been drawing down on him, had the situation been reversed. Often you suspect people of what you are capable of yourself.

Harding then seemed satisfied Johnny was not going to go for his gun, and he turned and strode away, back toward his tent. Johnny watched him walk away.

From somewhere off on a ridge, a wolf let out a lonesome call. Distinctly different than a coyote. The howl trailed off and then was gone.

Johnny stood by his campfire and thought maybe he knew how the animal felt. And he knew Carter did, too.

■ ■ ■ ■

INTERLUDE:
THE CABIN

■ ■ ■ ■

24

The cabin was actually a dugout. The back wall and both side walls were simply where the shovels had stopped digging when the cabin was built. The roof was also made of earth. Roots hung down, and more than once a snake had dropped onto the floor. Spiders tended to creep their way in. The floor was of hard packed dirt, and Jessica tried to keep the dust and rocks out, but working at it with a broom tended to just sweep up more dust.

The front of the cabin was made of logs, though the mud was dried and falling from the chinks, leaving openings the wind could creep in through. There was no door, save an old, ratty blanket nailed to the doorway overhead. Jessica hated the thought of spending a winter in this cabin, in these mountains. She would freeze to death. Against the front wall was a small cast iron stove, but she doubted it would do much against the cold, if the cold was anything like what she experienced in Vermont.

The cabin had two bunk beds, and a bed against the back wall. She shared one of the bunks with Cade, and Two-Finger Walker got the other bunk, and Vic Falcone and Flossy shared the single bed.

Jessica had not seen a bath since she had left with these men back on the trail. There was a creek within walking distance and she had taken a dunk in it a couple of times, but the water was ice cold and she didn't really feel any cleaner afterward than she had before. Her hair was filled with dust she couldn't quite get out, her cheeks were smeared with dirt, and her dress was torn at one sleeve and the hem was becoming frayed.

In the center of the small cabin was a table. Vic Falcone sat there, a bottle in front of him. His gun rested on the table beside the bottle. He hadn't shaved since leaving Cheyenne and now a wild looking beard was covering his jaw. He was in his undershirt with suspenders up and over each shoulder. His undershirt was stained with dirt and sweat. His hair was growing long and unkempt, and was sticking out in places.

This man had seemed so debonair when she first met him. So eloquent. But since Jessica had left her family, Falcone had descended into what he now was. He was sullen and quick tempered, and often simply wanted to be left alone. He sat with his bottle of whiskey, staring away into nothingness.

Sometimes he would sit outside on a hand-cut bench by the door and look off at a distant ridge. Sometimes Jessica thought he was a little scary, and sometimes just plain sad.

Jessica stood now, broom in hand, trying to decide if she should continue to attempt to clean this floor or just give up. She would steal an occasional glance at Vic. He simply stared. Then he brought both hands up and through his hair, and leaned forward on both elbows and buried his face in his hands. He sat like that for a moment or two, then reached for the whiskey bottle and took a pull.

The blanket hanging in the doorway was swept aside and Flossy came in carrying a heavy bucket of water with one hand. She had been down to the creek. If they needed water for any reason, it meant a walk down to the creek. And it usually meant a walk for one of the women. Jessica didn't notice any of the men doing a whole lot of work around here.

Flossy's hair was tied behind her head in a bun, but it was as dirty as Jessica's. Flossy wore the same low-cut dress she had back outside of Cheyenne, and sweat was glistening against her neck and collarbone and down to her cleavage. Daytime could turn off hot here in the mountains this time of year, and it was a long walk down to the creek and an even longer one back carrying a full bucket of water. Streaks of dirt worked their way up her neck and onto her face.

She sat the bucket down on the table heavily and stood for a moment catching her breath.

None of them were eating well. Often no more than one meal a day. Some rabbit, and once in a while maybe an elk. But that involved the men actually doing something productive like hunting, but they seemed more interested in sitting around with a bottle of whiskey, or wasting ammunition doing some target practice by shooting at tree branches. The only time Cade seemed to have any energy at all was when he was in bed with Jessica.

The thought of such activities in a room shared by others would have horrified Jessica at one time. And it indeed had, the first few times. But you get used to that sort of thing. Funny how easily your civilized tendencies can fall away, if you let them.

She thought of her mother and father once in a while. And of Age. Her brother. But she didn't really miss them. The life she had now could not really be called living, but neither could the life she had. The drudgery of the day-to-day labor on a farm. All she had to look forward to was going from the status of farmer's daughter to farmer's wife, once she found a sod buster willing to take her on.

The life she had now was really no better. She had gone away with these men seeking danger and excitement, and wanting to see the world. All she really succeeded in doing was exchanging one sort of hell for another.

Flossy looked at Vic. She said, "Vic? I just brought up some water. You want some coffee?"

His face was buried in his hands again. He didn't respond. It was like he hadn't heard her at all.

She tossed a concerned glance to Jessica, then said, "Vic? Honey?"

He said through his hands, "I heard you."

"Would you like me to make some coffee?"

"I don't truly care what you do."

Flossy tossed another glance at Jessica, who answered with a shrug of her shoulders.

Jessica said, "I'll take a cup. And a fire might take some of the dampness out of this place."

Flossy nodded. "Come help me get some firewood."

25

Two-Finger walker sat on an old stump, his gaze drifting toward the cabin. He had his bowie knife in his hand and was whittling at a piece of wood. Though he wasn't really doing all that much whittling. He was mostly just sitting with his knife in his hand, thinking about how insanely bored he was.

He looked down at the piece of wood. It was pine, soft enough that he might be able to carve it into something. When he had been a kid back in Minnesota, he had carved dogs and horses and such.

He had learned to hold the wood with his bad hand, gripping it with his thumb and his index finger, the only finger remaining.

White-Eye walked over. He had a rifle in one hand.

"Gonna do some huntin'?" Walker said.

White-Eye nodded. He was the only one never slept in the cabin. There weren't enough bunks, and he said he would rather sleep outdoors anyway. He usually made a small fire off a ways from the cabin and unrolled his blankets there. Between the three of them — White-Eye, Cade and Falcone — White-Eye was the only one Walker thought had any sand at all and would hold up in a fight. Walker was beginning to wonder why he ever signed on with this outfit.

It was down to just the four of them, now. They had left Lane behind. With the wrist of his gunhand broken, he would no longer be of any good to them. Not that Walker thought he was much good to begin with.

White-Eye said, "I'm gettin' tired of eatin' rabbit. And there's only two cans of beans left."

"I'm tired of eatin' beans, anyway."

White-eye nodded.

Walker said, "Is this all there is to riding with Vic Falcone? Hiding out in this old, two-bit cabin? What the hell are we waitin' for?"

White-Eye shrugged. "Didn't use to be this way. Used to be a lot of us. You ever hear of Kiowa Haynes?"

Walker nodded. He looked up at White-Eye, squinting in the sun. "Yeah, I heard a Kiowa."

"He used to ride with us. He was killed by the brother of that McCabe boy. Last summer. We used to have a big cabin and a good-sized bunkhouse in a canyon. Maybe a week's ride from here. Maybe more. Right near a little town. We had all the women and whiskey we could want."

White-Eye looked toward the log wall of the dugout. "This here cabin we found last fall, after we had to abandon the canyon. Made by an old prospector or a mountain man, I suppose. Don't rightly know. It was empty when we found it. Got through the winter here."

"What happened at the canyon?"

"Most of our men got killed. Started up in Montana, really. We was gonna raid a couple of ranches, and get some horses and supplies. Maybe even a woman, if we was lucky. But we rode down on the McCabe ranch. A couple of us spoke against it. Kiowa did, and me. And a gunhawk named Logan. McCabe has a reputation. It seemed riding down on his spread might not be the smartest thing to do, especially when there were smaller ranches in the area, with less men. Ranches that weren't run by Johnny McCabe and a small army of gunfighters. But old Vic — he wouldn't listen to reason."

"Doesn't seem like Vic listens to reason very much."

White-Eye shook his head, and spit a wad of tobacco juice into the grass. "Trying to be too much like Sam Patterson, I guess. Sam never listened to no one, but he didn't need to. Sam had instincts like a mountain lion when it came to survivin'. Just tag on along behind him, and you'd be all right."

"What ever happened to Patterson, any-way?"

White-eye shrugged his shoulders. "Just rode out one day. Said he'd had enough. That left Vic in charge. Vic tries to be like old Sam, but he just ain't cut from the same cloth."

White-Eye squatted down on his haunches. "Now, old Sam, he took in this orphan boy, one day. Back in Missouri. Back durin' the War. We was shootin' up this old farm. Burnin' the place. The farmer was a Union sympathizer, and we was told to burn him out. We did with a passion. Old Sam — he never did nothin' second-rate. But he saw this little whelp just lookin' up at him. The farm was burnin' and women screamin' and we was shooting guns off into the night. But the boy just stood and stared at Sam. So Sam — he just scoops the boy up and brung him with us. Said he always intended to find a good home for him, but somehow never found the time to. Sam ended up raisin' him like he was his own."

Walker shook his head. "Not the smartest thing to do, totin' around a kid."

"Nope. But Sam, he somehow made it work."

Walker was too bored with the chunk of pine to bother anymore. The stump he was sitting on had an exposed root that stretched out past his foot. He threw the knife at the root, and it landed tip first and stood there.

White-Eye said, "When the boy was maybe fifteen, Sam told him to make his choice. Either join us, or ride on. The boy chose to ride on."

Walker reached over and pulled the knife of the root, then sat back and threw the knife again. This time the tip of the knife hit at a slightly wrong angle, and the knife bounced off the root and landed in the grass.

White-Eye said, "Thing is, that boy turned out to be the bastard son of Johnny McCabe."

Now White-Eye had Walker's full attention. Walker said, "You serious?"

White-Eye nodded. "We never saw him again until last summer. Maybe five years had gone by. We was perched on a ridge watching the ranch house with a spy glass, and we seen the boy there. His name was Dusty. Well, old Vic always hated the boy. Kiowa did, too. They both felt the boy ate their supplies but never give nothing back. Didn't carry his own weight. But they was both too scared of Sam to say anything. Kiowa did say something once. Tried to scare the boy. I thought Sam was gonna gut Kiowa right there. He would'a, if Kiowa wasn't such a good scout.

"So, Vic sees Dusty down there at the ranch, and now all he wants is to ride down there and attack the place. Maybe kill Dusty in the process. I told him no. Made no sense. Logan said so. Even Kiowa. As much as he hated Dusty, to ride down on the McCabe place was suicide. But Vic wouldn't listen to reason.

"So, one night we rode in. All of us. Only half of us rode away. Then, Dusty takes to following us. Him and his brother. 'Cept we didn't know Dusty was McCabe's son, and we didn't know the other one was, either. They followed us to the canyon. Dusty killed Kiowa in a knife fight, and they had men positioned at the top of the canyon. Got Logan. I was positioned at the other end of the canyon as a guard, so I got away. And Vic and Flossy managed to get away with their hides intact. But that was it. Just the two of us. Vic ain't never really been the same. It's all been downhill since then."

"Where'd you find Cade?"

"In a saloon, down Colorado way."

"Should'a left him there."

White-Eye snickered. "Vic was desperate to find men who would ride with him. Cade was all that was available. Vic wouldn't listen to reason."

Motion at the cabin drew Walker's attention. The girls were stepping out through the blanket. Flossy, and the young one. Jessica.

Walker said, "Now that does bring a complaint of mine to the surface."

"What does?"

"Them women. We got two right here. But Vic gets one, and that useless good-for-nothin' Cade gets the other one."

White-eye nodded. "That's the way Vic does things. She wants to be with Cade, for whatever reason."

"Maybe it's time some things were done different around here."

"Like what?"

Walker retrieved his knife from the grass and got to his feet and tucked the knife into a sheath in the side of his boot. "Maybe it's time I had a little talk with Vic."

White-Eye had also risen to his feet. He shook his head. "Won't listen. Never does."

Walker nodded with a smile. "Oh, he'll listen to me. But before I do, I gotta ask. If it comes down to it, which side will you be on?"

White-Eye shrugged. "The side that works out best for me."

Walker nodded. Good answer.

White-Eye said, "I will admit, I am gettin' a little tired of waitin' here at this little cabin. Another winter here ain't what I have in mind."

Walker said. "Then, things are about to change around here."

And Walker started toward the cabin. White-Eye sat on the stump and laid his rifle across his lap, and watched.

26

Walker stopped maybe thirty feet from the blanket. He called out, "Vic! Come out here! We gotta talk."

He waited. It then occurred to him this might not be the best position, from a tactical point of view. There were no windows in the cabin, but there was a vertical slit cut at one side of the door, and another one at the other. Just big enough to fit a gun barrel through. Vic could shoot him where he stood, and Walker didn't think it wise to assume such a thing was beyond Vic.

There was no response from the cabin anyway, so he said the hell with it and strode toward the cabin and pushed aside the blanket. One of the nails holding the blanket in place popped free and landed on the dirt floor.

Vic was sitting at the table, a half-full bottle of whiskey in front of him. The women had come back into the cabin and were at the stove, getting ready to build a fire.

"Vic," Walker said. "I want to talk with you."

Vic looked at him wearily. "What about?"

"About this." Walker glanced about him, indicating with his eyes the cabin itself. "This place. What we're doin' here."

"What we're doing here is my business. You're on the payroll. You do what you're told."

"What payroll? I don't recall any money comin' our way since I signed on with you."

Vic nodded. "It will. You just have to be patient."

"That's where you're wrong, Vic. I don't have to be nothin'."

Vic looked at him a long moment. "You're free to ride on anytime. There's nothing holding you here."

"Yeah, there is. It's called money owed. You owe me for all the weeks I been followin' you around and waitin' here at this sad excuse for a cabin. You got the money to pay me?"

Vic shook his head. "Not yet."

Vic hadn't had enough whiskey to make his words slur, but his eyes looked a little glazed as he stared at Walker. His gun was still on the table beside him.

"Look," Flossy said to Walker. "We don't want trouble."

"Ain't talkin' to you, woman."

Jessica was truly scared. She had always been a little scared of Walker. She reached over to Flossy and took her hand.

"Now," Walker said, directing his gaze back to Falcone. "I signed on in the first place to have another crack at Johnny McCabe. When do I get that?"

Vic shrugged. "That opportunity has passed. Without having his son as a hostage, to just ride onto his ranch would be suicide."

"You sayin' you're afraid?"

"I'm saying I'm smart. Like I said, you're free to ride on any time."

"Just how do you figure on payin' me?"

"I have no money right now, but we're going to make some. You hang with me a little longer, and you'll see. There are gold fields up in Montana. We'll grab some money there. Sometimes a smaller group of men like we have here can be more effective than a large party."

"When we gonna do this, Vic?"

"In a while. You just need to be patient."

"I think I'm done bein' patient."

Walker suddenly sprang at Falcone. Falcone reached for his gun, but there was too much whiskey in him and his reaction time was a little too slow, and Walker was on top of him. Grabbing his hand and pulling it away from the gun. Walker then gave Vic a backhanded slap to the face, strong enough to send Vic falling backward in the chair.

Walker didn't wait for Vic to get to his feet. With one hand he grabbed the table and sent it rolling sideways. Flossy screamed. Jessica gripped Flossy's hand tighter.

Walker grabbed Vic by the suspenders and pulled him to his feet. Blood was streaming from Vic's nose and he was blinking his eyes. Your eyes tend to water when you get hit in the nose, and all the whiskey was making it worse.

Vic looked like he wasn't sure what was happening. Two-Finger didn't wait for him to figure it out. With his good hand, he drove a fist into Vic's stomach. Vic doubled over, all the way to the floor and lost much of the whiskey he had consumed. That which hadn't made its way into his system yet.

Walker then kicked him in the ribs and Vic flopped over sideways.

"Stop it!" Flossy screamed.

Walker grabbed Vic by the suspenders and pulled him to his feet again. The bunk beds were immediately behind Vic, and Walker placed a hand on Vic's forehead and drove his head back and into the wooden bunks. Once. Again. Vic's knees buckled.

Walker hauled Vic to his feet one more time. Vic was no longer fully conscious. His eyes were fluttering and his legs were wobbly. Walker dragged him out through the blanket and threw him on the ground.

Cade was standing there. He had been walking up to the cabin when Walker and Vic burst out through the hanging blanket. He now stood staring, a little shocked.

Walker said to Cade, sort of growling through his teeth, "Go get his horse."

Cade stood, staring.

"I said, get his horse. Fergit the saddle. Just the horse."

Cade hurried away.

Vic coughed and spit. Blood was still streaming out of his nose. He tried to wipe some away with his sleeve, then looked at the crimson color on his sleeve with surprise. As though his battered and whiskey-addled mind was just realizing he was bleeding.

He blinked his eyes and sucked in breath. His eyes found focus. He rose to his knees, and tried to fully stand but fell back to the ground, and rose to his knees again. One arm was folded in front of his ribs where Walker had punched him. He reached the other hand out to the ground to steady himself.

He looked over to where White-Eye sat on the stump. The rifle was still on White-Eye's lap. He was sitting contentedly, as though he were at the theater watching a show.

Jessica and Flossy stepped out through the hanging blanket. Jessica still had hold of Flossy's hand. With Flossy's free hand, she was covering her own mouth and looking with shock at Vic.

Cade climbed the grassy hill with Vic's horse. There was a hackamore over the animal's nose, but no saddle. Walker grabbed

Vic by the suspenders and hauled him to his feet one more time.

Walker grabbed Vic by the hair and pulled his head back until Vic was staring at the sky, and slid out his bowie knife and brought it to Vic's neck.

Walker said, "I ever see you again, I'll cut your throat ear to ear. You understand me?"

Vic tried to speak, but words didn't come. Between the bleeding nose and the wind being knocked out of him by the punch to the stomach and ribs, and his head being slammed into the wooden bunk. He drew a breath and tried again, and got out a hoarse, shaky, "Yes."

Walker stood a little taller than Vic, and was hard muscled. He grabbed Vic by the back of the suspenders with his mangled hand and the belt with his good hand and lifted and almost threw Vic onto the back of his horse. The horse was startled and shifted its hooves, but Cade held onto the hackamore and kept the horse in place. Vic was conscious enough to shift himself around until he was sitting astride the horse. He was still coughing, and he wavered a bit as though he was about to fall off the horse, but grabbed hold of the mane to hang on.

Walker pulled off his hat and struck it across the rump of the horse and the horse took off running, down over the grassy slope and out of sight.

White-Eye got to his feet and strolled over.

"What did you do?" Cade said. "He's our boss."

Walker said, "Not no more."

"But he'll die out there like that. Even if he gets down off this ridge, it's miles to any place."

"He'll die if he stays here, too. I'd see to it."

White-Eye chuckled. "He's been dyin' bit by bit for a long time, I think."

Walker pulled his hat back down over his temples, and said to White-Eye, "Well, are you with me?"

"You look like a man who can get things done." He nodded. "Yeah, I'm with you. What's the first order of business?"

"First, we're gonna leave this cabin behind. Maybe spend the night, then in the morning we're out of here. We're gonna head north. Like Vic said, to the gold fields. But there's also a man up there I need to see."

White-Eye smiled and nodded. "Johnny McCabe."

Walker held up his crippled hand. "Got me a score to settle with him."

"Keep in mind, Vic tried to take that ranch and lost half his men."

White-Eye said, "I don't plan to try and take that ranch. From the sounds of it, it would take a lot more men than Vic had to do that. I intend to face him. Finish what I

329

started, years ago."

White-Eye spit some tobacco juice to the grass. "Don't mean no offense, but if what they say about you is true, you faced him twice. Once he shot apart your hand, and the second time he gave you that there scar across your face and cost you an eye."

"That was years ago. I was young and stupid. I've learned a lot over the years. I can handle myself a lot better now than I ever could then. And McCabe is an old man. He must be pushing fifty. Cattle ranching."

White-Eye nodded. "There's a good chance he ain't the man he was."

"Hold on," Cade said. "I signed on with Vic Falcone. I don't know that you got what it takes to lead anyone. I'm fixin' to ride after him and get him back here and once he's cleaned up he'll decide what we're gonna do."

"You suddenly got some backbone, boy?" Walker said.

Cade's bullet wound was now half-way healed. And he was wearing his gun. He let his hand drop down near his holster. A smile crept across his face. "You don't know how fast I am with a gun."

White-Eye shook his head. "Boy, this man survived a gunfight with Johnny McCabe. You're way out of your class."

"No I ain't. He don't know what he's deal-in' with. I say Vic's in charge of this outfit."

Walker said, "And I say Vic's lucky I didn't

330

cut his throat right then and there. Probably should have been done a long time ago."

Walker turned his gaze to the women, who were standing by the cabin doorway. "And it's time you two started earnin' your keep. And I don't mean just cookin' and cleanin'."

Cade said, "You can't talk to my woman that-a-way."

Walker looked at him with a grin. Like a cat getting ready to eat a mouse, except the mouse didn't know how extremely over-matched he was. White-Eye was watching, chewing on some tobacco.

Walker said, "She ain't your woman, boy. Unless you want to try and make her your woman."

"You're gonna make me draw on you, ain't you," Cade said.

"Your choice. Draw, or shut up."

Cade went for his gun. He burst into motion, stabbing his hand at the gun riding low on his leg. But Walker was sliding his out of the holster and bringing his arm to full extension, cocking the gun as he moved, and squeezing the trigger. All in one smooth, fluid motion. Not as fast with his left as he was once with his right, before Johnny McCabe shot his hand apart, but fast enough. Cade's gun had barely cleared leather when Walker's bullet caught him in the chest. Cade's gun fired into the ground at his feet. He took a couple steps backward, staggering a bit, a look of shock on his face.

Walker squeezed off another shot for good measure. Put the bullet a couple inches away from the first one. Cade took another staggering step, then dropped to his knees.

He looked up questioningly at Walker. Then, as though he realized he was still holding his gun, he began to raise it toward Walker. Walker cocked and squeezed one more time, and the bullet tore into Cade's forehead, snapping his head back. Cade fell backward, his legs doubled up awkwardly beneath him. He twitched a bit, but otherwise didn't move. His eyes stared toward the sky.

"Cade!" Jessica screamed out. Flossy squeezed her hand more tightly. White-Eye spat some tobacco juice to the grass.

"Well, that's over," Walker said. Smoke was still drifting from his gun. He slid the gun back into his holster.

White-Eye walked over and pried Cade's revolver from his grip. He gave it a once-over. A Colt .44.

"Good gun," he said, and tucked it into his belt. "I wonder what size his boots are."

Walker turned to Jessica and Flossy. "You two. Into the cabin. Time for you to start earnin' your keep."

PART TWO:
THE VALLEY

27

The buildings of the little town weren't set up to form a particular street. They were just sort of scattered about.

Directly ahead of the settlers was a long structure made of logs and with a peaked roof, and a stovepipe stuck out of the wall at one side. Above the doorway was a sign that read HUNTER'S SALOON. A small walkway made of hand-cut boards lined the front of the saloon. Maybe two hundred feet in front of the saloon and off to the side a bit was another building, this one standing two floors high. Clapboard walls painted white, and again a peaked roof. This had a sign that read, simply, HOTEL. The sign was a bit faded and the paint was peeling. Another building stood beside it, long and with walls of upright planks, and a sign out front that read FRANKLIN'S EMPORIUM. A boardwalk connected the two. Off to one side, sort of at an angle to Hunter's, was a small square-shaped building, also made of upright planks and painted white, and with a steeple standing tall.

Brewster led the team of oxen pulling the first of his two wagons, and his wife walked alongside him. Behind them was their second wagon, with Age leading the team. The Brewster wagons always seemed to be first in line, followed by the brooding Harding, and then Ford pulling up the rear. Johnny had never asked, and had no idea if it was a pre-arranged thing or if the order of wagons seemed to reflect the natural pecking order that had developed among the settlers.

Johnny rode beside the first Brewster wagon, and without giving any specific suggestions or directions, rode toward Hunter's. Brewster simply kept his team of horses moving along beside him.

Johnny hadn't shaved since he and Dusty had ridden out to meet Jack over a week ago, and a thick mat of whiskers had grown. His sombrero was dusty, and his hair was tied into a tail and fell down over the back of his shoulders.

"So, this is it?" Brewster said. "The town named after your family?"

"Well," Johnny said. "It isn't really a town. Not officially. Just a collection of buildings. Hunter's an old friend, and he built his saloon where it is because the stage trail passes through here, leading north to Virginia City. After a while, a hotel was built. Then

Mister Franklin moved in and built his general store. Up ahead a little, there's a pass between two ridges that leads down into the valley, and when we first moved here we named it McCabe Gap. The folks here sort of appropriated the name for this little community."

Mildred said, "Jack mentioned that your family was the first in this area."

Johnny nodded. "At one time, the nearest town was Virginia City, a two-day ride away overland by horseback, and closer to three if you take the wagon trail. Fetching supplies was almost a six-day day trip. Three going, and three coming back. And in the winter we couldn't hope to get a wagon down those trails, so we had to buy our entire winter's supplies before the first snow. Then Bozeman started up and cut our supply runs in half, time-wise. This was all before Franklin moved in and built his store. Now we have it easy."

Mildred Brewster said, "Do many people live in this area now?"

"A couple of other ranches have set up within riding distance, and there are a few farms, too, further out. There are a few claims being worked between here and Helena."

Brewster said, "And you say this little valley of yours has some fertile earth and plenty of water?"

"Some of the best in this part of the territory, in my opinion. I grew up on a farm in

337

Pennsylvania, and even though I left the farming life behind me, I know good soil when I see it."

"If you don't mind my asking, why hasn't anyone built on it already?"

"Location, I suppose. Most folks want to be within reaching distance of either Bozeman or Helena."

They were now no more than a hundred feet from Hunter's front door.

"Pull up here," Johnny said. "There's someone I want you to meet."

Johnny rode up to the hitching rail and swung out of the saddle.

He called out, "Hunter!"

Within a count of three, a large man with a full dark beard was pushing his way out the door. His eyes lit up when he saw Johnny.

"Johnny!" Hunter called out.

Hunter stood a good six inches taller than Johnny, and wasn't just tall but big. He reached out to shake Johnny's hand, and his hand practically swallowed Johnny's. He slapped a hand on Johnny's shoulder and knocked him over a step.

Jack and Dusty came riding alongside Johnny, and Hunter did the same to Dusty, grabbing hand as he stepped out of the saddle. Then he grabbed Jack in a bear hug and lifted him from the earth.

"You've been gone too long, bear cub," Hunter said. He had given that name to Jack years ago.

Abel and Mildred were standing behind Johnny, grinning. Johnny glanced back at the Harding wagon, which was pulling up alongside Abel. Harding wasn't smiling, and Johnny doubted the man had much to smile about.

Hunter invited everyone in for a meal. "You folks have been riding for all these weeks. Come in and sit and let my cook whip you up something to eat."

"You hired a cook?" Jack said.

"Sure did. An old Chinese gent. Can cook like you can't believe. Almost as good as Aunt Ginny's."

The wagons were driven to a large grassy expanse that began near Hunter's and stretched off toward the nearest ridge. Teams were unhitched and rubbed down and left to graze while Hunter's new cook went to work frying steaks and potatoes.

Franklin came scurrying over with a side of bacon. He was a man a little shorter than Johnny and maybe ten years older, with a receding hairline and the beginnings of a pot belly. He shook hands with Johnny and the boys and was introduced to the settlers, and offered the side of bacon free of charge. Franklin was hospitable as all get out, Johnny thought, and never missed the chance to drum up new business.

Franklin glanced down at the twin Remingtons Johnny wore. Franklin said, "I wanted to tell you, I have a forty-four Peacemaker at the store. Only a couple years old. I've been holding it for you, in case you wanted a look. I know you've been looking for one."

Johnny nodded. "Once we're settled in, I'll ride back into town and check it out."

As dinner was being served, Johnny said to Brewster, "I won't be joining you. The boys and I have been gone from home for too long. We're going to ride out to the house. I'll be back in the morning, and we can check out that stretch of farming land I've been talking about."

As they swung into their saddles, Jack allowed himself a glance about. To one side of the town was a rounded slope covered with pines that led up to a razor-like ridge. On the other, another ridge gradually rose and then began to stretch out. This one was rocky in places, and in other places covered with pines. Further out, beyond town, the land gently sloped down to a dry gulch that flooded in the spring, and then up to another set of ridges. In places they were rocky with steep cliffs, and in others the slopes were more gently rounded.

This was all a grand vista taken for granted by the people who lived here. They could see this kind of thing every day. But for Jack, whose general vista was the inside of a classroom, this place was like something out of a storybook.

A wagon trail led from town through the pass and down into the valley, across a stretch of open meadow and then across a wooden bridge and up to the ranch house itself. Three miles in all.

Pa led the way, turning his horse around to the back of Hunter's saloon, and to a small path that cut into a forest of maple and alders. This was the secondary trail that would lead down into the valley, Jack knew. A precarious trail that could be navigated by a horse, but a man driving a wagon would have to take the longer route that led from the other side of town and through the main pass. The longer route added almost a mile to the ride.

They rode along in single file. Pa, then Dusty and followed by Jack.

Jack glanced about to the left and then the right as they rode, and then dropped his eyes to the ground to search for tracks. It was the way Pa had taught him to travel. Always looking, always watching. Never let yourself be taken by surprise. Expect anything, and be prepared for everything.

Aunt Ginny had once said about Pa that he was always in a state of perpetual war. This came back to Jack now, as he followed Pa and Dusty. Pa had taught him to ride as such, so he would always be ready for a surprise attack. As though there were Comancheros or highwaymen behind every rock, or snipers in every tree. Even now, Pa rode with the reins in his left hand, and his right resting by his revolver.

Jack thought, *God help the highwayman who actually tries to jump Pa.*

The trail cut through a thick stand of hardwood — mostly oak and birch and alders, and then up a slope and through a narrow, rocky pass, and then into a pine forest and down into the valley.

They emerged from the trail onto a long grassy expanse a mile wide and five miles long. Ahead of them, a half mile in the distance, was a structure two floors high, made of logs. It resembled the type of house popular back east, called a *Cape Cod.* Jack had noticed long ago that once you got outside of Boston, many of the homes were built with this design.

Rising above the roofline was a stone chimney and smoke drifted lazily from it. Too early in the day for a fire in the living room hearth, Jack thought. But the stove in the kitchen fed into the same chimney. This meant Aunt Ginny was working on dinner. One thing about the food at school, Jack never found it came even close to his aunt's cooking.

Standing near the house was a large barn, and beyond it was a long low structure Jack knew was the bunkhouse. Behind the house, stretching back to a line of trees that marked the end of the valley floor, a remuda of horses ran freely.

"Come on," Johnny said, and he and Dusty clicked their horses ahead.

Jack fell into place behind them, but he didn't do so with much enthusiasm. He had found home didn't really feel like home when he had been gone for a long time and was only back for a visit.

When you have been away for a long span of time, you often find the people you left behind are in different places in their lives. And things about the home might have changed. An end table might have been replaced, or a new chair had replaced an old one. Jack found one year an old horse that had been there as far back as he could remember, one of the first horses Pa had acquired when he and Ma were newlyweds, had died. No one thought to mention it in a letter and the horse had been gone eight months when he finally got back for his summer visit.

He didn't fault anyone for not writing about it. It would be impossible for anyone to capture in a letter everything he missed about this place.

Mainly what he missed was the day-to-day life. A colt born in the spring growing a little more every day. Some wild horses Pa caught needing to be broken. Sitting with the family by the hearth at night. The smell of Pa's pipe smoke in the air. Josh's foghorn voice and Bree's musical giggle. The timbers overhead giving an occasional creak as Jack lay in bed, waiting for sleep to take him. The sound of sleet in the winter against his bedroom window, or the crickets in the summer chirping from somewhere out in the night.

He thought about this as he followed his father and brother across the grassy meadow to the house, and his heart ached for times past that would never be here again.

As they covered the quarter mile from the edge of the woods to the house, Jack saw a man step out of the barn. He was long and angular, with a white shirt and suspenders and a dark sombrero. Even from a distance he knew the man was Fred Mitchum, the wrangler. Fred looked up at the sound of horses approaching and gave a big wave.

A small rectangular corral was set up near the barn and it was here the riders reined up and swung out of their saddles. Fred met them with handshakes and a wide grin.

"Glad to have you back, Jack."

Jack found himself smiling widely. He had always liked Fred. "Good to be back, Fred. How have you been?"

Fred nodded. "No complaints. No complaints."

Jack and his brother and father began the

short walk to the house. Jack couldn't help but notice how all three of them walked with wide, sort of bowing steps, and he had to repress a little grin. After being in the saddle so many hours, combined with the extreme tightness of riding boots, it was kind of hard to step along with a normal gait. Jack never walked this way at school, but now as he followed Pa and Dusty to the house, he found himself falling into pace.

The front door opened and Jack's sister Bree came bounding out. "Pa! Dusty! Jack!"

She was sixteen, with long dark hair tied up in a bun behind her head. Despite a cumbersome ankle-length skirt, she skipped down the stairs with almost the grace of a dancer and took Pa in a hug, then followed with Dusty.

"Jack," she said. "We've all missed you so much. It's good to have you home."

He nodded and forced a smile. It was indeed good to see his sister again. But would they be so happy to see him once they discovered the Jack they thought they knew didn't really exist? He put all of that aside as he pulled his sister in for a hug.

He then looked up at the porch and saw Aunt Ginny standing and looking toward them, a book closed in one hand. Not a tall woman, she stood with an almost regal quality. She had too much stately dignity to run to them, but a smile lighted her face.

"Jackson," she said as he approached the porch. "It is so good to see you again."

He climbed the steps and gave her a small peck on the cheek. "It's so good to see you again, too, ma'am."

Standing beside Aunt Ginny was a girl about Nina's age. Hair too light to be called brown but not quite blonde. Her hair was in a bun and she had a smattering of freckles across her face. Like God had been tossing freckles wildly and she had gotten in the way.

"Jackson," Aunt Ginny said. "Allow me to introduce you to Temperance."

"Pleased to meet you," she said.

"Likewise," he said, taking her hand gently. Aunt Ginny had mentioned Temperance in her letters. "I've heard a lot about you."

She suddenly flushed with embarrassment. "Oh, no."

"Only good, I assure you."

Aunt Ginny gave him a look up and down through spectacles perched on her nose. He stood nearly as tall as Pa and Dusty. His shoulders filled out his shirt with muscle he had gained from much time boxing in the gym and working with the college rowing team. He had seen little on Earth that could tax your muscles like being on the rowing team.

"My," she said. "We sent you off to school a boy, and every year you return more and more a man."

The others came up the steps behind him. Aunt Ginny took his arm and they started into the house.

"Come," she said. "Dinner's almost ready. You'll have to tell me all about school. It must be so exciting."

He managed a smile. "Yes, ma'am."

Aunt Ginny had a rule about dining at the McCabe ranch house, and she was not about to overlook it now, despite how happy she was to see Johnny and Dusty back. And how elated she was to see Jack home for a few weeks of vacation. He had not been home the summer before, so she had not seen him in two years. The rule was that you don't come to the dinner table covered with dust and sweat. You washed, and if you couldn't find the time to sit in a tub you at least did a thorough scrubbing in front of a water basin. She allowed a man to wear a gun at the table — a siege on the ranch house by renegade Sioux warriors a few years earlier had helped convince her of the practicality of keeping a gun close to hand, and Jack was sure the attack by Falcone and his men the summer before reinforced it. But you washed, you shaved, and you wore a clean shirt.

Jack climbed the stairs wearily and stepped into the bedroom he had shared with Josh when they were growing up. Bunk beds were at one wall, and against the other was a bureau upon which stood a pitcher and a basin. Jack noticed the pitcher was filled with water, ready for use.

His rifle was still in his saddle, and his bedroll was still tied behind the cantle. Fred was probably pulling the saddle off of the tired horse at the moment and depositing it all in the tack room. Jack would go down to get it all later. He had bought his horse in Cheyenne, and it would be the only animal in the remuda not bearing the Circle M brand of the McCabe ranch, or the Bar J Brand of Zack Johnson's spread.

He took a moment to sit on the bottom bunk and simply breath the air, taking in the scents of the old house. A waft of leather came by, from a set of Josh's chaps rolled up and dropped onto the bureau. Gun oil, from a rag on the bureau that Josh had probably used recently to clean his pistol with. There was also the smell of dried wood, from the boards underfoot and the pine logs the walls were made with.

Josh went to the window and unlatched it and swung the panes open. Down below he had a view of the ranch yard. He leaned over to one side and looked off toward the corral, and he could see the horses were no longer tethered to the rail. Fred was indeed taking care of them.

He decided he could wait no longer to begin preparations for dinner. The smell of fried steak and onions was wafting its way up from the kitchen. Aunt Ginny had a way of taking the steak and the onions and blending them together so the end product was greater than the sum of its parts. Jack lifted the pitcher and filled the wash basin. In the top drawer on the left side of the bureau had always been wash cloths and towels, and so he pulled the drawer open and found this tradition had not changed. He went to work on scrubbing away the trail dust, and then he found a straight razor in the drawer and went about shaving.

He decided to raid Josh's closet. They had been about the same height the last time Jack had been home, two summers ago. Jack found a white broadcloth shirt and shouldered into it, and found it fit reasonably well.

Now wearing Josh's white shirt, and with the dust brushed away from his gunbelt and his boots, and with his face freshly shaved and his hair wetted and combed, he climbed down the stairs to the kitchen.

He found Bree was there, setting the table. He decided to pitch in and placed water glasses at each setting. A bottle of red wine was on the table and had already been opened, and was breathing.

He lifted it and looked at the label.

"Cabernet," he said. "eighteen sixty-four."

Bree began dropping silverware at each setting. "Aunt Ginny had some wines delivered last spring, as soon as the snow was melted."

"Cabernet sauvignon. Should go well with the steak I've been smelling since we got home."

"You say that well. *Sauvignon.* You know your wines. Part of that education you're getting, huh?"

He shrugged and gave a laugh that was more rueful than he had intended. "I guess Aunt Ginny's money's not going totally to waste."

That got a curious glance from Bree, but she said nothing.

Jack said, "So, where's Josh?"

"He's out at the line cabin. The one at the northeastern range. A thunder storm last week scattered almost five hundred head. He and some of the men are out there trying round 'em up."

Dusty entered the room. His buckskin shirt had been replaced by one of blue broadcloth. His shoulder-length hair was combed and swept back, and his chin now smoothly shaved. He still wore his .44 Peacemaker riding low at his right leg and tied down. Pa soon followed, along with Aunt Ginny. Pa's beard was now gone, but his hair was still tied back in a tail. He wore a buckskin vest and a russet colored shirt. His guns were also in place.

They sat to eat, and Jack's first mouthful of

steak sent a rush of flavor clean down to his boots.

He didn't realize he had given a sighing moan as he chewed until he realized everyone was looking at him. He said, "You just don't get cooking like this at school. Or anywhere, for that matter.

He then decided to put on a little literary flair, which he knew Aunt Ginny would appreciate, and said, "Aunt Ginny, of all of the meals you have so incredibly graced my palate with over the years, fried steak and onions is my favorite."

She nodded with a smile. "I remember."

"How did you know we would be here today, though? Coming in on horseback with some covered wagons in tow, you must have figured we would be here sometime within the next few days, but . . ."

She said, "Intuition. I had a feeling. Like I've always said, go with your intuition."

"Your gut feeling," Pa said, tossing a glance at her.

She glanced back, trying to put on a scowl but not managing to hide the delight in her eyes. "If you must put it in such barbaric terms."

"What can I say, Ginny? I am what I am."

Jack and Bree exchanged quick smiling glances, and Jack shook his head. The game was on. The never-ending battle for one-upsmanship that had been going on between

Pa and Aunt Ginny for as long as he could remember. When it came to such a thing, Aunt Ginny was the only one Jack had ever known who could go toe-to-toe with Pa and come out unscathed.

"So," Jack said, as he lifted his glass of wine for a sip. "I was thinking maybe of riding out to the line camp tomorrow and giving Josh a little help."

"You don't have to do that," Pa said.

"Not at all," Aunt Ginny chimed in. "This is your vacation, Jackson. You've worked hard all year at medical school. And I'm sure the ride in from Cheyenne on horseback was not easy. Take this time to relax. Read a book. Maybe take a leisurely ride through the ridges."

Bree said, "I can join you. It'd be fun. Give us a chance to get caught up."

Jack nodded. "Maybe we can do that." And he returned to his food.

After dinner, they retired to the parlor, as Aunt Ginny liked to put it. Meaning they left the kitchen and went to sit down by the hearth. Pa stirred a fire to life, then he took a burning twig from the fire and lit his pipe, and took his favorite chair.

Pa's chair was one he had built himself years ago using oak wood for the frame, and a large piece of leather for the seat and the back. Aunt Ginny sat in a rocker that had been shipped from her home in San Francisco. She sat with a glass of lighter colored wine, sort of a faded yellowish color. Pinot Grigio, which Jack knew was one of her favorites. One of the more full-bodied white wines. She would do a red wine with beef, but generally preferred a white wine.

As Jack sat on the sofa facing the fire, he thought what he could really use was a good belt of Kentucky whiskey. But such a thing might have made Aunt Ginny widen her eyes with surprise. Kentucky whiskey was essentially made from corn squeezings, and it would have contradicted the sophisticated college man image everyone here seemed to have of Jack.

As the family sat in the parlor, they chatted about ranch business. And household business. Bree and Aunt Ginny told Pa of the storm that had scattered part of the herd. If Josh was not back within a couple of days, Pa was planning to ride out and see if he could lend a hand. Also, along with the lightning storm had come hail the size of eggs, which had torn up a couple of shingles on the barn roof. Josh had climbed up and found some boards were in the process of rotting and could use replacing, too, which he intended to do once he got back from the line cabin.

"I can take care of that," Jack said. "It would do me good to do some manual labor."

"No, I can take care of that," Dusty said.

Pa said, "I'd hate to think you came all the

way out here to see your family and the first thing we did was put you to work. Take some time and just enjoy your vacation."

Jack nodded and looked back to the fire. He could surely go for a taste of corn whiskey.

Aunt Ginny was looking at him curiously, but she said nothing. She took a sip of wine.

Dusty said, "I'd best go out and check on things. Walk the rounds."

Pa nodded. Walking the rounds was sort of a family term for taking a walk about the ranch house and the out buildings and just making sure everything was secure for the night. Checking in on Fred and getting his verbal report of the state of the horses. If any of them had developed a gimpy leg or needed a shoe replaced. Jack thought about offering to go with him, but decided not to bother.

After a time, everyone turned in. Everyone except for Jack. He stretched out on the bottom bunk in his clothes and waited while the household quieted down for the night.

Eventually, he got to his feet. His gunbelt was still in place and his boots were on his feet. He stepped out into the hallway and found it quiet. Pa's door was ajar. Bree's was shut. The door to Dusty's room was hanging open.

Jack walked quietly along. He knew Pa probably heard him, as Pa could awaken at the slightest noise. Jack never remembered his father sleeping so soundly you had to jostle him to wake him up. Not like Josh. That boy could shake the rafters with his snoring, and you had to almost kick him in the ribs to wake him up. But Pa could be awakened by the slightest creak of a floorboard. Part of being shot at once too often, Jack figured.

Jack descended the stairs and crossed the parlor floor. The hearth was now dark and silent, but he could still catch the gentle smell of the night's wood fire lingering in the air.

He stepped out on the porch and found Dusty standing there. He still had his gun in place, and a wine glass was in his hand.

"Just finishin' off that wine," Dusty said.

"Shame for it to go to waste," Jack said.

Dusty smiled. "Exactly what I was thinkin'. I never thought I'd develop a taste for it. An old, uncivilized gunhawk like myself."

Jack didn't know quite what to say. He was hoping the entire family was asleep so he could slip away into the night unobserved.

"Trouble sleeping?" Dusty said.

"Not really. Just something I've gotta do."

Dusty smiled. "You're heading into town. To see that girl. Nina."

Jack let out a sigh of defeat. "Is it that obvious?"

"It is to me. I saw how you two were looking at each other. Been there myself, so I know how it feels."

"You have a girl?"

Dusty shrugged. "Did have. A girl named

355

Haley I met down in Nevada. More than a year ago, now."

"Nevada's where you're from?"

"Arizona, before that. But the long trail that led me finally here began in Nevada. That's where I met Haley. Mahalia Anderson. I didn't know her long. But the time we had together was something I'll always remember."

"What happened?"

"When I went back to see her, before I began the ride north to Montana, she was gone. Her only family was her father, and the two of them lit out for Oregon. She left me a letter. Last year, after the fall roundup, me and Josh headed out to Oregon to find her. We were gone three months. We spent Christmas over a drizzly campfire. But we never did find her. We finally decided to come back because Pa would need help with the spring roundup."

"What do you suppose happened?"

Dusty was looking off into the darkness. "Hard to say. A young girl like that. She was about Nina's age. Maybe she met another man. I wonder if I'll ever know."

"I kind of figured you and Temperance had some sort of romance going on."

Dusty chuckled. "Temperance and me? No. All she can see is Josh. Those two are so hopelessly in love. When they're in the room together, you can almost feel it in the air.

Kind of like you and Nina."

"It's that obvious?"

Dusty nodded.

"Well, I'm going to go saddle up. But I'd appreciate if you don't tell Pa. After he cautioned us about her father, he might not think it's a good idea for me to go riding in to see her."

Pa had told Jack and Dusty about the threat Harlan Carter made when they were still a few days out of McCabe Gap.

Jack said, "Pa told me to have Fred leave your horse in the stable. He figured you'd probably be saddling up tonight."

Jack grinned. "No kidding."

"One thing I've learned about both Pa and Aunt Ginny. You can't put much past them."

"No, you can't."

"Want some company for the ride in? Just in case her old man takes it into his head to revert back to his former ways?"

So, that was why Dusty was out here. He was waiting for Jack.

Dusty said, "Actually, I have to admit, I have both horses saddled and waiting."

Jack said, "So you don't think I could handle Harlan Carter?"

"From what I've seen of you on the trail, you could handle him even if your arm was still in a sling. I gotta tell you, the picture everyone painted of you ain't exactly what I see when I look at you."

"What kind of picture did they paint?"

"A college boy. Soft hands but a sharp mind. Refined. A sophisticated gentleman who's at home in a tie and jacket. Not that you don't have a sharp mind, but what I see when I look at you is hard muscle and the eye of a gunhawk. You can talk a gentleman's talk, but it's like a role you play. It's not who you really are."

Jack didn't know quite what to say.

Dusty said, "Remember, I told you I was raised by Sam Patterson. He taught me about survival. And one thing he thought important toward survival is learning how to read people. You got refinement on the surface, maybe. But you're no one I'd want to tangle with. But Pa figured maybe if I went along, if Carter saw there were two of us, he'd feel a little less brave."

Jack said, "All right. I guess I wouldn't mind the company on the ride in. Let's go mount up."

28

They rode alongside one another, taking the main trail to town. It was a mile longer than the shortcut that would come out behind Hunter's, but the shorter trail went through patches of woods and narrow ravines, and at night was too dangerous to ride. A horse could step into a hole or trip over a rock. The main trail, however, cut through the middle of the valley. The land was open to either side of them, and in the light of the half moon overhead, Jack found he could see for a fair distance.

"So," Dusty said. "Wanna talk?"

"About what?"

"Oh, I don't know," Dusty said, in the way someone says when they actually do know. "Let's see. A college man who has invested two years in medical school comes home to see the family, but winds up taking the trip up from Cheyenne by horseback instead of by stage coach."

"Those families needed someone along

who knew something about the trail."

"So, you were planning to take the stage until they asked you to ride along with them?"

Jack said nothing. He had pretty much decided to make the way by horseback even before he joined them.

"That's what I thought," Dusty said, taking Jack's silence as confirmation. "There's a restlessness in you. Something I wouldn't expect from a college man who was following his life's goal of becoming a doctor."

Jack said, "You should play poker for a living."

Dusty snorted a chuckle. "So, like I said, anything you want to talk about? We're brothers, but we don't really know each other all that well. Sometimes it's easier to talk to someone you don't know."

"All right. What would you say if I told you I didn't really want to be a doctor?"

Dusty shrugged. "I don't know. I guess I'd say, 'Okay.' Maybe I'd ask what it was you did want to do."

"What if I told you I just wanted to be a rancher? I just wanted to work alongside you and Josh and Pa. I wanted to marry a good girl and put up a cabin, maybe here in the valley or somewhere nearby, and raise children and cattle and live my life right out here in these mountains?"

Dusty was looking at him curiously. "Then, why'd you go off to school in the first place?

Why didn't you just stay here and work with Pa and Josh?"

They still had a couple miles of trail left, so Jack told him the story. A boy who could remember everything he could read, who everyone thought was brilliant and should have a classical education. To live his life here on the frontier would be a disservice to him.

"So, Pa and Aunt Ginny sent me off to school in the East. I didn't have the heart to tell them all I really wanted was to be right here. It's not my fault I remember everything I read. I don't even like to read."

Dusty said, "Me, I can barely read at all. Like I said earlier, it took me two months to get through that Dickens book."

"Doesn't mean you're stupid. Just means you never had a chance to get education."

They rode in silence for a few moments. Then Dusty said, "Why didn't you just tell them you didn't want to go?"

"I didn't know how. Pa and Aunt Ginny were both so excited about giving me the chance for a higher education. Aunt Ginny offered to pay for the whole thing. She has a boatload of money."

Dusty nodded. "She never said exactly, but I kind of figured."

"Her father, our grandfather, was a merchant seaman. Had a fleet of three ships, making regular runs to China and back. Aunt Ginny grew up wanting for nothing.

"When Ma died, Aunt Ginny closed up her house in San Francisco and came to live with us, to help him with us children. When Pa moved us here, to this valley, Aunt Ginny came with us. The arrangement they made was Pa takes care of the ranching itself, but she has the household. This includes sending for some of her fancier belongings from Frisco, and even spending money on the household furnishings without Pa complaining. Pa's not normally one to accept charity. And she told him that he should consider my education as part of her contribution."

"I still think I would have said no, if I didn't want to go."

"You think so. You don't know what it's like growing up in that man's shadow. You're just like him, anyway. Probably wouldn't have bothered you. You look a lot like him. Walk like him. But for Josh and me, it's a different story. Maybe it's because of the larger-than-life way people have of looking at him. Josh and I found ourselves encouraged to look at him the same way. The two of us want nothing more than to earn his praises."

"Pa thinks the world of both of you. You should see his eyes glow with pride when he talks about you, off at that medical school."

"Part of me wants to die rather than disappoint that man."

"But you're not goin' back." It was more of a statement than a question.

Jack shook his head. "I'm not going back."

"So, when do you plan to tell them?"

"I wasn't really planning to. I don't really know how, so I was actually considering taking the coward's way out. I was just going to visit for a few weeks and then leave. Take the stage to Cheyenne. But instead of catching the train there, I was just going to buy a horse and keep on going. Maybe to California. Maybe Texas. I know enough about cowpunching to hire on somewhere. Or maybe work as a drover. Maybe use a different last name so people wouldn't look at me like I'm some sort of royalty whenever I tell them who I am. Maybe call myself Jack Brackston. Aunt Ginny's last name."

Dusty let his gaze travel along the trail ahead, looking for any sign of motion in the darkness. "But then Nina came into your life."

Jack nodded. "But then Nina came into my life."

"So, what're you going to do?"

"I really have no idea."

They rode in silence for a little while more. Then Dusty said, "They'd have figured it out anyway, you know. Sooner or later, they'd have figured out you never arrived at school. And wherever you went — California, Texas or somewheres else — they'd have figured out who you are there, too. Because you can hire yourself out as a cowpuncher all you want, or a drover, but the way you wear that gun and the look in your eye all say gunhawk. Two and two has a way of getting put together, and people would start figuring out who you must be."

Jack nodded. People did indeed have a way of putting two and two together. Dusty sure did.

"So," Dusty said, "how much does Nina know about what her father said to Pa?"

"Nothing. I didn't know how to tell her."

"I still say you could handle him. But that's a terrible place to put Nina in. She has no idea the kind of man her father is."

Jack nodded, and they rode along in more silence for a while.

Then Jack said, "I have a confession. When Aunt Ginny first wrote me about you, I was so jealous I couldn't see straight. All my life, I wanted nothing more than to be like Pa, and here you were, riding in out of nowhere and were more like Pa than I could ever be. But I have to admit. I'm glad you're my brother."

Dusty nodded. "Likewise, you know. But I will say I'm glad you're different than Josh. We get along fine, now. He's become one of the best friends I ever had. But it was rough goin' for a while. My face had the bruises for days."

Jack laughed. "That's Josh."

■ ■ ■ ■

They followed the trail through the pass known as McCabe Gap. A wide pass between two gently rounded slopes. Wide open and easy to navigate by moonlight. Then ahead were shapes that looked simply like chunks of darkness. Jack knew them to be the buildings of the little town most folks called by the name of the pass. They rode past a building that had no sign out front, but it was known by ladies in the area as *Alisha Summers' House of Ill Repute.* Most of the men simply referred to it as Miss Alisha's. The windows were dark, though Jack knew it didn't necessarily mean everyone was asleep, considering the activities that went on at Miss Alisha's.

Then they rode past Franklin's store. He lived in a small room out back. The store was dark, as could be expected at this time of night. Jack carried no watch, but judging by the position of the moon, he figured it to be somewhere between ten o'clock and midnight.

Dusty said, "These folks offered me a job last year."

Jack looked over at him.

"They wanted me to be the unofficial town marshal. I would have had no real authority, other than to lock up offenders and hold them until a territorial marshal could come and haul them away."

"But there's no jail."

Dusty nodded with a smile. "Franklin has a tool shed. Apparently they wanted me to use that until one could be built."

"I can't imagine a community this small has a need for a marshal."

"Doesn't look like it now. But last summer, folks were scared. Those raiders. They would camp in the mountains and light a huge bonfire, big as you please. Like they were saying to the world, 'Here we are, and there ain't nothing any of you can do about it. We'll take what we want, and you can't stop us.' "

Dusty indicated with a nod of his head the darkness off toward the eastern end of the small town. "The ridge up there — they had a fire going there one night. So big you could see it from Hunter's. And then off there," he nodded in the other direction. "Maybe a couple miles away, up on that ridge. It scared folks."

Jack nodded. "I guess I can see how it would."

"And there's prospectors up in the hills, diggin' and pannin'. Sooner or later one of 'em's bound to find something. They did out in Helena, which isn't all that far away. And in Bozeman. And when they do, folks will start swarming into the area."

Jack had never really thought about gold being found in these ridges. "You think that'll happen?"

Dusty shrugged. "I don't know. But the idea that it could makes people like Franklin think we'd be better off with a town marshal. I would have stayed at Hunter's, sleeping in a bedroll in one corner, or sometimes in a room at the hotel. And they were offering meals and ammunition. They couldn't really offer any pay."

They approached Hunter's, and Dusty swung out of the saddle.

"This is as far as I go," Dusty said.

"What are you going to do? Wait for me here?"

"I'll knock on the door. Wake Hunter up. Grab me a cold beer and sit on the porch. Or maybe challenge Hunter to a game of five card draw. Like you said, I make a good poker player."

"All right. I won't be long."

"Take your time. Remember, I know how it feels to have a girl like that in your life."

"I appreciate it."

"Oh, and one other thing." Dusty opened the flap on one saddle bag and produced a pair of buckskin boots. "I made these last spring, after Josh and I got back from Oregon. Pa always carries a pair with him. You and I look like about the same size. You'll want to go into camp in these, so you don't make too much noise and maybe wake up her gunhawk father."

Dusty tossed them to him.

"Thanks," Jack said. "I seem to be saying that a lot tonight."

"I'll get my turn. That's what happens with brothers."

"Absolutely."

Dusty knocked on Hunter's door. While he waited for the big man to answer, Jack sat in a wooden upright chair on the porch and began tugging at his riding boots. They were worn tightly by most cowpokes because you didn't want your foot to come loose in your boot while the boot was in the stirrup. They were hard to walk in, though, and even harder to pull off.

Finally, the boot he was working on came free. With a feeling of suction letting go, the boot slid off. Jack felt a wave of relief in that foot. He then went to work on the other.

Dusty heard Hunter's footfalls from behind the door.

Hunter called out, "We're closed!"

"Hey, it's me. Dusty."

They could hear a wooden bar being pulled back, and then Hunter opened the door. "What're you doin' way out here at this hour?"

Dusty nodded with his head toward Jack, who was still in the chair, pulling at his second boot. Dusty said, "He's heading over to the wagons to visit his lady."

Hunter's face broke in a smile. "I know who

you mean. I saw them two stealin' glances at each other."

Jack was finding this whole thing embarrassing. Despite his talk with Dusty on the way to town, he was starting to wish he had ridden in alone.

Hunter said to Jack, "You think she'll be awake at this hour? Must be close to midnight."

Jack sighed with resignation. He was going to have to tell them. "Last night, she and I met outside her tent after her father fell asleep. I told her once we were here, I would give a hoot owl call and she would know it was me."

Hunter's mouth fell open with a silent, incredulous laugh.

Dusty said, "A hoot owl?"

Jack said, "I do a really good hoot owl. I used to entertain the boys at the college with it, when we were having some drinks."

"I'll bet you had a lot of drinks."

Hunter said, "But what if a real hoot owl should call out, and she goes out and finds you not there?"

"I told her I would do two calls close together, wait a minute and then do another."

Hunter was shaking his head.

Dusty said to Hunter, "Hey, I could use a cold beer."

"Go in and help yourself."

"Want to lose some money in a game of cards?"

"Lose some money? Me? Are you forgetting who you're talking to?"

"How much did you lose last time we played?"

"That's not the point. I'm feeling lucky tonight."

Dusty tossed a glance to Jack. "I'll be here when you're ready to go home."

Jack's second boot came free with such violent force that he was almost knocked from the chair. He then began pulling on the buckskin boots. They were cut like moccasins, rising almost to the knee and tying with a strip of rawhide.

Jack stood his leather boots beside the chair and then stepped off and toward the meadow where the settlers were camped. These buckskin boots felt good after having his feet packed into tight-fitting boots. And he could feel the contours of the earth in the soft buckskin soles. Every little tuft of grass, every rock. At one point he stepped on a dead stick that would have cracked under his weight, but he could feel it through the buckskin and pulled his foot back.

He decided he was going to have to make himself a pair of these. He didn't know exactly where he was going when his visit home was done, but he knew it would not be back to school. And he figured wherever it was, he would need a pair of boots like these.

Not that he could imagine being anywhere without Nina. Her presence in his life sure complicated things.

The wagons were ahead of him. Four of them. One buckboard, which was the Harding's wagon, and three conestogas. Two of the conestogas belonged to the Brewsters, and one to the Ford family. The white canvas of the conestogas picked up the moonlight and took on a sort of dull gleam. The grayish tarp over the cargo in the buckboard didn't do so as much.

The tent by the buckboard was where Nina would be. Jack stood in the darkness at the edge of camp and let loose with his hoot owl call.

He had learned this from Pa, when he was a kid. Pa had learned it from a Shoshone warrior when he had wintered with them in this valley, years ago.

Jack waited a bit, then made the call again. High pitched, forming his mouth in just the right way. Pa said it would not have convinced an expert in such things, like the Shoshone themselves, but it could fool pretty much anyone else.

He then made the owl call a second time, like he told Nina he would. Two calls, then a hesitation. The he waited. The oxen were down for the night, in the grass off to the edge of the pasture. In the moonlight, one lifted its head and looked Jack's way, but otherwise didn't react. After all, the oxen were all familiar with Jack.

After a time, the tent flap opened and Jack could see someone step out. He couldn't see precisely who it was, but it was not tall enough to be Harlan Carter. It was either Nina or her mother, and he doubted it was her mother. He felt his heart beat pick up in anticipation. He started toward her.

As he drew closer, he could see in the moonlight it was indeed Nina. Her hair was tied into a braid that was flipped over one shoulder. She was in a robe tied together in front.

She saw him approach and broke into a broad smile. They didn't dare speak should her father hear them, but they needed no words. They collided with each other, wrapping their arms around each other and diving into a deep kiss. One of her feet came off the ground. His hat fell to the grass.

"Come on," he whispered into her ear.

With her hand in his, they walked from the meadow and out into the open expanse between Hunter's and the hotel. The expanse that would probably develop into a street, Jack figured, if more people moved in and this place developed into an actual town.

"Jack," she said. "I was hoping you'd come."

"Did you really think I could stay away?"

She drew in a deep breath of mountain air,

letting her gaze travel from the hotel to Franklin's. "Oh, Jack. It's just what you said it would be. It's so beautiful here. The mountains and ridges that surround this place."

"Wait'll you see the valley. And as soon as we can, I want to get you out to the house to meet Aunt Ginny and Bree. Josh is off with the herd, but he should be back in a few days."

Her gaze drifted over to a building beyond Franklin's. "What's that place down there?"

"Oh, that belongs to Alisha Summers. She runs a . . ." He wasn't sure quite how to put it. "Let's call it a men's club."

"Oh." She got the meaning. "I wouldn't think a town this small would have need of such a place."

"There are five cattle ranches within riding distance, including ours. Cowhands work hard, and men who work hard tend to play hard. Not only is Hunter's filled on the first Saturday after payday, but there's a small barroom in the hotel that fills up, too. Even a town this small can turn into a wild place when it's overrun by cowhands who have worked hard all month and want to howl. Miss Alisha finds wall-to-wall business. Even on a regular Saturday, between paydays, cowhands come in on a Saturday night looking to make some noise."

Her gaze remained on the Summers establishment, and she grew silent. Jack could guess why.

He said, "I've never been a customer there, in case you're wondering."

"No, I wasn't."

"Yes, you were."

She looked at him with a guilty grin. "Yes I was."

They strolled about, hand-in-hand. They talked of nothing and yet somehow everything, in the way a couple has of doing when they are falling in love. Occasionally they would stop to kiss. And then they would walk on.

She asked him about his boots. He told her how his father always carried a pair.

"They sure would have come in handy out on the trail," Jack said. "When I was going in on foot to pull you out of Falcone's camp. These are a Shoshone design. This pair is actually Dusty's."

"So, things are working out well between you and Dusty?"

He nodded. "Surprisingly well."

"How about the overall problem?"

He shrugged. "It's all still there. Nothing's really changed. I don't know how to tell any of them how I feel. Aunt Ginny is so excited to hear any story I can tell her about school. I kind of think maybe she wanted to pursue higher education but in her day, a woman going to college was unheard of. It practically is today, too. I think that's part of it. And part of it is she truly wants what she thinks is best for me, and can't even conceive of the idea of me being content roaming these hills and building a cattle ranch when I could be in Boston or New York, working at one of the finest hospitals."

"How long do you think you can put off telling them?"

He smiled. "As long as I possibly can."

Their stroll eventually brought them back to the meadow where the settlers were camped.

She said, "Is there any chance I can see you tomorrow?"

"There's every chance. My father is going to show the valley to Brewster and Ford and your father. I intend to come along. If you are with your father, then I'll be riding along to help show you the valley. If you stay behind at camp, then I'll be staying to visit with Hunter, and eventually make my way over to your camp."

She was smiling. "You have it all figured out."

He raised his brows in a sort of shrug. "I have very little in life figured out."

He walked her to her tent and gave her a silent kiss, and waited until she was safely in the tent and then turned and headed back to the saloon to see how much money Hunter had lost to Dusty.

29

The following morning, Jack followed the enticing smell of coffee and bacon down the stairs and to the kitchen. Since he had very little clothing that was range worthy, and the clothes he wore at school were in his trunk in the marshal's office in Kincaid, he borrowed one of Pa's range shirts. This one was gray, and his vest was in place and his gun was buckled on.

Pa was in his customary place at the head of the table. Temperance was at the oven, removing a batch of biscuits. An apron was tied about her waist and a bandanna about her head.

Pa said, "Temperance, breakfast is great. You outdid yourself."

Temperance and Bree usually exchanged breakfast duties.

"Thank you, Pa," she said. She had tried calling him *Mister McCabe* when she first came to live here, but he had corrected her on that. *All the kids here call me Pa.*

He directed his gaze to Jack and said, "I didn't expect to see you so early."

Aunt Ginny was at the table with a cup of tea in front of her. "Why? Did something happen last night?"

Jack went to the stove, and found things as he remembered them from previous mornings in this house. A pot of coffee and a kettle of hot water for tea.

Ginny said, "That's trail coffee. I probably should have made a pot of normal, civilized coffee for you."

"No need." Jack grabbed a cup and saucer and filled the cup with black coffee. "This is how I drink it."

"Even at school?"

"Especially at school, when you're up half the night studying."

She gave a grimace at the thought of drinking the stuff, and Pa chuckled.

There was also a large plate on the counter heaping with strips of bacon, and on the stove was a skillet with some fried eggs ready to eat. Jack normally wasn't hungry in the morning, so he decided to opt for the coffee only.

Aunt Ginny looked at Jack as he sat at the table. She said, "You didn't answer my question."

"I just took a little ride last night, that's all."

Bree was stepping in through the back

door, a basket of eggs in her hand, and she heard what he said. With a smile, she said, "Must be a girl involved to get a man out in the middle of the night. I heard you both ride away."

Jack said, "Doesn't anyone sleep in this family?"

Aunt Ginny said, *"Both?"*

"Yes, ma'am. Dusty rode with me."

"I was just couldn't sleep, that's all," Dusty said, striding into the kitchen and heading for the coffee pot. He was once again in his buckskin shirt, and his Peacemaker was tied down to his leg. "Thought I'd ride along with Jack, and give him some company."

Jack's gaze met his and Jack gave a slight nod. His way of saying, *thanks for not saying anything about Harlan Carter.* No need to worry Aunt Ginny unnecessarily.

Pa said, "I'm going to ride into town today. Gonna show the settlers the acreage at the center of the valley. There's a good water supply and should be good for farming. Not really enough acreage for a herd our size. Not that we haven't used it before, but even a couple hundred head of longhorns can graze it down to nothing in just a couple of weeks."

Bree filled a plate with bacon and eggs, and she grabbed one of Temperance's biscuits. Temperance filled a plate for herself and they both went to the table.

Aunt Ginny took a sip of her tea. The

fragrance of Earl Grey was gently drifting about, competing with the smell of coffee.

She said, "It would be good to see that land put to use. And we need more families here if we intend to build a community."

"There's land available here. Good water. About a square mile at the center of the valley."

Jack decided he was hungry after all. He got to his feet and went to the cupboard for a plate, and began serving himself some eggs and bacon. He said, "There's more acreage than that in the valley, Pa. Almost three square miles that's hardly used. Once in a while in the summer, if there's a drought. But moving the cattle in and out of the valley is a lot of work. Not cost efficient."

"But most of that land is too far from the lake for anyone to use the water."

"There's always irrigation."

Dusty looked at him skeptically. "You mean, digging trenches all the way from the lake out to the fields? That's a lot of digging."

"No. They could dig wells. Water isn't far from the surface down in the center of the valley. They could use windmills to pump the water. If they put the well in the center of their fields, maybe even a couple of wells powered by windmills, then irrigation would be feasible."

Pa nodded. "That what they're teaching you at medical school?"

"One of my . . ." He was about to say *drinking buddies,* but quickly amended it before the word could get out, "buddies is majoring in agricultural science."

"You mean," Dusty said, "he's goin' to college to learn how to farm?"

Jack chuckled, and returned to the table. "Does sound kind of foolish when you look at it that way. But what he's studying is new farming technology. Such as using a windmill for a pump."

Pa said, "I really doubt these farmers from Vermont know a lot about building windmills. Is that anything you could help them with?"

Jack nodded. "Maybe. I read the textbook on it. Interesting material. And as you know, I tend to remember most of what I read."

He had woken up Aunt Ginny's curiosity. "What else is this friend of yours learning about agriculture?"

"Cattle breeds. There are new breeds being raised in Europe, and even back east. Herefords, gurnseys, and such. Animals with a lot more beef on the hoof than a longhorn. Maybe twice as much."

"Twice?" Dusty was a little incredulous.

Jack nodded, and cut into his bacon. "Sounds a little farfetched, I know, but I've seen them. Trouble is, they're much shorter legged and can't cover a lot of ground."

"Sounds like they'd be easy to handle."

"For a short distance, yes. But it would be

380

impossible to do a drive to market with them."

"Doesn't sound like they'd be much good out here."

Pa said, "I've heard of some of those new breeds. It'll only be a matter of time before the railroad is up in these parts. Cattle will all be marketed by train. The long, overland drive is gonna become a thing of the past."

Jack swallowed his bacon and took a sip of coffee. "I really think these new breeds are going to be the way of the future. With more beef on the hoof, you can get a higher price. And they're shorter horned, which makes 'em easier to transport by train. Less likely to gouge each other up."

"The last herd we brought down to Cheyenne, we had to saw off the horns. That took some man-hours."

"And from what I understand, these newer breeds don't roam free over an open range, like longhorns. A longhorn can eat pretty much any kind of grass, but the newer breeds are more selective. Generally, they're kept in pastures where they can graze a bit, but they're also fed a lot of hay. That hay is grown on farms, and so in parts of the east and Europe, a sort of symbiosis is forming between farmers and ranchers."

Bad choice of words. Aunt Ginny understood the word *symbiosis*, but Pa and Dusty probably would not. They were not stupid by any means, but symbiosis was one of those ten-dollar words you just didn't hear much outside the classroom.

Jack decided to rephrase, without making it obvious. "I see communities developing where farms sell hay to the ranchers, and the ranchers in turn sell beef to the farmers. That's what I was thinking when I met those folks and agreed to lead them out here. They had heard there was good farming land in this part of the country and I brought them to this little valley because I think they're folks you," he looked at Pa, "could work with. Especially Brewster and Ford."

"I don't know," Dusty said, shaking his head and reaching for his coffee. "Farming and ranching has never mixed."

"That's because the longhorn requires so incredibly much open range, and farming requires a set piece of earth to plow and plant. Farmers staking claims tend to reduce the amount of open range available."

Pa was smiling, obviously proud of his son. He glanced at Ginny, who was also smiling. Pa said, "It's the wise man who looks to the future."

"I guess I just don't like seeing things change," Dusty said. "Things that are good enough just the way they are. I like the open range. I like the feeling of freedom you get, just you and your horse and all those miles of open country around you."

Temperance said, "You sound like Josh."

"And that's a good thing?"

She beamed the kind of smile a woman has only when she's talking about the man she loves. "I think it is."

Jack said, "I didn't say I approve of the change. I would hate to see this country around us chopped up into claims. But I really think it's inevitable, and we should try to get the jump on it the best we can. And part of that involves bringing in people we can work with."

Johnny drained his coffee, and rose to his feet and headed for the pot. "Jack, how long do you think you'll be here before you head back to school?"

Here we go, Jack said. Back to pretending he was only here for a visit before going back to medical school. Now was not the right time to spring the news on them because it would turn into a long family discussion, and he and Pa needed to be saddling up to get into town. So he decided to fake his answer.

"Well, the semester starts September fourth, and you need to allow three weeks to travel, just to be on the safe side. And a week to settle in."

"End of July, then?"

Jack nodded uncomfortably, hoping no one would notice. He had been a good poker player back at school. Darby could testify to this by how much Jack had drained Darby's bank account. Jack was hoping that experience would come in handy now.

Johnny filled his cup and sat down.

Ginny said, "What's going on, John?"

"Well," he hesitated. What he was about to say was something that weighed on him a little. He now had everyone's full attention.

Bree said, "What is it, Pa?"

"Well, I did some thinking during those days on the trail with Jack and Dusty. There's something I've gotta do."

Aunt Ginny said, "Visit Lura's grave."

Pa nodded. "I've been wanting to do this for a while. But last summer I was shot up so bad, and I was a while recovering. Then there was the fall roundup. And then," looking at Dusty, "you needed to go to Oregon, and that was important. And then came the spring round up. But now, both you and Josh are here, and it's time for me to go."

Temperance glanced questioningly from Pa to Bree. Bree said to her, "Ma's buried in California."

Jack figured Temperance had gotten much of the back story of this family but was still putting some of the pieces together.

"John," Ginny said. "Will you at least consider taking a train?"

He shook his head. "You know how I travel, Ginny."

She nodded with a suddenly weary resignation. "Overland. Through the mountains.

Like some sort of Indian."

"Well, in many ways, I guess I am some sort of Indian."

Jack said, "That's a long trip to be taken that way."

"It's the only way I travel. Sleeping under the open sky. Feeding myself from the land along the way."

Jack understood, more than anyone here except Dusty knew.

Pa said, "I've got to get not only through the Rockies but also the Sierra Nevadas before first snow. I figure I can visit with Matt and his family for a while. Visit some old friends. Then in the spring head back home."

Dusty said, "Josh and I can handle fall round-up. And spring, too, if you're not back yet."

"That's what I figure."

Bree said, "But you won't be here for Christmas. Seems like the family is never together for Christmas, anymore. Jack," she looked at her brother, "you haven't been able to be here for Christmas for years, and Josh and Dusty were both away last year."

"Sorry, Punkin," Pa said. "Can't be helped. It's something I've gotta do."

Pa looked at Jack. "I don't want to lose any time with you. But I don't think I can wait until the end of July to head out."

Jack nodded. "I understand. Maybe we can get some time together. Maybe ride through the hills and bring some venison home. And besides, we had some time on the trail."

Pa nodded with a smile. It was good his son understood.

Aunt Ginny said, "When do you think you'll leave?"

It was July first. He said, "Maybe in a couple of weeks."

She nodded and took a sip of tea.

"Don't worry," he said to her and to Bree. "I'll be coming back."

Ginny said, "It's just that it's hard not to worry when you're out there all alone on horseback that way. And California is so far away."

"Not like I haven't made that ride before." He had visited Lura's grave five years earlier. "Zack was on the ranch then, and he and Josh ran things until I got back."

"But, John, you're not getting any younger."

He shrugged. "Such is the way of life. You can't stop living, though."

The eastern sky was lightening but the sun hadn't yet come into view when Pa had Jack dropped a loop on a couple of geldings and threw saddles on them. Dusty was bracing a ladder against the side of the barn and getting ready to climb up. He wanted to get the roof repair done before the day got too hot.

Dusty looked at Jack. "You're more than welcome to stay and lend a hand."

"What?" Jack said with a playful smile as he swung into the saddle. "I'm on vacation, remember?"

Dusty threw a grin back at him. He began his climb up the ladder with a bucket of tar in one hand.

Pa called out to him, "We should be back before dark."

They found Brewster had rented a buckboard from the livery. Not that they had any money to spare. Most of their cash had been spent outfitting themselves for the journey west. But old Jeb, who ran the livery, let them have it on credit.

Jeb was near eighty and a little bent at the shoulders and back. Bent in the kind of way a lifetime of hard work can do to a man. But he still had a strong grip and could heft a saddle with one hand. He wore a sombrero over white hair, and a corn cob pipe was always in his mouth like it had somehow grown there.

He said, "Most of the folks around here live on credit. They run a tab until they sell some beef, and then they pay everyone they owe and start the cycle all over again."

Brewster said, "To be fair, at best it'll be over a year before we can harvest any crops. It's way too late in the season to plant now."

Old Jeb waved the idea off, like he was swishing his hand at a fly. "You're friends of

Johnny McCabe. Good enough for me. Don't come no more stand-up than him."

When Johnny and Jack emerged from the patch of woods behind Hunter's, they found the wagon hitched to a team. Brewster was in the seat, the reins in his one hand. Ford was sitting beside him, and Harding, dark-eyed and sullen as ever, was in back.

Pa said, "So, just you men are coming?"

Brewster said, "It's been a long journey. We figured to let our families rest a bit."

" 'Sides," Harding said, "This is men's business."

Jack glanced at his father and had to repress a grin. Just let him say that to Aunt Ginny. She wouldn't care if he was a gunfighter or not. She would cut him down to size.

Jack said to his father, "I think I'm going to visit with Hunter a while. Maybe have a cold beer. It's hard to find cold beer, even in Boston."

Pa nodded. He knew fully well why Jack was staying behind, and it had nothing to do with cold beer.

From the back of the wagon, Harding was staring at Jack. Jack met his gaze. Harding was giving a dark glare, trying to reinforce his warning. Stay away from his daughter or things would get rough. Jack met the gaze, trying to say with his eyes, *You want a piece of me? Bring it on.*

Jack knew a fight with Harding would be

bad for Nina, no matter who won. In fact, a fight with him would probably lead to gunplay, and only one would walk away. To do that to Nina would be callous and unthinking. But Jack also had his father's temper. It wasn't loud and explosive like it was with Josh, but it was there nonetheless.

Pa saw the silent exchange and said to Brewster, "All right. We're wasting daylight. Let's get moving."

Jack sat in the saddle and watched the wagon bump its way along the dirt expanse that passed for a street, and then turn off and toward the trail that would take them into the valley. Pa was riding alongside the wagon, sitting in the saddle and rolling his hips gently with the motion of the horse as though he were born to it. His graying hair fell in a tail from under his sombrero to his shoulders, and his twin Remingtons were buckled in place. Harding was sitting in the back of the wagon, getting jostled with every rut and rock the wagon wheels found. Served him right, Jack thought with a smile.

Once the wagon was out of sight, he turned his horse toward the meadow out beyond Hunter's.

Johnny led the farmers through the opening in the ridges known as McCabe Gap. They followed the wagon road down and into the grassy valley floor, where it intersected with

389

another trail that cut its way along the entire length of the valley. A turn to the right would take them to the ranch, but Johnny turned led the settlers to the left.

Brewster handled the team well with but one hand, Johnny thought. Amazing how a person can adapt to hardships unimaginable by another.

Johnny rode with the rein in his left hand, and almost absently brushed his fingers across the pistol riding low at his right side. Brewster's one-handedness and the pistol at Johnny's right side sort of made his mind segue to what Charlie Franklin had said the day before. He had a Colt Peacemaker at his store, waiting for Johnny to try it out. A Peacemaker could be reloaded so much faster than the old Remingtons Johnny used. With these new Peacemakers, you needed only one gun. Funny, Johnny thought, the way the human mind will sort of wind its way along from one trail of thought to another.

All the time he scanned the ground ahead of them for tracks, and then would lift his gaze to the edge of the pine forest that stopped at the base of the ridge to their left, now a half mile in the distance. Always looking for any sign of anything amiss. Tracks that shouldn't be there. Riders that shouldn't be there. His gun at his right side was ready, as was the one at his left. His Sharps rifle was in the saddle boot just below his saddle horn.

"How long is this valley?" Brewster asked, his voice cutting into the silence.

"About five miles," Johnny said. "Further down the stretch, at the other side, is a small ranch owned by Zack Johnson. Used to work for me. I've known him a lot of years."

"Heard the name," Harding said from the back of the wagon.

I'll bet you have, Johnny thought. Zack Johnson's name didn't have the growing fame Johnny's did — no writers from New York seemed to be wanting to write dime novels about him, but among gunhawks Zack's name was well known.

Johnny said, "This valley is really not big enough to keep a herd the size of ours or Zack's. Further to the east, the ridges begin flattening out kind of quick, and there's a lot of grass. Miles of open range."

At a point four miles from town, Johnny reined up. Around them was open grassland. In places the land rose and fell in low swells, and in others it was flat like a small plateau. And all of it was covered with tall, green grass. In some places tall enough that it brushed the belly of Johnny's horse.

"Well," he said, "this is it. All around here. A couple thousand acres of fertile land."

The morning had been turning off hot, but now there was a coolness to the breeze and a smell of water.

Johnny said, looking off toward the north-east, "There's a small lake in that direction. Not a quarter mile from here. It fills quite deep in the spring with the runoff from the melting snow. By August the water recedes quite a bit, but the lake never fully dries up. We've used this lake before a couple of times during droughts."

Harding had climbed out of the wagon and was standing in the grass. "Then why would you want to give it up?"

"It's not officially ours. In fact, none of it is, because this section of the territory hasn't been officially opened for settlement. But it is going to be sooner or later, and there's only so much land that can be claimed. We're going to claim the side of the valley we're in, the ridge immediately east of there, and maybe twenty thousand acres east out into the open range beyond the valley. The valley itself, as big as might seem standing here, is actually too small for a herd of longhorns the size of ours. It wouldn't take long for even a few hundred head to graze it down to nothing, and moving the herd in and out through the gaps in the ridges is harder than it might sound. And besides. We're looking to the future. There's gonna come a time when farmers and ranchers will be working side-by-side."

Harding said, "I find that hard to believe."

"Every change is hard to believe, until it happens."

Ford looked at Harding. "What do you think?"

Harding said, "I don't know."

Brewster said, "This grass is green and rich. The sign of good soil."

He climbed down from the seat, and grabbed a shovel and dug into the sod. He then pulled up a chunk of grass and shook loose the dirt, and then scooped the dirt up in his hand. "Rich, black loom. Look at that. I've never seen dirt this rich."

Johnny knew *loom* was what New Englanders called *loam.*

Harding had strolled over. Ford had jumped out of the wagon seat and was standing by.

"Look, Harding," Brewster said. "Tell me you've seen dirt any better than this anywhere."

Harding scratched his bearded chin and said in his tight-lipped way, "Gotta admit. I haven't."

Johnny swung out of the saddle and loosened the cinch.

"So, McCabe," Brewster said. "What's the process for building here?"

Johnny strolled over and gave a shrug of his shoulders. "I suppose you just move the family out here, pitch your tent, and call it yours. Like I said, this section of the territory isn't open for settlement yet, but as soon as it is — the first day it is — you file your claim at the land office."

"Where's the nearest land office?" Ford said.

"Right now, Bozeman."

Brewster shook the loose dirt out of his hand, and stood. "I say we pack up the families in the morning and bring them out here."

"First we have to decide who gets which section."

Johnny said, "From the ridge over yonder," he pointed with one hand toward the piney ridge now a half mile in the distance, "to the other one at the other side is roughly two miles. Not all of it's this rich. But with irrigation, you could grow a fine crop."

"Irrigation?" Harding said.

Johnny nodded. "Jack can tell you more about that than I can."

Harding looked away like had suddenly gotten a bad taste in his mouth.

Brewster said to Johnny, "We're sold. Thing is, we're going to have to bring timber down from those hills if we hope to build."

"Can be done quite easily. Those hills don't belong to anyone, either. The timber's just there, ready for the taking. One of the benefits of being some of the first to move into an area."

Ford said, "I was expecting to farm, but it's not like that's my only choice. I ran a sawmill back east. I brought some blades with me. I could set one up here."

Johnny said, "This area could sure use a saw mill."

Brewster was smiling. He looked at Ford, who was looking about with as big a smile.

Johnny said, "That lake is a central supply of fresh water. I'd recommend building all three places so the lake is right between all of you. It'd make it hard for anyone to claim it out from under you someday. And if you were to dig a well, I don't think you'd find you have to dig very far. According to Jack, you can use windmills to pump water for irrigation. I have to wonder if a windmill might be a good source of power for a sawmill, too."

Ford said, "I noticed what looked like a small river when we were riding in here."

Johnny nodded. "It's running really well right now because of spring runoff. This time of year you can actually take a canoe from one end of the valley to the other. But come August and September there may not be enough current for a water wheel."

Harding looked at him skeptically. "Windmills? I don't know anything about building windmills."

"Jack can help you with that, too."

Harding didn't like the sound of that, either. "I really don't know. I was originally thinking of Oregon, and I'm still thinking maybe that's the place for me."

Brewster said, "Well, while you're busy not

knowing, I'm going to tell Mildred we've found our new home."

30

Jack was sitting in an upright chair in front of Hunter's with a cup of coffee, when the buckboard came clunking down the center of the little town with Pa riding alongside it. Jack got to his feet and walked over.

Jack said to Brewster, "What did you think?"

Brewster was all smiles. "I can't wait to tell Mildred. We've found our new home."

Jack smiled. "I thought you'd like it."

"Tomorrow, I'm taking the family out and we'll stake out our acreage."

Ford said, "I'm doing the same."

"Maybe I'll ride out and pay a visit," Jack said.

Brewster nodded to him with a smile. "You're always welcome."

The sun was riding low in the sky. Pa said to Jack, "Come on. Let's get home. I heard Aunt Ginny mention something about sending Dusty out for venison."

Jack had eaten venison a lot on his ride up

the Bozeman trail with the settlers, but he never tired of it.

Brewster turned the wagon toward the livery barn and they returned the rig to Old Jeb, then he and Ford and Harding began back on foot to the meadow where the families were camped.

Brewster said, "I wish you would reconsider, Harding. You saw how good the dirt was. And you'll never find finer neighbors than this lot seems to be."

Harding shook his head. "This place is not for me. That's all."

Ford tossed a weary look at Harding. "It's because of how your daughter feels for that boy, isn't it?"

"That's none of your concern. I have to make the decision that's best for my family."

Brewster had to agree with that. "So do we all."

Brewster parted company with them and meandered toward the tent and the two wagons that belonged to his family. Mildred had a cook fire going and was working at a pot of stew. Age ran out to meet him.

"Is it what they said, Pa?"

Brewster smiled. "All that and more."

Ford said to Harding, "I wish you'd reconsider, Carter. We've come all this way together, and we knew each other for years back in Vermont. It would seem strange not to have you and your family with us as we become part of this community."

Harding said, "You're more than welcome to come with me. Oregon has dirt every bit as good as this. Or so they say."

"That's just it. *So they say.* We're here, and we've seen the dirt they have right here. And we've seen these people. And Oregon is more than five hundred miles further on. Five hundred rough miles. At this rate, it'll be a push just to get a cabin up before winter."

"Then we better not be dallying here. My family and I leave in the morning. We'll follow the Bozeman Trail back to Cheyenne, and then pick up our way to Oregon."

Ford shook his head. "We're staying right here."

"Suit yourself."

Without another word, Harding turned and started for his tent with his long, loping gait. Ford stood a moment watching him walk away, shaking his head. He then turned and headed for his own tent.

Emily Harding had a pot of baked beans heating over a fire. Nina was with her, a kerchief tied over her hair. Nina looked up and said, "Father's home."

Emily gave her husband a welcome-home smile. "So, tell us all about it."

He gave her a peck on the cheek. He had to bend over a ways to do it, because he was so tall and she was so not.

"Not much to tell," he said. "It's not right

399

for us. The water source isn't as good as the McCabe boy made it out to be. There's timber, but it'll be a long haul to get it from the ridges to where the house would be. And the land isn't even open for settlement, yet. When it eventually is, there's no guarantee we'd be able to keep our land, if someone else beat us to the claim."

Nina was staring at her father with a little dismay. This was not what she had been hoping to hear.

Emily said, "What does Abel say? And Jacob?"

Harding shrugged. "They're staying. They said the dirt is some of the best they've seen. And I agree. It's just the other factors are too stacked against us."

He glanced at Nina. "And I don't like the neighbors. I think they'd be trouble."

Nina's dismay was starting to shift into annoyance. "You mean Jack."

"I mean the entire McCabe family. And that big grizzly bear of a bartender. They're all gunfighters, Nina. Men like that attract trouble like honey to a bee. You saw what happened out on the trail. We almost lost you. None of that would've happened if Jack McCabe hadn't been with us."

"You don't know that."

"Those men are enemies of the McCabes. Not us. No, Oregon is for us. Your mother and I talked about Oregon in the first place, and we let ourselves get sidetracked here. We need to get moving so we can get a cabin up before the first snow."

"When do we leave?" Emily said.

"Tomorrow. In the morning we leave for Oregon."

"Just like that?" Nina said. Her annoyance was starting to shift to outright anger. "We ride out just like that? Without any further thought?"

"No," he said. "Not just like that. A lot of thought has gone into this."

"I don't even get a chance to say goodbye to Jack?"

"It's best this way. The sooner he's gone from your life, the sooner you can forget him."

"Forget him? Father, I love him!"

He looked at her wearily. "You don't know the first thing about love. You're a child."

Emily placed a hand on his arm, but he shook it off. He said to Nina, "You're my daughter, and you'll do like I say. It's in your own best interest. You have to trust me."

Tears were filling Nina's eyes. Tears of fear. Tears of rage.

She turned and ran.

"Nina," he said.

Emily said, "Let her go, Carter."

"Nina!" he roared after her.

Emily grabbed his arm firmly. "Let her go."

He turned his gaze to her, looking down at

her from his height. His eyes were not friendly. "This is part your fault, you know. You encouraged her from the start. You think I don't know you two were conspiring behind my back so she could see that boy."

"Carter . . ."

"Them beans smell like they're burning. Why don't you tend to 'em. I'll go after her and make sure she's okay. I don't like her runnin' out there by herself. This is big country."

She stood firing a gaze at her husband that said she was angry enough to eat nails. But he ignored her and began way from their camp, navigating through the tall grass in his long-legged gait that took him to the edge of the meadow.

The girl was nowhere in sight.

He called out, his normally simmering baritone rising to a roar, "Nina!"

He waited. Nothing. A bird took flight from a tree at the edge of the woods. He sucked in air and cut loose with his daughter's name again. He heard a small echo fade in the distance.

A voice came from behind him. Brewster's. "Carter, what's wrong?"

Harding looked back at him. "Nina's run off."

Brewster stopped beside him. His one hand was hooked into his belt. His beard was thick and shook a bit as it caught the wind. He stood as high as Harding's shoulder in height.

"What happened?" Brewster said.

Harding hesitated, as though he was considering telling Brewster it was none of his affair, but then said, "She doesn't like the idea of goin' on to Oregon. Got mad and run off."

Brewster said, "She doesn't want to leave the McCabe boy."

Harding hesitated again, as though saying the word would leave a bad taste in his mouth. "No."

"I'll get Age and Ford and Ford's boy. We can go look for her. Those are deep woods."

"I'm sure she'll be all right. She's probably out there with that boy, now."

Brewster shook his head with a little disbelief at what Harding was saying.

Harding said, "They met together after we were all asleep almost every night along the trail. You know that? They thought I didn't, but I did. And Emily went right along with it. Encouraging her. Helping her."

"Well, if she's with Jack, then she's safe. He knows this land."

"If she's with him, then safe is one thing she's not. I know that kind of boy. We never should'a brought him along. It was all your idea. As long as he's in her life, she's in danger. Look at what happened to your Jessica."

Brewster kept his gaze on the trees at the edge of the woods. Harding looked at him suddenly, realizing he had crossed a line, but then looked away, damned if he would apologize.

Brewster was silent for a few moments, then said, "The men she ran off with are nothing like the McCabes."

"They're gunhawks. All of 'em. They live by the gun. They die by it. I don't want Nina caught up in any of it. If I knew where their ranch house was, I'd ride out now and take care of things."

Brewster looked at him, his brows rising like brows tend to do when you hear something absurd. He said, "What — you would strap on your gun and have it out with the boy?"

"If'n I had to. Don't think I can't." Harding then looked at him suddenly, realizing he had said too much.

But Brewster said, "Oh, for goodness sake, Harding. I know who you are."

Harding stared at him.

Brewster said, "I was in the war." He held up his left arm, which ended right at the wrist. "I know what it is to kill a man. I still see those battles in my dreams. And you have the look in your eye. I could tell when I first met you that you had killed before."

Harding continued to stare at him.

Brewster said, "Vermont is not all that isolated from the world. I read newspapers. I hear talk. It didn't take long to figure who you were. I never said anything, but I heard others talking and more than one person has figured it out."

Harding was staring at him intently. Disbelief. Anger.

Brewster said, "None of us cared who you were. We cared about who you are now. What you brought to the community. What kind of man you are. What kind of husband to Emily. What kind of father. You're a good man. It doesn't matter who you were."

Brewster turned to fully face him. "If you rode out there, maybe you could beat that boy."

"I know I could."

"Maybe. I'm not so sure. But you'd also have to kill his father. And his brother. And I hear there's another brother, too. You willing to kill all of 'em?"

"If'n I have to."

"Listen to yourself. Isn't that exactly what you want to protect Nina from?"

Harding didn't know what to say. He turned his gaze back to the woods. He called out her name again.

Brewster said, "Then, consider this. If you do fight that boy, it will be Nina who's caught in the middle. Either that boy will shoot you, or you'll shoot him. Or maybe you'll both kill each other. But either way, whatever happens, you'll be hurting Nina. Think about that."

Harding stood silently, looking at him.

Brewster said, "Now let's get the men together and find your daughter. It's going to be dark soon and these are mighty big woods."

Nina ran. She was angry and hurt and scared, all at once. And so she ran.

Father was going to rip her away from Jack. She had found something that made her feel like she was walking on air. A kind of wonderfulness Mother said came along at best only once in a life time, and often not even then. And now Father was going to rip her away from the man she loved and take her to another part of the world and she would never see him again.

And so she ran.

She heard a noise. A sort of roaring sound from somewhere behind her, in the distance. It was Father, she realized, calling her name. She didn't care. She was not going back. She kept on running.

She paid no attention to where she was going. She had covered the small expanse of meadow between the family camp and the edge of the woods in maybe twenty seconds — she had always been a good runner. It was her running ability that helped get her away from those outlaws back on the trail. Yes, Jack had certainly rescued her. But he wouldn't have been in a position to do so if she hadn't taken off from the camp like a rabbit and put some distance between herself and those men.

Distance is what she wanted now. Distance from her father. Despite his towering demeanor that others thought intimidating, and his dark eyes and his tight-lipped almost snarly way of talking, and his voice that seemed to rumble deep in his chest, she had never doubted that he loved her. Not until tonight.

And so she ran.

She quickly found the forest here was much different than it had been back in Vermont. The woods she had known at the edge of her family's farm were tangled with underbrush. Thorns and junipers and such. And the ground had been covered with dried leaves. But these woods were clean. There was an occasional bush or a deadfall that she had to run around, but for the most part there was very little underbrush. The trees were pine and grew straight and tall, and sometimes as many as a few yards apart. You could ride a horse through these woods, she thought. And the earth was covered with pine straw, which allowed her to run almost silently. Occasionally she would step on a dried stick and it would crack, but otherwise there was none of the noisy crunch-crunch you would get in a forest back in Vermont.

The smooth soles of her shoes were slippery on the pine straw, and at one point a foot slid out from under her and she fell. Her momentum carried her face-forward into the pine straw.

She waited a few moments, her heart hammering in her ears, while she waited for any pain. There was none. She seemed to be able to wiggle both feet. She didn't think she had hurt herself.

She pushed herself to her feet and continued running.

Her dress was cumbersome and her shoes kept sliding on the pine needles, but still she ran. Sweat began to roll down her face and neck and soak her dress through the back, but still she ran.

She realized she was running uphill. The land now rose before her. She was running up a slope. Her feet began to slip more now, and soon she was walking more than climbing. The slope became steeper the more she climbed.

A rabbit darted away from fifty yards ahead of her. A bird that sounded like the crows back home called out from somewhere above. Probably perched on a tree branch.

The slope leveled out and she came to an open area. She stood on an outcropping of bedrock and looked at the open space that fell away beneath her, and her jaw fell open. For a moment her anger at her father was forgotten.

The pines covering the slope below formed

a dense blanket of green, and beyond them was a large grassy area. Maybe the valley floor Jack had spoken of. There was a house that looked tiny in the distance, and she could see smoke rising from a stone chimney.

Beyond the house was another ridge, this one a dark green because of more pine growth, and with a sharp rocky promontory toward the top. The breeze was strong and cool and refreshing at this height.

A dark bird with a large wing span was sort of gliding about in the winds overhead. She didn't know what kind of bird it was, but the feathers at the tips of the wings sort of looked like fingers. She thought it must be a hawk of some sort.

She untied the bandanna from her hair and used it to wipe the sweat from her face and neck.

She wondered if the house was Jack's. The McCabe ranch house. She was suddenly filled with the feeling that she wanted to see him. She wanted to be in his arms. Everything felt all right when she was with Jack. And his father would be there. Jack was right about the man's presence. It was almost like there was some sort of aura about him. You just felt reassured that everything would be all right when he was near. She could see how growing up in this man's shadow could be intimidating, but right now she needed the reassurance that being with Jack and being in the company of his father brought.

She looked toward the west. There were ridges in the distance, and very far away, a rounded peak. And the sun was drifting down near them. She realized it was going to be dark soon. If she was going to make the house with the stone chimney before nightfall, she had best get moving.

She tied the bandanna back over her hair and began down the slope. She didn't quite run as the slope was steep and the pine needles underfoot slippery, but she didn't walk, either. She was not good at guessing distances, but she thought she had at least half a mile to cover. Maybe more. She didn't want to be caught in these woods after dark.

The land began to level out a little, and she increased her pace. Soon she was running again.

She hoped she was holding to a straight course. She had heard of men getting turned around in the woods. She had no compass and no real way to gauge the direction. The woods about her were becoming kind of dark as evening came on.

One foot slipped and both feet went out from under her and she went sliding a couple of feet on her butt.

She was glad no one was there to see that. The puffiness of her skirt and the layers under it had cushioned her fall, but had not protected her pride from being bruised.

She got to her feet and continued running.

The hurt and the anger toward her father was now pushed to the back of her mind while she focused on getting to the bottom of this slope and to the open, grassy valley floor before it got too dark to see. She ran along, not quite going at top speed as it would be too difficult to maintain her footing in these slippery shoes. But she maintained a steady pace. She was breathing deeply, sucking in air as she ran. Sweat was again running down her neck and back.

Then the earth suddenly seemed to give way beneath her. She didn't know what was happening but she was suddenly falling. She reached out wildly with her hands, grabbing at wet bare earth. A sort of wall of dirt. And then she slammed hard into something.

It took her a moment to catch her breath. She then looked about her and saw she was in some sort of pit. It was maybe four feet wide, and there were rocks at the bottom. And a little water and a lot of pine straw. The sides of the pit were earthen and almost perfectly perpendicular to the pit's floor. Like they had been dug with a shovel or a pick axe.

The pit looked deep. Maybe six or seven feet. She would have to climb out. She could see pines overhead, outside the pit. They were dark, as sunset was fast approaching. It was even darker here in the pit.

She could afford to waste no time, she knew. She had to get out of these woods before it became fully dark. She rose to her feet and then felt sudden, sharp pain in one ankle. She fell back to the wet pine straw at the bottom of the pit.

She reached for her ankle. It was not particularly sore to touch, but when she tried to wiggle her foot sharp pain shot through the joint.

I've broken my ankle. Here I am, at the bottom of a pit in the middle of the woods and it's getting dark and I've broken my ankle!

She sucked in air and let out a loud, shrieking, "Help!"

But there was no one on the slope to hear. She waited, breathing heavily while the sound of her scream faded in the distance. She was alone, in the middle of the woods, in some sort of pit. Her ankle was broken, and it was getting dark fast.

31

First thing Brewster did, before it was even light and before his first cup of coffee, was to knock on the door of the man called Hunter.

He explained the situation. "Harding's daughter ran off after an argument, and she's been gone all night."

"In these woods?" Hunter was a little incredulous. He was also blinking his eyes with sleepiness. He stood in his undershirt and Levi's, with a gun in his hand. Someone starts banging on the door as frantically as Brewster had been before the sun is even in the sky, he answered the door with a gun.

"We were hoping you could help."

Within five minutes, Hunter was in a range shirt and a sombrero, and a gunbelt was buckled around his waste. He was not a fast draw and had no pretenses of being so, and did not wear his gun hanging low or tied down. It was up on his hip where he could reach it if need be, but otherwise out of the way. He was striding toward the meadow where the settlers were camped. Brewster was almost having to run to keep up with him.

The sky was growing lighter as sunrise was drawing closer. The woods were filled with the sort of hush that comes right before the night ends and the day begins. Sort of like the Earth is holding its breath, waiting for the majesty of the coming of the new day.

Harding glared at Brewster. "What do you think he can do?"

Hunter didn't wait for Brewster to answer. He said, "I can track. I been living out here most of my life. I was raised in these mountains, about two hundred miles south of here. Been livin' in this valley or near it for more'n ten years."

"Then, let's get going."

"Harding, it's not light enough. We gotta be able to see the tracks to follow 'em."

Mildred Brewster said, "I can put some coffee on."

Hunter looked from Harding to Brewster. "Sometimes the best thing you can have when you're tracking is patience. It's more important than luck."

Emily Harding was there, looking like she was standing so alone even though her husband was only a few feet from her.

Hunter said to her, "I'm sure she's all right."

Emily nodded.

Harding said, "I'm sure she is, too. But I'll

feel better once we find her."

Emily gave him a look. A long, hard look. Then she turned and walked away toward their tent.

Hunter thought sometimes a woman can say more with just a look than she ever could with words.

The coffee was brewed and Hunter was handed a tin cup. He stood and drank coffee while the others standing about him did the same, and they waited for the sky to lighten.

When Hunter's cup was empty, he handed it back to Mildred Brewster, then he drew his revolver and checked the loads. It was a Colt Army .44, a cap-and-ball revolver which meant you had to manually load powder and a bullet in each chamber and then put a percussion cap on a short metal tube called a nipple toward the front. Kind of time consuming. Those new Peacemakers that took metallic cartridges, like the one Dusty had and Franklin was holding for Johnny, could be reloaded in a fraction of the time. Hunter carried in his vest pocket a pre-loaded cylinder so if his gun ran out of bullets he could pop out the spent cylinder and put in a fresh one and keep on firing. Johnny McCabe just carried two pistols so he could get off ten shots before reloading.

The loads all looked good. Hunter kept one chamber empty, and repositioned the cylinder so the empty chamber was in front of the hammer, then slid the revolver back into the holster.

It was light enough for him to see the percussion caps in his pistol, so he decided it was light enough for him to see tracks.

He said, "Let's go."

Oftentimes grass will bend beneath the foot of a person or an animal, and it can be a few hours before the grass stands fully upright again. However, too many hours had passed since Nina had run through the grass between her family's camp and the edge of the woods.

Hunter said, "Do we know if she ran straight towards the woods, or if she ran through the meadow back toward town?"

Harding said, "If she had run back toward town, I would have seen her when I went after her. I've gotta figure she ran straight to the woods."

Hunter nodded. Good enough for him. He headed for the woods. The others followed. Ford was with them, as was Age. The grass was still a little wet with morning dew, and Hunter felt the wetness soaking into the knees of his pants.

Once they were in the woods, he found a tuft of kicked-up pine straw. Then another a little further ahead.

"Was she running?" he said.

Harding nodded. "Most likely."

"This was kicked up by something running.

Probably her."

They followed a little further along. Trouble with tracks was that even though Nina's footsteps might have been consistent, the earth beneath her feet was not. In some places the pine straw was thicker than others. In some places it was a little damp, in others it was dry. The kicked-up tufts of pine straw were not consistent. Hunter would find one, and then no more for maybe fifty feet.

Finally, as they began to climb a slope, he could find no others. He found a broken stick on the ground and knew it might have been cracked by Nina running across it, or it might have cracked for any number of other reasons.

He shook his head.

"What's wrong?" Brewster said.

"This is gonna be half guess-work and half luck. We need a real tracker."

Harding said, "I thought you said you were a real tracker."

"I can track. But I ain't no expert at it. Not a trail like this, made by a girl afoot more than ten hours ago. We almost need a Shoshone for this. Or the next best thing."

He looked to Age, and said, "Who's the fastest rider here?"

Age said, without hesitation, "Me."

Hunter thought so, which was why he looked at Age.

Hunter said, "Run down to the livery. Tell Old Jeb I sent you. Tell him to give you a horse and to saddle it mighty quick. I want you to follow the trail that starts in the woods just behind my saloon. Follow it all the way through. It's marked right clear and is easy to follow. Follow it all the way to the end. It comes out in the valley. Where the trail ends, at the edge of the woods, you'll see a house maybe a quarter mile away. That's the Mc-Cabes' spread. Tell 'em what's goin' on and bring 'em back fast as you can."

Age glanced at his father who gave a nod of his head, and Age said, "Yes, sir."

And Age turned and began back toward the meadow at the kind of light, quick-stepping sprint only a boy can muster.

Harding turned his dark eyes onto Hunter. "We don't need their help."

Hunter said, "Beggin' your pardon, but I think we do. Johnny McCabe can track a fish through water, and Dusty's about as good. Jack and Josh ain't much behind 'em. If you want to find your daughter in these woods, we need men who can do the job."

The McCabes were just sitting down to breakfast when Age came galloping in. It was Bree's turn to make breakfast. Jack had a cup of coffee in his hand and was about to attack a couple of strips of bacon. Aunt Ginny had just poured a cup of Earl Grey and was gently lowering herself into her chair. Aunt Ginny never simply dropped into a chair.

418

"Who could that be at this hour?" Ginny said at the sound of drumming hooves from outside.

Frantic knocking began on the kitchen door and Dusty opened it to find Age. It took Age maybe twenty seconds to explain the whole thing, out of breath and rattling off his words, and the men left their breakfast behind and went to grab their guns. Bree went out to tell Fred to saddle three horses. Within ten minutes, Johnny and his two sons were gone, riding toward the trail that would take them out behind Hunter's.

Age was going to join them, but Aunt Ginny insisted he stay and have something to eat, and give his horse time to rest. It looked like he had ridden the animal at break-neck speed all the way from town. The horse was covered with lather at its neck and shoulders and flanks.

Bree sat at the table and reached for her cup of tea, and she thought a moment. Three of them trying to track the girl from the meadow. It would take them maybe half an hour to get from the house to the meadow, and then it would be a case of following her tracks. If they could find them, after all these hours."

Bree said, "Age, you said Nina ran straight into the woods?"

"Yes'm," Age said. "Mister Hunter thinks she went straight up the ridge behind town."

Bree looked at Aunt Ginny. "It might make sense to have someone approaching town from the opposite direction. Going through the woods from the valley and up the slope."

Aunt Ginny gave her a look that said, *oh no you don't,* but Bree said, "I can ride as well as any man on this ranch. Better'n some. I know these ridges like the back of my hand. And Pa's shown me how to shoot a rifle. I'm almost as good a shot as Josh."

Aunt Ginny looked like she wanted to protest, but the words wouldn't come.

Temperance was sitting beside Aunt Ginny. She said, "I can ride, but not like you. I'd come, but I'm afraid I'd just be in the way."

Bree got to her feet. "Could you have Fred saddle a horse for me?"

Bree went upstairs. She was in a gingham blouse and a dark skirt that fell to her knees. Aunt Ginny hated it when Bee wore Levi's — *no woman back in San Francisco would be caught dead in men's pants,* Aunt Ginny had said more than once. But Bree had reminded her this was not San Francisco. Bree had a lot of miles of riding ahead of her, and riding side saddle would just not suffice. She pulled off her dress and the petticoats beneath it, then pulled open the bottom drawer of her dresser and found her solitary pair of Levi's. She pulled them on, then reached for her riding boots. She grabbed a gray sombrero from a nail in the wall and pulled it down over her head.

Downstairs, she stopped at the gun rack. A couple Winchesters, an old Henry, and Pa's even older Hawken muzzle-loader. There were empty spaces as Pa had grabbed his Sharps this morning, and Dusty and Jack had each grabbed Winchesters.

One of the Winchesters standing was a .44-40, and took seventeen cartridges. The other was a shorter carbine, a .44 caliber, and it took twelve cartridges. This was the rifle Bree preferred as it was a little easier to handle. A little more maneuverable, especially from horseback. It was the one she usually used for target practice.

The gun was loaded. Pa kept all the guns loaded. If you need a gun, an empty one is of no use to you. Keep them loaded, and treat them like they're loaded. Regardless, she pulled the lever down partway and opened the chamber a little to reassure herself there was a cartridge there. Something else Pa had said. Always check your loads.

She pulled open a drawer of the cabinet the gun rack stood on and grabbed a box of extra cartridges, and then went out and climbed down the front steps. A horse was saddled and tethered to the top rail of the corral, and Fred was standing by looking restless.

"Are you sure about this, Bree?" he said. "I can saddle up and go with you."

"I'll be fine, Fred. You should stay with Aunt Ginny and Temperance."

He nodded reluctantly.

Aunt Ginny had stepped out the kitchen door and was walking toward the corral. Bree was expecting her aunt to give her grief about the Levi's, but Ginny said nothing.

Bree slid the rifle into the saddle boot, and then swung up and into the saddle.

Aunt Ginny said, "You really are your father's daughter."

Bree smiled and nodded. "I'm heading straight up and over the ridge. I'll be in McCabe Gap in probably two or three hours."

"Be safe, child."

Bree turned her horse and was off at a light canter across the grassy valley floor.

"Fred," Ginny said. "Hitch us up a wagon. Temperance and I will take Age back to his parents. We'll wait in town for any word on Nina."

Bree turned her horse into the woods. This horse was a buckskin, caught in the wild by Pa a couple years ago. Broken by Josh. But a mountain horse is never fully broken. This horse had spirit and was one of Bree's favorites to ride. It had a mane so blonde it was almost white and one matching stocking, and was full of spirit.

The horse wanted to move, to charge

through the trees, but Bree kept it on tight rein. She looked about as she rode.

At one point she reined in the horse and sat in the saddle and called out, "Nina!"

She waited. There was no response. She checked the reactions of the horse. Pa had said a horse can smell things and hear things that a human never can. Watch your horse and let its motions tell you what it is hearing or smelling.

This horse was flicking its head back and forth and lifting its fore hooves impatiently. It wanted to run. Bree nudged it on but kept it under rein. She didn't want to cover ground too fast and miss something.

She rode on maybe five hundred yards, then reined up and called out again. Nothing.

Fred had hung a full canteen from the saddle horn, so she grabbed it and pulled the cork free and took a swig.

"Where could she be?" she said to the horse, though she didn't expect the horse to understand her. You do a lot of horse riding, you end up talking to your horse. "She's out here somewhere."

The horse snorted and flicked its head again. It didn't know what she was talking about, but wanted to run.

"You be patient, boy. After we climb this ridge up and down, you'll have your work-out."

She nudged the horse ahead again. The

ridge flattened out to a small plateau, and there was a grove of birch. The bark was a yellow-white, and the leaves were fluttering in the wind.

Bree sat in the saddle and waited. She guessed they were almost half-way up the ridge. She had left the ranch house maybe an hour earlier.

Maybe she should ride laterally for a while and cut for sign. That's what she figured Pa might do. Or Dusty. She turned her horse and began a slow ride across the side of the ridge.

She left the birch grove behind her, and was in pines again. At one point she emerged from the pines onto a rocky section of slope.

She dismounted and let the rein trail — ground hitching they call it. She loosened the cinch and let the horse rest a bit. She pulled the rifle from the saddle because she was not going to be caught unarmed should the horse for any reason decide to bolt. She was Pa's daughter, and had learned to think like him.

The wind shifted. The breeze was picking up. The clearing she was in provided an open view of the sky, and she saw some dark clouds toward the north.

"We're gonna get some rain, boy," she said to the horse.

The horse lifted its head. It sniffed and it shifted its hooves nervously. Something on the breeze had caught its attention. It hadn't been there a few moments earlier, but when the wind shifted it brought this new scent to the horse.

"What is it, boy?" Bree said, gently reaching for the rein. "Is there a mountain lion up there? Or a big ol' grizzly?"

She wasn't afraid. She had her rifle and was a crack shot. She had gone hunting with Pa and Josh once, a couple years ago, and brought down a mountain lion with this very rifle.

She tightened the cinch and stepped up and into the saddle.

"Let's go check it out, boy."

She nudged the horse ahead, but she rode with the rifle across the front of her saddle.

Nina was at the bottom of the pit. She had tried to rise to her feet three times, and all three times had collapsed with stabbing pain in her ankle. It had gotten dark, and spent the night in the wet pine straw in total blackness.

Animals called from the night. A wolf howled from somewhere up on the ridge.

Nina curled up, shaking with fear. And she was cold. She cried at one point. Then she decided not to let herself cry anymore. She had to be stronger than that. Her ankle was starting to hurt even when she wasn't trying to stand on it and her shoe was feeling tight. This meant her ankle was probably swelling.

She reached down in the dark and unlaced her high-top shoe and gingerly pulled it from her foot.

She then curled up again on the cold, damp pine straw and stared up at the darkness overhead. She half expected a wolf to suddenly peer down at her with glowing eyes.

But no wolf showed. Somewhere in the night she fell asleep. She awoke shivering, laid there awake for awhile, then slept some more.

Eventually morning came and she became aware of how god-awful hungry she was. And thirsty.

I'm gonna die in this pit and no one will ever know, she thought.

Her anger at her father now seemed so distant, like it had been long ago. Her thoughts were of Jack. She wanted him to hold her one more time. She wanted to taste his kisses one more time. She didn't want to die like this. Like some wounded animal at the bottom of some strange pit dug in the middle of the woods.

She heard a noise up top. She wasn't sure what it was. She waited and listened again. And she heard it again. A sort of snorting sound. Like what a horse makes.

"Hello?" she called out. "Help!"

A girl then poked her head into view at the top of the pit, looking down at her. The girl had a gray sombrero on her head.

"Are you Nina?" the girl said.

Nina nodded, not knowing what to say.

"Hi. I'm Bree. Jack's sister. Give me a couple minutes and I'll have you out of this hole."

Jack felt a sort of fear he had never known before as he rode along the side of the ridge. He was cutting for sign. Sign that was just not there. He called out Nina's name and listened for an answer that never came. The woman he loved was out here somewhere in the woods. She might need his help, but where was she? Was she even still alive?

Pa had said maybe they should split up so they could cover more ground. Pa rode in one direction. Dusty in another. Hunter in yet another. Harding could ride a horse and had come along, and took a fourth path along the side of the ridge.

Nina had run away from Harding the evening before. The man who was really Harlan Carter wouldn't say what the argument was about, but Jack could only guess.

Jack shouldn't have had a thought like this, a thought of revenge, but it suddenly crept in on him. If something happened to Nina, then Carter would have the gunfight he seemed to itching to have. Jack was his father's son, after all.

There were no more tracks to follow. The trail was too old, and to make matters worse, it was starting to rain.

Around noon, they began converging at the settlers' camp. First Johnny, then Dusty and after a while, Hunter. The women were preparing food as the men would need to eat. Aunt Ginny and Temperance were there, and helping. Ginny had used her credit at Franklin's to stock up the settlers' supplies so a full meal was being prepared. Chicken, potatoes, biscuits.

Aunt Ginny told the men that Bree was out in the woods searching, too.

Johnny stood by Ginny, a tin cup of coffee in his hand. He said, "We'll take a few minutes to eat, then we'll continue the search. Right up until dark."

Dusty was standing by him, a plate of food in his hands.

Ginny said, "I told Fred if Josh should come riding in, to send him into town to help."

Johnny nodded.

Jack came riding up and swung out of the saddle. "I'll take some of that coffee."

Aunt Ginny said, "You should eat."

"I'm not hungry. I just want a quick drink of coffee and then I'll switch saddles with a horse from Old Jeb's remuda, and then I'm off again."

"You need to eat, Jackson."

Pa said, "Your aunt's right."

Dusty looked up. Motion at the edge of the

meadow had caught his peripheral vision. Bree was on a horse and behind her on the saddle was Nina.

"Jack," he said. "Pa. Look."

They followed his gaze. Aunt Ginny had just poured Jack a cup of coffee, and he let the cup go flying into the grass and ran toward them.

"Easy," Bree said. "The girl's got a badly twisted ankle."

Jack reached for her, anyway. She reached down for him and slid off the back of the horse. Jack took her in his arms.

Her blouse had dirt stains on the elbows and shoulders. Her hair had come mostly free of the bun and was flying wildly. There were dirt streaks on her cheeks. Jack didn't care. He held her tightly like he was afraid to let go.

"Are you all right?" he managed to say.

She nodded. "Bree found me. I'm okay."

Jack looked up at Bree, tears in his eyes. He couldn't find the words. Bree gave a nod and a smile.

They were quickly surrounded. Questions were being asked, all at once.

Nina was saying, "I fell into this pit. I twisted my ankle. I thought it was broken."

"Give the girl some room to breathe," Ginny said. "Let's get her back to her family's camp."

Harding looked at her and she looked at

him, and then he took her in a big hug.

"I'm so sorry," he said.

"Father, I'm staying. I'm not going to Oregon."

"We can discuss it later."

Nina said, "We can discuss it anytime you want. But I'm staying."

Ginny said to Bree, "You must be hungry."

Bree said, "I don't normally drink coffee, but I have to admit that smells almighty good."

With a grin, Dusty poured her a cup. It was thick and black. Trail coffee. She took a sip.

"I found her in a pit, up on the eastern side of that ridge," she said. She looked at Pa. "Prospectors were in these hills off and on even before we moved in. I figured it was an old claim that showed no color, so it was abandoned. It looked like it was hand dug. Maybe six or seven feet deep. It's been empty a long time."

She took a sip of coffee. "Looked like a deadfall had covered most of it, and pine straw had collected on the deadfall. When it was getting dark, maybe at first glance Nina thought it was just a lumpy spot on the ground. When she stepped on it some branches must have broken and down she went."

Johnny put his arm around his daughter. "Have I ever told you how proud I am of you?"

She gave a wicked grin. "Not today."

"Well, Punkin', I'm proud of you."

She took another sip of coffee. "You know, I think I'm starting to understand why you men like this stuff."

"Oh, Lord," Aunt Ginny said.

Bree went on to explain that Fred had included a length of rope on the saddle. Fred never saddled a horse without including a length of rope and a canteen of water. Bree tied one end of the rope to a tree and then using the rope, climbed down into the pit. After she was sure Nina wasn't hurt too badly, she tied the rope around Nina's middle, then climbed out and tied the rope to the saddle horn and had the horse back up.

"The horse pulled her right up and out of the hole, as quick as you please."

Since Nina was a little shaken up but could ride, Bree brought her to Granny Tate's. "Granny said it's sprained quite bad. There's swelling, and she's not to step on it for a while. Granny wants to see her again day after tomorrow. She splinted it up to help her keep the foot still."

Bree then sighed with exasperation. "You know what I did? I forgot to fetch Nina's shoe. It's still at the bottom of that pit."

They all laughed. Ginny gave Bree a hug. Ginny said, "You did fine. You did really fine."

Jack looked over toward the Hardings' tent.

Nina was sitting in a wooden chair and devouring a plate of food. Her ankle was indeed in a wooden splint. Thin planks six inches wide, tied together with a strip of bedsheet. Jack knew Granny Tate's improvised splints were better than anything he had ever seen a doctor devise.

He decided to go over and see how she was doing.

Pa stopped him with a hand on his shoulder. "Not now, son. Let them talk. They have a lot to discuss."

Jack nodded.

Harding was standing about awkwardly while his daughter ate. She devoured a chicken breast and a baked potato and her mother filled her plate again.

Finally, Nina looked up at him. "I'm staying," she said.

He began to say something but she cut him off before he could get the first word out.

"No," she said. "You crossed a line last night. As I lay there in that pit, thinking I was going to die, I had a lot of time to think this over. You can go to Oregon if you want. But I'm staying. And if Jack McCabe asks me to marry him, I'm going to say yes. Simple as that."

Emily looked at her husband. "Carter, I love you. You know that. So believe me when I tell you how hard it is to say this. If she

432

stays, I'm staying too. Whether you do or not."

Harding looked long into his wife's eyes. He then looked to his daughter, who was once again focused on the food in front of her.

Jack stood with his coffee in one hand. Bree was telling in greater detail about how she found Nina and got her out of the pit. Pa was beaming with pride. While they talked, Jack allowed a glance toward Nina. He couldn't tell what she had said to her father, but he watched Harding back up a step. Harding stared at her while she focused on the plate of food in her lap. Jack watched as Harding turned and strode away.

Jack didn't realize Aunt Ginny was watching the Hardings too until she said to him, "That man is trouble."

32

The little collection of buildings known as McCabe Gap went wild on the fourth of July. Cowboys and the families they worked for swarmed into town. It was like Saturday night, except women and children were there too. Frank Shapleigh, who owned the hotel, hung a banner with the colors of the flag and the words JULY 4th over his door. He had been doing this every year since he arrived, and a couple bullet holes in the fabric were mementos of previous July fourths.

Hunter had ordered extra kegs of beer and extra crates of bottled beer and whiskey. Franklin had dug a barbecue pit off beside his store, and smoke was currently pouring from it and the savory smell of roasting pork was filling the air.

The stretch of dirt between Hunter's saloon and the hotel was filled with people. Most of them were afoot, but riders were also trying to make their way through to Old Jeb's livery so they could deposit their horses for the night. These riders were cowhands from ranches in the surrounding area, and they knew they would probably be staying the night. It was Friday, and even though they had been paid the Saturday before, many had held onto their wages for this weekend. Their evening would begin at Hunter's and then work its way over to Miss Alisha's, and then they would bunk either in the livery or camp outside of town, and begin it all again Saturday evening.

Aunt Ginny sat on the boardwalk in front of Hunter's. She had brought a wooden kitchen chair with her. She was in a dress with a high collar, and a pill box hat was pinned to her hair. Bree stood beside her, looking wide-eyed at all the excitement before her. She had left her Levi's home and was also in a dress. Hers was a sky blue with a neckline of white lace. She wore no hat and her hair wrapped on her head in a fashion she had seen in a magazine from St. Louis. Or as close as she could approximate it with Temperance's help.

A cowhand rode past Hunter's, and reared his horse and fired his pistol into the air. A man with a beer bottle in one hand raised in the air and screamed out like he was on the warpath. People on foot scurried past.

"Oh, Aunt Ginny," Bree said with a smile of wonder. "Isn't it all so grand?"

Ginny smiled. "I don't know if that's the

435

word I would use for it."

Hunter stood on the boardwalk in front of his doorway. His arms were folded over his barrel chest, and his thickly bearded face was breaking into a wide smile. Across the crowd, on a porch built onto the front of the hotel, Frank Shapleigh stood. He was a long, thin man, and a derby covered his head. He normally wore a string tie, but at the moment his shirt collar was open.

He looked over at Hunter, and they exchanged a smile. All of these people meant money would be flowing. Or at least credit would be. And these people were good for the money they owed. One thing about a community like this — it survived on honesty. And besides, you knew where everyone lived.

Hunter raised a hand in a wave, and Shapleigh returned it with a big smile.

Dusty stepped out of the doorway and around Hunter to stand beside him. Dusty was in a white shirt and a black string tie. His Levi's were clean, and his Peacemaker was tied down to his right side. He held a mug of beer in one hand.

"Gonna be a wild night," Dusty said.

"That's right," Hunter said. "This is your first Fourth of July in this town."

Dusty nodded. "Last year at this time, Josh and I were on the trail, tracking those raiders."

"I missed it, too. Zack and Fred and I were

right behind you on the trail. Franklin tried to handle the saloon for me, but when I got back the door was off the hinges."

Dusty nodded with a laughing smile. He remembered.

Hunter said, "This night and tomorrow are gonna be the two wildest nights of the year. Wilder than the wildest Saturday night. We have more people in the area than we did last year. There are prospectors in the hills a few miles west of here. There's a gulch a bunch of 'em are working."

Dusty said, "I've heard. They're calling it William's Gulch. I'm not really sure why."

"And there's a ranch, the Bar W. Their men used to ride clear into Bozeman, but we're a little closer, and more and more of 'em are riding in here to let loose. I expect. I would sure appreciate it if you and your brothers could be around tonight."

Josh had ridden in from the line cabin the night before. There was still work to be done, but he didn't want to miss the Fourth of July in McCabe Gap. He had missed it the year before, and didn't intend to miss it again. He had given the men with him the weekend off, too.

Temperance had been the first to greet him. As he had been riding toward the house, she charged down the stairs and ran toward him. He scooped her up from the ground and pulled her onto the back of the horse with him and held her in a long kiss.

"Miss me?" he said.

She smiled. "Maybe a little."

He now walked arm-in-arm with her. Her hair was done up under a hat that sort of reminded Dusty of a canoe. She was in a gingham dress, and about her neck was a chain and small diamond locket Aunt Ginny had given her for Christmas. Josh was in a flat-brimmed sombrero, and his hair was pulled back in a tail, like Pa's. He was in a white shirt and string tie, and his pistol was at his side.

They strolled like a couple in love, aware only of each other. People pushed past, and the cowboy on the horse fired his gun in the air again, but it was like they didn't even here.

Hunter said, "When's that boy going to ask her to marry him?"

"Been kinda wondering that myself."

Out beyond the hotel and Franklin's General Store was a large outcropping of bedrock, and it was on this that some tin cans had been placed.

Johnny McCabe stood fifty feet away. In his hand was the Colt Peacemaker Charlie Franklin had been holding for him. The gunbelt that went with it was buckled on, and the single holster was tied down to his leg. On the ground at his feet was the gunbelt he normally wore, with the twin Remingtons.

Johnny brought the gun out to arm's length,

cocking it as he moved, and squeezed off a shot. One can jumped away.

Franklin was standing at one side of him, and Zack Johnson at the other. Zack stood just a foot or two back, because experience had taught him if you do this, then the noise of the gun won't hurt your ears as much. He didn't understand the science behind it and he didn't care to. He only knew it worked. Franklin had never discovered this, and stood immediately beside Johnny and was holding his ears as the gun went off.

"Slight pull to the left," Johnny said.

"That can be corrected," Franklin said. He was, among other things, a fairly adept gunsmith.

"Not necessary. I can compensate. Never met a gun that was exactly perfect. My Sharps pulls a little to the left."

Johnny snapped a sudden shot, and a can flew away. Franklin couldn't get his hands up to his ears in time, and winced as his ears protested.

Johnny was in a range shirt, but he had taken the time to put on a string tie. He wore his buckskin vest, and his brown sombrero was pulled down to his temples.

Zack said, "Let's see how fast you can clear leather with that, old man."

"I bet I'm faster with this new gun than you are with that old rusty one on your belt."

In the holster tied down to Zack's leg was a

Remington .44. Not unlike those Johnny normally wore. And not unlike Johnny's, it was well-oiled and in good firing order. But Johnny and Zack never missed an opportunity to needle each other over anything at all.

"It's no older than those two you normally swagger around with."

"Of course," Johnny said, "I hope it's not lost on you that I'm looking at a newer gun."

"Are you saying yours are old and rusty?"

Others had gathered. Whenever Johnny McCabe or Zack Johnson were willing to put on a shooting display, people gathered to watch. These two were almost legendary, and you didn't miss a chance to watch someone like this showing off their shooting.

"Come on," Zack said. "Let's see how you can handle that new shootin' iron. Five dollars says you can't get five cans with five shots."

Johnny said, "How about six cans?"

"Six cans with six shots? Making it even harder on yourself."

"How about six cans with five shots?"

Zack rubbed his chin. "Five dollars? I hate to take your cash that way."

Franklin turned to the people behind him. Eight or ten had gathered. Mostly cowhands. Wide sombreros and loose fitting pants tucked into high riding boots. Pistols worn at their hips. There were a couple with narrower-brimmed hats and boots that laced up. Franklin didn't know them. Probably prospectors from over at William's Gulch.

"Five dollars!" Franklin called out. "Who's willin' to put up five dollars to say Mister McCabe can get six cans with five shots?"

One man called out, "Five says he can't."

Another said, "Ten says he can."

Zack said to Johnny, "So, now he's a bookie too?"

Johnny nodded and snorted a chuckle. "He's a roofer and a gunsmith and a barber and a store keeper. I suppose out here you have to be a little bit of everything."

While Franklin was collecting the money as the new self-appointed bookie of McCabe Gap, Johnny flipped open the loading gate of the pistol and dropped out the empties, and then loaded five new cartridges.

"Damn, but this is convenient," he said.

"Sure does load faster than these Remingtons. I bet it'll seem strange not to carry two guns, though."

Johnny snapped the loading gate shut. "Been carrying two guns ever since I was seventeen years old. Over twenty years now."

"Closer to twenty-five."

Johnny shot him a side-ways glance. The old joke that Johnny was getting old, made by a man who was a year younger. "Not that much closer."

"Close enough. Just lookin' at all those gray hairs you got."

Johnny said, "You want to try your hand at shooting those cans?"

"Oh, not me. I let you do all the fancy shooting. That way when the young bucks come looking to make a name, they'll look right past me."

"Scared?"

"Smart."

Johnny cracked a half smile.

Zack said, "All right, old man. Let's see what you got."

Johnny wasn't going to try a quick draw. He had been wearing this holster not even ten minutes. With the gun already in his hand, he brought his arm out to full extension, cocking the hammer as he did so, and let loose with five shots. Four cans leaped away from the fence as though they had a life of their own. The fifth can spun, as the bullet had grazed it, and then in its spin hit the sixth can and both fell to the ground.

A chorus of hoots and cheers rose from the crowd. Those who had won their bets. A few foul words rose from those who had lost.

Johnny looked at Zack. "Did you really think I couldn't get all six?"

Zack reached into his vest for his wallet. "I just wanted to see you do it. That's all. Bet you can't do it again."

"And you think you can?"

Zack handed him five ones. "All right, old man. You and me and a rail full of cans. Ten dollars. Whoever has the fastest draw and gets all five cans wins. Franklin can be the judge."

Franklin held out both hands. "Oh, no. Not me."

But men were slapping him on the back and cheering his name, the way a man will do when he has a little too much beer in him. Hunter had begun serving early in the day.

Johnny reloaded the Peacemaker and slapped it in the holster. "You know, I've never really practiced drawing with this gun, in this holster."

"So, you're saying you want to back out?"

Johnny grinned. "Not a chance."

Zack looked over at Franklin. "Oh, Franklin, Johnny will buy the gun. That is, if he has any cash left."

Ten cans were stood on the fence while bets were made in the crowd behind Johnny and Zack. The crowd had now grown to more than twenty. A young man in a black jacket and shirt and a white collar, the town minister, said, "I'll put five on Mister McCabe."

Franklin turned to look at him with surprise. "Parson?"

"Well, it's for the church."

Johnny said to Zack, "Who goes first?"

"I say we both go at once, so Franklin can more accurately judge."

Franklin said, "Look, I don't really think I should be doing this."

One man called out behind him, "You better get this right, Franklin."

Johnny and Zack both squared away at the fence. Johnny said, "All right, Franklin. On the count of three."

Franklin's voice shook a little as he called out, "One . . . two . . ."

The crowd of men behind them shouted out, "Three!"

Jack had ridden out early that morning to the lake, and the section of land Harding had reluctantly set aside as his. The tent was set up, and the wagon was beside it. Jack had brought a buckboard from the ranch so Nina and her mother could ride. Jack found Harding had set out that morning on foot, angry at the world about him and announcing he wasn't going to the festivities in town.

Nina said, "He's so angry, Jack. I've never seen him like this before."

Again Jack considered telling her what he knew, but then decided against it. Not now, as they were heading into town for what was supposed to be a good day.

They sat up in the shade, beside Hunter's. They had brought wooden kitchen chairs in their wagon from Vermont, and Jack had tossed them in the buckboard. Emily Harding had wanted four, in case Carter should show up.

Jack lifted the chairs out of the wagon and set them on the ground, trying to find as level

444

a spot as he could. Mrs. Harding was looking off into the crowd, and Jack knew she was hoping beyond hope she would find her husband, having a change of heart and deciding to join them. Jack hoped he never caused Nina the kind of pain Harlan Carter was causing his wife.

With the women sitting comfortably, he took the team to the livery and then fetched a pitcher of lemonade and three glasses from the hotel. Shapleigh didn't have cold beer to offer like Hunter did, but his wife put together some of the best lemonade Jack had tasted.

What Jack really wanted was a cold beer, but he knew from things Nina had said that her mother was a strict Baptist, as were the Brewsters and Fords. The Baptists Jack had known considered beer to be a drink of evil. Pa had said before that nothing is really evil. Beer or guns or anything else. It is what you do with them can be defined as evil or not. But Jack decided now was not the time for a philosophical debate with Nina's mother, so the lemonade would suffice for now.

Jack navigated his way through the crowd, and rejoined Nina and her mother.

There was a roar of gunfire from the other side of the town. Mrs. Harding said, "It sounds like there's a war going on over there."

Jack said, "Target practice. Probably Pa and Zack. It usually comes down to them."

445

"Oh," Nina said. "Would you like to go watch?"

Her ankle was still bound tightly in a splint, and Jack knew it would be nearly impossible for her to make it that far.

"No," he said with a smile. "I don't want to spend a minute out of your company."

That got a smile from her. The kind of smile a woman reserves for the man she loves.

After a time, Jack saw Hunter step out of his saloon. He stood on the boardwalk in front of the doorway and searched with his eyes through the crowd like he was looking for someone in particular. Then he saw Jack sitting with Nina and Emily, and walked over.

"Ladies," he said. He wore no hat, but he bowed his head slightly toward each.

"Mister Hunter," Nina said.

"Now, what have I told you? It ain't *mister.* Just Hunter."

Nina smiled with a little embarrassment, even at being playfully admonished. "Hunter."

Hunter fixed his gaze on Jack. "Can I talk to you a minute?"

"Sure." Jack got to his feet. "If you ladies would excuse me?"

Jack had removed his sombrero while he was sitting with Nina and her mother. He now pulled it on down over his head, and followed Hunter back up onto the boardwalk in front of the saloon.

Hunter said, "We got a problem. In there."

Jack stepped into the barroom. In one corner was Harlan Carter. He was sitting at a table in one corner, his back to the wall. In front of him was a bottle and a glass. Even sitting, he was a tall man. He was leaning on his elbows and his gaze was fixed on the bottle in front of him, but Jack knew he was missing nothing going on in this room.

Jack left his hat in place as he crossed the room to stand in front of the table.

"Leave me alone, boy," Carter said. He barely moved his mouth when he spoke, but his voice carried.

Jack said, "Since when do Baptists drink whiskey?"

"I said leave me alone."

"Or what? Are you going to gun me down? Like you threatened to do with my father back when we were on the trail."

Hunter was looking at Dusty with a look that said *you gotta be kidding me.* Someone threatening to shoot Johnny McCabe wasn't usually still walking around afterward.

"I meant what I said. I told him to keep you away from my daughter. But there you are, outside with her and my wife."

"Well, someone had to bring them into town. You were too busy storming off by yourself, and coming in here to drink whiskey, so someone had to do it."

"Don't push me, boy."

Jack felt his father's temper rising inside him. For a moment he had a visual of his fist connecting with this man's face, and it made him feel mighty good, but that would be the wrong thing. For Nina. So he drew a breath in slowly and forced himself to be calm.

"We could fight, if that's what you want. But either way, no matter who wins, Nina will be hurt."

"You been talkin' to Brewster? He said the same thing."

"And he was right. Look, Mister Harding, you don't have to like me. But I love your daughter."

"Love?" He chuckled bitterly. "What do you know of love?"

"What do *you* know of it?"

Harding glared at him. "I know more of it than you think I do. I know enough about it to know I'd die before I'd let harm come to my daughter."

"And yet you sit in here, drinking whiskey, and wanting to fight me. It's purely by charity that my father didn't take you down that night."

"Ain't a man alive that can take me down."

"That's the whiskey talking."

"I suppose you told her all about me."

Jack shook his head. "I haven't said anything. I don't think I'm going to. That's your place."

"I tried to take her out of here. I wanted to

448

take Emily and Nina to Oregon. But they won't have none of it. Nina chose you over me. And Emily's backin' her play. So stand there and gloat all you want, boy. But leave me alone."

Jack didn't know what to say. He stood and looked at Carter Harding, or Harlan Carter, sitting at the table with his whiskey. Harding dropped his gaze from Jack back to his whiskey.

Jack said, "At least do yourself a favor and when you leave, use the back door. I don't want them to have to see you like this."

He turned and strode away from him. Dusty was behind the bar, pouring a beer for a cowhand who had just bellied-up.

Jack said, "Keep an eye on him, will you? Come get me if you need to."

Dusty nodded.

Jack stepped out and stood a moment on the boardwalk just breathing the air and letting his ire calm down. He turned toward the patch of earth to the side of the saloon where Nina and her mother were sitting, and found Nina was watching him. She had been since he stepped out of the building.

He returned to the chair he had vacated and gave her a smile. She said, "Is everything all right?"

He nodded. He was about to say it was just a cowhand from the Circle M who had a little too much to drink, but then he thought better of it. He was not going to lie to this girl. So he said, "Everything's fine."

"What happened?"

"Nothing important." He took her hand and looked off at the crowd.

The cowhand who had been rearing his horse in the air slid from the saddle and landed hard on the ground. But he got up laughing. Too drunk to feel pain, Jack figured.

Nina said to him, "You're not going to tell me, are you?"

"Not right now. Later. I promise."

She nodded, apparently deciding to let it go for now.

The crowd eventually cleared for a horse race. Josh and Dusty took part in that, along with men from the McCabe's ranch, and others. Josh was on the horse Bree had playfully named Rabbit, the fastest horse Jack had ever seen. Until today. Jack came in second to a man from the Bar W.

Then there was a pie-eating contest. Come dark, torches were set up to provide light and a small band began playing. A cowboy from the Bar W could pay a fiddle. Fat Cole, a cowhand from the McCabe's ranch, could pluck a banjo reasonably well. Fat was a little older than Jack and stood tall and thin. Jack didn't know if the name was a play on the way he was built, or short for the cowboy's full name of Jehosaphat. Or both. Franklin, it turned out, could play a harmonica. They did their best to improvise the Vienna Waltz, which Jack wouldn't have recognized if he hadn't been told what it was supposed to be, then they started in with square-dance music.

After a time, folks began to head out. Families with children, especially.

Age Brewster had offered to drive Nina and her mother back to the land that was to become their farm because Jack had been asked by Hunter to stay and help out at the saloon.

"How will you get home?" Nina said.

"I'll rent a horse from Jeb Arthur at the livery."

Jack, with his jacket removed and his sleeves rolled up, began to work behind the bar, filling mugs from the kegs.

The room was full. Card games were in progress, and Jack guessed as many as fifteen were standing at the bar and three times that were milling about on the floor watching the games in progress.

Dusty was behind the counter also, pouring beers and filling shot glasses of whiskey.

"Cash only tonight," Hunter announced to Jack and Dusty. "No way to keep track of any tabs."

An order came from one card game for four mugs of cold beer. For this, Jack had to climb a ladder down to the root cellar and fill the mugs and then climb back out, balancing the tray. He decided to pour five.

Once the beer was served, he took a moment behind the bar and took a big gulp. "Been waiting for that all day."

Josh was there, working his way through the crowd. He was taking orders for drinks, and also being a presence to help remind people to behave themselves. Hunter was doing the same.

Around ten o'clock, the peace was broken at one card table. One of the players was in a tie and jacket and neither of Jack's brothers recognized him. Jack figured he was a gambler, trying out the area. One of the cowhands at the table accused him of cheating. The cowhand rose to his feet and made like he was going to for his pistol. The card shark produced a derringer — Jack didn't see where it came from — and a shot was fired nicking the cowhand on the arm. The table was then overturned on the card shark and punches were being thrown and money was flying about on the floor.

The fight soon spread, the way fights will, and the entire room exploded in mayhem. Two cowhands crashed into the bar, which was nothing more than two planks laid across upended beer kegs. The planks were jarred and slid away, and a beer keg went over, and Jack was knocked backward by one of the planks. Dusty was slammed into a shelf on the wall behind the bar, a shelf that contained bottles of whiskey and vodka. The shelf collapsed and the bottles landed on the floor.

Dusty got to his feet and grabbed the two cowhands, who were now grappling on the floor, but before he could do more another cowhand who had taken a punch was driven into him and both went crashing to the floor.

Josh was punching one man and then two grabbed him from behind. Jack grabbed both men, pulling them from Josh. Jack stood at least an inch taller than Josh and was heavily muscled from his time on the boxing team and the rowing team at school, and he used this muscle to slam both cowhands into each other.

Hunter was in the middle of the fray, grabbing one man and throwing him into another, a wide grin on his face. He was enjoying this, Jack knew.

Josh was about to swing a fist at a man, when his attention suddenly was drawn to the doorway. Jack tried to follow his gaze but there were men in the way and then two were tackling him to pull him down. Josh was then punched by a man from the side, and he was down. And then Jack was up and swinging fists. He realized he was smiling, too.

After a time, things calmed down. A number of cowhands were ejected from the place bodily. Hunter's door was off the hinges again. A bottle of whiskey was shattered on the floor, and a beer keg had been cracked and half the brew had drained away.

Jack was sitting on one of the kegs that had supported the planks that made up the bar. He was laughing. His hair was flying wild and his shirt was soaked with sweat and his tie was crooked. A couple buttons had been lost from his shirt and there were a couple of blood stains. His knuckles were skinned and bruised and one was bleeding, and the side of his face was numb from a punch he had taken and he was tasting blood.

"Damn," he said with a smile. "I haven't had so much fun in a long time."

Dusty was holding a bandanna to his nose, which had pretty much stopped bleeding, and a bruise was rising on one cheekbone.

Dusty said, "I love this place on a Saturday night."

Hunter was talking with the remaining customers. Card games had resumed, and some were milling about chatting or nursing wounds. Hunter had given everyone a round on the house, the best way to heal wounds.

He was righting some tables that had been tipped over. Two chairs had been broken and their pieces were lying on the floor.

"What a night!" Hunter was still smiling.

Dusty said, "You lost an entire bottle of whiskey and half a keg of beer."

"Yes, but I made up from it." He pulled from his pants a fistful of dollar bills. "I took this from the floor. The money on that table was going everywhere. No way to tell who it belonged to. Some of it might as well go to the damages."

Jack laughed. "I could use a cold beer."

"Me too," Hunter said.

Josh had taken a couple of punches to the face and one eye was swollen shut. Aunt Ginny was going to give them the lecture of their lives, Jack thought.

But Josh wasn't smiling. He said to Dusty, "I saw someone. In the middle of that fracas. He was standing by the door."

Now he had the attention of Dusty and Jack. Dusty said, "Who?"

"A man from that canyon, last summer. One of Falcone's men. The one with the blind eye. It's all milky white."

Dusty nodded. "White-Eye. He was here?"

"I only saw him for a second. He was standing by the door. Then I was hit and there was a crowd around me, and when I got a clear look at the door again, he was gone."

Jack was looking at both of them curiously.

Dusty said to him, "One of Sam Patterson's men. Lost the eye when a knife slashed down his face. It was long before I knew him. They called him White-Eye."

Jack said, "A long knife scar starts above the eye, and goes down through it to his cheek?"

Dusty nodded.

"I think I know the man. He was with Falcone outside of Cheyenne."

Dusty said to Josh, "Are you sure it was him?"

"I only saw him for a second. I wouldn't stake my life on it."

Dusty headed out the door. Josh and Jack followed. Hunter followed them.

Dusty stepped down from the boardwalk and walked out maybe fifty feet from the building. The torches had long been taken down and the town was now dark and empty. Lamps were on at the first floor of the hotel and they could hear a piano. And the front room down at Miss Alisha's was lighted. But otherwise, all was dark. The ridges beyond the town were lost in the night.

"What are you looking for?" Jack said.

"Campfires."

Jack nodded. Aunt Ginny had written how the raiders had lit a huge bonfire every night, almost announcing their presence in a show of daring and arrogance.

"I doubt they would be that brazen again," Josh said. "If Falcone's back, he would know better."

But the hills and ridges were all dark.

"It may not have been him," Josh said.

Dusty said, "Sam Patterson taught me never to take chances. I think we should assume it was, until we can prove otherwise."

Jack said, "Should we tell Pa?"

"Not yet. He's leaving in a week to go and visit your mother's grave. If he thinks something's wrong, he won't leave. And he's been needing to do this."

Josh said to Dusty, "Come morning, maybe you and I can go into the ridges and cut for sign. Look for any tracks made by a lone rider. Any cowhands coming from the ranches in the area will be using one of the trails. Let's hold off on telling Pa anything unless we need to."

33

Breakfast at the McCabe house was a mixture of Aunt Ginny scowling and scolding the boys for reckless behavior, Pa laughing at the way they looked, Bree eagerly wanting to know all of the details, and Temperance fussing over Josh and his black eye.

Pa told them to take the day off. Jack found a punch he had taken to the ribs that hadn't hurt much at the time now hurt, and he had to be careful and not take in too deep a breath. If it wasn't a lot better by morning, he would have Granny Tate had a look at it to make sure it wasn't broken. Josh's eye had darkened and swollen and a bruise on his cheekbone had darkened so much of one side of his face was purple. The bridge of Dusty's nose had swollen and when he rose from a chair he did so gingerly. He had at one point flipped backward over a table, but said he was fine as long as he didn't move too quickly.

They made their way outside. Jack announced he was thinking of riding out to check on the settlers. Josh mentioned maybe riding into town to help Hunter fix his saloon back up. Repair tables, and put the door back on its hinges. Dusty said he should really lend a hand, too.

They had Fred saddle some horses for them, and then began a ride toward town.

Josh said to Jack, "You handled yourself pretty well last night. You left a lot of those boys in worse shape than they left you. How's a city boy from college learn to scrap like that?"

"The boxing team. And I'm on the rowing team. And some friends and I hit some taverns on the Boston waterfront more than once."

Josh's brows rose with surprise. "Really? My little brother brawling in waterfront taverns? Do Pa and Aunt Ginny know this?"

Jack shook his head. "And I'd rather they didn't."

Josh nodded. "So, you gonna ride down the valley to see your girl?"

"Not this morning. I'm riding with you two."

Josh shook his head. "I don't know, Jack. We've gotta cover some ground, and if we find this White-Eye man, it could get a little rough. It's likely he won't be alone."

Dusty said, "He can stand alongside us. He has what it takes."

Josh gave him a curious look.

459

They rode onto the trail that cut from the valley floor out and to the small town, coming out behind Hunter's.

"All right," Josh said to Dusty. "Since you know how they think, where would you be hiding out in these hills if you didn't want to be found?"

"Since they made such a show with those bonfires last year, I think I'd be in the ridges on the other side of town. Send lone riders out to scout about, but do it a lot quieter. A lot more low-key. Which is what Sam Patterson would have done in the first place."

Jack said, "From what Aunt Ginny told me of it in her letter, it sounded almost like they were posturing. Like a bully does before he strikes."

Dusty nodded. "Not a whole lot of difference. Vic Falcone made a good right-hand-man for Sam, but he was never really a leader. He showed it last summer. He was trying to intimidate everyone. Trying to show how strong he was, and that he could just ride in and take what he wanted whenever he wanted. All he did was give us time to prepare. And he greatly underestimated his opponent, being Pa."

Josh said, "It's amazing he's lived this long."

"Vic always had a knack for survival. Notice how he was one of the few who got out of that canyon alive."

"Well, if we find them out there, we end it. Now."

Dusty nodded. "That's my line of thinkin'."

Jack said, "Agreed."

They stopped in at Hunter's and explained what they were going to do. They asked him not to tell Pa, should Pa come riding in. Pa was due to leave for California in a week or so, and they didn't want him burdened with this.

Then they rode out to the ridge beyond town. A ridge visible from Hunter's front porch but was actually five miles away.

At this point, the mountains form a sort of series of long lines. Jack always thought from a bird's-eye-view they might look like the kind of ripples ocean waves can make in sand. Some of the ridges extended for miles. The valley Jack and his brothers called home was really an extra wide spacing between two series of ridges. He had taken a geology class once as an elective, and the professor had explained about the theory of the ice age, and how glaciers had carved out valleys that once might have been V shaped and made them more U shaped, and gave them floors that were almost flat. Jack didn't know if he really believed all of that theoretical stuff — sometimes he thought its only value was to give bored scholarly types something to think about — but if it was true, then glaciers would have carved the valley by digging out

461

the ten-mile-long gulch between ridges.

Once they were beyond town, they began cutting for sign. Riding sideways along the ridge, watching for any tracks that might have been made by a lone rider, or a small group of riders on their way to town, or away from it.

They rode with their pistols loose in their holsters. Josh had an old Navy .36 which he hoped to eventually replace with a Peacemaker. Dusty had the Peacemaker he had taken off the gunfighter he had been forced to kill back in Nevada over a year ago. And Jack had the Peacemaker he had brought west with him.

Josh was in the lead, with Jack immediately behind him, and Dusty bringing up the rear. Until Dusty rode up beside Jack.

"That's quite a gun you have there. I've been meaning to ask you about it."

He nodded. "I bought it in New York, last year. Five-inch barrel for a quicker draw. I'm not like you and Pa. I'll take whatever advantage I can get."

Dusty gave a nod and a grin. "I get the impression you don't need much of an advantage in anything."

They rode along the ridge for a couple of miles, then stopped to let the horses rest a bit.

Josh said, "I don't know these ridges outside the valley near good enough. Don't get out here nearly enough."

They took some water from their canteens, then mounted up and continued on. After a time, they doubled back and then tried a ridge line south of the valley. They found some bear tracks a day or so old. They found deer droppings and moose droppings. But nothing to indicate any riders had been through here.

They returned to Hunter's late in the afternoon and had a cold beer. They had been in the saddle all day and so they opted to stand at the bar.

Hunter climbed down to the cellar and emerged with four mugs of cold beer. He handed one to each of them, and took the fourth one himself.

He said, "Did you boys find anything at all out in them ridges?"

Josh shook his head. "Maybe it wasn't the same man I saw. I just thought I did. It was only a glimpse, for maybe a second or two."

Jack said, "Well, at least we looked."

Dusty took a sip of cold beer. "There's a lot of ground to cover, though. If I didn't want to be found, then I could find a way to do it."

Josh said to Jack, "Was there anyone with him that good? Back in Cheyenne?"

"There was one gunhawk by the name of Two-Finger Walker."

"Two-Finger. Pa's mentioned him once or twice."

Dusty said, "I've heard the name a few times over the years. He's a killer. Fierce. Deadly. But I've never heard anything about him being any kind of a scout. And White-Eye was dependable and a little cold-blooded, but Sam never relied on him for scouting or tracking."

Josh said, "He used that one you fought. Kiowa Haynes."

Dusty nodded. He then looked to Jack, "So, what're you gonna tell everyone back at the house? You told them you were going to check on the farmers today."

Jack shrugged. "I'll tell them you two had decided on taking a ride through the hills and doing a little hunting, and that sounded kind of good. Besides, I don't really want Nina to see me all beaten-up like this."

Dusty nodded. Josh said with a smile, "You do kind'a look like hell."

Jack said, "You looked in the mirror lately?"

Dusty said, "He looked like hell before the fight."

Hunter was laughing. He took a big chug from his mug.

Jack said, "I don't like lying to the family, but I really don't want anything to happen to keep Pa from riding out to visit Ma. He's had a really hard time dealing with all of it over the years. He never really got over the loss."

"He's been different this past year," Josh said. "There's a sort of ease on him. Like he's somehow found some sort of peace inside him. Like he came to some sort of understanding about it."

Pa could become very long winded when talking philosophy, Jack thought, but when it came to talking about himself he was like a closed book. "Well, if that's the case, then it's more important than ever that we let him go to California without burdening him with any of this. Besides, we don't really know if it was indeed White-Eye that Josh saw."

Hunter said, "Are you sure that's wise? If it is Vic Falcone out there, with a new gang of outlaws, maybe we need your Pa right here."

Josh shook his head. "We're men now, Hunter. And you're here, and Zack is just down the stretch. And we have an extra gun in Jack, too, until the end of July."

Dusty glanced at Jack, but said nothing.

Over the next few days, Jack and Pa went hunting in the hills surrounding the valley. Pa brought his Sharps and let Jack use it to bring down an elk. And he and Pa stood on the porch at night a couple of times, watching darkness descend on the valley. Pa talked philosophy, going on about Shoshone beliefs and ways.

"Their village wasn't far from where those settlers are building their homes." Pa had his pipe in his left hand. His right was resting on the handle of the new revolver tied down at his right leg. Jack didn't know if he would ever get used to the sight of Pa swaggering around with only one gun. "We hunted these hills and we roasted elk and venison by an open fire at night."

"That must have been quite a time for you."

Pa nodded. "It was one of the best winters of my life. At that time, there were no settlements here in Montana Territory. No Bozeman. No Helena. There wasn't a white settlement north of the Oregon Trail. Just these mountains. I would stand on a cliff off on that ridge west of the valley, and just stare off at the valley floor and the ridges beyond. All of it was covered with a blanket of white. And I just felt like I was in country undisturbed by the white man. Country that was as God made it. There was such a feeling of peace and calmness and stillness that just sort of settled through me."

Jack knew the ridge. Pa still rode out there every so often.

Pa said, "I sometimes wonder if I did right by you and Josh and Bree, bringing you all the way up here after your mother died. Maybe I should have left us right where we were. Only a couple days' ride north of San Francisco. Out here on the remote frontier, life can be hard. Last summer, especially, I started having doubts. That fire fight we had with Falcone and his men — that was a bad one."

"No, Pa, overall I think you made the right decision. I can't imagine a better place for the family to call home than right here."

At the end of the week, it was time. When the eastern sky was just starting to lighten, Johnny dropped a loop on the stallion he called Thunder, his favorite mount. The one he preferred to ride when he was going on an overland trip. He saddled Thunder and left him tethered to the rail at the front porch. He then went in the house for his bedroll and saddlebags and his rifle. He would travel with his Sharps only.

He stepped outside and tucked the rifle into the scabbard, and tied his saddlebags and bedroll in place.

His sombrero was in place, and he wore a waist-length canvas jacket the color of desert sage. Tied down to his right leg was his new Colt Peacemaker.

He looked up as the door opened. Jack stepped out, followed by Josh and Bree and Dusty. They filed down the stairs. Jack was in a white shirt and vest, and Dusty in his buckskin shirt. Josh's hair, the color of corn silk, was falling to his shoulders. Long, like Pa's. All three boys were wearing their guns.

"I thought we said our good-byes last night," Johnny said.

They had sat long by the hearth and talked, and Bree had given him a big hug before she went to bed, and the boys had each given him a handshake. He had words for each of them, telling them each how proud he was of them. Of the man Josh had become. Of the son Dusty was, and how glad he was Dusty was now in the family. Of how proud he was of Jack, off at that school in the east, getting an education that would allow him to make a difference in the world.

"We did," Bree said. "But we can't just let you ride away without being here to see you off."

On the porch was Ginny. She was in her robe, with a cup of tea in one hand and her tiny spectacles perched on her nose. Temperance was beside her.

He said, "Take care of the house."

She said, "I always do. Take care of yourself."

"I always do."

"There's no chance we could talk you into taking a stage coach like a normal person, is there? Hop the train in Cheyenne."

He grinned. "Not a chance."

She returned the grin. "Somehow, I didn't think so."

He said to Temperance, "Take care of my boy. Sometimes it's not an easy job."

She smiled. "No, it's not. Ride safe."

It was time. Johnny gave Bree another big hug. Then it was handshakes for the boys. To Josh he said, "Take care of things while I'm gone."

Josh said, "I will, Pa."

"I know you will." He looked to Dusty. "I know you both will."

He looked to Jack. "Travel safe. It's a long way back to Massachussetts."

Jack had made the journey many times. A journey he didn't intend to make again. But all he said was, "I will."

They watched their father swing up and into the back of Thunder. He sat in the saddle for a moment, looking at his family.

Pa does indeed sit tall in the saddle, Jack thought. His wide hat, his wide shoulders, the gun at his side. A man worthy of the legend he was inspiring.

Pa then turned and Thunder started away at a loping trot. Bree reached up to wipe away a tear, and Dusty put an arm over her shoulders.

Dusty said, "He'll be all right."

She nodded, but said nothing.

They watched as Pa rode down toward the wooden bridge. In the distance, he became little more than a shapeless moving object in the grayness of pre-dawn. They heard the clopping of Thunder's iron shoes on the wooden bridge. And then he was away.

34

The man most knew as Carter Harding walked away from the family tent. In one hand was a whiskey bottle he had paid for by dipping into the meager supply of cash they had remaining. He and Emily had sold their farm in Vermont and outfitted themselves for the trip west. To find a spot of land, preferably in Oregon, and start over in some place where maybe he wouldn't be recognized.

It hadn't come as a total shock that Abel Brewster had figured out who he was. He had heard people talking. And Emily had. He knew sooner or later he would be exposed, and then it would be off to prison or the gallows. He didn't want to leave his wife without a husband. Or even worse, his daughter without a father. There had been a mild drought the year before and they had lost some crops and what they could manage to harvest barely covered the debts they owed. As with any farming community, they lived on credit all year long and they paid everything up at harvest time. Anything left over was profit. And then they started the whole cycle over again. He and Emily decided to use the drought as an excuse, claimed they lost too much money, then sold out and headed west. Brewster and Ford apparently did lose some money and had to sell their farms to pay their debts, so they joined the Hardings.

Carter hadn't really wanted them along. It would be easier for his family to lose themselves in some remote corner of the frontier if he didn't have neighbors from Vermont tagging along. But he could find no effective argument for talking them out of it.

But now it was all going to pieces. The life he had tried to protect his daughter and wife from was catching up with him. His daughter's heart had been stolen by a gunfighter. And the gunfighter and his family of gunfighters all knew that Carter Harding was really Harlan Carter. Notorious outlaw. Wanted dead or alive in three states.

His last hope was to get his family out of this little section of Montana. Away from the McCabes. Oregon still awaited, and if they left soon they could still get there in time to put up a cabin. One appealing aspect of Oregon was they had reasonably warm winters, much unlike New England, or even this god-forsaken stretch of mountains. And it rained much of the time in the winter, making it ideal for planting alfalfa, so a farmer could get in two crops. A more traditional crop in the summer, and then alfalfa in the winter.

If they had left this valley now, they could be back in Cheyenne hopefully by August. With any luck, they might be in Oregon by the end of September. Put up a cabin and get in an alfalfa crop. But no, here they still were, and the women had no intentions of leaving.

And so he walked. Whiskey in one hand, gun belt buckled about his hips.

When he went east and began using a different name, he had gotten rid of his revolver. He hadn't worn a gun belt in over ten years. But when Jack McCabe gave him one he had taken from the outlaws who had taken Jessica Brewster, it felt so natural. A little bit of the man he had left behind, the man called Harlan Carter, seemed to come alive inside him again.

He hadn't tasted whiskey in more than ten years either. But it seemed like the next natural step. He had gone to such drastic lengths to keep his daughter from the life he had left behind, and yet now it was all proving futile. He was in the process of losing her, and possibly even his wife. So, why not allow a little whiskey?

A tree grew near the side of the small lake. About the only tree growing on the valley floor. An oak, tall with green leaves stretching out to the sun. He strode through grass as tall as his knees, walking toward the tree.

He stopped maybe a hundred feet from the tree. He faced it. He reached for the pistol in his holster and gave it a look. An old-style Army .44 revolver. Out of production now, replaced by the newer guns that used metallic cartridges. This one had been refit to take cartridges, but it was still inferior to the newer guns. The balance wasn't as good. And the bore had too many years of corrosion eating away at it. Black powder was highly corrosive. Enough of that and the rifling would be damaged, further impeding the gun's accuracy.

He knew a lot about guns. Knowledge he wished he didn't have, because that knowledge came from his years as Harlan Carter. Years he would like to put behind him, and yet was finding he could not.

He had hid from himself behind a plow. But it seems no matter how hard you might try to hide from yourself, you eventually catch up with yourself.

He slid the gun back into the holster, and took a swig of whiskey. It was his fourth or fifth this morning. He wasn't really keeping track. But he could feel the whiskey reaching into him, working its magic, making the pain a little less hurtful. And yet it somehow brought out an anger in him.

He reached for his gun. Harlan Carter had been known for a quick draw. And yet, his fingers fumbled with the handle of the gun and he couldn't quite get a grip on it. Lack of practice. He steadied himself and tried again. This time he got the gun in his hand and brought his arm out to full extension, cocking the gun as he did so. And he fired. And the tree just stood there like nothing had happened.

He had been aiming at a lower branch. He had missed cleanly.

He slid the gun back into the holster and repeated the procedure. Draw, cock and fire. A little bit of wood on the top side of the branch splintered. He had grazed it.

He shook his head with anger at himself. If he had been drawing down on a man, he would now be dead. Even a cowhand with average skill with a gun would have dropped him.

Maybe that would be for the best, he thought, and took another drink of whiskey.

Emily spoke from behind him. "Carter, what on Earth are you doing?"

He turned at the sound of her voice. She was striding through the tall grass toward him, her skirt parting the grass like the bow of a ship cutting through water. Nina was a few feet behind her, doing her best to keep up with her ankle all trussed up in a wooden splint and with a cane in her hand. Age

Brewster had cut the cane from the branch of a tree a day earlier.

"What does it look like I'm doing?" he said.

"Carter, are you drinking? I thought I smelled it on you last night."

Nina said, "Father, it's not like you to drink. I've never seen you take a drink."

He said, "You know nothing about me, little girl."

And he turned and faced the tree again.

"Carter," Emily said.

He ignored her, and drew down on the tree again. Again he missed. Damn, he thought, I can't even outdraw a tree.

Nina hobbled around to face him, driving her cane into the ground angrily as she did so. "Father, I want to know what's going on with you. What do you mean I don't know anything about you?"

"You don't even know my name, little girl. Even when you call me 'Father,' it's a lie."

"Carter," Emily said again.

He slid the pistol back into its holster and began pacing. And he talked. He was generally a man of few words, but whiskey has a way of loosening the tongue and the words flew out of him. He told her how his name was really Harlan Carter. A farm boy from Michigan who had gotten caught up with some guerrilla raiders during the war. They had operated out of Missouri, burning bridges and farms and shooting down farmers who were Confederate sympathizers.

"And something inside me liked it. I hated to admit it, but it was there. A certain thrill when the night exploded in flames and gunfire and chaos."

"Father . . . ," she said quietly.

"After the war, I kept doing what I knew how to do. I couldn't imagine going back to a life behind a plow. So some of the men and me, we started hitting banks and trains and stage coaches in Nebraska and Missouri and Kansas. And we killed. And we stole. And we burned."

Tears were in her eyes. "Father . . ."

Emily said, "Carter, I think that's enough."

But he continued. "But then it happened. You know what happened? I shot me a preacher man. I shot him and killed him. He was a Mexican padre, in Texas. We rode right into his mission. He had gold there. And we took it. And I put a bullet right into his chest and watched him fall to the floor and then stepped right on over him to get the gold cross standing on the altar behind him. And then you know what he did? Layin' there in a pool of his own blood, he looked me right in the eye. Stopped me dead in his tracks. And you know what he said? He said he forgave me."

Harlan let out a bitter laugh and ceased his pacing and looked at Nina. "With his dyin' breath, the sumbitch looked me in the eye and said, 'I forgive you.' "

He resumed his pacing. "I tried to put that behind me. But it stayed with me. It kept comin' back to me in my dreams. That padre, layin' there in that puddle of blood. And he forgave me.

"I got to the point I couldn't do it anymore. We had us a little hideout. An old sod cabin in Kansas. It had been abandoned by some farmer who must've tried to make a go of it but couldn't. I just left the men I rode with. They were layin' around drunk one night. I just saddled up and rode out. Rode east. Ended up in Vermont. Changed my name."

He had stopped pacing, and Emily walked up to him. "And married me."

Nina said, "What did you mean about me being wrong when I called you my father?"

Emily said, "He meant nothing."

Carter looked at his wife. "She should know the truth, Emily."

Emily sighed and looked at her. "I was married once, to a man named True Gallagher. We weren't much older than you. We moved to Vermont where land was available and tried to build a farm, but he got pneumonia one winter and was gone. You were barely a year old. Carter had newly arrived and he married me. And he's been a father to you."

Nina barely whispered the words. "You're not my real father?"

Carter said, "I'm not really anything. I'm

not a real father. Half the time I'm not a real husband."

He looked to Emily. "I've never been able to really reach out to you the way a husband should. I've always been so closed up. In many ways a stranger to you."

"You've carried a lot of pain for a lot of years. I understand that, and so I know not to push. But you've always been a good husband."

He said to Nina, "I've always tried to keep you shielded from the kind of life I led. From the kind of man I was."

Nina said, "You've always been a good father."

"I've tried to be the kind of father I wished I had. But sooner or later, I knew Harlan Carter would catch up to me. And he has."

"How? No one knows."

"Everyone knows. Everyone. Abel Brewster told me the other day he had it figured out. So does Ford. And the McCabes all know."

Her eyes widened with surprise. "Jack knows?"

"Oh, yeah. His father figured it out. His father's a gunhawk just like I was. Just like I *am.* Takes one to know one. He could tell by the look in my eye. It was just a matter of time for him to put two-and-two together. And his boys all know. That boy, Jack, he's just like me. He might not be exactly like I am, but it's close enough.

"A life with him will put you in danger. His mother was killed by a bullet meant for his father. I don't want you to have to live that kind of life."

"But I love him."

"Honey," he shook his head sadly. "You're young. You don't know what love is."

It dawned on her. "That's why you wanted us to leave for Oregon."

He nodded. "There's still time."

"But don't you see, Father? We'll still be running. And then when someone there figures it out, what do we do? Run some more? Where? Canada? Alaska? Sooner or later we'll run out of places to run to."

He shook his head.

"Carter," Emily said, "we can't keep running forever. This is good land. You've said yourself the dirt here is some of the best you've seen. And the neighbors are good people."

"They know who I am, Em. It's just a matter of time before the law comes for me. And it'll be the gallows."

"You're not that man anymore."

He touched a hand to the side of her face, letting the fingers trail along her cheekbone. "The law won't see it that way. And, really, I am. Deep down, I am. I can run from myself for a while, but eventually you can't run no more."

Nina said, "Jack won't tell. I know he won't.

And I don't believe his family will, either."

He shook his head. "You're asking me to trust my entire family's well-being to a group of people who are gunhawks themselves. Not much better than I was. You can bet Johnny McCabe couldn't even tell you the number of men he has killed. And even though that boy, Jack, may have been off at school in the east, you can see it in his eye. And the way he carries that gun."

"He's a man of honor. All of the McCabe men are. And Bree saved my life."

He shook his head sadly. "There ain't no honor in killin'. Men of the gun are really all the same, for the most part."

"Carter," Emily said, "come back to the camp. Put the whiskey down. We can have some coffee and talk this out. Decide what to do."

"No need, Em. I've given it all I could. Protected you both from my past and that kind of life all I can. And now it's all caught up with me."

He turned and started to walk away, the bottle of whiskey still in his left hand.

"Father," Nina said, and began to hobble after him.

"No," Emily caught her arm. "Let him go. Sometimes a man needs to be alone."

"Mother . . ."

"In some ways, I think he has really always been alone."

They stood, the wind rippling their skirts, watching Harlan Carter walk away. His head down, his shoulders bent. A bottle of whiskey in one hand, a gunbelt buckled about his waist. Emily reached out and took her daughter's hand.

Harlan Carter wandered. He was angry. He was saddened. He would take a pull from the whiskey bottle and he kept on wandering.

At the edge of the valley floor he came to the woods. Mostly pines, standing tall. He was at the opposite side of the valley from the pass leading to the town. This was good. He wanted to be alone. He didn't need any rider passing by on his way to town.

He wandered through the woods. He took another drink of whiskey. He walked, and he cursed the name of Jack McCabe. If not for meeting him back in Cheyenne — if not for Abel Brewster insisting they ask him to come along as their guide — then Carter Harding would not have been exposed as Harlan Carter. He wouldn't be on the verge of seeing his daughter immersed into the very life he had tried to protect her from. And he wouldn't be facing a noose. Sure, Brewster knew who he was, and apparently Ford did, but Harding didn't think he had to be concerned about them.

He wandered through the woods. Sweat was soaking his hair and his shirt.

He realized he wasn't feeling well. His legs were wobbly and he felt a little light headed. Dehydration. He needed water. It was hot out, and the only fluids he had taken in for the past couple of hours were from the whiskey bottle.

He staggered down a slope, slipping a little on the pine straw but managing to keep his footing. At the bottom was a small stream, barely more than a long, thin puddle moving along between rocks. He didn't care. It was wet. He knelt down and with his hands he scooped water into his mouth.

It was a little brackish. Only a few inches deep, and the bottom of the stream was covered by brown pine needles.

He scooped a few mouthfuls, the water spilling down over his beard and onto his shirt. He then took a chug from the whiskey bottle to cover the taste of the water, and pushed to his feet and continued on.

He was steadier, now. The light headedness was gone and his legs felt stronger. He walked aimlessly, following a downhill slope. He didn't realize he had changed direction, but he came back out onto the long grassy meadow that covered the floor of the valley.

His vision was a little blurry. The heat, maybe. And the whiskey. He looked out from the edge of the woods, surveying the scene before him, but realized he couldn't see it all that well.

He was feeling tired, suddenly. Drowsy. He realized he was standing by a tall pine at the edge of the forest, and he was in the shade. He sat down and leaned his back against the tree. It was actually surprisingly comfortable. He drifted off.

He awoke sometime later. He had no pocket watch. He glanced up at the sun and saw it was somewhere between its zenith and the western horizon. Mid afternoon, maybe. He had been gone for hours. He didn't really care. Emily and Nina didn't need him anymore.

His vision was a little clearer now, and he realized he could see a house from where he was. It was a ways in the distance. Half a mile, maybe. Made of logs, and with he could see smoke rising from a stone chimney. A barn stood in front of the house, and another long building that was one floor high. A bunkhouse, maybe.

Must be the McCabe spread, he figured. And there, he would find the source of his problems. The one who had ruined his life. The boy, Jack.

He pushed himself to his feet and started through the tall grass. He took another pull of the whiskey bottle as he walked along. He then drew his gun and checked the loads. He had done some target shooting this morning and he had no cartridges on him. His gun-

483

belt had no loops for cartridges. But there were two shots left in his gun. One was all he would need.

35

Jack and Dusty rode up to the corral and swung out of the saddle in front of the corral. Sweat was streaking the back of Jack's shirt from under his vest. Dusty wore no vest, and his shirt was visibly wet down the back. They had taken the day to ride through another set of ridges, looking for tracks. Josh had intended to join them, but Dusty talked him out of it. Josh and Dusty were leaving for the line cabin in the morning to finish up rounding up any strays, and Dusty thought Josh should spend the day with Temperance. He and Dusty would probably be gone three or four days.

Jack had volunteered to go too, but Josh had said, "No need for that. You're here for a vacation, not to work. Spend some time with Aunt Ginny and Bree, or seeing your girl."

Fred had heard the hoofbeats as they rode in, and was stepping out of the barn. "See anything?"

Jack shook his head. "A few bear tracks. We

scared up an elk but we couldn't get a shot at him. No signs of riders, though."

Fred glanced toward the ridge to the west. There were dark clouds rising like a mountain floating in the sky. "Looks like rain, anyway. Any tracks that might be there will be washed away by morning. Want me to take care of these horses?"

"If you don't mind," Dusty said.

Fred led the horses away. Jack walked over to a water trough and pulled his hat off and dipped it deep in the water, and then held it up and let it flow down over his head like a small waterfall. He dipped his hat again, when something caught his eye. "What's this?"

It was an empty whiskey bottle, lying on its side by the water trough. He picked it up, and looked at Dusty.

Dusty's hat was off and he had been about to dump water over himself, too. "Who's could that be? Pa doesn't allow any drinking on the job."

Then they heard the voice of Harlan Carter from behind them. "Don't neither of you move. I got a gun trained on you, and I still remember how to use it."

Jack said, "Carter. Nice of you to come pay us a visit."

"Quiet your tongue, boy. You done caused me enough trouble. I could just shoot you down now, for all you done."

"Does Nina know you're here?"

"Don't matter no more. I lost her."

Dusty said, "Look, Carter, you shoot us down and you're gonna be in a world of trouble. Do you really want Johnny McCabe on your trail? Or our brother Josh?"

Fred, however, had stepped into the barn but could hear the exchange. He pulled a Winchester from one of the boys' saddles. He jacked the lever very slowly, chambering a round quietly so the sound wouldn't carry, then he stepped out of the barn and brought the rifle to his shoulder and leveled it at Carter.

"Drop that gun," Fred said. "I got me a Winchester here. It'll blow a whole the size of a silver dollar in you from this distance. I may not be a big, bad gunhawk like you, but if you think I can't plug you from here before you can fire that gun, you got another thing comin'."

Jack turned to face Carter. "Do you really want it like this? An exchange of gunfire? You might get me, but Fred and Dusty will riddle you with holes."

Carter said, "He don't even have his gun out."

"You've never seen him draw." Not that Jack had, either, but he had heard the stories.

"So, you got me. Now what? Send for the territorial marshal?"

Jack unbuckled his gunbelt. "You've been

487

wanting a piece of me for a while. Now's your chance. Let's settle this like men. Face-to-face."

"With our fists?"

"What — are you afraid, old man?"

Carter's shirt was soaked with dirt and sweat. His hair was wet and plastered to his skull, partly from sweat and partly from dunking his head in the water trough, when he had set down his whiskey bottle. From where he was standing, Jack guessed he had been hiding in the tack shed, waiting for Jack. The tack room was a small lean-to built to the side of the barn with a doorway that opened to the outside, but another that opened into the barn.

Carter holstered his pistol, and unbuckled the gunbelt, letting it fall to the ground.

Jack said to Dusty and Fred, "Don't either of you interfere. This is between Carter and me."

"That's right," Carter said, balling his hands into fists. "This has been a long time comin'."

Dusty leaned back on the fence. "Oh, I ain't gonna interfere. I'm gonna enjoy this."

Fred lowered his rifle and walked over to Dusty, and leaned one elbow against the top rail. "Too bad Hunter's not here. He always enjoys a good scrappin'."

Jack and Carter circled each other. Carter stood a good four inches taller, with a lean, hard muscled body. Jack's frame was more compact, but with cleanly defined muscle from his boxing and his time on the rowing team.

Carter said, "I fought men to the death before you were even born, boy. You're goin' down."

Jack was eyeing Carter warily, but he couldn't help a grin forming. He had to admit, he liked this. "I hear the talk, old man. But I'm not seeing any results."

Carter then charged, swinging his fist at Jack's head with the same motion. Jack ducked and swung a hard hook into Carter's midsection. Carter's stomach was solid muscle, but Jack threw his own hard muscle into it, grunting with the effort, and Carter's own momentum helped.

Carter went down to one knee, one arm wrapped around his stomach, and the other hand flat on the ground. He huffed for air.

"You're stronger than you look, boy."

Jack stayed a few feet back, bouncing a little from one foot to the other. He often did this in the ring. He found if he was already in motion, he could react to his opponent better than if he was standing flat-footed.

"You done?" Jack said.

"I don't know. I'm a lot older'n the last time I did this."

Jack waited. Carter huffed for air. Jack danced back and forth on his feet. Carter shook his head defeatedly, and Jack stopped dancing.

Carter then sprang from his kneeling position directly at Jack and wrapped his arms around Jack's chest and lifted and threw. Jack came to a sliding stop in the dirt. Before he could begin to rise, Carter was on him, grabbing him by the shirt and pulling him to his feet. His shirt tore and some of the material came loose in Carter's grip.

Carter then drove a right hook into the side of Jack's jaw. Jack heard a crunching sound and saw black as his feet went flying out from under him and he landed hard on the ground.

Carter then walked warily around Jack while Jack blinked his eyes. Black spots were floating about. The side of his face felt numb.

Carter stopped and looked down at Jack. Carter said, "I'm gonna enjoy this."

And Carter drove a foot down at Jack. However, Jack was in motion, lifting his knee and driving a foot up and into Carter's groin.

Carter staggered back, and then dropped to one knee again. Jack rose to his feet, staggered a bit, and then held his balance.

Carter looked at him with hatred, but some of the fire was gone.

Jack said, "Old Shoshone trick. They taught my Pa how to fight. He taught me."

"It'll take more than tricks to handle me, boy."

Carter rose to his feet, and they charged at

each other.

Carter swung a fist, and Jack ducked. Jack drove one into Carter's midsection. Carter wrapped his arms around Jack and lifted him from the ground, but Jack had one arm free and drove a fist into Carter's face. The fist caught his nose, but Carter wouldn't release the grip. Jack struck again and caught him in the eye. This time, Carter let go.

Jack stood with his feet far apart and drove punch after punch into Carter's midsection. Carter staggered back a bit, then came in for a punch but Jack ducked, and then stepped in with more punches to the midsection.

Dusty said conversationally to Fred, "This is where a smaller man has the advantage. In close like that. Jack knows what he's doin'."

Fred nodded. "He was taught by the best."

Blood was streaming down Carter's nose, and one eye had swollen shut. Jack added to his woes by driving an uppercut into his jaw. Carter's knees buckled and he went down.

He rose to his hands and knees, his head hanging. He was coughing, and he spit a little blood. He wasn't faking this time.

He tried to get to his feet, but couldn't. He fell back to sit in the dirt. Blood was streaming down over his chin onto his shirt. He tried to say something, but only coughed some more.

"All right," Dusty said, stepping in between them. "You're both done."

Harding rose to his knees, and Fred grabbed him by one arm and helped pull him to his feet. Harding staggered back a couple of steps, but managed not to fall over. Fred handed him a bandanna that he held to his nose.

Fred said, "We should get you home."

"I can get myself home."

"You can hardly walk, and it's almost two miles to your camp. I'm gonna fetch a horse for you."

Harding didn't say no.

"Come on," Dusty said to Jack. "Let's get in the house and get you cleaned up."

Jack started toward the house with Dusty. He had taken a serious punch to the side of his jaw, and he felt a little unsteady. Maybe a concussion. He thought he maybe should go into town and see Granny Tate. It wouldn't hurt to have her look at his shoulder, either. It hadn't been bothering him at all for a while, but now he could feel it stiffening up a little. And it was hurting to move his jaw.

He said, "The worst part of all this will be facing Aunt Ginny."

Dusty shook his head. "The worst part of all of this will be explaining to your girl how you beat the hell out of her father."

36

Harlan Carter hadn't ridden a horse since he became a farmer, but he found it all came back to him and despite his injuries he was able to keep from falling out of the saddle. His head was pounding and he wasn't sure how much of it was from the whiskey, and how much from the pounding Jack McCabe had given him.

He hated to take the horse offered to him by the McCabe's wrangler. He hated to take anything from those people. But there was no way he could have made it back to the camp, as beaten up as he was.

He had taken numerous punches to the stomach and ribs — more than he could count, and he felt every one of them as he swung out of the saddle.

It was near dark. Nina had been in the tent and had heard the horse approaching. She stepped out and saw him half-fall out of the saddle. She screamed, "Father!" and went to him, managing a hobbling run.

Emily had been at the cookfire, maybe twenty yards behind the tent, focused on roasting a haunch of venison. Age Brewster had gone hunting that afternoon, and returned with a large buck, and the Brewsters shared the meat with everyone. Emily hadn't heard the horse approaching, but she heard her daughter scream and looked over at the sound.

"Carter," she said, and left the fire and went running over.

Carter stood, wavering a bit, one arm wrapped about his ribs. The blood had stopped leaking from his nose, but his shirt was stained with it. Emily didn't know if he had been shot, or what had happened to him.

Even though Nina needed a cane to help her get along on her sprained ankle, she sidled up to her father and pulled his arm about her shoulders to try to help him stand.

"Father," she said. "What happened?"

"Wasn't sure you'd want to call me that, after you knew the truth."

"Come on. Let's get you sitting down."

The two of them started a hobble toward the cook fire. Emily took his other arm, and they got him to one of the wooden chairs they had brought from their farm back east.

Emily grabbed a bucket of water and a cloth, and began cleaning his face.

Nina said to him, "I'll always call you *Father.* You are my father, and always have been.

Maybe you weren't there when I was born, but you've always tried to give Mother and me the best you could. Now that I know the truth, and what you have been trying to protect me from, I love you even more."

He gave her a long look. "I thought I had lost you."

"Not ever."

She wrapped her arms around him in a hug, but he winced from the pain in his ribs and she pulled back.

"What happened?" Nina said. "Were you shot?"

"No." He shook his head with an embarrassed smile. "I got into a fight."

"A fight?"

He nodded. "At my age."

"Who on Earth with?"

He looked at Nina. "With your boyfriend."

Nina said, "Jack?"

He nodded and chuckled. "For a college boy, he packs a whale of a punch."

Nina said, "Let me get this straight. You got into a fight with Jack?"

He nodded. "It's my fault. I have to admit. I went over there lookin' for trouble."

Nina wasn't pleased. "It doesn't matter. You're my father. It takes two to fight."

Brewster and Age came walking over.

"I heard you call out," he said to Emily. "Is everything all right?"

Then he saw Harding, and said, "Good

Lord, man, you look like you were run over by a team of horses."

"Feel like it, too."

Carter told what happened. "The only consolation I have is I left him in almost as bad condition."

Emily cleaned the cut on his face made by Jack's fist. He then turned and spit some blood. He said, "I cut my tongue, on one of his fists. I will say this for the boy — he's a scrapper. I've met some real hardcases in my time, but he could hold his own with any of 'em."

Brewster said, "Are you still thinking of lighting out for Oregon?"

Carter said, "I'd like to, but the women like it here."

Emily said to Brewster, "You and Mildred are here. And the Fords. And we do have good neighbors. There are good people in town.

Brewster said, "Harding, you don't have to go to Oregon. We all want you and your family to stay here."

Carter said, "It's only a matter of time before they send a territorial marshal for me. I'm a really bad man, Abel. There's wanted rewards offered for me in three states."

"What proof do they have? If someone sends for a marshal, all we have to say is you're Carter Harding. From Vermont. Whoever thinks you're Harlan Carter is wrong. I

496

can say I've known you all my life, back in Vermont. I've talked to Ford about it, and he's willing to say the same thing."

Carter shook his head. "I hate to ask people to lie for me."

"You're not asking. And besides, it's not entirely a lie. You're not Harlan Carter. Not anymore. You forget, Harding, I've been in the war. I've seen men kill. I've seen men who like to kill. And I've done some killing. The look in your eye is not the look of a man who is a killer. Maybe you've killed. But that's all behind you, now. I can look anyone right in the eye and tell them honestly that you're not Harlan Carter."

Carter gave him a long look. "I don't know what to say."

"It's called having friends."

"I guess . . ." He hesitated, partly from the emotion welling up in him, and partly because his wounded tongue and his bruised up ribs made it kind of painful to talk, "I guess I've just seen myself as one man against the world for so long, I've kind of forgotten what it means to have friends."

Brewster smiled. "Well, get used to it."

"I made a real fool of myself, over these past few days."

Brewster nodded. "We all do, from time to time. It's called being human."

Emily said, "Does this mean you're staying?"

497

Carter nodded, and managed a smile. "I couldn't go nowhere without you and Nina. You two are my life."

Nina had stepped away from them while they talked. She was leaning on her cane. She was glad her father was all right, but she was also furious. But not furious at him.

"Age," she said. "Come morning, can you hitch up a team and drive me over to the McCabe house?"

"Sure," he said, questioningly.

Carter heard her and looked over at her, but before he could say anything, she said, "I need to talk with Jack. I have a lot of questions, and he'd better have some answers. And I don't want to hear any sass from you."

Carter looked at Emily and said, "Well, I guess I've just been told what-for."

Emily said, "Maybe someone should have a long time ago."

He gave a nod. "Maybe so. Can you forgive one man's foolishness?"

She couldn't help but smile. "Carter, I think I could forgive you anything."

She leaned in for a kiss which he started to return, but then pulled back. He found his teeth also hurt from the uppercut punch Jack had given him, and thought maybe one had been broken off. Kissing hurt awful. He said, "Easy woman, I've had me a hard day."

Emily couldn't help but laugh.

■ ■ ■ ■

The following morning, Fred saddled three horses and had them waiting by the corral. One of them was Rabbit. One was a buckskin Dusty preferred, and one was a bay with two white stockings that Jack preferred.

The three brothers stepped out from the kitchen door. All three had their guns in place and tied down, and sombreros over their heads.

Josh said, "I was gonna ride out to the line shack today, but maybe I should hold off."

"No," Dusty said. "I'll ride along with the fighter, here, to make sure he gets to town. I'll ride out and join you afterward."

"Funny, funny," Jack said. "I can ride into town all by myself. I've been taking care of myself for years."

"Well," Dusty said, "you sure took care of Harlan Carter yesterday."

The side of Jack's face was purple and swollen, and he couldn't open his mouth more than a couple inches. He was on his way to Granny Tate's. He had expected the tongue-lashing he would have gotten from Aunt Ginny to be worse than the fight itself, but all she did was look at him disappointedly, and then walk away. He found that was even worse than the tongue-lashing he had been expecting.

He said to Dusty, "I'm serious. I'll be all right. Go on out with Josh. I can ride into town myself."

Dusty was a little hesitant, but then gave a sigh of resignation. He was about to say, *well, all right,* but then he heard the clatter of iron-shod hooves and steel rimmed wheels on the wooden bridge in the distance.

The barn blocked their view of the trail down to the bridge, so he said, "Sounds like we might have company."

They waited until the wagon pulled into view. It was Age Brewster holding the reins, and Nina was on the seat beside him.

Josh said, "Well, looks like we're not needed here."

He and Dusty both swung into their saddles as Age gave the reins a tug and called out, "Whoa," to the team. Once the wagon was stopped, he reached up with one foot and pushed down on the brake.

"Good mornin', Miss Nina," Josh said, reaching up with one hand to touch the brim of his hat.

"Miss Nina," Dusty said, doing the same.

Josh said, "We were just riding out."

She said, "Good morning, boys. Don't let me keep you. I was just here to talk to Jack."

Dusty said to Jack, "We'll see you in a couple days. Three at the most."

And they turned and rode off.

Nina started climbing down from the

wagon. Jack hurried over to offer a hand for assistance. Not that a woman couldn't climb down from a wagon herself, but chivalry required him to offer a hand, which he did. She accepted the hand.

He leaned in for a kiss. She didn't do the same. He stepped back, thinking, *Uh-oh.*

"We need to talk," she said.

Age said, "I'll just wait right here."

He wasn't just being polite. He really wanted to be nowhere near the two of them right now, considering how riled Nina was.

"Come on," Jack said. "Let's walk."

He offered his hand. She didn't take it.

They started off, away from the corral and the house.

He said, "I was just heading into town to see Granny Tate. My jaw's so bruised up I want to make sure it's not broken. And I think I might have a concussion."

She was still using a cane, but her ankle was no longer trussed up. She had pulled a shoe on over her foot.

He said, "I see you've taken the splint off of your ankle."

"My ankle isn't the issue."

Now he knew she was angry. He decided it might be best to just be silent and give her the time she needed to explain what was going on.

She said, "I can't believe you."

He nodded. "Fighting with your father. I

know. I'm so sorry. I let my temper get the best of me. But, in all fairness, he did come looking for a fight. He actually was holding a gun on Dusty and me at one point."

"You don't see, do you?"

Now he was confused. "I guess not."

"My father sat up with Mother and me into the night, telling us step-for-step what happened. He was wrong, and he knows it. But so were you. You didn't have to fight. You could have refused."

"I know. And I'm so sorry. I have my father's temper, and sometimes it gets the best of me."

"I can't believe you knew all along."

He was even more confused. "I knew?"

"You knew all along, but you didn't tell me. I can't believe you didn't share that kind of knowledge."

Now he knew what she was talking about. "He told you."

"Yes, he told me. But what I don't understand is why you didn't tell me."

He shrugged. "I guess I was waiting for the right time."

"The right time?" she stopped walking and faced him. "The right time to tell me something that important? That big? The right time was as soon as you found out. Jack," she sighed with frustration and looked away for a moment, gathering her thoughts, and then looked back to him, "how can we even hope to build a life together if you can sit on knowledge like that and don't even share it?

"According to my father, you knew back when we were on the trail. He talked to your father about it days before we even arrived in town. And from what your father said, my father gathered he had figured it out before that. Which means you knew, too. When did you find out?"

"My father told me who he suspected your father was back at the way station."

"So, you knew for the past few weeks."

He nodded a little sheepishly. "Yes. So it seems."

She turned away. "I thought I knew you."

"Look at it from my perspective. If I had told you, it might have looked like I was trying to drive a wedge between the two of you. Especially considering how he felt about me."

"All right. Granted. I guess maybe I can see that."

She stood still for a moment, looking off at the trees.

"So," he said, "are we all right?"

"I don't know." She turned to face him. "Jack, what you did. Fighting my father. It's no small thing. It's made me see things in a little different light, I guess. It's made me think my father might be right."

"Right? About what? He's not right about anything."

"Jack, you're a gunfighter. I've heard you

use the word *gunhawk*. I think I understand what that means now. It's a certain way of doing things. Of approaching life."

"I am so sorry about fighting your father. I know it was wrong. I think a small part of me knew it then, too."

"And yet, you did it."

He was silent. He didn't know what to say.

"It's not a case of forgiveness, Jack. I do forgive you. But it's a case of no longer being sure about you."

"Nina . . ." Now he felt his own ire rising a bit. "It was a lack of judgment on my part. I have already apologized. It doesn't affect how I feel about you."

"But it does affect who you are. You're a man of violence. You wear that gun on your leg like it's somehow a badge of honor. You see fighting as an end to a means. When my father confronted you, you knew he had been drinking. Fighting him shouldn't even have occurred to you."

He nodded. "Yes. I was wrong. And I've said I was sorry."

"It's not a case of forgiving you."

Despite his ire, he had to admit he was confused again. "Then, what is it?"

She said, "I've thought about this long into the night. I sat up by the fire just thinking. It's hard to say this, but I think we need some time apart."

Now he was really getting angry, but he

tried to keep his voice to an even level because he loved her. "Are you telling me you've never done anything wrong?"

"It's not that I haven't made mistakes. We all do. But do I want to build my life with a man of violence? Do I want him to be the father of my children?"

"A man of violence."

She nodded.

"A gunhawk," he said.

She nodded again. "I guess what I'm saying is I need time. I have to think."

"I don't see what there is to think about. Your father is Harlan Carter. A wanted outlaw. A killer. A gunhawk, if you want to use that word, and much worse than I've ever been. I've never had my name on a reward poster."

She shook her head. "He's my father, Jack. He's always been there for me. Maybe the man you describe is what he once was. But the only man I've ever known him to be is strong and sometimes stern, yes. And sometimes too closed-up for his own good. But everything he did was to protect Mother and me. He worked hard to build a home for us. He always put us first. He's a good man, Jack."

"So it's okay for him to see me as no-good, but I have to accept him as a good man?"

She shook her head. "Don't come see me, Jack. I need some time away."

He nodded. Part of him wanted to plead with her not to do this, but part of him wanted to simply turn and walk away. His temper versus his love for her. And at the moment he felt like it was about to tear him in two.

"So, you're going to be living just two miles away, building a farm, and I'm not allowed to come visit?"

She nodded. "For now."

His turn to look away. He wanted to cry. He wanted to shout with rage. He had never felt this way before.

She said, "I need to go home, now."

He nodded, and almost said, *Yes you do.* But he caught his tongue before it could slip out. It would be too easy to say something he might later regret. He walked her back to the wagon.

Fred was in the corral, leaning against the fence and chatting with Age. He stepped away as he saw Jack and Nina returning. She began to climb back up and into the wagon. Jack offered her his hand, but she ignored it.

"Please take me home," she said to Age.

Age looked like he wanted to crawl away under a rock somewhere. He raised his brows in a sort of shrug at Jack, then disengaged the brake and clicked the team forward and turned them around, and headed away along the trail.

Jack pulled his horse's rein free of the corral and swung up and into the saddle.

Fred said, "Are you all right?"

"No," Jack said simply, and kicked the horse into a gallop toward town.

37

Jack's bruised face healed slowly, but it did heal. Granny Tate had told him she didn't think it was broken. And she found his shoulder was healing well. The bullet wound had left a furrowed scar that she said would never go away, but the force of the bullet plus landing hard on it when he fell after being shot apparently wrenched the shoulder. Such a thing can be a long time healing fully.

He never told the family the details of his conversation with Nina, only that she wasn't seeing him anymore. Aunt Ginny gently touched his arm but said nothing. Temperance looked at him sadly but also said nothing.

Bree, however, had less patience for subtlety. She said to him, "I'm not going to ask what happened, because that's for you tell if and when you're ready. But I just need to know if you're all right?"

"I suppose I will be," he said. "We're McCabes. We're survivors, right?"

She nodded, "That's one thing we are."

He saddled up the next morning, and rode off into the hills. He never felt more at home anywhere in the world than when he was riding through these hills. Letting his horse find its way through the pine trees, gradually climbing a slope. He hadn't been riding anywhere in particular, but he found himself on the rocky cliff where Pa used to stand and look off at the valley during that year he wintered here with the Shoshone, before he married Ma. Jack dismounted and loosened the cinch and let the horse graze, as a little grass grew near the cliff. And he stood and simply looked off toward the distance.

One ridge across the valley gently declined and then melded into the next. They were covered with pine. Overhead, a chicken hawk glided about in the wind.

Beneath the cliff was a grassy slope that dropped sharply down before leveling off a little. A couple hundred feet down he saw a grizzly lumbering its way along. The bear was no threat to him. If it started working its way up the hill, he would just get his horse and continue along.

He wondered how it felt back years ago, when Pa had stood here looking off at this very scenery. Back when the only people within a hundred miles were the Shoshones who had set their village up on the valley floor. From what Pa had said, it wasn't far from the lake. Not far from where Nina and the other settlers now were.

The following day, he did the same thing. Saddled up and rode, with no particular destination in mind. Around noon he shot a rabbit, and built a small fire from a deadfall and roasted the animal and ate his lunch.

That evening, Josh and Dusty returned from the line cabin, and Jack gave them the news. "I might have won that fight, but Harlan Carter won the war. He has his daughter, and I'm out of his life."

Josh said, "I'm not so sure I'm comfortable with the thought of an outlaw the caliber of Harlan Carter living this close to the ranch."

He rode out the next morning. Aunt Ginny said to Dusty, "I don't like the idea of him just riding out there, alone."

Dusty said, "Sometimes a man just needs to be alone. Work things out for himself."

Jack had been intending to simply ride the ridges again, but found himself at Hunter's. As he stood at the bar with a glass of whiskey in front of him, finding this stuff compared poorly to Kentucky bourbon, he found himself missing Darby for the first time since leaving school. Maybe it was time to write him a letter. Explain everything that had happened. One person he had always been able to talk to was Darby.

"Hunter, do you have a pen and paper? I'd like to write a letter."

Hunter got him a couple sheets of paper from the back room he used as a bedroom, and a pen and bottle of ink. Jack sat down at a table with his glass of whiskey and put pen to paper. At first he didn't know how to begin, but once he had, he found the words flowed. He told of how it felt to be home, and how he had found the girl of his dreams, and then lost her. And how when his visit was finished here, he didn't know where he was going.

Darby had never been one to take much seriously. He had always said Jack took things way too seriously, which was why they made such a good team. Maybe old Darby was right.

When it was finished, Hunter found an envelope and Jack addressed it to Darby Yates, Cooperstown, New York. Jack figured the way the mail moved, Darby should get the letter in maybe three weeks.

Jack said to Hunter, "Will you make sure to put this letter on the next stage?"

Hunter nodded. "It's due in tomorrow. I'll make sure."

Hunter set the letter behind the bar, then returned with a glass and the whiskey bottle. He set the glass in front of him and filled it, then refilled Jack's glass.

"I can tell the look," Hunter said. "Trouble with your girl."

Jack looked at him with surprise. "Am I that

easy to read?"

Hunter nodded with a small grin. "Anyone who's been there knows the look. I had me a girl once. A couple different ones, over the years. And yet here I am. Alone, running this saloon. Believe me, I know the look."

Hunter's saloon didn't have swinging doors like some of the establishments in bigger towns like Bozeman or Virginia City did, so he just left his door open so business could walk in. He heard footsteps at the doorway. "Got me a customer. Be right back."

Jack sort of half-interestedly watched the big man walk across the floor to the bar.

"Welcome to Hunter's," Hunter said. "What can I get you?"

It was a Tuesday afternoon. The town that had been so alive on the Fourth was now almost dead. Jack, Hunter and the new customer were the only three in the barroom.

Jack idly thought he recognized the man. Black suit jacket, a checkered tie. He wore a short-brimmed black hat, and a gun on his hip. The man had a black mustache that covered his upper lip, and his jaw was gray with a few days' worth of whiskers.

"You Hunter?" the man asked.

"That I am." Hunter was stepping behind the bar. "What can I get you?"

Then, Jack recognized the man. He was the gambler from the night of the Fourth. The one who had been in the card game and was accused of cheating, and pulled a derringer on the man accusing him, which had sent the barroom exploding into a brawl that almost tore apart the place.

As Jack was realizing he knew him, the gambler pulled his pistol. The gambler said, "I'll tell you what you can give me. I had two hundred and twenty dollars worth of winnings on the table on the night of the Fourth, before all hell broke loose. That's a lot of money. I'm here for it."

It was indeed a lot of money, Jack thought, especially out here on the frontier. Some ranches paid their cowhands twelve dollars a month and keep. Two hundred and twenty dollars was almost two years' pay.

Hunter said, "I'm not looking for trouble. But your money's gone. There was money all over the floor and everyone was grabbing at it. No way to tell whose money it was, or where it went."

"Well, now, that's your problem, not mine. I want two hundred and twenty dollars. And I want it now."

Jack rose to his feet, and the gambler swung his gun toward him. "Hold it right there, cowboy. Don't make a move, or I'll cut you down."

Jack said, "Takes a brave man to come in here at gunpoint and start giving orders. Put that gun away and let's see how brave you are."

Jack still had his glass in his hand. It was in his left hand, so his right was free to go for his gun.

The gambler walked toward him, his gun aimed at a point between Jack's eyes. "How good do you think you are with that gun, cowboy? I see how you wear it. Low and tied down. Do you think you can draw that gun before I can shoot? What kind of odds do you think you have?"

Hunter said, "Your gripe's with me, not him."

The man turned to look at Hunter. "If I was you, big man, I'd be getting me my money."

Jack tossed his drink into the man's face. Jack had gotten a face full of whiskey, once. Back at school, too drunk to walk steadily, he had fallen with a glass of bourbon in his hand. He had landed on the floor, and the bourbon in his eyes. He didn't forget it. And he was not surprised when the man screamed and took a step back, clawing at his face with his free hand.

Jack reached down and grabbed the table by the edge with both hands and flipped it over on the gambler, who went down under it. His gun fired, the bullet tearing into the table.

Jack then pulled the table away and landed with astride the gambler. With one hand he grabbed the gambler's gunhand by the wrist, and he drove the other fist into his face. Hard. He put his shoulders into it, using the muscle he had gained rowing and boxing. He pulled his fist back and let it go again. A second punch was all that was needed, and the gambler went limp.

Jack rose to his feet, and pulled the gun from his grip.

Jack said to Hunter, "We don't have a jail here, do we?"

Hunter shook his head. "Franklin's got a tool shed, but that's about it."

Franklin, almost on cue, came running in. "I saw that man ride in. I thought he looked like he was no-good, and then I heard the gun go off."

The gambler was stirring, and rolling over. He would be awake in a few moments, Jack thought. But it would be his turn for a concussion.

Hunter came over and Jack handed him the gambler's pistol, and then reached into the man's coat and vest for any papers that might identify him. He found none.

The gambler groaned a bit, then tried to sit up.

"What's your name?" Jack said.

The gambler didn't answer.

"All right. Then," he looked at Franklin, "if we could borrow your tool shed. You might want to empty out anything sharp like saws."

"I'll be just a minute," and Franklin hur-

515

ried out.

The gambler said, "You're gonna lock me in a tool shed?"

"Best jail we got," Jack said. "We'll be sending for the territorial marshal in the morning. Hopefully you won't have to sit in there more than a week."

"That ain't humane."

"Best we got. You should have thought of that before you came in here trying to rob the place."

"I wasn't trying to rob anyone. Just trying to get what's mine."

"Tell it to the judge." Jack grabbed him by the arm and pulled him to his feet. "Let's move."

Once he was locked in the shed, Franklin and Jack and Hunter reconvened at Hunter's for a cold beer.

Franklin said, "This is exactly what I've been saying. We need a lawman. You could have been killed, Hunter."

Shapleigh stepped in, and joined them. He asked what the fracas had been about, and they told him.

"I fully agree, Charlie," he said to Franklin. "We need to hire some sort of lawman for our town. You saw how wild things got the night of the Fourth. They get fairly wild almost every Saturday night. Especially the Saturday after the cowhands all get paid."

Hunter said to Jack, "How long do you

really think we can keep him in a tool shed?"

Jack shrugged. "Not long, I wouldn't think. The ground's not all that hard. He will probably dig himself out tonight. Besides, I don't even know where he would have been taken for court. There's no circuit judge who comes through here."

"Bozeman, I suppose."

Shapleigh said, "This place is growing. Mark my words. If we're going to attract the right kind of people here — more people like those settlers down in the valley — then we're going to have to have some sort of way of enforcing law and keeping the peace."

Come morning, Jack sat down to a plate of steak and eggs. It was Bree's turn to fix breakfast, for which he was grateful. Not that Temperance didn't cook well, but Bree did a little something with the steak that made it extra good.

She sat beside Josh at the table. Conversation drifted casually about as they ate, but when Josh and Temperance thought no one was looking, they would steal a glance at each other. *Just the way Nina and I were,* Jack thought.

He started thinking maybe it was time he cut his visit here short. He had told them he would be here until the end of July, but he was suddenly feeling a restlessness.

Dusty said, "Tomorrow's Saturday. Think

it'll be wild in town?"

"Could be," Josh said. "The Bar W pays on the third Saturday of the month. Their hands'll be in, shooting up the place."

"Nothing Hunter can't handle, I suppose."

Josh cracked a grin. "Well, maybe we should ride in. Just to check things out."

Jack said nothing. His steak and eggs were untouched.

Aunt Ginny said, "Are you not hungry this morning, Jackson?"

"No, for some reason I'm not," he said, rising to his feet. "If you'll all excuse me, I'll take my coffee on the porch."

With his coffee cup in hand, he strode from the room.

"What's wrong with him?" Bree said.

"I don't know," Aunt Ginny said, staring after him. "He has not seemed quite his normal self to me since he got home."

Josh said, "Could just be Nina. I remember how hard it was for you," he looked over at Dusty, "when we couldn't find Haley last winter, in Oregon."

Dusty nodded. "It still is hard."

"Maybe," Aunt Ginny said. "But he's seemed somehow different since he got home."

She stood, and with her tea cup in hand, she said, "Maybe it's time I had a talk with him."

Dusty said, "With all due respect, sometimes a man just needs to be by himself. To work things out."

She gave him a look that told him she was suddenly aware that he knew more than he was letting on. He found it uncanny how this woman could seem to look inside your mind.

She said, "Excuse me," and followed Jack out to the front porch.

She found him standing by the porch railing, cup in hand, gazing off toward the ridges at the far side of the valley. The sky was lightening with the coming of morning, but was still a steel gray, the way it is right before the sun shows itself. Overhead the sky was clear, but there were clouds drifting far to the north.

He glanced over his shoulder at the sound of the door opening. He said to his aunt, "I remember when I was younger, growing up here. Seeing Pa every morning, standing out here with his coffee.' "

Ginny stood beside him, and took a sip of tea. "It is time for you to talk to me, Jackson. Since you have been home, you have been evasive, restless, and at times even reckless. None of the qualities I normally see in you."

"I guess I've had a lot on my mind."

She shook her head. "No, Jack. Not to me. You've always been able to talk to me."

Jack took a sip of coffee. "I had to write a paper, a few years ago. It had to be about the most influential person in my life. Of course, everyone who knows me knows how much Pa means to me. The entire class was looking forward to me writing about Johnny McCabe, the gunfighter, the former Texas Ranger. I think even the professor was. But that would have been too easy."

"So, who did you write about?"

"I wrote about you. And I found describing you to be less than easy. You're a complicated woman."

"I think we are all complicated in our own way."

"Perhaps. But everything that Josh is, you can see in him plainly. There's nothing hidden about him. He simply is what he seems to be. I'm finding Dusty the same way. And it's never a secret how Bree feels about anything. You, however, seem to make an art form out of being complicated."

She chuckled. "So, how did you finally describe me."

"I summed it all up with two words. Caring, for one. Caring, and yet caustic."

That drew a smile from her. "I have been called a lot of things over the years. A witch, and something that rhymes with witch. But caustic? I think I like it."

He returned the smile. "I thought you might."

"You must understand, Jackson, that I worked many years at being caustic."

"Most young women growing up in a

wealthy family in San Francisco would try for *charming,* I would think."

"Most of them did. Charm can open doors for you. But I found I didn't want doors opened for me. I wanted to open them for myself. Besides that, my father was caustic by nature. I had to be able to hold my own with him."

"That's what you taught Bree, Josh and me, too."

"You see, Jackson, this is a man's world, but there is plenty of room for a woman who relies on charm. Such a woman can even attain power, after fashion, pulling strings from the background if she has a strong husband to stand in the foreground. There is little room, however, for a woman who wants to stand in the foreground herself. I found that if I were to attain this, I would have to learn to push my way into that foreground.

"That is why I developed what your father calls *the Gaze.* A firm stare that can turn a man's knees to rubber and his spine to butter. Actually, I learned that from my father, too."

She took a sip of tea. "Do you know what it was about your father that first impressed me?"

Jack had heard this story before, but he liked to hear it so he let her continue.

She said, "Your father did not wither away under the Gaze, as did so many men. He shot it right back at me. Right then, I knew your mother had picked a good man."

She took another sip of tea. "Of course, we are drifting from the matter at hand, which I suppose could be your intention."

He shook his head and tossed her a smile. "I'm not that good a politician. Besides, I don't believe there's a person alive who could manipulate you."

"Some have tried, God help them." She smiled. "Though, it is clear you don't want to talk about what is troubling you, so I will begin. You, Jackson, are a terrible house-keeper."

This caught him a little by surprise, but he couldn't deny it. "You should see the room I share with Darby. No, on the other hand, maybe you should not."

"Darby is your friend from school. You've mentioned him in letters."

Jack nodded. "Probably my best friend in the world. Strange, because we sometimes seem to have such little in common."

"It is because of your terrible housekeeping skills that I was in your room yesterday morn-ing, gathering up dirty socks and preparing to give the room an over-all straightening, and the floor a good sweeping. How you man can live with gravel underfoot and never seem to notice it is beyond me. Anyway, this was when I accidentally knocked over your saddlebags. You had left them perched rather precariously at the side of your bed, and they were unlatched. All of the contents spilled on the floor.

"I won't even comment on the bottle of whiskey. But as I picked up the mess from the floor, returning it all to your saddlebags for you to sort through later, I found your train ticket. Jackson, it is a one-way ticket."

There, he thought. Finally. The proverbial cat was out of the bag. Not to mention the train ticket.

Aunt Ginny said, "Jackson, are you in some sort of trouble at school?"

That brought a surprised chuckle to the surface. "No. I'm in no trouble, believe me. Or, at least, I'm in no trouble at school?"

"Then, where are you in trouble?"

"Well, I'm going to be in trouble here, if this conversation continues much longer."

She took another sip of tea. The cup was pretty much empty, now. "I'm waiting."

"Aunt Ginny, please don't think me un-grateful for all you have done for me. For all of the money you have put forth for my schooling."

"But you're not going back." It was more of a statement than a question. "Is it because of the girl?"

"She would have been a very good reason not to go back. But no, I had already decided before I met her. I bought that one-way ticket a month before I met her."

"And you didn't think you could talk to your father or me about it?"

"How could I? I so do not want to disappoint either of you. After all you have done for me, and Pa is so proud of me. How do I tell him I don't want to be a doctor?"

"What do you want to be?"

And so he told her. For the first time, he explained to her all he had ever wanted was to ride beside his father, to be like his father. To raise cattle, and help him build this ranch. And maybe, if he should meet the right girl, to build a home with her in this valley, and to raise children with her.

"I thought I had met the right girl with Nina. I thought at least that part of the equation had been fulfilled. But apparently not."

Jack had forgotten about the cup and saucer in his own hand. He took a sip and found the coffee was growing cold. Aunt Ginny was staring with a sort of stillness toward the floor of the valley, toward the wooden bridge and beyond. Jack wasn't sure if she was angry, or hurt, or what.

He said, "Please don't think me ungrateful. I know what an opportunity you and Pa have given me. But it's not an opportunity to do what I want. It's as simple as that."

"Jackson, don't you think your father would have leapt at the opportunity for a classical education, and go on to be a lawyer? Or a doctor? Or a professor at a fine school? With his mind, he would have been successful at whatever endeavor he chose. He could have been a Senator. With your father's capabilities and leadership skills, who knows? He might have had a chance at the presidency. But school costs money, and he was born to a farming family. He didn't have the opportunity that you now have. By going to school, you are, in a sense, following the path he might have chosen had things been different."

Jack shook his head. He didn't disagree with his aunt lightly and frivolously, and surely didn't do it simply for the sake of doing so. But he did disagree with her. "He might think he wanted a classical education. But I don't think he would have been happy."

Ginny had been staring off to the valley floor, but now she turned to face her nephew. It wasn't often anyone other than John himself openly disagreed with her.

Jack said, "I've seen the serenity in his eyes when he looks off at the mountains. When he is riding through the ridges, with his horse beneath him and his guns at his side, he is at one with himself and the world around him. Had he been off in school at Harvard or Oxford or some such place, he never would have spent that winter in this valley with the Shoshone, years ago, he never would have found the peace and harmony he now has within him. Shoshone beliefs and religion is such a part of him. Of who he is.

"Aunt Ginny, the grass is always greener, like they say. And sure, Pa might stare into the fire at night sometimes and wonder what-if. But one thing the Shoshone taught him and he taught me was we are each guided along the path we are supposed to be. He had the opportunities he was supposed to have. I think, in the long run, he would have felt as out of place at an Ivy League school as I do. Maybe even moreso."

"So, when would you have told us all of this, had I not dragged it out of you this morning?"

He shrugged. He looked down at his cup of coffee, and saw it was mostly empty. The bottom of the cup was filled with the sludge that tends to settle at the bottom of a cup of trail coffee. "I was considering leaving in a couple of weeks, as though I was going back to school, then maybe going off to sea, or something. But that would be the cowardly way, and that wasn't the way I was raised. And then I met Nina, and suddenly things were a lot more complicated. And now Nina's out of my life, and I'm back to not knowing what I'm going to do."

"You could simply stay here, at the ranch. Work alongside your father."

He shook his head. "I don't really belong here."

"Jackson, this will always be your home.

Whether we understand your decision or not. Being family isn't about agreeing with each other or even understanding each other. It's about loving each other, regardless."

"I appreciate the offer to stay here. Really, I do. And working alongside Pa is something I yearned for every single day that I was off at school. But when it comes to operating this ranch, I'm an outsider. Family, yes. But I've been away too long.

"Dusty fits in here like he has always been here, and maybe that's because he's so much like Pa. You said it yourself, in a letter you wrote last winter. The way he moves, the shape of his face. He's like a younger version of Pa. But I've found, even more than that, his attitude and the way his mind works is all so much like Pa.

"Maybe it's time for me to admit to myself that I am not like Pa. I am myself. Similar in some ways, maybe, but distinctly different in others. I have to start making my own way in this world."

"And that way does not involve school, or being a doctor?"

He shook his head. "I'm sorry, but no."

She drew a lungfull of air and let it out slowly, and then let her gaze drift back to the valley again. Clouds off to the north were now taking on a reddish hue.

"You know," she said, "Joshua has had similar problems. Oh, the details might be different, but at the core, it's the same situation. Wanting to be able to ride alongside your father and be the man he is, and yet finding his presence seems to somehow make it difficult to be an individual. He seems caught between the man he thinks he should be, and the man he needs to be."

Jack nodded. "I didn't know that. Part of being away from the family for so long. But I'm not surprised to hear it."

Ginny looked at him. "Your father is a good man. But he's just a man. Human. He's not a god."

"He's practically a living legend, Aunt Ginny. Did you know there's a writer in New York who's writing dime novels about him? The man contacted me last year, wanting to pick my brain about Pa. I declined."

"I didn't know that."

"They talk about him in saloons and cattle camps from the Rio Grande to the Canadian border."

She nodded. "That I did know. And his exploits seem to grow with the retelling. Not that they weren't sometimes fairly incredible to begin with. But despite all of this, he's not really a legend. He's not really larger-than-life. He's not a dime novel hero. He's just one man."

Jack nodded ruefully. "Maybe so. But that one man's shadow is mighty large, and mighty hard to step out of. It seems to follow you wherever you go."

"So, where *will* you go? If you're not going back to school, and you're not staying here?"

His turn to let his gaze drift off toward the center of the valley. Toward where the settlers were building their farms. It had been nearly two weeks since his fight with Harlan Carter. Two weeks since Nina had told him not to come see her anymore.

When he had told Aunt Ginny, she had said for him to give it time. But how much time was he to give her?

"I don't really know. But I think it's time for me to find out. The longer I stay here, the more uncomfortable it's going to be. Dusty already knows. He knew something was wrong, and we talked about it, and I think he understands. But to explain all of this to Josh, and then to Bree, and then eventually to Pa. I really just need some time to sort out my thoughts and let myself find my way."

"Will you at least send me a letter to let me know where you alight? So I'll know you're safe?"

He smiled. "Absolutely. And as soon as I can, I'll begin repaying you for all of the money you spent on my schooling."

"I'll have no such thing."

"But my education is wasted."

She shook her head. "No education is wasted. Like what the Shoshones taught your father, we are guided along the paths we are meant to follow. I've always believed that sort of thing, too. If you hadn't been meant to go to school for the years you did, then you wouldn't have. You were meant to learn what you did for a reason. You owe me nothing."

"I am so grateful to you, and to Pa. I hope you know that."

"Your father and I have an agreement we made long ago. I handle the household, and he manages the ranch itself. So, maybe I'm overstepping my authority a little, when I tell you this — if you must go, then take the best horse from the remuda. It's yours. Take whatever rifle you want from the rack, and all of the ammunition you need. And anything else you need from the ranch."

"Thank you."

"So . . ." She hesitated, as though she dreaded to ask this question. "When do you think you will be leaving?"

"I think in the morning. Before first light."

She nodded. "I assumed as much."

And then she took her nephew in a long hug.

Ginny said nothing about it the rest of the day. This was Jack's to tell, when he was ready, and to tell in his own way. So she went about household duties. She and Temperance took a buggy into town to Franklin's to buy some supplies. Then Ginny and the two girls took rugs out and gave them a good beating.

This was a process that took most of the afternoon because furniture had to be moved in order to free the rugs so they could be rolled and carried outside. Then dinner had to be prepared. This involved going out back and fetching a couple of chickens to be prepared.

Ginny sometimes smiled with amusement at what the high-society ladies of San Francisco could see her killing and plucking and cooking a chicken. But such had been her life for years.

The family sat about the hearth that night. John's chair was empty, as it always was when he was away. There were no household rules against sitting in his chair, it was simply not done. Josh put the fire together and poked at it. Temperance sat on the sofa, looking at Josh like every man wishes the woman in his life would.

They talked idly of things. How crazy the town would become tomorrow night, when cowhands from the McCabe spread and the Circle W and others within riding distance descended on it. Even though it was not payday, and would not be quite as wild as it had been the night of the Fourth, it would still be wild.

They wondered where John was. He had been gone for days, now. Meandering peacefully through the mountains, she figured. Making his way gradually south and west, toward California. Sleeping under an open sky, and sitting in the evening by a fire.

Josh and Dusty talked about moving the herd. The grass on the section of range they were using, in the lower grassier hills east of the valley, was close to becoming grazed out.

And Jack said nothing. He simply sat. He poured himself a glass of whiskey from the decanter on the small table in the parlor, and sat and stared into the flames.

Such a complicated young man, she thought. Before he had returned this summer, she would have been willing to bet her life that she knew this boy inside and out. Now she realized she had actually known little about him all along. She wondered how she could possibly have been so oblivious.

Morning came, and she was the first one to the kitchen. The morning was chilly, as it often was at this altitude even in the summer. She built a fire in the stove and began heating water for tea.

She was sitting at the table with a steaming cup in front of her, the comforting aroma of Earl Grey filling the air about her, when Temperance stepped into the room. It was her turn to fix breakfast. But the first thing she did was to put on a pot of trail coffee, because the boys would be wanting it. They drank it like it was the elixir of life. Ginny only hoped Bree didn't want a cup this morning. Ever since Bree's jaunt in the mountains rescuing

Nina Harding, she seemed to be developing a taste for it, also. Oh well, Ginny supposed. Bree was her father's daughter.

Dusty drifted into the room. He was in a range shirt, and his gunbelt was in place. The boy never seemed to wear a vest. He poured a cup and then stood by the counter. The boys often preferred to stand when they were in the house, as they would be spending the day in the saddle.

"Josh and I'll be moving the herd Monday. No sense to try to start today, with it being Saturday."

Bree came downstairs and offered her good-mornings to everyone, and then said, "Where's Jack?"

Dusty gave a sort of half shrug. "Upstairs, probably."

"No, his room's empty."

Josh stepped into the room and went directly to the cupboard for a cup. "What's going on?"

Bree said, "Jack's not here."

"Oh?" he said absently, reaching for the coffee pot. "Where is he?"

"Maybe he's off riding in the hills again," Bree said.

Dusty said, "He doesn't usually leave this early."

"He's been acting kind of strange ever since he got back from school."

Ginny finally said, "He's gone."

All were silent now, looking at her. Then Bree said, "Gone? Gone where? He's not due to leave for school for another week."

Ginny shook her head. "He's not going back to school."

Josh stepped forward. "Not going back to school? Then, where's he going?"

Ginny said, "If I only knew."

38

Jack didn't necessarily intend to wind up at Hunter's.

He was in no specific hurry to leave the valley, as this place would always be home in his heart, and he didn't know when he would be back. If ever. So as the sun climbed gradually into the sky, he meandered through the ridges one more time.

He stopped at a small meadow and watched a white-tail buck and three does grazing contentedly. Polygamists, he thought with a smile. Then the wind changed and the buck caught the scent of Jack and his horse. The buck raised its head and the three does followed, then they bolted for the trees at the other side of the meadow and were gone like they had never been there. Jack turned his horse and they started away.

Jack had his bedroll and saddle bags tied to the back of his saddle. Two canteens were full and slung over the saddle horn. In the scabbard was a Winchester carbine. He had thought about taking a long rifle, which could hold seventeen cartridges, but then decided on the shorter gun which held only twelve, because it would be easier to pull quickly from the scabbard and was more maneuverable. Two boxes of cartridges were in his saddle bags.

He was in a faded blue range shirt and he wore a vest that actually belonged to an old suit. It was now worn and a little tattered. He was in Levi's, and his revolver was at his side and tied down. He had no suit jacket or dress shirt or ties with him. He had left them at the ranch house, because he figured he wouldn't need them any more. His sombrero was pulled down about his temples.

He roamed along, eventually working his way to Pa's rocky cliff. He waited there a long time, looking off into the distance. He had to admit that, as much as an outsider as he felt at the ranch, he felt a pang of sadness at riding away from this valley. It was even stronger than what he felt when he left to return to school, because he knew where he was going. This time, his entire future felt wide open.

For years, he had felt like his entire life was planned for him. School back east. Then medical school. Then interning at a hospital in Boston or New York. Then becoming a surgeon and making his mark on the medical world and making lots of money. Now, it was just him, his horse and saddle, and what little he had in his saddle bags and wrapped up in his bedroll.

The sun was high in the sky when he finally pulled himself away from Pa's cliff, and followed a high pass that would take him out of the valley.

As he descended the slope on the other side, he knew he would come out maybe a mile from the small town of McCabe Gap, and the thought of a cold beer suddenly seemed good. After all, he didn't know when he would find cold beer again. This was how he wound up at Hunter's.

He swung out of the saddle and gave the rein a couple turns about the hitching rail, and stepped into the barroom.

Hunter and Franklin and Shapleigh were there at a table, having coffee. From the position of the sun, Jack figured it was late morning. It was Saturday, and tonight the town would go wild for a little while, but right now it was dead quiet.

Henry Freeman was there, too. A former slave, and now the blacksmith of this community. He ran a small farm outside of town, and his grandmother, a granny doctor from back in the Appalachians, served as the local doctor.

It might have seemed odd to some for a man of color to be sitting at the same table as a bunch of white men, but in many places on the frontier, equality was seen as something earned, not granted or denied simply because of heritage or the color of your skin. Henry had long since shown himself to be a stand-up sort of man, and that was all that mattered to men like Hunter or Franklin.

Miss Alisha was also with them. A woman about forty, with maybe a little too much pancake on her face, and her brows dark like she had taken a paint brush to them. She was in a simple dress that buttoned to the neck, but anyone taking a look at her knew she was no farmer's wife.

They all looked up at him.

"Jack," Hunter said. "What brings you to town?"

Franklin said, "Good morning, Jack."

Miss Alisha nodded her head at him.

Jack had come in intending to have a cold beer and take a last look at a place he might never see again. But as he stood in the doorway looking at them, he found himself saying, "You folks have been looking for a town marshal. Well, if the terms you offered my brother apply to me, then you've got yourself a marshal."

Franklin looked uncomfortable, and looked to Shapleigh, who gave a small shrug and looked at Hunter.

Hunter said, "What about medical school?"

Jack shook his head. "I'm not going back."

"I guess I shouldn't be surprised. There's been something different about you this visit."

538

Hunter looked to the others. "Well? What do you think?"

"Well . . . ," Franklin said, "we appreciate the offer, but . . ."

Hunter said, "You handled that gambler well enough. And Dusty told me about how you handled yourself back on the trail. You might be a college boy, but you're your father's son."

Franklin looked like he was trying to find a way to argue that, but couldn't. Franklin had always reminded Jack a little of a nervous chicken. Squawking about what he didn't have, but then squawking even louder when he did get it.

Miss Alisha gave him a surprisingly motherly smile. "I think being his father's son is about as good a recommendation as a boy can have."

Shapleigh nodded and said, "I'm sold."

Hunter got to his feet and crossed the floor to Jack, and extended his hand. "You got yourself a job, Marshal."

■ ■ ■ ■

PART THREE:
THE TIN STAR

■ ■ ■ ■

39

Henry Freeman was a skilled smithy, and he hammered out a tin star with a long thin pin in back. Jack pushed the pin through his shirt on the left side, just inside the line of buttons, and the tin star hung on his shirt like it belonged there.

Henry stood maybe three inches taller than Jack, and was muscled like a circus strongman. His hair was short and tightly curled, and had been black when he and his family first moved to this town but was now showing gray.

He had a lantern jaw and a wide, toothy smile, and he was showing that smile now.

"Looks good on you, Jack," he said.

"Thanks Henry. What do I owe you?"

"Nothin'. We can't pay you, but what we can do is offer our services for free."

Jack grinned. "Now, I wonder what Aunt Ginny would say at Miss Alisha's part in that."

Henry laughed. A large, from-the-heart

laugh, like he always did. "Now, I'd like to be a fly in the wall for that conversation."

Jack found, as expected, the gambler had dug through the earthen floor of the tool shed and squeezed out from under the wall, and had been long gone by morning.

"We need a jail," Jack said to Hunter and Franklin and Henry. "Nothing fancy. None of us can afford that. But some sort of structure. Maybe made of logs. And we have to have some sort of floor so no one being held there will be able to dig their way out."

"A wooden floor," Franklin said.

Hunter nodded. "Ford, down in the valley, is setting up a saw mill. We can maybe get him to donate some lumber. After all, they're going to be part of this community."

"In the morning, I'll take a ride out and have a talk with him."

By four o'clock, a few of the local cowhands had begun to trickle in. Jack saw one horse at Hunter's hitching rail had a Circle M brand, so he went in to see who it was.

He found Fred Mitchum at the bar, with a mug of cold beer in his hand. Fred was wearing a baggy white shirt and suspenders, and a dark, wide-brimmed sombrero.

Fred broke into a wide grin. "Well, look at you. When you rode out this morning, I figured you had a long ride ahead of you."

Jack said, "I thought so, too. But I ended

up here."

"That badge looks good on you. I'm heading back to the ranch after this here beer, and I'll tell everyone. Aunt Ginny will be specially pleased, I reckon."

Jack said, "You're not staying in town for the festivities tonight?"

Fred shook his head. "I'm too old for a Saturday night in a cow town."

Eventually, Fred rode out, and more cowhands rode in. Jack didn't figure it would be as wild as the first Saturday after payday, but he knew it wouldn't be a quiet night, either.

As dusk was casting the land into shadow, Josh and Dusty reined up in front of Hunter's. Jack was standing on the porch.

"Well, looky here," Josh said with a wide grin. "I guess the rumors are true."

Dusty stepped out of the saddle and shook Jack's hand. Dusty said, "I'm glad you didn't ride off. Aunt Ginny's really happy, too."

Jack said, "I'm riding down into the valley tomorrow to talk to Mister Ford. I'll make sure and stop at the ranch to say hello."

Josh slapped Jack's shoulder. "They couldn't have picked a better man to wear that badge."

By eight o'clock that night, Hunter's was half full, and in front of the Shapleigh's hotel there were some horses tethered, and the piano in his barroom was filling the night with an old tune. Normally played on a fiddle, Jack thought. Might have been *Sally Gooden,* but he wasn't sure. He doubted any of the patrons cared.

Jack strolled about the town, stopping in at the hotel to make his presence known, then crossing the wide expanse of street to Hunter's to do the same. He then checked Franklin's to make sure the door was locked, which it was. He then headed down to Miss Alisha's to stick his head in the lobby and door and let them know the law was present.

Miss Alisha was sitting on a sofa with tattered, old velvet upholstery.

Jack said, "If you need anything, just give a holler. I won't be far away."

She gave that strange smile, whorish and yet motherly. "I know we picked the right man for the job."

The night was going smoothly, he thought. The two barrooms were doing a steady if not explosive business. He figured Miss Alisha would have a fistful of cash before the night was done, too. Looked like the night was going to pass without incident.

However, before the night was done, he found his first day on the job was going to include having to kill a man.

At about ten o'clock, he was walking toward Hunter's when he heard the sound of voices raised and it sounded more like anger than the sort of hooting and hollering drunk cowhands will engage in when they're having a good time. He ran the last few steps and in through the open doorway.

A table was overturned, and one cowhand was standing with a knife in his hand. Jack didn't recognize him. A sombrero with a floppy brim and a rawhide chinstrap hanging loose. He wore his gun hanging down on the hip a bit, but not tied down. He was cowhand through and through, but the way he wore his gun told Jack he fancied himself as a gunman. The other cowhand was Fat Cole, from the McCabe Ranch. The Circle M.

Hunter was in the small crowd that had gathered around them, and was saying, "Put that knife down."

Jack said, "What's going on?"

Fat was more scared than angry. He said, "He accused me of cheatin', Mister McCabe. I ain't no cheat."

Josh and Dusty were in the crowd, too. Dusty said, "I've known Fat for a while, now. I can vouch for him."

Josh was focusing his attention the other cowhand. His normally booming baritone dropped a notch and he spoke through tight lips. "Put that knife down or I'll put it down for you."

The McCabe temper was rising up. Jack didn't think it rose up stronger in anyone else than it did in Josh.

Jack stepped forward. "I'll handle this."

The cowhand said, "Get out of the way.

This is between me and Stringbean."

Jack stopped between the cowhand and Fat. "Not anymore. There's law here, now. Put the knife down, and leave."

The cowhand was maybe Jack's age. Maybe a little more. But on the frontier, he might have been a cowhand for three or four years already, making him a seasoned veteran of the range.

He was smiling, though there was no humor in his smile. He said to Jack, "You gonna make me?"

Jack was not smiling. "If I have to."

"Even better." He stepped back, and slid his blade into an empty sheath at his left side. "You got that gun on, and you carry the name McCabe. Let's see if you have what it takes to earn it."

"Turn around," Jack said, "and walk away."

Jack wanted to tell the cowhand he would spend the night behind bars, but there was no jail. Telling him he would spend the night in a tool shed just didn't carry the same weight.

The cowhand's right hand dropped down to his gun. He was drunk enough to be foolishly brave, but not enough to lose his steadiness. He said, "Is that gun you wear for show, or do you know how to use it?"

"Don't do this," Jack said. "It's not worth dying for."

"I ain't the one what's gonna do the dyin'."

"Don't," Jack said again.

The man went for his gun, but Jack was faster. The cowhand's gun cleared leather, but Jack's was already out at arm's length and firing. One shot. The bullet caught the cowhand in the chest. His knees buckled and he landed on the floor on them, looking down at his chest and then up at Jack with surprise. As if he suddenly realized the foolishness and the seriousness of the game he was playing, but it was too late to go back.

Blood was already soaking into his shirt. Must have hit a major artery, Jack thought. Or pierced the heart muscle itself. The cowhand fell backward and stared at the ceiling. He twitched a bit, kicked a couple of times, then his eyes lost all life and he stopped breathing.

Josh and Dusty were suddenly at Jack's side.

Josh placed a hand on Jack's shoulder and said, "It wasn't your fault. He would've killed you."

"Why, though? Why did he force my hand?"

Dusty said, "Josh and me — we've been here for a while, Josh especially, and we have a reputation."

"But they all see me as nothing but a college boy."

Hunter knelt by the cowhand and touched two fingers to the boy's neck to feel for a pulse, and shook his head.

Dusty said, "I know what you're capable

of. I saw it back on the trail with the settlers. But the folks here, they're gonna have to learn what you're all about. Some folks have to learn the hard way."

Jack slapped his pistol back into his holster. "I suppose. But that's a hard way to learn."

40

The following morning, Jack hauled a wooden chair from Hunter's barroom out to the boardwalk in front of the saloon.

Hunter said, "I'm gonna have to build me a bench out front, the way Shapleigh has in front of his hotel."

Jack rocked the chair onto its back legs and rested it against the wall, and took a sip of coffee. Chen was Chinese, but he made trail coffee as good as Jack had ever tasted.

"Nothing to it," Chen said. "Just put it on the fire and let it boil over three times. By then it has turned to mud."

"That's about it," Jack said.

It was Sunday morning. The wildness of the night before was gone as though it had never happened, and now Jack sat and drank coffee and watched people drifting in for church. The only game in town was Baptist, as that was the denomination of the young minister.

Hunter stepped out, a cup of Chen's coffee

in his hand. "Hard thing for church goin' folks. If you're not a Baptist but you want a church service, you sort of gotta bite the bullet."

"I started attending a Methodist church in Boston a couple years ago. I went most Sunday's, except when I was too hung over."

As they watched, the Carters rolled in. Or the Hardings, as most folks in the area knew them. They were using the buckboard they had acquired when their original conestoga wagon broke an axle. He and Emily were at either end of the seat, with Nina tucked in between them.

The wagon was being driven by a team of horses. Must have bought some somewhere, Jack thought. Possibly from old Jeb. He doubted Carter would want to do business with Dusty or Josh.

Nina looked over at Jack and Hunter as they rolled past. Jack raised a hand to touch the brim of his hat. She nodded back, but then turned her gaze away.

"That girl sure holds a grudge," Hunter said.

"It's more than that," Jack said. "She doesn't want to build her life with a gunfighter. And maybe she has a point."

"You're bein' too hard on yourself."

Jack shook his head. "Not really. I think in her place I might have made the same decision."

"Sounds like you've done a lot of thinking about it."

"That's about all I think about." Jack got to his feet. "I'm going inside. Suddenly I have a thirst for something stronger than coffee."

That afternoon, Jack rode out to the ranch and had tea with Aunt Ginny. Then he headed down to the center of the valley to visit Ford. To do so, he had to ride past the acreage Harlan Carter was claiming.

The trail took him to within a quarter mile of the Carter camp. He could see a stack of logs, and someone moving about. Probably Carter, cutting the logs and getting ready to put up a cabin. The tent still stood, and the buckboard rested idly nearby. Their horses grazed contentedly off to one side. There were no oxen in sight, so Jack figured Carter must have traded them for the horses. Old Jeb would have no need for oxen and Jack saw no oxen grazing at the ranch, so he had to wonder if Carter had ridden all the way down the stretch to Zack's ranch to do business with him.

Jack wanted nothing more than to ride in. To ask how they were doing. Specifically, to ask Nina how she was. He was also thinking maybe he owed Carter an apology. Nina was right — Jack shouldn't have given in to his temper. Regardless of how badly Carter seemed to want the fight, he was Nina's father and Jack should have respected that. But he forced his gaze away from their camp and continued riding along.

Ford had a cabin partially built. He and Brewster and Carter had been cutting logs on a nearby ridge and hauling them down with horses.

Jack explained the situation. He and the others in town were planning to build a jail, but they needed lumber. They were hoping Ford would be able to donate some.

"I'd be pleased to. Problem is, I won't have a sawmill up and running until next spring. I'm going to build a water wheel for power, but the stream feeding this lake only runs fast enough to power a water wheel until maybe May or June. So any mill business will have to be done in the spring months."

Jack said, "I don't know if we should wait until then."

"Well, maybe Abel and I could cut some logs and haul them into town for you. You and Hunter and the others would have to do the building. Maybe even Carter would help out, if we caught him in the right mood."

Jack shook his head. "I wouldn't gamble the farm on that."

Ford grinned. "Abel and I and my boy should be able to handle it. And Abel's son Age. The boy works like a man."

"You have to in this land, if you hope to survive. As soon as you're grown enough to handle an axe or a shovel, you're expected to do the work of a man."

Come Monday, Brewster and Ford rode into town and announced they were headed off into the ridges to cut wood. Age was with them, and Ford's son Randall. Jack joined them, as he didn't expect to have to do a whole lot of marshaling on a Monday, and Hunter came along, too. The stage was not due until Wednesday, which meant his only customer would probably be himself.

They hauled logs down to the location Jack had picked out. A flat, grassy area maybe a hundred feet to the right of Hunter's.

Jack said to Hunter, "Since most of the men I lock up will probably be coming from your establishment, it'd be easier if the jail is next door."

That evening, Jack sat at Hunter's and wrote Darby another letter, bringing him up to date on events. He sent it off with the Wednesday stage.

The following day, Jack and Hunter went to work notching the logs and setting them into place. Franklin and Shapleigh joined in, though neither of them had ever built a log cabin before, so it was a learning experience for them. Henry Freeman joined in, and Josh and Dusty rode in from the ranch to lend a hand.

By the end of the week, a cabin stood on

the spot that had been simply a flat stretch of grass. The front section was to be Jack's office, with a couple of bunks against one wall. The back section was a holding cell. Essentially, it was a room with a one foot by one-foot window cut into the back wall — enough to let light in but not large enough for a man to crawl through. A second window was on the back wall of the office so Jack would be able to check on any potential prisoners without having to unlock the door. The floor was made of logs they split in half, with the flat ends aiming up.

Josh said, "There's an old cabin, maybe four miles north of the valley. Used to belong to an old trapper. It's been deserted for years."

"I remember the place," Jack said.

Josh said to Dusty, "Pa used to take us out there, sometimes. It was a good place to spend the night if we were deep in the hills and wouldn't have time to get back home before nightfall. Often we slept under the stars, but sometimes we used the cabin."

He said to Jack, "I was out there a couple years ago. The stove was still in good shape. Maybe we could haul it down here and set it up for you."

And so they did. The stove was small and the three of them were able to carry it from the cabin and tie it onto a travois pulled by a couple of mules. They managed to drag it down to the base of the ridge and then load it onto a buckboard. By the end of the day, it was standing in the front of the jail building, its stovepipe protruding through a small hole in the wall.

Hunter took a wide wooden plank and painted the word JAIL on it in black letters, and they nailed it to the front wall just above the door.

With an old wooden roll top desk that had been at Franklin's and unable to find a buyer, and a couple wooden chairs, one from Hunter's and one from Shapleigh's, Jack's marshal's office was complete.

There was no boardwalk. You simply stepped from the front door down onto a plank and then into the mud. And there was no actual lock on the door leading to the single jail cell. There were two steel brackets nailed at either side of the door, and a two-by-four dropped into place served to hold the door shut.

Jack stood outside with Dusty and Josh, looking at the cabin.

"It's not fancy," Jack said, "but it doesn't have to be. It'll do nicely."

The days passed. Life about the small town of McCabe Gap was slow and simple. Jack would have breakfast at Hunter's, prepared by Chen. And then he would walk about the town. Stop in and visit Franklin, or Shapleigh.

Saddle up sometimes and ride about the area. Visit with the Freemans, or ride down into the valley and visit the ranch or the farmers. Essentially, making a visible presence of the law. He avoided the Carter farm, though. Jack figured there was no one there who wanted to see him.

At night he would have dinner at Hunter's, or sometimes ride out to the ranch for a taste of Aunt Ginny's cooking. And he would walk about the town, checking the locks on the buildings. Walking the rounds, he had heard lawmen calling it.

He knew he had no actual authority. All he could really do was lock up a miscreant and hold him until the territorial marshal could come and take the prisoner away. But it was more than the town had before Jack took the job.

One morning, he went to Hunter's for breakfast, and then took his coffee on the front boardwalk. On the boardwalk was a bench Hunter had built from split logs.

"Well," Hunter said, "what do you think?"

Jack sat on the bench, and nodded. "Good and solid."

Hunter leaned in the doorway, a tin cup full of coffee in one hand.

"Been doing some thinking," Jack said.

"What about?"

Jack took a sip of coffee. A cloud hung high in the sky overhead, and a light breeze worked its way down from the nearest ridge. It brought with it a hint of balsam.

"July Fourth," Jack said.

Hunter shrugged. "Almost a month ago."

Jack nodded. "Been thinking about the man Josh thought he saw. That outlaw they call White-Eye."

"You boys rode all through the hills. Didn't find anything."

Jack shook his head. "Of course, he could have just stuck to the trails."

"Not the way of that outfit."

"Not the way they did things last summer. Doesn't mean they haven't learned something."

Hunter nodded thoughtfully and took a sip of coffee. "If it was actually him Josh saw, do you think he's still in the area?"

Jack shook his head. "Got no reason to think so at all. I don't really have any reason to think it actually was White-Eye. Josh isn't even sure. But I have this nagging feeling of warning. Right here." He reached a hand to the back of his head.

Hunter said, "A wise man listens to his gut feelings."

"That's what Pa always said."

"And your Pa is a wise man. Have you talked to Dusty and Josh about it?"

Jack shook his head again. "They're off moving the herd. And besides, they've done enough to help. If I'm gonna be the marshal here, I have to handle some things myself."

They were silent for a few moments. Jack took another sip of coffee, finishing off his cup.

He said, "If they're in the area, they need to eat. That means they need supplies. And I can't see men like that looking for honest work."

"That means they must be stealin.' "

"Indeed. When the stage was last in, I asked Walt if he had heard of any robberies in the Bozeman area, or if there had been any problems at any of the way stations between Bozeman and Cheyenne."

"What'd he say?"

"Said he hadn't heard of any. But there was a small mining operation robbed up near Helena. A man was killed, his cabin looted and burned. But those things happen in mining areas."

"They do. But you still got that naggin' feelin'."

"I do."

"Then, you gotta act on it. Your Pa would do no less."

Hunter went back into the saloon, and Jack sat and looked at the town. Things were quiet at the hotel. Franklin was on the boardwalk in front of his emporium with a broom in his hands. He had swept a pile of dirt out onto the boardwalk and was now sweeping it away into the street. The church was quiet.

Hunter was right. The robbery and murder up Helena way was probably not in the slightest bit related to the man Josh thought he saw July Fourth. But Jack couldn't let it rest. Not until he was sure. After all, this was why he was wearing the badge.

He decided to walk over to Jeb Arthur's livery and saddle his horse, and take a ride.

Jack headed into the valley and rode down the stretch to the Johnson ranch.

When Zack Johnson visited the McCabes or stopped in at Hunter's for a beer, he was usually clean shaven. But Jack caught him working, and he was covered with sweat and dust and had a week's worth of whiskers on his jaw.

Johnson and his men had caught some wild mustangs, and had them in a circular corral within view of the house.

The Johnson spread was smaller than the Circle M. Not quite a thousand head. The house itself was a single-floor shack made of upright planks nailed into place, and had a stone chimney. The house was built on a flat stretch, and in the distance was a pine covered ridge.

Johnson was standing by the fence, watching one of his men saddle a mustang. Johnson turned to look over his shoulder at the sound of an approaching horse.

He broke into a smile. "Well, the law

decides to pay us a visit."

Jack reined up. A layer of dust had settled on his sombrero and along his vest and the tin star pinned to it.

Jack said, "Thought it was time for a visit. Been many a moon since I've seen your place."

"Not changed much."

Jack swung out of the saddle and shook hands with him.

Johnson said, "We heard the news, that you're the town marshal. That badge looks good on you."

Johnson called his wrangler over to tend Jack's horse, and they stood and watched Ramon, Johnson's ramrod, climb into the saddle of the mustang. The mustang began bucking and humping, but Ramon held onto the saddle, with one hand holding the reins and the other out beside him.

The cowhands were whooping and calling out, "Ride 'em, Ramon!"

Jack counted maybe five seconds before Ramon became airborne and landed hard in the dirt. Two other cowhands hopped down from the fence and ran toward the horse, which was bucking away as the though rider was still on its back. Mad as hell and trying to rid itself of its saddle. Ramon rose to his feet a little slowly and hobbled his way back to the fence. He slid out between two rails.

"You all right?" Johnson said.

Ramon nodded. "I'll live."

Johnson looked to Jack. "Want to give it a try?"

Jack shook his head with a grin. "Not me. I'm just a college boy, remember?"

Johnson slapped him on the shoulder. "Come on. Let's go to the house. Got a bottle of Scotch that needs a little emptying. Ramon, you comin'?"

Ramon nodded. "After that ride, I could use a little Scotch."

The house was a one-room structure, with an iron stove and a set of cupboards on one wall, a line of bunks on the other, and a table in the center.

Johnson went to the cupboard and produced a bottle. No need for glasses, Jack figured, this far out from civilization.

Jack pulled out a chair and settled into it. Ramon dropped into his chair a little gingerly.

"You sure you're okay?" Johnson said, handing the bottle to Ramon.

"Nothing a little of this won't cure." Ramon Cormier was a little older than Jack, with black hair that curled out from under his sombrero. He had a beard and mustache that was black and fine. Not so much a fashion statement as a simple lack of shaving. He was no gunman and wore his pistol high on his belt and a little to the front, but Jack knew Ramon was no pushover in a fight. He had been with Zack Johnson the summer before, helping defend the McCabe ranch. Such things are not forgotten.

Ramon took a pull from the bottle and handed it to Jack.

They talked about the price of cattle. Rumors that Walt had heard and told Jack about.

Johnson said, "I'm thinking next summer I'll have enough of a herd to maybe make a drive down the Bozeman to Cheyenne, then east to one of the railheads. I want to talk to your Pa about that. Combining both herds will make the drive a lot easier."

They talked about Pa's overland trip to California, to visit Ma's grave.

"He's been gone a few weeks now," Jack said. "We don't really expect to hear from him until maybe next spring."

The bottle went back to Johnson. "I was there, when your Ma was killed. I was in the stable rubbing down a horse. I heard the gunshot. We trailed that man well into the Sierra Nevadas, but then the trail went cold."

Ramon said, "You never found out who did it?"

Jack shook his head. "At this rate, I doubt we ever will."

They talked a bit about the old days. Zack Johnson talked about his time in the Texas Rangers. With some whiskey in him, he became quite the storyteller. He told once again about catching a Comanche arrow in

564

the leg and being knocked from his horse, and Pa taking down ten Comanches with as many shots. And he told of tracking Mexican border raiders south into Mexico.

Then Jack told about how Josh thought he saw one of the men who had ridden with Falcone the summer before.

Zack Johnson suddenly got serious. "You should've said something sooner than this."

Jack shook his head. "Not much to tell. Josh saw him for only an instant. It might not have been him. We rode through the ridges cutting for sign, and found none. I did some riding through the ridges myself in the weeks after that, and saw nothing."

"Still," Johnson said, "I'm gonna take me a ride into the hills this afternoon and take a look around. Bronc bustin' is over for the day. Ramon," he looked at his ramrod, "I want you to take Coyote and ride up the stretch and stay at the McCabe place until Josh and Dusty are back. That is, if you're wounded pride can sit a saddle that long."

Ramon grinned. "I'll manage."

Johnson said to Jack, "Coyote Gomez is one of my top hands. Can track a man through a river at midnight, and he's a crack shot."

Jack rode back across the valley with Ramon and Gomez. Aunt Ginny invited them all for tea.

As they sat on the porch, Ramon and Coyote in their oily and dusty chaps as they hadn't taken time to clean up, Aunt Ginny said, "I really feel badly about you boys coming all the way out here. I hate to be a burden."

"No burden at all," Ramon said.

After their cup was finished, Ramon and Coyote headed for the bunkhouse, and Ginny walked with Jack to the corral. Fred had dropped a loop on a fresh horse and switched saddles, and the new horse was tethered to a fence rail, waiting for Jack.

"Jackson," she said, "I've given some thought to your decision not to return to school. It's a shame you couldn't have told your father before he left."

He nodded thoughtfully. "A shame? I suppose. And yet, I have to admit, when it comes to telling him news that might disappoint him, I find myself a coward."

She shook her head. "I doubt anyone would ever use the word *coward* when referring to you. Not after the way you conducted yourself on the trail keeping those settlers safe. Rescuing Nina Harding. And then facing down that cowhand a few weeks ago when he drew on you."

He looked at her with surprise.

She said, "Oh, yes. I've heard. People are talking about you, Jack. I find it's difficult for a McCabe man to go long without people talking about him. A McCabe man tends to cut a wide swath through life."

"Well, I still don't know how I'm going to tell Pa. Facing him and giving him news he won't want to hear."

"What makes you think he won't want to hear it? You boys think you know your father, but I sometimes wonder if you really do. You spend too much time comparing yourself to the legend instead of simply looking at the man."

"With all due respect, ma'am, I don't see much difference between the legend and the man."

Jack slid the rein free from the rail.

"Jackson," Aunt Ginny said, "have you considered writing him a letter? Explaining it all to him?"

He looked at her. He hadn't considered that.

She said, "Address it to him at your Uncle Matt's ranch. He'll likely be spending part of the winter there. You can send the letter out on next Wednesday's stage. It should be at Matt's before the summer's out."

He nodded. "I'll consider that. Thank you."

He gave her a peck on the cheek and then swung into the saddle. She stood and watched the young man she thought she knew so well but realized she was only beginning to know, as he rode away toward the trail that would take him out of the valley.

41

Jack wrote his letter. He sat at his desk in his little office with a candle burning, and tried to put pen to paper. He found he was getting nowhere, so he then decided to move the project over to Hunter's. A shot of whiskey might make the words flow more easily.

He sat and filled the page. And the following Wednesday, he handed the letter to Walt.

Walt was a tall man with stooped shoulders and a beard that was mostly white. Jack didn't think Walt was much older than Pa, but he had an old way about him. Some men have an old way about them even when they're young. Jack figured Walt was probably one of them.

Walt said, "I'll have this down to Cheyenne in a week, and then it'll be on a train bound for San Francisco."

"Thanks, Walt."

The days blended together. Jack began each morning at Hunter's for coffee and eggs, prepared by Chen.

Chen was small and elderly. A long white braid ran down his back, and he had a thin white goatee. And yet he moved like a young man. He stepped lightly and quickly, and he was quick to laugh. And the most important thing, Jack thought, was the man could cook. Before Chen, Dusty would sometimes serve as cook at Hunter's, but generally if you wanted a meal in this small town, you headed for Shapleigh's. Now things had changed. Stage passengers who were hungry were heading directly to Hunter's. Shapleigh had even asked Hunter if Hunter would loan Chen to him sometimes.

One day, Hunter said to Jack, "Chen's also gonna tend bar for me on Saturday nights."

Jack said, "How's this little guy gonna keep a couple dozen rowdy cowhands from walking all over him?"

Hunter grinned. "That's your job, since you're wearin' that tin star."

"I can't be everywhere at once."

Jack was sitting at a table with a plate of eggs and a couple strips of bacon, and a cup of trail coffee. Hunter looked across the room where the old man was pushing a broom. He didn't look like much, Jack thought. Small and thin. He couldn't have weighed more than a hundred pounds. He wore a flannel shirt that bagged on him, and Levi's maybe a size too big that were held together with a length of rope through the belt loops.

"Hey, Chen," Hunter called out. "Come on over here."

Chen came over, broom in hand. "Yes, Boss?"

"Jack, try to push Chen down."

Jack looked at him as if to say, *you've got to be joking.*

Hunter said, "Go on. Give it a try."

Chen was standing there, grinning.

Jack said, "This is foolishness."

Hunter said, "Afraid to try, huh?"

Jack sighed with disbelief. He couldn't believe Hunter was going to go that route. Challenge his courage.

Jack got wearily to his feet. "All right."

He placed a hand on Chen's shoulder and gave a gentle push.

"That all you got?" Chen said. He spoke with a hint of an accent, but he had apparently been on this side of the ocean a long time.

"Go ahead," Hunter said. "Push him right onto the floor. If you can, I'll give you ten dollars."

Jack looked at him. He had to be kidding. Ten dollars? That was almost what a cowhand made in a month. But to push down an old man just seemed wrong.

Chen reached out with the broom and cracked Jack in the ear with the end of the handle.

"Ow," Jack said, stepping back. He had to admit, the old man had moved faster than he would have thought.

Chen said to Hunter, "He can't push me down, I get the ten dollars."

Hunter said, "It's a deal."

All right, Jack thought. Let's get this farce over with. Jack was six inches taller than the old man, and had probably fifty more pounds of muscle. He reached his hand to the old man's shoulder and gave a shove.

Except the old man was no longer there. He had stepped aside, not seeming to move quickly but he somehow had, and Jack found himself pushing at empty air. He managed to hold his balance, but just barely.

The old man was smiling. Hunter was grinning.

Jack then placed his hand on the old man's shoulder to give a shove, but the old man reached up and grabbed Jack's thumb with a hand that was surprisingly strong, and he twisted and Jack found pain shooting through his hand. The old man pulled downward as he twisted, and Jack was forced down to one knee. The old man was still holding onto the broom with the other hand.

"Hey," he said.

Chen then gave him a light tap on the head with the broom. "This a knife or a club or a gun, and you're dead."

He released Jack, who rose back to his feet.

His thumb and wrist were a little sore.

Chen looked at Hunter and said, "Ten dollars."

Hunter nodded with a grin. "I'll go get it. It's in the box in my room."

The box in Hunter's room was what passed for a safe.

"How'd you do that?" Jack said.

"You push, and I move. You strong like the oak, I am strong like the wind."

An old man who speaks in poetic nonsense, Jack thought. "Can you show me how you did that?"

Chen shrugged. "Can you learn?"

"Can I learn? Until last spring, I was in medical school at Harvard."

Chen shrugged again. Apparently this meant nothing to him. Jack realized the old man might never have heard of Harvard.

Chen said, "You need to unlearn what you've learned. Strong is good, but quick is better. Huh?"

Jack shrugged. The boxing coach at Harvard had said something similar once. In fact, Pa had also when he was teaching Jack and Josh some Shoshone wrestling tricks.

Hunter returned with the ten dollars. "You're not gonna believe how old he is."

"Ninety-two," Chen said.

Jack looked at him incredulously. Not for the first time this morning. "Ninety-two?"

Chen took his ten dollars from Hunter, and

then went back to sweeping the floor.

Hunter said, "I think he'll be able to handle himself behind the bar."

August blended into September. The days became a little less hot, and the nights were cool enough at this altitude that sometimes Jack needed to wear a jacket.

Aunt Ginny and Bree and Temperance came into town for supplies a couple of times. Jack would stop in on the local businesses every morning to make certain all was well. Every night, he walked his rounds, which didn't take long because the town was so small. He also rode out to the Freemans' cabin two or three times a week to make certain all was well.

A couple of times he saddled up and took a ride through the ridges around town, looking for tracks or signs of camps that had been made. He found none. And all this time, there was no sign of White-Eye. He was starting to think more and more that the man Josh had seen was indeed someone else.

A couple of times a week, he met with Chen out behind Hunter's for some lessons in Chinese wrestling. Maybe less athletic than Shoshone wrestling, it seemed to be mainly based on not giving your opponent a solid target to strike, and twisting thumbs or fingers to bring a man to his knees.

One Saturday night, a cowhand with too

much whiskey in him had reached across the bar to grab a bottle. He was new to the area and didn't yet have a tab, and had run out of cash. Chen brought an empty beer mug down across the back of the man's hand, striking at a sensitive place on the wrist, which stopped the man in motion. Chen then brought the mug up and into the man's face, catching him in the nose.

While the man stood, his hand hanging awkwardly in the air because he had lost all feeling in it, and the other hand up at his nose while blood streamed down and he blinked away tears, Chen said, "You leave."

Jack stepped up behind the man. "You heard him. Vamoose."

The man nodded, and without a word turned and left.

Chen grinned at Jack. "Quick, not strong."

The second week of September, Jack rode out to the middle of the valley to visit with the farmers. He saw them ride into church every Sunday and sometimes got a quick hello from them, and a silent stare from Nina, but he hadn't really talked with any of them for a couple of months.

The Carter cabin was now fully built, with smoke drifting from a stone chimney. Carter himself was out front, sawing at firewood when Jack rode up.

"The place looks good," Jack said.

Carter looked up at him, a buck saw in one

hand. "I learned me a few things about cabin buildin' over the years."

Jack nodded.

Carter said, "How's things in town?"

"Quiet. Not so quiet on Saturday nights," he grinned, and Carter returned the grin, "but generally quiet."

They heard the sound of the door knob turning, and looked to see Nina standing in the doorway. Carter said, "Maybe I'd best take a little break. Get me a drink of water. Been workin' up a sweat."

Jack nodded. "The day has turned off warm."

Carter strolled away from Jack, toward the cabin. Nina reluctantly stepped aside to let her father past.

Jack nudged his horse ahead until he was only a few feet from the door, and he reached up to touch the brim of his sombrero in the cheating tip-of-the-hat most cowhands used when greeting a lady. "Good to see you, Nina."

She nodded.

He said, "I miss you, you know."

She closed her eyes in a silent sigh. "Jack, I don't want to go into this again."

"Nina, I made a mistake. I admit that. But can't you find it in your heart to forgive? Even just a little?"

"It's not that you made a mistake, Jack. It's that you revealed a side of your character that

I didn't know was there. A side I really don't think I could live with."

He was about to say, *People can change.* And yet, he didn't really believe they did. People might learn things and as such alter their behavior a little, but they really couldn't change their nature. So he said nothing.

She said, "My father talked to me long about the hazards of being with your kind of man."

"*My* kind?" He felt his ire rising again.

"What he calls a gunhawk. I didn't really know what he was talking about until the two of you fought."

"Doesn't that name apply to him, too?"

She nodded. "But I was talking about building a life with you. Bringing children into this world with you. I don't know that I want a gunhawk to be the father of my children."

He didn't know what to say about that. This girl who saw him so clearly, moreso than anyone in his own family, didn't approve of him. Talk about a blow to your self esteem.

She said, "I think you'd best be going, Jack."

He nodded. "I think you're right."

Without another word, he turned his horse and started away down the trail.

Carter stepped out of the cabin. "Don't you think you might have been a little hard on him?"

"What? You were eavesdropping?"

He shrugged. "It's not that big a cabin."

"It's what you wanted, wasn't it? You didn't want me with a gunhawk. Well, now I'm not. You two both proved your point very successfully." And she pushed past him and back into the cabin, and slammed the door shut.

Jack had dinner at the ranch a few times. Josh and Dusty, long finished moving the herd from one section of range to another, rode into town once in a while for breakfast with their brother. They were also present every Saturday night.

One such night, a cowhand with a few too many glasses of whiskey actually swung a fist at Chen, even though Chen was old enough to be his great-grandfather. Chen merely stepped aside, doing his wind-thing, and the cowhand's fist slammed into the wall and he broke a knuckle. Jack escorted the man down to Granny Tate.

It was the fourth week of September as Jack sat on Hunter's porch, watching the weekly stage roll in. In his hand was a tin cup filled with trail coffee. Walt threw him a wave, then hopped down and opened the stage door. The first passenger off the stage was in a brown jacket and matching vest and derby. His hair was red, and Jack would have recognized his freckled face anywhere.

"Darby," Jack said, rising to his feet. He

called out, "Darby!"

He set his coffee on the bench and strode over to the where the stage had come to a stop, in front of Shapleigh's.

Darby Yates broke into a big smile. "Jacko."

They took each other in a big hug that saw them spinning around, first one lifted from the ground, then the other. Then they stepped back and Darby raised his fists playfully and Jack snapped a couple light boxing jabs into Darby's shoulder.

Then Darby stepped back. "Look at you. A full-fledged cowboy. Right out of a dime novel."

"What brings you here?"

"I got your letter. I had to see it for myself. The little town and the valley that had so captured the heart of my best friend."

One porter from Shapleigh's climbed up on the stage and handed down Darby's trunk.

"Come on," Jack said. "I want you to meet Hunter, and have a taste of the coldest beer east of the Divide. West of it, for that matter."

They stepped into Hunter's. Hunter gave the man a handshake. "Let me get both of you a beer from the cellar."

Jack and Darby took a table, and Hunter returned with two cold mugs of beer.

"The keg's fresh from Saint Lou," Hunter said. "The Plank Road Brewery. Some of the best around."

Darby took off his derby and dropped it to the table.

"Darby," Jack said. "What an incredible surprise."

He shrugged. "I thought about writing you that I was coming, but the way the mail moves out here, I figured I'd be here before you got the letter."

Jack nodded with a smile. "True."

"In fact, I was halfway here when the porter on the train handed me your second letter. It was dated more'n a month ago."

It then occurred to Jack what the date was. September 24. "Darby, what're you doing here? I mean, why aren't you in school? The semester must have begun three weeks ago."

He nodded. "That it did. But I've been doing some thinking. A lot of thinking, in fact. I said goodbye to my family and got on the train, but then I kept right on going. Booked passage to Cheyenne, then hopped the stage here."

"How long can you stay?"

Darby shrugged. "As long as you can have me, I guess. I have no plans. And I brought you a little present."

He reached into his trunk and pulled out a bottle of Kentucky whiskey.

Jack broke into a grin. "It's going to be a long night."

Darby nodded. "But a good one."

They drank into the night. Hunter joined

579

them. They slept late into the morning, Darby on the top bunk and Jack on the bottom.

Jack was awakened by the door opening and Chen stepping in with two cups of coffee.

"For you both," he said.

Jack sat up on the bunk and took a cup of coffee. Darby said, "Could someone shut the door? It's bright in here?"

"No wonder," Chen said. "You two drank an entire bottle of whiskey last night. Drink your coffee."

Jack and Darby had both poured down the whiskey the night before, but Darby drank three glasses to every one of Jack's. Like he usually did. And he usually paid for it in the morning.

Chen handed the second cup of coffee up to the second bunk, but Darby pushed it away, spilling some on the floor.

"Hey!" Chen called out. "That's hot."

"Keep it away. My head feels like there's a gong going off inside."

"It going to feel much worse if you do that again."

Jack smiled. "Take the coffee, Darby."

Chen reached the mug up to Darby again. Darby reached down to push it away, but Chen grabbed his wrist. Darby was pulled from the bed and slammed to the floor. Jack was laughing. He had seen that coming.

Chen said, "Now your head is hurting

worse, and the coffee is all over the floor. Now you have to walk all the way over to Hunter's yourself and get another cup."

As they sat at Hunter's and drank coffee, Jack said, "You know, I've got a job here. I can't fill every night with whiskey like I did last night."

"What kind of job?"

With one finger, Jack tapped the tin star on his shirt. "This is real."

"What can possibly happen in a little town like this?"

"Not much, most of the time. But it can get wild here on a Saturday night. The townspeople need me functional."

Darby nodded. The gong going off in his head had quieted a little after three cups of coffee, so he was able to nod his head without too much pain. "How'd that old man throw me on the floor like that?"

"He's a man of mystery."

"Well, I won't get in the way of you doing your job." He took a sip of coffee. "Where's the bank? I've gotta withdraw some funds."

Jack shook his head. "Darby, there is no bank. You saw the entire town when you came in."

"What about that building down past the store?"

Jack chuckled. "That's a brothel. The nearest bank is a two-day ride away."

Darby looked at him with dead seriousness in his eye. "Jack, I only have two dollars and twenty cents in my pocket. I tipped the stage driver a dollar yesterday. This is all I have. I figured I'd withdraw some cash when I got here."

The smell of bacon was in the air. Chen was at the stove, cooking.

Darby said, "Mister Hunter told me this meal's on the house, and I appreciate that. But I can't keep living like this. I have to get down to that bank."

"I have another idea. It'll involve a walk down to the Freeman cabin. After you've got enough coffee in you so you can walk."

Jack called a meeting at Hunter's. It was a Thursday afternoon, which meant business was pretty much dead anyway, so the business leaders in town were able to spare a few minutes. Franklin was there, along with Henry Freeman and Shapleigh, and Miss Alisha.

Darby stood beside Jack. The white shirt the day before was looking a little rumpled now, and he had discarded his jacket and tie, and his vest was unbuttoned. Pinned to his shirt was a tin star Henry had made.

Franklin said, "I'm not sure we need a second lawman, Jack."

"I think you might. There are times, like on a Saturday night after payday, when this town

582

can almost explode. It's not fair to keep expecting my brothers to ride in and help. It's not their job. And there are times when I need to be gone for a while, like if I'm going to scout the hills, or ride into the valley. It would be good to have a deputy on hand."

"But," Franklin said, "no offense intended, but can he hold up in a fight? I mean, he looks like a city feller."

"He was on the boxing team with me, back at school. Knocked me on my butt a few times."

Darby nodded with a smile. "More'n a few times."

"And maybe Mister Chen can teach him some wrestling tricks."

Henry Freeman said, "Can you shoot?"

Darby shrugged. "I've shot a pistol before. In the woods outside of Boston, Jack and I did some target practice. And I've gone hunting a few times with an uncle of mine on his estate in upstate New York."

His estate, Jack figured. Darby wasn't winning a lot of points with these people.

Jack said, "I'll vouch for him."

Franklin gave a reluctant nod, and looked to Shapleigh, who did the same. Miss Alisha was giving her strange motherly smile. She said, "For what it's worth, I'm a good judge of character, and I think he's a stand-up sort of man."

Hunter said, "All right, Jack. If you'll vouch

for him, then I say it's worth giving it a try."

They went to Franklin's to see if he had a pistol for Darby, and then they went out behind the marshal's office for some target practice. Darby held the pistol out at full extension and squeezed off a shot. He was aiming at a branch a hundred feet away. When the sound of the shot died away and the smoke dissipated, they could see the branch was untouched. He brought the arm back up to full extension and emptied the gun at it.

Jack said, "You didn't hit the branch at all."

"I think I came close once."

Jack shook his head. "Let's reload and try it again."

Darby was using a Colt Dragon .44. Long since out of production, it was cap-and-ball, but it had been retooled to use cartridges. Darby reloaded it.

"Show me how to do the fast draw," he said.

"You don't have a gunbelt. And besides, I don't think you're ready for that. You need to be able to hit a target a hundred feet away."

"How'd your father teach you?"

"He began by having me shoot at a target a hundred feet away."

Darby squared away at the tree branch. "All right, you rascally branch. You have breathed your last."

And he brought his arm out to fully extension and cocked the gun, closing one eye as he tried to draw a bead on his target, and fired. The branch remained unharmed.

Darby said, "How many tries did it take you to hit a target the first time?"

"This isn't about me, it's about you."

"Come on, Jack. How many? More than seven?"

"It took me nine. But I was only ten years old."

"Ten years old, huh?" Darby threw his shoulders back, and aimed the pistol. "I can do better than that."

"Don't aim the gun. Just point it, like you're pointing a finger."

Darby fired. The bullet kicked up a piece of bark on a tree behind the branch.

Darby fired all four remaining shots, and when the smoke cleared, the branch made it clear it was going to live to fight another day.

Jack gave the pistol back to Franklin, and got Darby a shotgun.

The following morning, Jack was at Hunter's, sitting at a table with a cup of coffee in front of him. Darby was taking the morning rounds. Chen sat across the table from Jack. He was about to start cooking, but wanted to finish his coffee first.

"Hey," Jack said lightheartedly. "I thought Chinamen all drank tea."

"I've been in this country a long time. I

developed a taste for this brackish brew you call coffee."

Jack took a sip. "So tell me, Mister Chen. What's your story? What brought you here?"

"I probably shouldn't tell you this, because you're a lawman, but I'm on the run. There's a price on my head."

Jack looked at him with surprise.

"I wasn't always as I am now," he said. "Once, in China, I was *si guang chu li.* You would say in your language . . ." He was searching his memory for the word. "Mercenary, I think."

"You were a mercenary?"

He nodded. "I rode for a warlord, who became an ally of the emperor. I was the warlord's number one."

"Si gong . . . how did you say that?"

"Si guang chu li."

"So, how did that lead to a price on your head?"

"I became a lover of the emperor's niece. And she was married."

Jack was incredulous. "No kidding. And here I thought you were this man of great wisdom."

"I am now. Mistakes when we are young is how we become wise when we are old. As long as we learn from those mistakes. If we don't learn, then we sometimes don't live long enough to be old. Now is your time to make mistakes. It is my time to be wise."

"So, how is it you can be so old, and yet are more capable than many young men?"

Chen shrugged. "I awaken in the morning before first light. I walk to a secluded place and meditate. I then stretch, and I breathe."

"Well, everyone breathes."

He shook his head. "Everyone sucks in air and then blows it out again. Few people actually breathe."

"You're a man of mystery, Chen."

Chen smiled. "Not so much. Not really. I'm a man who has made mistakes and learned from them so I could live to be old."

"I hope I didn't make a mistake with Darby."

"He's your friend. You should know him well enough to know if he can do the job."

"That's just it. He's my friend, and we spent a lot of time together back at school. We drank a lot of whiskey. But I never really told him much about myself, and I know little about him. I know he comes from a wealthy family, and they expected him to be a lawyer. But we never really talked about any of it."

"He was unhappy, as were you."

Jack nodded. "Yeah. I guess I always knew that, at least to some degree. But we never talked about it."

"You merely drank whiskey and shared each other's misery."

"Yeah. I guess that's the situation."

"What does your heart tell you?"

But before Jack could consider the question, Darby called from outside. "Jack! Jack!"

Jack sprang to his feet and ran for the door.

Darby was standing in the open expanse of dirt between Hunter's and the hotel. A girl was sitting on a horse. Darby was holding his shotgun in one hand, and grabbing the horse's reins with his free hand.

The girl seemed to be only partially conscious. She was swaying in the saddle, her eyes fluttering. Her age was difficult to guess, but she was not old. Her hair was chestnut colored and long and matted and tangled. Part of it was tied onto the back of her head in what was at one time probably a bun, and the rest was falling about, down her back and along one arm. Her face was bruised in places like she had taken a beating, and her dress was worn and sooty and muddy.

Jack suddenly realized he knew her. It was Jessica Brewster.

Jack ran to her, just as she toppled from the saddle. Darby let his shotgun drop to the mud and caught her with both arms, and he lowered her to the ground.

"Jessica," Jake said.

She was now fully unconscious. Her nose was swollen like it had been struck, and Jake saw some dirt along her face that wasn't actually dirt but dried blood.

Hunter and Chen were standing behind Jack. Shapleigh was hurrying from the hotel, and Franklin had stepped out of his store to see what all the commotion was about.

"Hunter," Jake said. "Run and get Granny Tate. Hurry."

42

They moved Jessica to a room on the second floor of the hotel. Granny Tate examined her and determined the girl was suffering from exhaustion and dehydration. She also looked like she hadn't had a decent meal in a while. Jack knew the medical term to be malnutrition.

Granny Tate was about Chen's age, and she wore spectacles balanced on her nose. A scarf was pulled about her hair, and she walked with a cane. And yet the woman was a wealth of medical knowledge. She was what they called back in the Appalachians a *Granny Doctor.* She had trained at the side of another granny doctor when she was young, and had been a doctor her whole life. She was what Jack's professors would call a *folk* doctor, and they would say it with a little scorn or amusement. And yet this woman could look at a patch of woods or a meadow and see a natural pharmacy. She could cure fever or infection. She could set a broken bone better than any medical school graduate Jack had ever seen. One time three or four years ago Pa had been thrown by a bronc and his back was hurting even days later. He went to Granny Tate, and she had her grandson Henry push on Pa's back in a given spot and the bone snapped like a stick, and Pa's pain was gone.

"Let's see one of them big city doctors do that," she said.

Granny had the men leave while she performed an examination on Jessica. Henry's wife Mercy had come along and was acting as nurse. Jack and Darby waited in the hallway.

While they waited, Jack informed Darby about his adventures coming up from Cheyenne along the Bozeman. In the first letter he had written, he included much about Nina but little else. Now he told Darby about the girls being kidnapped and the bullet wound he took to the shoulder, and about riding out to rescue them. And how Jessica refused to come back with him.

Darby said, "She chose to remain with those men?"

Jack nodded gravely. "It was a painful thing for her family. Her father didn't talk much about it, but I could see it in his eyes."

"Why would she do that?"

Jack shrugged.

Mercy finally opened the door. She was

about thirty, also with a bandanna tied about her hair. "You boys can come on back in."

Jessica was lying in bed with the covers pulled to her chin. She looked to be sleeping.

Granny Tate said, "We got some water into her. We'll try food in a little while."

"What kind of shape's she in, over all?" Jack said.

"Them men, they used her somethin' fierce. And they beat on her. She got a tooth knocked loose, and might have to come out. She got a concussion from where she was hit on the side of the head. Got a little blood in one eye. Two broken ribs, near as I can tell."

Mercy said, "I've got to get home for a little while, to cook dinner. I'll be back this evening. And Granny has got to get out to the Bar W."

Granny Tate said, "Tom Willbury's daughter is due to deliver. 'Spect she'll do so tonight."

Jack knew Tom Willbury to be the owner of the Bar W. His daughter Eugenia, not much older than Bree, had married his ramrod. Jack hadn't heard she was with child.

Granny said, "Jack, could you sit with her until Mercy can get back?"

"Darby, her family has got to be told. Will you ride out?"

"If it's all the same, Jack, I'd like to sit with her. If it'll be all right," he looked at Granny.

She nodded. "I s'pose it'll be all right. She's out of the woods, for the most part. A strong girl. Now it'll just be a time of healin'. Have Mister Chen fix her up a steak and some spinach when she comes around. She'll need greens, and she'll need red meat."

Iron, Jack knew. The girl needed iron.

Jack looked at Darby and saw he was staring at Jessica. Jack said, "All right, Darby. I'll be back in a couple of hours. Probably bringing Mister and Missus Brewster with me."

"I'll be right here."

Darby sat in a wooden chair beside the bed and stared at her. The curve of her cheekbones. The way her face sort of settled gradually down to her chin. Her hair was still a tangled mess, and it was spread out on the pillow around her face.

He said, "You have to be the most beautiful girl I've ever seen."

She was breathing gently, and her eyes were shut. He knew she wasn't hearing a thing he said.

Granny Tate and Mercy Freeman had gotten her dress off of her, and she was in petticoats and the blanket had now slipped to her shoulders. One hand was free, so he took it in his.

"Jessica Brewster," he said. "I don't even know you. Not at all. But I know this. I want you to get well."

She stirred a little, but then settled into peaceful sleep.

"What did they do to you?" he said. "How could you have gone with those men? If I can get my hands on them, they'll learn a whole new definition of the word *suffering.*"

She continued to sleep.

He said, "Look at me. Sitting here, in a cowboy town, out in the wild west. I should be back in law school. I should be starting my third year. I was going to be an attorney. My father has plans of me eventually running for the Senate, you know that? My father has been a senator for years, like my grandfather before him. Lots of success, lots of money. The grandfather retired to a lavish estate in upstate New York. Has enough money to choke an elephant.

"I didn't want that. I didn't want law school. You know what I do want?" He shrugged. "Damned if I know. I just know I wasn't happy. You know when I was happiest? When I was filling myself with whiskey with Jack. We'd get drunk and act foolish and laugh like idiots. We'd go into Boston and hit some of the waterfront bars. Put to the test things we had learned in boxing club. He knew a thing or two about Indian wrestling, too. Some sort of Indian tribe. *Shohonee* or some such thing. Sometimes we'd go to a baseball game." He chuckled. "You haven't seen anything until you've seen a National League baseball game. The hooting and hollering, fights breaking out in the stands. A wild time.

"But really, how long can a man hide from himself behind wild times and whiskey? I suppose if I were to write my autobiography, I'd call it *Wild Times and Whiskey*. That's about all I have to show for my time on this earth. That, and two years toward a law degree I don't even want."

She began to stir again, and then her eyes fluttered open. He let go of her hand.

"Hello," he said.

She looked at him with a little surprise. He got to his feet. "Darby Yates. Deputy Marshal of McCabe Gap, at your service."

"McCabe? Is Jack McCabe here?"

Darby nodded. "He's the marshal. He's gone to get your family."

"No." She dropped her head to the pillow. "I don't want to see them. I don't want them to see me like this."

"Do you think they love you?"

She looked at him curiously. What kind of question was that? "I suppose so."

"There's no suppose about it. Do they love you?"

She shrugged, though the motion caused her a little pain. "I suppose every parent loves their child."

He shook his head. "Mine love what they want me to be. Not who I am. Do yours love you? It's a yes-or-no question."

She looked at him long. He could tell she

didn't know what to make of him. "Yes."

"Then they need to see you. And it won't matter what condition you're in, or what you've done. All that'll matter is you're all right."

She said, "Who exactly are you, Darby Yates?"

He smiled. "I'm the man who's going to make sure no harm comes to you ever again."

43

Granny Tate had said she didn't think Jessica's broken ribs would fare well on a wagon ride to the cabin in the valley, so Shapleigh said she could remain at the hotel until she was well enough to travel. Jessica was able to sit up and walk a bit, and she had her meals in her room. Her mother and father and Age spent most of the day with her.

Toward evening, as they were climbing into their wagon to begin the ride back to the valley, Jack walked over and said to them, "How is she?"

Mildred had tears in her eyes, and merely shook her head but couldn't say anything.

Abel bucked up and managed to find the words. "She's not our Jessica. At least, not the Jessica we knew. I mean, she's the same person, obviously, but when she looks at you, it's not the same look in her eye."

Mildred then managed to say, "Whatever those men did to her, they beat the spirit out of her."

Abel shook his head. "She's our daughter, but it's hard to admit she's not the girl we thought she was. Not that I mean to lift any of the blame from those men. They need to be brought to justice. But the Jessica I thought I knew never would have run off with them in the first place."

Jack nodded. "I expect Granny Tate will be checking in on her tonight, after she's done at the Bar W."

Abel Brewster climbed into the wagon seat. He looked years older than the last time Jack had seen him. His shoulders were a little bowed, as though he was carrying a weight that only he could feel, and there were lines on his face Jack didn't remember seeing before. This whole thing with Jessica was apparently taking a lot out of him.

"It's getting late," Abel said. "I'd like to get us home before dark."

Jack nodded. "Be safe."

Abel took the reins in his one hand and gave the horse a *giddyap,* and they started away. Age was sitting in the back of the buckboard, and gave Jack a wave as they rode away.

Darby strolled up to Jack, his shotgun cradled in one arm.

Jack said, "It's really odd the way those men treated her. Beat her the way the did, and apparently used her. You don't usually see that sort of thing out here. Unmarried women of

598

marrying age are so rare, they're often treated almost reverently, even by the worst cut-throats."

"Not in this case, apparently."

"Apparently. It tells us a lot about these men."

Darby said, "I'm going to go up and check on her."

"Darby," Jack hesitated because he wasn't quite sure how to say this. "Darby, I got to know that girl a little on the trail up from Cheyenne. She's not Becky Thatcher."

Jack figured Darby would know the reference. From the book by Mark Twain published three years earlier. Jack had taken out a copy from the public library in Boston, and he knew Darby had read at least part of it.

"Jack," Darby said, "has it ever occurred to you that maybe she's a girl who no one understands? Not even her own family? Maybe she's reaching for something in life and doesn't know what it is? Does any of that sound familiar? I know it could apply to me, and I think it could probably apply to you. All right, so she made a wrong decision. She needs support, not criticism."

Darby turned and walked toward the hotel.

Jack saw Chen sitting in front of Hunter's. Chen had a knife in one hand, and was carving away on a long stick. Jack walked over.

"Good afternoon," Chen said.

Jack nodded.

"How are things going with your friend, the deputy?"

Jack let out a long exhale of exasperation. "I think he's falling in love with Jessica Brewster. It seems to me that's akin to ramming your head into a wall again and again."

Chen chuckled. "Some women are like that. Maybe he is just seeing what he wants to see. But maybe he sees something you don't."

"Why is it you have a way of saying things that make me feel like my legs have been kicked out from under me?"

Chen shrugged. "Just a talent, I guess."

Jack looked at the stick. It had to be four feet long. "What is that you're whittling?"

"I'm making a *goon.* What you would call, I suppose, a stick. Or a staff."

"A weapon?"

Chen shrugged again, carving his knife along the stick. "This is a rough land. I don't use a gun. Never really had the chance to learn. But in my youth, I was a fair hand with a sword and a staff. I don't see any swords for sale at Franklin's, but I can make my own staff."

Jack said nothing while he watched Chen work. Chen then said, "Your friend has to find his way. Just like you do, and just like I do. One question — does he have a good heart?"

Jack knew he was asking about Darby's moral fiber and intentions, not the physical organ pounding away in his chest.

Jack said, "Yes. He has a good heart."

"Then I think you have little to worry about."

"You know, Chen, my father is due back sometime next spring. I hope you're still working at Hunter's. I'd like him to meet you. I think you two would get along well."

Darby found Jessica feeling a little stir crazy.

She said, "I spent the entire day with my parents. People who are like strangers to me. I know they love me, but they think they understand me but they don't, and they want me to fit into their little world, but I can't. I need to get out of this room. To get some fresh air."

"Well, Granny Tate said you shouldn't travel."

"I can at least maybe make the stairs. With a little help."

And so he helped her down to the hotel's small dining room. They moved one step at a time, with her holding the railing with one hand and the other elbow braced against her ribs. She was in a dress her parents had brought with them, and her mother had helped her wash her hair and comb it out and wrap it in a bun.

The dining room wasn't as lavish as the hotels Darby was accustomed to back east. The floor was bare boards and the walls were papered but starting to look a little dingy. The doorway leading out to the lobby was a bit uneven. But it was made of actual boards, not logs. Shapleigh must have had them hauled in from Bozeman or Helena.

Darby pulled a chair out and Jessica lowered herself gingerly into it.

She said, "Wow. That winded me. It was a longer walk than I realized."

"Now we should try to get you something to eat."

"I am a little hungry."

Shapleigh heard the voices and stepped in from a small office he kept off of the lobby.

Darby said, "Mister Shapleigh, are you offering dinner this evening?"

"I'm sorry to say, no. We don't usually have much business this time of week. The stage isn't due for a few more days."

"Well, then," Darby said to Jessica. "Maybe I could go over to Hunter's and see if his coolie cook could fix you some dinner. He's really quite good."

"Darby," she said, "sit a minute."

He slid out a chair and dropped into it. She glanced across the room to see if Shapleigh was still there, and found he wasn't. He had probably gone back to his office.

She said, "Darby, you've been very kind to me. Much moreso than you need to be."

"I meant what I said upstairs, yesterday."

"Darby," she shook her head with a little

disbelief. "Darby, I'm a whore. That's what I am. You have to face it. I belong down the street at that brothel. I made choices and they didn't work out, and they led me down this path. But I can't go back to the life I left. My parents want me to live with them in their little shack in the valley and return to the life I had, but I just can't do that. I'd die if I did that."

"You're not a whore. You can't be held responsible for what those men forced you to do."

Her voice rose a little with exasperation. "They didn't force me, Darby. That's just it. I did what I did because that was the payment required for being there. They provided for us. Me and another woman, Flossy. Then when I decided I didn't want it anymore, they beat the hell out of me and sent me on my way. One man in particular. Two-Finger Walker. He did most of the beating. Then he put me on a horse and sent me away. I wound up here."

He reached out for her hand, but she pulled it away.

He said, "You made some wrong decisions. But I totally understand about not wanting the life your parents have set up for you. I'm the same way. I totally understand."

"Do you really? Does anyone?"

He nodded thoughtfully. "If you let some people in, you might find more of us understand more than you might think. Now I'm going to go and get you some dinner. Then if you want me to go, I'll go and not come back. It's up to you."

Darby found Chen in front of Hunter's, carving on a stick. Chen had left some venison stew on the stove to simmer, so he went in and fetched Darby a small pot of it. Darby brought it back to the hotel, and Shapleigh produced a bowl and a spoon for Jessica, and a cup of tea.

Jessica said to him, "Darby, you don't even know me. Why are you taking such care of me?"

He shrugged. "Maybe I do know you. Maybe I see some similarities between you and me."

"Trust me. There's nothing similar." She dipped her spoon into the stew and took a sip. "I have to admit, this is good. The best cooking I've had since I don't remember when. Yes, I do. Since I left the wagons, back on the trail."

She looked at him. "What do you possibly think we could have in common? Look, I appreciate you helping me down the stairs and getting me supper. And sitting with me upstairs. I really do. But you don't know anything about me, Darby. I made some really bad decisions. Did things I never thought I would do. We drank an awful lot of whiskey, and that was part of it, too. It has a way of clouding your mind. I doubt I would have stayed as long as I did, otherwise. I don't care if I have another drop of the stuff as long as I live. But now I've got to figure out where to go from here."

"Maybe the best thing to do is just eat your stew. Take care of immediate business. Take care of tomorrow when tomorrow gets here."

She took another spoonful of stew. "Bad things label you, Darby. Do you really want to be with a woman who has been labeled like me? Look at you. Educated. Handsome. You can do so much better than me."

"So, you don't believe in second chances?"

She looked at him with a little disbelief. "Do you? Really? In this world?"

"Yeah, I do." He nodded and pulled out a seat and dropped into it. "I think you knew in your heart you can't just be a farmer's wife. It's not right or wrong, it's just who you are. You need something more out of life. You got a little crazy, maybe, and made an impulsive decision. Kind of like I did, leaving school behind and taking the train out here. It turned out your decision was a wrong one, but maybe now it's time for a new beginning. To start over."

"I'm a whore, Darby. That label is there and it's never going away."

"There you go with labels."

"I can't help it. The world is a place of labels. You're a good person, or a bad one.

You're smart or stupid. A hard worker or lazy. The things I did, I'll carry the label of whore the rest of my life. I can try to hide from it, but these things have a way of making themselves known."

"I think maybe you don't want a second chance. Maybe you want to punish yourself for making a wrong decision."

"Darby, there's something I have to tell you. Then you can decide if you really want to stay or not."

He waited.

She said, "I think I'm with child. I'm sure Granny Tate suspects. It belongs to one of those men. I have absolutely no way of knowing which one. That's why I wanted to leave. I couldn't deliver a child in that little cabin with them. I sure couldn't raise it there. Now what do you think of me?"

He said, "You really don't understand, do you?"

She shook her head.

"It's not about mistakes you've made, or things you've done. It's about who you are."

"But you hardly know me."

"I think we both know a whole lot more about each other than we realize."

He reached his hand out to her, and this time she took it. She looked at him as though she wanted to say something, but then her eyes began filling with tears.

"Eat your stew," he said, "before it gets cold."

44

Jessica sat at Hunter's with a cup of hot coffee in front of her. It had been three days, and she was now able to cross the street without a whole lot of pain. She was at a table and Darby was with her. Sitting across from them was Jack.

She said, "That man, Two-Finger, hates your father, Jack. Hates him something fierce. Flossy told me the story about how he lost three fingers on one hand in a fight with your father, and then lost his eye in another. He's here to gun him down."

Jack said, "He'll have to wait until next spring, because Pa's long gone. On his way to California."

Darby said, "Jess, you mentioned a cabin you were staying in."

She nodded. "There's a cabin, maybe a few miles off in the mountains. I'm not good with directions. It wasn't very big, and it had no stove."

Jack looked at Darby. "I think I know which

one she's talking about. That stove is in my office now."

Hunter was putting on another pot of coffee, and was within hearing distance. He called over, "If we know where they are, then why don't we just ride out and take care of business?"

Jack shook his head. "That place is on a small plateau on an otherwise steep slope. It's easy to defend, and would be mighty hard to attack. Pa might have attempted it by himself. One man might have a chance. But I know my limitations."

Jessica said, "Jack, it's starting to look like you don't have a whole lot of limitations. But I doubt they're there now. They move around a lot. As soon as I left, they probably up and moved again."

Darby said to Jack, "Let's get your brothers."

"They left for the fall roundup four days ago. I don't expect to hear from them for two or three more weeks."

Jack said to Jessica, "What about Vic Falcone? Is he still in charge?"

She shook her head and explained what happened to Falcone, and to the one she had originally left her family to be with. Cade. And they had sent Lane on his way because he had broken the wrist on his gunhand and would be of little use to them.

Jack said, "So there's only two of them?

Walker and White-Eye?"

"There's a gambler who rode in. We were staying maybe two or three days south of here at the time. He said he had a run-in with you. You locked him in a tool shed." She snickered. "Did you really do that?"

Jack nodded and reached for his coffee. "That was before we got the jail built."

"And since then Walker's got two others working for him. Two brothers. They robbed a farm down south of Bozeman. Shot the farmer and got some sacks of flour and a couple horses. The law down there is looking for them."

Darby looked at Jack. "What are we gonna do?"

"I'm going to ride down the stretch in the morning and see if there's anyone at Zack Johnson's spread. He and most of his men are very likely conducting their own fall roundup, but he might have left someone at the ranch. I'm going to see if anyone can be spared to stay with Aunt Ginny and the girls. You'll all be okay here while I'm gone. You have that shotgun. And Hunter's here, and Chen."

"Chen?" Darby tossed a glance at the old man behind the bar. Chen was wiping glasses and beer mugs. His long white braid fell down his back. "That old coolie?"

"Don't call him that. He's one of the best men I've ever known, and I'd lay odds on him in a fight against most anyone."

"Seriously?"

"Remember when he pulled you out of the top bunk and slammed you on the floor?"

Darby gave a dismissive shrug. "I was hung-over."

Jack called out to Chen and asked him to come over.

"Darby," Jack said. "I want you to try to push Chen down."

Darby was looking at him like he had lost his mind, but Chen grinned. Chen said, "Can I have ten dollars if he can't?"

Bree had Fred saddle a horse for her. He picked the bay gelding she had ridden the day she rescued Nina. With a rifle in the scabbard, she stepped up and into the saddle. She was in a split skirt and riding boots, and a sombrero was pulled down to her temples. Aunt Ginny hated to see her wear that thing, but it was ideally suited for riding through these hills. It kept the sun off of her head and out of her eyes, and helped cushion her head from any low hanging tree branches. Not that she made a habit out of riding into tree branches, but it was good to be prepared.

"I'll be back in a while," she said to Fred.

She rode at first aimlessly through the pine forest that covered the ridge on the western side of the valley, and then got a hankering to visit Jack. So she turned her horse down toward the pass and the small trail that cut through it, and came out behind Hunter's. She rode toward the jail, and swung out of the saddle. There was no hitching rail yet, so she left the horse ground hitched — which is to say with the rein trailing — and stepped in.

She found the place empty. Both bunks were in disarray. One of the cowhands working for the Circle M had told her a friend of Jack's from school had come west and Jack had hired him on as a deputy. Apparently he was as inept as housekeeping as Jack was.

She saw a Winchester leaning in a corner and picked it up. It was one of the rifles from the ranch. She thought maybe when the boys got back from the roundup she would ask Josh to build him a gunrack. Josh was not a finished carpenter, but she thought he could put together a reasonably functional rifle rack. Bree had seen the town marshal's office in Bozeman once, and he had a rack filled with rifles.

She heard footsteps at the door and turned expecting it to be Jack, or maybe his deputy friend. But this man looked like no one who would belong at Harvard. He looked like he had been on the trail a long time. He was a little taller than Jack, and his shirt was darkened from one sweat stain on top of another. His face had a bushy beard, and his hair was long and stringy. He wore a battered looking sombrero, and one eye was milky white with a long scar that ran from above his brow to his cheekbone.

"Anything I can do for you?" she said.

He grinned. But it was not a pleasant one. She was reminded of a cat about to pounce on a mouse.

"Yeah, missy. You can come with me."

"And what, on Earth, would make you think I would want to go with you?"

"I been watching your house for a while. I trailed you into town. I'm to fetch you and bring you back. Then when your Pa comes to get you, we'll be waitin' for him."

"You're dreaming if you think I'm going anywhere with you."

His grin got wider. "Don't make it hard on yourself."

He began walking toward her, and reached a hand to her. "Why don't you just give me that there gun."

She realized she was still holding the rifle. She had to think quickly. He was too close, and approaching too quickly, for her to jack a cartridge into the chamber and have any hopes of getting off a shot. She didn't really want to kill anyone, anyway.

She had to think quickly. Pa had never actually trained her the way he had Josh and Jack, but she had watched him train them. And he had given her a lot of advice on how to survive, as well as showing her how to shoot and ride.

This man had only one eye that worked. She quickly lunged forward, driving the muzzle of the rifle into the other eye. She didn't hit the eye but caught his brow, but it was enough.

"Hey!" he called out, pulling back and away, squinting his eye shut and reaching up with one hand.

She then swung upward with the rife stock, catching him in the groin. His eyes widened and he went down on one knee. She then jammed the muzzle of the gun into his ear.

He yelped and folded downward to the floor, one hand covering his ear and the other at his eye. Blood was seeping through his fingers from the gash above his eye. His knees were locked tight.

She pulled the pistol from his holster and set it on the desk, then jacked a round into the chamber.

"All right, get into the cell," she said. "The back room."

He got to his knees, then pushed himself to his feet. He was wiping blood away from the gash over his one good eye, and with the other hand still hanging onto his ear.

He turned to make a break for the door, but she fired and a section of wood at the doorway tore up and splintered, and he jumped back. She jacked the gun again, and made certain she was back far enough that he couldn't lunge at her.

She said, "Get in that cell, or the next one takes out the one good eye you have left. Your choice."

He stared at her a minute, then turned and walked into the cell. She shut the door, and slid into place the two-by-four Jack used as a bar. The man with the white eye wasn't getting out.

Jack came running, bursting through the door. Another man about his age was behind him, and wearing a tin star. Must be his friend from back east.

"I heard the gunshot," Jack said. "We were over at Hunter's."

"A man was here, threatening to kidnap me. I arrested him."

Jack looked through the window into the cell. "White-Eye?"

White-Eye said, "I need me a doctor. That wildcat out there near killed me."

Jack looked at her with amazement. "You arrested White-Eye?"

She gave him a smug smile. "I *am* a Mc-Cabe."

45

Darby fetched Granny Tate to come and work on the prisoner. Bree sat behind Jack's desk. His rifle was once again standing in one corner, and she had gotten hers from her saddle and it was laid across the desk.

Jack said, "You really probably ought to go home, Bree."

"I think I'll stick around. Looks to me like you need a second deputy."

Jack rolled his eyes and tried to repress a huff of exasperation. Bree's sense of humor could be maddening sometimes.

Jack heard the clopping of horse hooves on the ground and the creak of wagon wheels in motion. "Sounds like Darby's back."

Jack opened the door, and held it as Granny Tate stepped in. She leaned on her cane as she walked.

"Thanks for coming, Granny," Jack said.

White-Eye was watching through the tiny window in the cell. "*That's* the doctor? I never seen a sadder lookin' doctor."

Jack said, "Shut up, White-Eye, or I'll let my sister beat on you some more."

He scowled, but Bree was giving her smug grin again.

Jack said, "White-Eye, we're coming in. If you do anything out of line, there won't be anything left of you to turn over to a territorial marshal."

Jack unlocked the door and he and Granny went in. She examined the wound over his eye and thought it needed maybe a couple of stitches.

White-Eye said, "That wildcat jammed a rifle into my ear, too."

Granny looked in his ear. "Aside from enough dirt in there to plant a potato, I think you'll be all right. You got a small gash, but it should heal."

Jack said with a grin, "Should we give it the corn liquor treatment?"

She returned the smile. "I don't think we have to put him through that right now."

"Just wishful thinking."

Darby was standing in the doorway to the cell. He said, "Considering what they put Jessica through, he's lucky he's still alive at all."

White-Eye said, "You ain't got what it takes, city slicker."

"No?" Darby charged in, shotgun in hand, pushing the muzzle into White-Eye's face. White-Eye backed up until he was against the wall. Darby said, "I'll pull the trigger and blow your brains all over the wall."

Jack grabbed Darby and yanked him back and pushed him out through the cell door. White-Eye stepped away from the wall, and Jack pulled his pistol from his holster, cocking it with the motion, and had the gun up and in White-Eye's face before White-Eye could blink.

Jack said, "Don't try anything fancy, White-Eye, or I'll finish what he started."

White-Eye apparently knew a hopeless situation when he saw it. He stood his ground while Jack held the door and Granny Tate hobbled her way out into the main office. Jack then stepped out and shut the door and slid the bar back in place.

White-Eye called out, "They'll be comin' for me. Just you wait."

Jack called back, "Shut up, or I'll hog-tie you and muzzle you."

Something in Jack's tone must have been convincing. White-Eye shut up.

"Bree," Jack said. "Take Granny Tate home, will you please? And bring a rifle with you."

Bree got to her feet and grabbed her Winchester from the desk.

Jack escorted Granny out to the wagon, and held an elbow while she worked her way up and into the wagon seat.

"Thanks for coming, Granny," Jack said. "I may have been a medical student, but you're the doctor around here."

"You need anything, you let me know. His wound starts showin' any signs of infection, you send someone for me."

"Thanks, Granny. We will."

Bree hopped up onto the wagon seat and freed the brake and turned the team around.

Jack stepped back into the office and shut the door behind him. Darby was sitting on the edge of the desk. He had laid the shotgun down across it.

Jack stood a moment, looking at his friend, deliberating the entire situation. How to best handle this. He decided to let his temper win out, and he charged at Darby and grabbed him by the lapels of his vest and pulled him off the desk and slammed him into the wall.

Jack said through clenched teeth, "I went out on a limb talking these town folks into letting you stay on as deputy. And by God you're going to take the job seriously. Do you understand me?"

He let Darby free. Darby took a step to steady himself, then smoothed out his vest.

Jack said, "This isn't just some lark. These are good people here, and this job has to be taken seriously."

Darby nodded. "I know, Jack. I know."

Darby began pacing, reaching with one hand to the back of his neck. "It's just that, well, when it comes to Jessica . . ."

"I know. You're taken with her."

He nodded. "I guess I am."

"Can I ask, why? I mean, I knew her back on the trail. She was trouble all the way."

"I guess it's just that I see a kindred spirit in her. To some extent, at least. Someone who's direction in life has already been mapped by her family. But she doesn't want that direction. Trying to follow that direction just chokes her off. She had to get away before it killed her. Now, the decision she made to leave the wagons and go with those men was the wrong one. Granted. And she knows that now. But she had to do something. There are people who would say that I made the wrong decision running away from school the way I did to come here."

It was now fully dawning on Jack. "That's why you came here."

"My grandfather sat on the Supreme Court. My father is a senator. They've been talking to me about the Senate and possibly the presidency since I was ten years old. Scared the life out of me. I've been dancing to their music every step of the way."

"I guess I did always know you were running from something. I guess maybe that's at least partly why we became such close friends."

"It was that letter from you, telling me you weren't going back to school. That's what gave me the courage to step away, too. Don't you see? You, me, Jessica. The situations are different on the surface, but down deep, we're

620

three proverbial peas in a pod."

Jack nodded and raised his brows. "I guess I never saw it that way."

Jessica suddenly spoke, from the doorway. "You understand me, Darby. Like no one else."

Jack and Darby both turned to the doorway. Jack had no idea how long she had been there.

She stepped in and said to Jack, "So, cowboy. You still disapprove of me?"

Jack took off his hat and tossed it onto his desk, then sat at the corner of desktop. "I guess I was passing judgment on you. I apologize. An old Shoshone chief who was one of my father's teachers said once we should never judge each other. We're all equal in the eyes of the Great Spirit."

She went over to Darby, who took her in a hug.

"So," she said, "what do we do now? Where do we go from here?"

White-Eye was in the cell, looking out the window into the office. He said, "Well hello there, Missy."

She looked up at the sound of his voice and clung onto Darby tighter.

Darby said, "I'm gonna kill him."

"Outside," Jack said. "Both of you."

Darby and Jessica stepped out the door, and Jack followed. He said to Darby, "Why don't you get her back to the hotel. I'll stay and watch the prisoner."

After Darby had returned, he found Jack had put on a pot of coffee. Jack poured coffee into a tin cup and handed it to Darby.

Jack said, "Look, I know you want to put a bullet in him. But we wear these badges, and with them comes a public trust."

"To hell with public trust. This is too personal."

"Then think about what it would do to you. It would make you one step closer to what he is. You can't do that to Jessica. She needs you now."

Darby gave a reluctant nod. "All right."

Jack placed a hand on Darby's shoulder. "Maybe it'd be best for you if you stayed away from the jail while he's here. There's other marshal stuff you can do. Walking the rounds, and such."

Darby nodded.

White-Eye said from the cell, "That's right. You keep that boy away from me. I'll turn him inside out, you give me the chance."

Jack said, "Tomorrow, I'm going to see if Ford has some lumber and I'm going to make a door so we can shut that window."

White-Eye said, ignoring Jack, "Let me tell you about that little girl. What I done to her. I used her real good. More'n once. Let me tell you all about it."

Darby let the coffee cup fly. "I'm gonna kill him."

Jack stepped in front of him. "Give me the

shotgun first."

Darby handed Jack the shotgun, then lifted the two-by-four from the cell door, unbarring it.

White-Eye was grinning and taunting. "You let that boy in here, and I'll give him the thrashing of his life."

Darby charged into the cell. Jack called out to him, "He's going to fight dirty! You have to do the same!"

Then the sounds of a fracas filled the air. Jack went to his desk and laid the shotgun across it, and took a sip of coffee.

He heard grunts. Hard breathing. The sounds of fists colliding with skulls. A crashing sound on the floor. Something slamming into the wall. Jack took another sip of coffee.

Then all was quiet in the cell. Jack waited, and after a couple of moments Darby stepped from it. Darby's face was bloodied. One eye was swollen shut. His shirt had been torn open, and his badge was gone. His derby had been on his head when he went into the cell, but it was also gone, and his hair was flying like he had just stepped out of a heavy wind. The knuckles of his right hand were battered and bleeding.

"Is he still alive?" Jack said.

Darby nodded. At that moment, Bree came in the door. With all of the commotion, Jack hadn't heard the wagon outside.

"What happened?" she said, horrified, staring at Darby.

Jack said, "You better bring back Granny Tate."

46

Darby sat on a small bench in front of the hotel.

It had been two days since his fight with White-Eye. One of Darby's eyes was still swollen shut, and a gash on one cheekbone had scabbed over. He had lost a back tooth, as White-Eye had nailed him with a hook punch in the side of the jaw and the tooth had shattered. It took three plugs of whiskey before he was numb enough for Granny Tate to pull the remaining shards of tooth from his gum with a pair of pliers, then she got out some thread and sewed the gum shut. During the fight, Darby had grabbed White-Eye by the head and pulled him down and brought his knee up and into White-Eye's face, and now his knee was swollen and it hurt to walk.

Jessica was sitting next to him, close enough that their hips were almost touching, and she was ever so slightly leaning into him, a subtle gesture but one with proprietary meaning.

"Does it hurt much?" she said.

"Only when I smile." He couldn't help but grin, but then winced. "Like then."

"You shouldn't have done that, you know. Fighting White-Eye. He could have killed you."

"He didn't stand a chance. I had too much to fight for."

That got a smile from her.

He said, "And I had the element of surprise on him. Boxing class at Harvard. And Jack and I were on the rowing team. That kind of thing can build muscle like nothing else. And we got into a few scraps in a couple bars down on the Boston waterfront. Let me tell you, those boys in those waterfront bars know how to scrap."

She ran a hand along his arm. "You are rather tightly muscled for a scholar."

He smiled. Then winced again.

"Sorry," she said.

"Jess, I've got to ask you something. I know you don't know what it is you want in life."

She shrugged. "Do you?"

"Maybe not long-term. But for now, I think I'll be content to be a deputy, working for Jack. He's right. These people here need us, and they're good people. They deserve someone who will take this job seriously. That is, if you think you might be content to be a deputy's wife."

"Why, Darby Yates. Are you asking me to

marry you?"

He looked at her slyly. "Maybe. Would you say yes if I asked you?"

"Maybe," she said, putting on the coyness. "Sometimes, you just have to go out on a limb and take a chance."

He said, "I don't have a ring. I do have funds, but I don't have immediate access to them. Out here, in the middle of nowhere, I don't see any way to get you one."

"Sometimes, a girl doesn't need a ring and finery and such. Sometimes a girl just needs the right man making the right offer."

He reached over and took her hand. "I don't know what tomorrow will bring, or where it will lead us. I don't know how long I'll be content to remain here wearing this tin star. It might be a week or it might be ten years. But I know I want you at my side. Jessica Brewster, will you consent to be my wife?"

She looked away, still doing the coy act, but with a grin breaking through. "Well, I don't know . . ."

He grabbed her and pulled her in for a kiss. She wrapped her arms around him. Suddenly neither cared that they were in a public place and potentially making a spectacle of themselves.

She pulled back, by only an inch or two. "I knew I would marry you, back in the hotel when I told you my secret, and you could

627

either stay or go, and you chose to stay. Right then, I knew I'd marry you if you asked."

"Somehow I knew that very first day, when you rode in on that horse, almost falling out of the saddle. Right then, I knew I never wanted you out of my sight. Strange, isn't it?"

She shrugged. "I don't know. Some people know each other for years before they marry. They have long courtships. But I think there's a moment, somewhere along the line, when they just know. It's a yes-or-no moment. And my heart says yes."

"You're pretty smart, for a farm girl."

"Oh yeah?" She was smiling as widely as she could. "*Farm girl,* is it?"

He was grinning, too. It was killing the side of his jaw, but he was just too happy not to.

She said, "I do have a question, though."

"Anything."

"I'm with child. I went to Granny Tate yesterday and she confirmed it. She's as sure as a body can be, this early on. What are we going to do? I really don't even know who the father is."

He shook his head with a smile. "Silly girl. *I'm* the father. I'm going to raise this child with you. We're going to be the parents. It doesn't matter what happened before. This child is ours."

She suddenly had tears in her eyes.

"All right, farm girl. You're not going to go

and get all weepy on me, are you?"

She laughed through the tears. "I'm just realizing I don't think I ever knew what the definition of the word *happy* was. Until now."

Jack had gone to Hunter's for a cup of coffee. He now stepped out of the barroom and stood for a moment on the boardwalk in front of Hunter's and took a look about the town. *His* town, he sort of thought of it now. Not that he had any illusions about it belonging to him, but when you were responsible for something you sort of developed a sense of ownership about it. He was sure Chen felt a certain sense of ownership toward Hunter's, even though the establishment belonged entirely to Hunter.

It was only a few months earlier that he had been packing his trunk back at Harvard, leaving school for what appeared to be his usual summer trip home, but knowing he would never be returning to school. Saying goodbye to Darby and figuring he would probably never see his friend again. And now here he was, the town marshal of this little community.

He thought about the letter he had sent Pa. It had been a few weeks, now. The letter was probably halfway between here and San Francisco. He wondered where Pa was. Since Pa was in no hurry, and meandering through the mountains was somehow rejuvenating for him, Jack figured Pa to be anywhere between one hundred and five hundred miles away by now. Sleeping under the open sky in the mountains. Hunting elk or deer for his dinner. Drinking from cold mountain streams. Standing on high cliffs, looking off at the vistas before him. Mountains standing tall with rocky ledges and forests of pine.

He hoped Pa understood. He had told Aunt Ginny, and though it was a little difficult for her to accept that she actually knew so little about the nephew she thought she knew so well, it had not been a disaster. Surprisingly, once she got past the initial surprise of it, she understood. Jack experienced a similar thing with Josh and Bree. Dusty was the easiest to tell, because Dusty had no preconceived notions about Jack. The last hurdle, he knew, would be getting past Pa. Would Pa understand and be accepting, or would he look at Jack with disappointment?

Jack saw Darby and Jessica sitting in front of the hotel. Jessica was someone else he thought he would probably never see again, after she rode off with Vic Falcone and his little band of outlaws. And just two months ago, if anyone had been willing to bet him that Nina would be out of his life, and it would be Darby and Jessica, probably the oddest couple Jack had ever seen, sitting in front of the hotel hand-in-hand, he would have taken that bet.

Jack had known other girls before, but none had taken hold of his heart like Nina had. Aunt Ginny had said he needed to give it time. His heart would heal, and he would be able to put her behind him. And yet, he wondered how much time had to pass? It had been weeks, and yet the pain sometimes seemed as fresh as the first day.

He crossed the open expanse of earth between Hunter's and the jail, and went in. His rifle was where he had left it, leaning in one corner.

Hunter had asked if Jack really thought it safe to leave his prisoner unattended, and Jack thought it would be safe for a short time. Long enough for him to grab a cup of coffee. The only real danger to the prisoner was from Darby, and he was across the street.

Jack stepped up to the small window and looked into the cell. White-Eye was stretched out on the bunk. His head was resting on the tattered old pillow Jack had found for the bunk, and he had one arm up and across his eyes.

"You still alive?" Jack said.

"Barely."

White-Eye had emerged from the fight in worse shape than Darby. Jack had found him on the floor, unconscious. Granny Tate had determined he had a concussion, but she didn't think his skull was fractured. At one point during the fight Darby had slammed

White-Eye's head repeatedly into the log wall.

Well, Jack thought, apparently he and his brothers had made the wall tight and solid.

White-Eye's face was bruised and swollen. He had taken a punch into his good eye, which was now nearly swollen shut.

White-Eye said, "You know, Walker's gonna be comin' for me. And when he sees what you did to one of his men, he ain't gonna be happy."

"Walker comes for you, and I guarantee my first bullet will be for you."

"You keep that deputy away from me."

"You talk about that girl again the way you did, and next time I'll let him kill you. We're a long way from the main trail, White-Eye. Remember that."

Jack again gave serious thought to building a small door so he could shut the cell entirely off from the office.

He sat down behind his desk, and looked at the empty coffee cup on the desk in front of him and the kettle standing on the cold wood stove. Another cup would do him well, he thought, but it was already turning off warm outside and to start a fire in the stove would heat the place up intolerably.

It was Thursday. The day before, he had sent a letter off on the stage with Walt addressed to the territorial marshal. Walt said he would deliver it to the town marshal's office in Bozeman the next day, which would be today. There it would wait until the territorial marshal came through, which he tended to do once every month or so. Essentially, White-Eye could be in this jail for awhile.

A problem, Jack could see, was going to be resources. To keep a prisoner in this jail for what could turn out to be many weeks was going to require resources. Three meals a day. The community was already providing this for Jack and now for Darby. He wondered if Franklin or Shapleigh or Hunter had put any thought into how expensive having a lawman in town could actually be.

This community was large enough that it needed law, even an unofficial lawman like Jack.

"Hey, McCabe," White-Eye called out.

"What now?"

"I'm hungry."

Jack pulled a pocket watch out of his vest. It was eighteen minutes to eleven. "It's not even noon yet. You gotta wait."

Jack reached for a newspaper. It was a couple weeks old, put out by a press in Virginia City. It had been on the stage the day before. Out here on the remote frontier, getting the daily paper was unheard of. At Harvard, he had read the Boston Globe every morning, but here he would have to take whatever paper he could find.

Jack flipped it open. On page two there was

an article about Senator Fenton D. Yates, Sr., D-NY, announcing he was seeking re-election. Senator Yates was Darby's father. Darby was actually Fenton D. Yates, Junior. The middle initial was for Dobbins, which is where the nickname Darby came from.

Amazing how much Jack knew about Darby, but apparently without really knowing much about him at all.

"Hey, McCabe!"

Jack shook his head. He had the passing thought of asking Granny Tate if she had anything that could act as a sedative and knock White-Eye out for a few hours, so he could have some peace of mind.

"Can't you be quiet?" Jack called back.

"I was wonderin' what yer holdin' me for? You never did actually charge me with any crime."

Jack was new at being a lawman, and didn't really know any of the protocols. He supposed they probably didn't really apply here, because his position was little more than honorary. His tin star was more symbolic than official.

"Well, I'm sure you're guilty of something. You ran with Vic Falcone long enough. I'm sure Dusty could testify to some of the raids and robberies you were involved in."

"You think that would hold up in court? I 'spect I'm gonna be a free man once you get me in front of a judge."

Jack hadn't thought about that. At the moment, the main thing he wanted was to hand White-Eye over to the marshal and get him out of here.

Jack actually knew the territorial marshal. He was a half-Cheyenne by the name of Dan Bodine who had been a cowhand on the McCabe ranch years ago.

"One thing you haven't thought about, White-Eye. You were arrested and beaten-up by a sixteen-year-old girl. That kind of thing can stay with a man. That'll follow you around for a while."

There. White-Eye was quiet. Finally. Jack figured White-Eye hadn't counted on that. Jack went back to his paper.

He then heard the clip-clip of a horse outside. It sounded like it was coming away from town. In one direction was the town, and in the other was the mountain pass the town was named for. The pass leading into the valley. This meant it was probably someone coming from either the McCabe ranch or Zack Johnson's' ranch at the far end of the valley. Or maybe one of the farms.

He heard the horse stop outside the door, so he put the paper down and waited. The door opened, and he got a surprise. It was a woman, maybe a little taller than Jessica. She looked to be maybe mid-thirties. Jack found it tough enough to guess a woman's age, and here on the frontier hard living tended to age a woman early. This woman's dress was tattered and streaked with dirt, and her face smudged with soot and dust. She looked almost as bad as Jessica had when she rode into town, but there were no signs of bruising. She was just many weeks removed from a bath.

Jack got to his feet. "Ma'am?"

She said, "You Jack McCabe?"

He nodded. It occurred to him that he had seen her somewhere before, but he couldn't quite remember where.

"I come with a message from Two-Finger Walker. He says he's comin' tomorrow at noon for the man you're holdin' in the cell."

Now Jack remembered where he had seen her. At Falcone's camp outside of Cheyenne, when he and Marshal Kincaid had ridden in to fetch Jessica.

White-Eye called out. "Flossy? That you?"

"Yeah, White-Eye. You okay?"

"You tell Walker they done beat me somethin' fierce, and now they're starvin' me."

Jack said, "He didn't get the beating he deserves, I promise you that."

She said to him, "Look, I don't want no trouble. I'm just deliverin' a message for Walker. He says if this White-Eye isn't on a horse, saddled and waitin' for him, then he's gonna burn this town to the ground."

"So, he sent you to town to tell me that?"

She nodded. "Look, McCabe. You don't

636

seem like a bad sort. But you can't stand up to the kind of man Walker is. He's a killer. And he means what he says. You don't turn White-Eye free, he's gonna kill you and everyone else here."

47

"Flossy," Jack said, "is that your name? Where's his camp?"

"You think I'm gonna tell you that?"

"I think you should. Considering what he and his men have done to Jessica, and are probably doing to you. Considering they are killers and robbers, and will probably continue to kill and rob. Also, think about this. There's probably a reward on them. At least on Walker. That money could be yours if you turn them in."

White-Eye was at the jail cell window. "Don't you do that, Flossy. Walker finds out you tried to turn him in, he'll kill you. You know that. This here boy won't be able to help you. Not at all."

Jack said, "Shut up, White-Eye, or I'll tell everyone you were arrested by a sixteen-year-old girl."

Flossy's eyes lit up with a smile. "That true?"

Jack nodded. "My sister. She almost blinded

him and emasculated him. Good thing he caught her in a good mood."

Jessica came running in, or as close to a hobbling run as she could manage with her broken ribs. Darby was with her.

"Flossy," she said. "I thought it was you. We were sitting in front of the hotel and saw you ride up."

"Jessica," Flossy said.

They looked at each other for a moment, then took each other in a hug.

Flossy said, "You cleaned up right nice."

Jessica nodded. "They're taking good care of me here."

Flossy touched a hand to the side of Jessica's face. Almost motherly. "I'd like to stay and talk, but I have to get back. Walker said to come in and tell McCabe what I had to, and then to come on back."

Jack didn't want to let her leave. He needed information on Walker and his little gang. As much as he could get. He had to think fast.

He said, "You're not going anywhere. You're under arrest."

She raised her brows puzzledly. "What for?"

"I'll think of something. Vagrancy, maybe."

He couldn't really arrest her for vagrancy because there were no town ordinances, but he thought she might not know that.

"So, you gonna lock me up?"

He shook his head. "Not with White-Eye. It wouldn't be decent. And we don't have any separate cell for a woman. Instead, we'll take you over to Hunter's for a meal and then figure something."

Jack grabbed his Winchester and he stepped to the doorway, and with a hand motioned for Flossy to come along.

Outside, he said to Darby, "Go back to that bench in front of the hotel and position yourself there. Watch this building like a hawk. If anyone comes near it, call out to me."

"Where are you going to be?"

"In Hunter's, questioning the prisoner. Jessica, I'm going to need your help."

She gave Darby a long look and a little smile, sort of saying, *Don't worry, I'll be all right.* Jack figured if he was in Darby's place, he wouldn't want Jessica associating with the very people she had run away from any longer than necessary. Jack gave Darby a nod, and he and Jessica escorted Flossy into Hunter's.

Darby returned to the bench he and Jessica had been sitting on, and fixed his gaze on the marshal's office.

In the barroom, chairs were all upside down on the tables. Jack righted three of them, and held two as the women sat down. The air was filled with the aroma of venison stew, something Chen had made more than once and as far as Jack was concerned, he could make it as much as he wanted. The very smell sent Jack's mouth to watering.

"Mister Chen," Jack said. "Do you have enough stew for the three of us?"

Chen nodded. "I always make extra, just in case."

"Well, I'd appreciate if you could serve up three bowls. This is marshal business. I'll square it up with Hunter later."

Jack sat down, and leaned the rifle against the edge of the table. Chen took a ladle and scooped stew into three bowls, and set them down in front of Jack and the women. The stew was brownish, with chunks of venison floating in it.

Flossy took a spoon and gave a tentative taste, then began slurping one spoonful after another.

Jessica said, "Living with those men, you don't eat regular. We did a little better when Vic was in charge, but after Walker drove him out, we were lucky to get one meal a day. And we ate after the men did, getting whatever leftovers there were."

Jack shook his head. "Absolutely barbaric."

"A ten-dollar word, but it hits the nail right on the head."

"Why did you stay? Why did you tolerate that kind of treatment?"

Jessica shrugged. She was about to say something, but Flossy cut her off. "There weren't no place else to go. What're we gonna do? Whore it up in a saloon some place? Twenty or thirty customers on a Saturday night? Sleep in beds filled with lice and bed bugs? At least with these men, it was the same regular customers. And they didn't treat us too bad. In a saloon, you don't know just who you're servin'. He might be the kind who likes to beat on you."

"They beat on Jessica pretty bad."

"That was because she said she wanted to leave."

Jessica said, "Flossy, you don't have to go back."

Flossy nodded. "Yes, Sweetie, I do. They'll kill me if I don't. Walker made that clear when he sent me down here. He said what you got would be nothin' to what I would get if I tried to run out on them."

Flossy took another deep spoonful of venison stew. "Jessica, get out of town. I was serious what I said. Walker intends to burn this place to the ground. He'll do it if White-Eye isn't turned free, and he'll probably do it anyway. He'll kill anyone he finds here."

"Why?" Jack said. The more he could learn about Walker, the better.

"He has a powerful hate for your father. He knows it would be suicide to ride on your family's ranch. Vic proved that last summer. So instead, he intended to kidnap your sister and then kill your father when he came for her. That didn't work. It just got White-Eye arrested. So now he's just gonna burn the town and kill anyone here. That'll draw him out."

Jack shook his head. "My father isn't even here. He rode out weeks ago. We don't expect to see him until next spring sometime."

That caught Flossy by surprise. "I don't think Walker knows that. I doubt it'll stop him, though."

Chen had drifted over. "Who these men?"

"Killers," Jack said. "Raiders. They take what they want, killing anyone who gets in the way. Robbing stages and way stations and farms or ranches. They ride away into the mountains, and there's not enough law out here to chase after 'em."

Chen said, "There are men like that in China, too."

"How do you deal with them there?"

"The army hunts them and kills them."

"That's about what's gonna happen here, too."

Flossy shook her head. "You're a good man, McCabe. And you mean well. But it's just you and that city slicker to stand against these men. They're professional killers. How many men have you killed?"

Jack had to admit, until this summer he had never killed any.

She said, "That's what I thought. A man like Two-Finger, he can't count the number he's killed. He and his men are gonna ride over this town, and they ain't gonna leave nothin' behind."

Word moved quickly through town. Fred rode into Hunter's for an afternoon beer and rode back to the ranch with the news. Brewster and his son pulled up in front of Franklin's with their wagon to buy supplies, and they heard the entire story from Franklin.

Hunter found Jack in his office. Hunter said, "You and Darby aren't standing alone against these men. I'll be standing with you. I may not be a gunhawk, but I stood alongside your Pa more'n once against Indian raiders, and rustlers."

Jack wanted to say no, it wasn't Hunter's job to do this. Jack was here wearing this tin star so the townspeople wouldn't have to be at risk. But he knew Flossy was right. He and Darby alone wouldn't be able to stop Walker and his men. Jack's brothers were too far away to get back in time to be of any help.

"Thank you," Jack said. "That means a lot to me. But I hope it doesn't get you killed."

"So, do you have any thoughts about how to defend this town? Maybe Darby could be on the roof of the hotel with a rifle."

Jack shook his head. "Darby couldn't hit the side of a wall if he was standing ten feet from it. But I do have a couple of ideas. First, though, I want everyone cleared from town. Miss Alisha and her girls. Everyone. I want every building deserted. I'd like you to coordinate it. I want everyone out by sunset."

Hunter nodded. "I'll get right on it."

Miss Alisha currently had five women in her employ, and they rode up to the McCabe ranch in a wagon with Hunter driving. Aunt Ginny stood on the front porch and watched Hunter pull the team to a stop in front of her.

"They can stay in the bunkhouse," Ginny said. "I'll have Fred move the men out. They can sleep in bedrolls outside. And Alisha?"

"Yes, ma'am?" Alisha said. She was sitting on the wagon seat with Hunter.

"You and your employees are guests here, but you're not working. Not even for free. Do you get my meaning?" Ginny fixed her with the Gaze.

Alisha dropped her eyes and nodded. "Yes, ma'am."

Hunter smiled. The law had spoken. He turned the team around and headed them down to the bunkhouse.

Temperance stepped out of the house to stand beside Aunt Ginny.

"Temperance, we have guests for dinner. A lot of them. We'll have to prepare more food."

"Yes, ma'am."

"Where's Bree?"

Temperance said, "I haven't seen her in a while."

"Well, find her."

■ ■ ■ ■

Bree was out back, a lariat in her hand. The house was three hundred feet behind her as she walked toward a chocolate brown gelding. She wore gloves so the rope wouldn't rough-up her hand. Fred did this barehanded every day — she didn't know how he managed it.

She had waited by the kitchen and watched while Hunter drove Miss Alisha and her girls to the bunkhouse, and then she saw Hunter leave again for town. It was then that Bree headed out back to the remuda. She didn't need anyone seeing her and telling Aunt Ginny where she was. Then Aunt Ginny would call to her, and Bree didn't need the bother of the argument that would ensue.

"Easy, boy," Bree said, walking up to the gelding. His head was down and he was munching on some grass. Mountain horses weren't tall, and this one was just barely fourteen hands. But like most mountain-bred horses, he could run hard and all day.

Bree twirled the loop and dropped it on the gelding. First try. She could handle a rope as well as any man on this ranch. After all, she was Pa's daughter. The boys weren't the only ones living in that man's shadow.

The horse lifted his head suddenly as the loop slipped down his neck, as if to say, *Hey,*

I was eating.

Bree slipped a hackamore over the horse's head, and said, "Come on, boy."

The horse twitched an ear at her, then reluctantly started following along.

She led the horse into the barn and a stall, where her saddle waited for her. She had already hauled it in from the tack room. A Winchester was tucked in the saddle boot; she had seen to that.

She fixed a bridle in place, and then dropped a blanket over the horse's back. Then she grabbed the saddle with one hand on the horn, and hefted. It was heavy, but she was stronger than she looked, and dropped the saddle onto the horse's back.

That was when the barn door opened and Temperance walked in. "Bree. There you are. I've been looking all over for you."

"Well, here I am." She went to work tightening the cinch. Or the girth, as Pa always called it. Pa was forever falling into Texas talk.

"What're you doing?" Temperance said. "We got a lot of mouths to feed tonight. Aunt Ginny's going to need help."

"You'll have to do it without me. I'm riding into town."

Temperance stood silently for a moment. Then she said, "Aunt Ginny's not going to like that."

Bree stopped working with the saddle and turned to face Temperance. "That's why you're not going to tell her. I fetched this horse myself so Fred wouldn't have to do it, so I wouldn't have to deal with him. I don't want anyone knowing."

"But . . . what am I going to say?"

"Tell her you couldn't find me."

"I can't lie to that woman, Bree. She can cut me in half just by looking at me."

Bree nodded. "Okay. Then just wait here until I'm gone."

Temperance was relieved. "I can do that."

Bree led the horse out of the barn and stepped up and into the saddle.

Temperance said, "It's gonna be dark in a few hours."

"It's okay. I won't be coming back tonight."

Temperance gave her a little frown. She wasn't sure just what Bree had in mind.

Bree said, "Take care of things while I'm gone."

And she turned her horse across the grassy meadow and toward the small trail that would come out behind Hunter's.

Temperance shook her head. She had come to love Bree like a sister, but sometimes didn't know just what was going on in that girl's head. She turned back toward the house and saw Aunt Ginny standing on the front porch. At first she felt a small wave of panic begin to rise, but then realized Bree had told her she didn't have to lie. She walked toward the house and climbed the steps to the porch.

Temperance said, "I told her we needed her help, but she told me you and I would have to handle things ourselves."

Ginny was looking off toward Bree, who was already tiny in the distance.

Temperance said, "She said she's going off to town, and won't be back tonight. I declare, I sometimes have no idea what she's thinking."

Ginny said, "I do. She's being her father's daughter."

Emily Harding, or more properly Emily *Carter,* stepped into the cabin to find Carter buckling on his gunbelt. The one Jack McCabe had taken from the outlaws, back on the trail.

"Carter," she said, "what are you doing?"

He said, "Going into town."

"What on Earth for? You know what's going on there?"

Abel and Age Brewster had just come by on their way home from town, and had told them all about it.

"I can't let that boy stand against those men alone."

"Carter."

He pulled the pistol and checked the loads, and as he slapped the pistol back into the holster, Nina stepped in.

She said, "Father, what's going on?"

Emily said, "Your father is going into town,

to help Jack McCabe face down those outlaws."

"Father? No. You can't."

He nodded. "I have to. I can't let him face
them men alone. Just him and that city
slicker."

Emily said, "One minute you hate that boy,
and the next you're willing to do this?"

"I never hated him." Carter grabbed his
floppy, wide-brimmed hat. "I just didn't want
Nina to build a life with a man like that."

He looked at Nina. "But maybe I was
wrong. That man's the same kind of man I
am, and I did okay by you and your mother."

Nina was standing wide-eyed. She couldn't
speak. She couldn't even breathe.

Emily stepped in front of her husband.
"Carter, you could get yourself killed."

He said, "Part of bein' the kind of man him
and me are."

He stepped around her, then stopped and
gave his daughter a peck on the cheek, and
then was out the door.

Jeb Arthur had a wagon hitched. Flossy was
already sitting in back.

"Jeb," Jack said, "I want you to take the
women out to the ranch. And stay there
yourself until this is over."

Jeb nodded.

Jessica stood beside the wagon, looking first
to Jack and then to Darby.

She said to Darby, "I don't want to go."

He said, "You have to."

"Then, come with me. You don't have to stand here and face these men."

He nodded. "Don't you see? I have to, if I'm going to be the kind of man who's worthy of being by your side."

"That's nonsense. You'll get yourself killed."

"No, it's not nonsense. Jack explained it to me a couple different times over the years. It all seemed fun, hearing this talk of western bravado. But now I think I understand it. In a land like this, a man has to stand as a man."

"Darby . . ."

She had tears forming, and so he pulled her in for a hug. He said, "When it's over, I'll come out and get you."

He then helped her up onto the wagon seat, and old Jeb gave the reins a little snap and the team started forward.

"Darby," Jack said, "just when I thought I knew you, you pull another surprise on me."

"I'm wearing this tin star," he said. "I've got to prove I'm worthy."

Jack gave a slap to his friend's shoulder, and they headed back to the jail. The way the livery was positioned, they were in view of Hunter's, and Jack saw a rider reining up in front of the building. It was Bree.

He said, "What in the world is she doing here?"

Jack and Darby walked over as she was pulling the Winchester from the saddle.

She said, "I was going to have old Jeb take care of my horse, but I guess I'll have to do it myself."

"Bree," Jack said.

"Reporting for duty as your deputy."

"Bree, you can't be here. It's going to be dangerous."

"Looks to me like you need all the help you can get."

"But you're a girl."

That was an argument that he knew carried little water out here on the frontier, and he knew he had lost as soon as he said it.

"Yeah?" She held up the rifle. "Well I'm a better shot than most any man with this. Better than you."

Darby looked to his friend. "Have you ever won an argument with her?"

She said, "No. And he's not going to now."

Jack said, "How can I ever face Pa if I let anything happen to you?"

"I'm Pa's daughter. As much as you're his son."

"Bree, you don't know these kind of men. What they're like. What they'll do if they get hold of you."

"They're not going to get hold of me. If we lose this, I'll save my last bullet for myself."

"Bree . . ."

"You know about the cellar we keep under the kitchen floor. It's where Aunt Ginny and

I hid last summer when the raiders attacked the ranch. There's a gun there, and Pa said to make sure they didn't take Aunt Ginny or me alive. It's no different now."

"Bree, I appreciate you wanting to help. Really, I do. But I can't allow this."

He had been so focused on Bree that he hadn't heard the horse walking up behind him. But he heard the deep foghorn voice that belonged to Harlan Carter, "If her daddy taught her to use that rifle, and she's as good as she says she is, I don't see how you've got a choice."

Jack turned to see Carter sitting tall in the saddle, a pistol at his side, a floppy hat pulled down over his temples.

Carter said, "I'll be here, too. You're gonna need all the guns you can get. And I've seen more'n one woman who could hold her own when the bullets start flyin'."

They heard the sound of a wagon clunking its way along the rough road into town. It was Hunter. He had to return from the ranch taking the wagon road through the pass, and was only now arriving. And they could see Henry Freeman on foot, walking toward them, a rifle in one hand.

He said, "Where I'm from, we had men like the ones you're getting ready to fight. They wore white sheets, but they weren't much different. I stood against them then, and I'll do it now."

Jack said, "Where are your wife and daughter, and Granny?"

"I sent them into the valley, to your ranch. Just in case those jackals decide to hit my little cabin on their way into town."

"All right, boss," Darby said to Jack. "You've got yourself a team. What did you say it's called? A posse?"

"Yep," Carter said, swinging out of the saddle. "That's what we are. Never thought I'd be on this side of one, though."

"A posse, then. All right, boss. Let's try to figure the best place to position everybody."

Bree said, "One of us should be at the jail. That's the first place they'll head for, I would think."

Jack nodded. "But they won't find White-Eye there."

All eyes were now on him.

"I have some ideas. Let's talk."

48

Walker and his men came riding in. They slowed their horses to a walk when they came within sight of the buildings. They pulled up side-by-side, and approached the log cabin that served as the marshal's office.

There were now seven of them. To Walker's right was the gambler. He went by the name Eb Markle. His black jacket was tattered and his checkered vest was streaked with dirt. He wore a short-brimmed hat that was dusty and becoming tattered, and holstered at his belt was a revolver.

The two brothers were there, also. The Volmer boys. Two-bit outlaws who had joined Walker a few weeks ago. One was tall and wore a hat and jacket that might have been brown once, but campfire smoke and dirt and ground-in dust had turned them a sort of dark gray. He had a long face and scraggly whiskers, and his brother looked about the same but was a little shorter.

There was also a man with two guns holstered at his belt and turned backward for a crossdraw. His name was Lucas Jordan, a sometimes horse thief and sometimes cattle rustler but who was good with a gun and wanted to ride along to see Johnny McCabe beaten. Walker knew of the man's reputation. Also a pair of cattle rustlers they had sprung from a jail in a small town a day's ride south of Bozeman. The town was barely a crossroads, but they had a jail. Now the marshal there was dead, and the two rustlers rode with Walker.

They reined up in front of the jail.

Walker called out, "McCabe!"

There was no reply. Walker called out again.

"Hey, Walker," Markle said. He was looking off toward the other buildings. Walker followed his gaze.

From here, you could get a better view of Hunter's and the hotel, and beyond them the livery and the church. Standing in front of Hunter's was Jack McCabe, a rifle in his hands. And beyond him, at the barn, or rather dangling from a timber above the hayloft, was White-Eye.

The timber had a block and tackle driven into it, and it was how hay was lifted up and to the loft. Only now, Walker was hanging from the rope, maybe fifteen feet above the ground. His hands were tied behind him, and the rope he was hanging from was wrapped around his chest.

"Now, that can't be too comfortable," one of the Volmer brothers said. The younger one, Clyde.

White-Eye was kicking in the air and began calling out, "Walker!"

"That son-of-a-bitch," Walker said. "I'm gonna really enjoy this."

They rode toward Jack and reined up a hundred feet in front of him.

Walker said, "I don't know what game you think you're playin', McCabe."

"I'm not playing any game, Walker. You and your men throw down your guns now and no one'll get hurt."

Walker had to crack a grin at that. "There's only one of you. You, and that city boy. But he don't count. There's seven of us."

Jack said, "First of all, my deputy is man enough that he nearly beat White-Eye to death. Second of all, he and I are not alone. I have a rifle trained on you right now. One of the best shots with a rifle you'll ever meet."

That morning, Jack had taken a look at the roof of the hotel. Hunter's idea of having someone there with a rifle wasn't a bad one, it was just that Darby was not the right man for the job. Bree was one of the best shots with a rifle Jack had ever seen, so he decided to put her to good use.

Jack said, "Any of you men go for your guns, and the first bullet will take your head off your shoulders, Walker."

Jack could tell Walker wasn't sure. He stared long and hard at Jack. Walker then said, "Where's your daddy? He's the one I have a beef with."

"He's not here. This is between us. This is my town, and you're under arrest. I'm going to hold you for Marshal Bodine."

"Well, then. Maybe what I'll do is just gut you right here on the street, and then just wait for your daddy." Walker glanced to his right. "Eb, go and cut down White-Eye."

Jack called out, "Darby!"

Darby stepped out of the barn, his shot gun to his shoulder and aimed at White-Eye.

"Terrible thing," Jack said, "to be hanging like that and just get riddled with buckshot if that shotgun goes off."

"No matter," Walker said. "He's just one man. I don't really need him, anyway."

"Loyalty doesn't run very deep with you, does it?"

Walker sat silently, staring at him. As though by doing so he could somehow bore a hole through him.

"I think you're bluffin'," Walker finally said. "You don't have nobody. The men from your ranch are off on a round-up. We done some checkin' to see what we'd be ridin' into."

"Drop your guns," Jack said. "Last chance."

Clyde, the younger of the two brothers, went for his gun. Whether Walker had given him some sort of signal, or the boy was just

658

too young and couldn't take the strain of this stand-off, Jack didn't know.

Bree fired from the roof, and Clyde was knocked out of the saddle, and then the others were drawing and so was Jack, and bullets were flying. Hunter stepped out of his saloon with a Winchester in his hands and Harlan Carter was on the porch of the hotel with a revolver drawn, and both were firing.

Horses reared and spun in the chaos. Jack's rifle was at his shoulder and he was firing and jacking the rifle and then firing again. A bullet tore through his sleeve but he didn't think it found any flesh.

The second brother fired toward the roof of the hotel, but then a rifle shot from the roof and a bullet from Carter both caught him and he was slammed out of the saddle.

A bullet caught Harlan in the leg and he went down. Jack's rifle was empty so he threw it aside and drew his revolver and began squeezing off shots.

Eb Markle rode away, straight toward the barn. Whether he was trying to free White-Eye or just trying to escape, Jack didn't know, but Darby was there and emptied one barrel of his shotgun into Markle's chest, and Markle fell from the saddle to land bouncing and flopping in the dirt, and the horse ran on without him.

The older of the Volmer brothers had felt a bullet tear into his shoulder, but he decided to get as far from this chaos as he could and see how badly he was hurt later. He tried to turn his horse but the animal was panicking because of the roar of gunfire, and it reared and he felt himself come free from the saddle and he landed in the dirt. He scrambled to his feet and ran toward the side of Hunter's saloon. Get beyond the line of fire as fast as he could.

He then found himself facing what looked to be an old Chinese man, who had a long stick in his hand.

"Get out of the way," the Volmer brother called out, raising his pistol.

But Chen brought the stick down on top of the man's hand and the hand went numb and his gun fell free, and then the stick came into contact with the side of his head, and his knees buckled and he went down.

Walker wheeled his horse, and it took off in a gallop toward the jail. Guns were fired at him, and bullets whizzed by him or tore up the dirt near him. Hitting a moving target is harder than it seems, especially in the heat of battle. Walker leaped from the saddle and ran for the front door.

And then all was quiet, except for the ringing in Jack's ears. A cloud of dust hung over the street, from the horses' hooves and gunsmoke. Four of Walker's men were down. A fifth, the gambler, was lying in the dirt over by the barn. White-Eye was still hanging and kicking from the barn.

Jack looked toward where one of the brothers had run off, beyond the side of Hunter's saloon, and saw Chen standing there.

Chen called out, "One of them is over here."

Hunter was running toward him. "You all right?"

Jack nodded. "You?"

"I'm fine. I think Carter's hit, though."

"Go tend to him, then. I'll go get Walker."

Jack started toward the jail, and Walker fired at him from a window. Jack ran, cutting to the side and the rear of the jail. Walker fired from the window, but also found hitting a moving target was harder than it seemed.

Jack stopped at the back of the jail, and quickly checked his loads. His pistol had one bullet left. He dumped the empties and thumbed in five fresh cartridges.

He stepped around the corner, gun ready, expecting Walker to have come out of the building and to be waiting for him, but Walker was not there.

He made his way along the wall, ducking under a window, and then to the front. Then he kicked in the door and charged in, finding Walker standing in the center of the floor, pistol aimed at him.

Walker pulled the trigger, but the hammer clicked harmlessly. Either the gun was empty, or a cartridge had misfired.

Jack had him. A gun fully loaded. Jack said, "Drop the gun."

Walker did so. But then he felt his McCabe temper rising. This man had caused him so much grief. He thought about the danger he had presented to the town, and the beating he had given Jessica.

Jack eased the hammer of his gun back to a resting position and holstered the gun. He then unbuckled his gunbelt and let it drop to the floor.

"It's your funeral," Walker said.

"No," Jack said. "I'm going to enjoy this."

Walker charged at him. But Jack remembered the teaching Chen had given him, and instead of meeting Walker's charge head on, he side-stepped and grabbed Walker by the jacket and wheeled him right into the wall face first.

Walker staggered a bit, then pushed away and swung a fist that caught Jack on the cheekbone. Jack, his knees bent and his legs spaced apart in a boxing stance, snapped a couple hard jabs at Walker that bloodied Walker's nose, then a right cross that drove Walker back into the wall.

Walker lunged at Jack and this time caught him and they both went down to the floor. They each clawed and wrestled. Walker was a little taller, but he didn't have the muscle Jack had put on boxing and rowing. Walker dug his fingers into Jack's face, catching an eye, and Jack pulled the hand away and twisted a thumb, the way Chen had shown him. Walker yelped and pulled away.

Both were then on their feet, circling each other. Walker pulled a knife from a sheath in the side of his boot. Jack grabbed the empty coffee kettle from the stove.

Walker lunged with the knife but Jack parried with the kettle. Jack then threw the kettle into Walker's face, and while Walker was ducking to one side to avoid it, Jack charged at him and grabbed Walker's knife hand by the wrist. He then drove his free elbow into Walker's face.

Blood was now streaming from Walker's nose, down over his chin and onto his shirt. He was a little staggered by the elbow that caught him in his already broken nose, and Jack took the moment to grab Walker's knife hand with both hands and bring the wrist down over his knee like he was breaking a stick. Walker's knife fell free.

Jack then planted his feet and began driving punches into Walker's midsection. Walker's knees buckled and he went down to the floor.

He began to get up, but the fight was gone from him, and he fell back to the floor.

Jack stood, heaving for breath. His shirt was torn open and blood was trickling from the corner of his mouth. Somewhere along the line he had bitten the inside of his cheek. A bruise was already forming on the side of his face from a punch he had taken, and he had some gouges on one cheekbone and on his brow from when Walker had tried to claw at his eyes. His fists were scraped and one knuckle was bleeding.

Bree was standing in the doorway, her rifle in her hands. "Did you enjoy that?"

He didn't realize she was there until she spoke. He nodded, a little surprised by his answer. "Yeah. I did."

"You gonna arrest him once he wakes up?"

"Why don't you do it?"

She grinned. "I seem to be doing a lot of that."

He reached to his mouth with the back of his fist to wipe away the blood. "Where's White-Eye?"

"Darby and Mister Chen are cutting him down from the hay loft. Darby let him fall the last five feet kind of hard, but I suppose White-Eye had it coming."

Jack nodded. "There is justice."

"But Mister Harding's in bad shape. He took a bullet in the leg, and Hunter's trying to stop the bleeding."

"All right. I'll be right over. I'll send Darby in to help you with this one."

Walker sat up, pushing himself as though the effort was great. He found himself staring into the muzzle of Bree's Winchester.

She said, "Oh, I don't this one's going to

give me any trouble. Not if he knows what's good for him."

Jack hurried to the hotel, which was where Carter had been standing when he went down. On the way, he passed Darby and Chen bringing a seriously battered White-Eye back to the jail. White-Eye's hands were still tied behind his back. They also had the one Chen had stopped with his wooden staff. The boy had regained consciousness but was walking a little unsteadily.

"You might want to hurry," Jack said. "Keep Walker safe from Bree. I want him alive for the territorial marshal."

He found Carter and Hunter where he expected to. On the boardwalk in front of the hotel. Hunter had torn away part of Carter's trouser leg. The bullet wound was a few inches below the knee. It was not a neat wound, but a large torn hole. Like someone had driven in an iron spike and then twisted. Hunter had wrapped a bandanna around it, trying to slow the bleeding.

"You look like hell," Carter said.

"Looks worse than it is," Jack said. "How're you doing?"

"Got in the way of a bullet."

"Not the smartest thing to do."

He shook his head. "No one ever accused me of being smart."

Hunter said, "Looks like the bone's broken. And I can't get the bleeding to slow down."

Jack said to Carter, "Give me your belt."

Carter unbuckled his belt and slipped it off. Jack then buckled the belt about Carter's leg just above the knee, pushed Hunter's rifle in between the belt and the leg, and began twisting until the belt was pulled as tightly as it could go.

Carter winced a bit on the last couple twists.

"Sorry about that," Jack said. "It's going to be a little uncomfortable. It's called a tourniquet. It'll stop the bleeding for the moment. Hold onto the rifle and hold this in place."

Jack said to Hunter, "Granny Tate's at the ranch. It'd be quicker if we can get Carter out there to her."

"I can travel," Carter said.

Hunter hitched the team to the wagon he had used the evening before to transport Miss Alisha and her girls, and he and Hunter lifted Carter to the wagon seat. Jack saddled a couple of horses, and he and Bree rode alongside the wagon. Darby, who had no illusions about being a horseman, jumped into the back of the wagon. Chen stayed behind, as they now had three men in the jail.

"Are you sure he can handle the jail all by himself?" Carter said.

"Oh, yeah," Darby said, from the back of the wagon.

They had to take the long way around,

which meant through the pass and down into the valley. Three miles. Hunter kept the horses to a steady pace. Carter rode with one hand holding the rifle in place, which in turn held the tourniquet tightly.

Carter glanced at Jack and said, "You look like hell, you know."

"Hey. I just had the fight of my life."

"You look worse even than when I was done with you."

"If I remember right, I beat you in that fight."

"I was drunk."

Jack had to give him that. "All right. Granted. But let's not have a rematch. I think I'd rather have you on my side."

"I guess we can call that a deal."

Jack looked at Bree and gave a shrug. Who would have thought, two months ago, that he and Harlan Carter would be exchanging good natured jabs at each other, or fighting alongside each other?

Jack said, "Your daughter won't speak to me."

"Yeah, I know. Partly my fault."

"I thought it was all your fault."

"You didn't have to fight me. That part was your fault. It just sort of reinforced all the warnings I was giving her about building a life with a gunhawk."

"That part was your fault, though."

He nodded. "Yeah. I take the blame for that."

"Could you talk to her?"

He looked at Jack. "Me? Hell, no. One thing I've learned these past few months is I can't talk to the ladies in my life. They talk to me. They don't let me talk to them."

Jack nodded. "Kind of like it is at my house."

"Hey!" Bree said.

Jack said to Carter, "See what I mean?"

Carter nodded. "Our lot in life."

They rode along further. Two ridges rose on either side of the trail. Long, gently rounded slopes covered with pine. Then the trail dropped down and past the ridges, and they were into the wide open grassy valley floor.

"Trouble with a gunfight," Carter said, "my ears are still ringing and all I smell is gun smoke."

From the back of the buckboard, Darby said, "They don't mention that in the dime novels. I've read a couple of them. All sorts of guns going off. But they don't mention how loud a gun battle actually is, or what it smells like. Or the screams of the men as they're dying."

Jack nodded. "That's because the writers are sitting behind a desk in some place like New York, rather than being out here where it's actually happening."

Carter said, "What's a dime novel?"

Jack explained it to him.

Carter said, "You gotta be kidding me."

They could see the ranch house ahead in the distance. Bree said, "I'll ride ahead and tell Granny we're coming."

She kicked her horse into a gallop and covered the distance within minutes.

When Hunter pulled the team to a halt by the front porch, Aunt Ginny was already there to give instructions.

She said, "Bring him in. Set him on the sofa in the parlor."

Fred was there to help Jack lift Carter off the wagon seat and up the steps.

Aunt Ginny said, "Someone should go and tell his family."

Hunter nodded. "This team needs a rest. I'll go saddle a horse and ride down to the farm."

Jessica hurried down the stairs and threw her arms around Darby and planted a long kiss on him.

She said, "I was so worried."

"I told you I would be all right."

Jack and Fred carried Carter into the house. Granny Tate said, "Set him down on the couch boys. Gentle. Be gentle."

Even so, Carter winced as they set him down. Aunt Ginny had already draped a sheet over it.

Hunter called Jack aside and said, "I've

seen men with those kinds of wounds. He's gonna lose that leg."

Jack nodded gravely. "Maybe."

Temperance was there. "What can I do?"

Granny said, "I'll let you know in a minute, child."

Bree had followed the men in, and was standing her rifle back in its place in the gun rack.

Aunt Ginny said, "You're okay?"

Bree nodded. Aunt Ginny gave her a hug. She said, "You had me scared, child."

"I had to go."

"I know you did."

Granny Tate knelt by the sofa and was giving Carter's leg a thorough examination. Jack stood beside the sofa.

She said, "The bone's broken, all right. I think the bullet might have splintered."

Everyone seemed to be gathering about the sofa. Aunt Ginny said, "Come on, everyone. Let's give Granny some room to work."

Jack indicated with a nod of his head for Darby to follow him. Jack led him to the end table at the other side of the room and poured a couple glasses of whiskey.

He said, "It's not Kentucky whiskey, but right now, it'll do."

They each knocked it back.

Darby said, "I killed a man today, Jack."

Jack nodded. "How do you feel about that?"

He shrugged. "I don't know. Maybe I'm just kind of numb all over from the whole thing."

Jack went out to a horse trough and cleaned up a little from his fight with Walker. He washed off the blood, and dumped a hatfull of water down over his head. He then went up to his room and took a clean shirt from the closet.

When he came downstairs, he found Granny Tate with Aunt Ginny in the kitchen, getting a cup of tea. Bree was there, and Darby and Jessica.

Granny was saying, "The bullet broke the bone. It's a clean break, but the bullet is in at least two pieces, and I can't get to them without cutting him wide open. The worst thing is one of the pieces of lead nicked an artery. That kind of bleedin' won't stop on his own."

"What does that mean?" Bree said.

Aunt Ginny knew the answer, but she remained gravely silent and let Granny answer the question.

Granny said, "It means, child, his leg has to come off."

Bree brought a hand to her mouth.

Granny said, "The sooner the better. As soon as that tourniquet is let off, the bleedin's gonna start again. And if he keeps the tourniquet on much longer, he's gonna lose the leg anyway."

Darby looked to his friend. "Jack?"

Jack knew what he was thinking. One thing about his and Darby's friendship, they tended to talk shop a lot. They even read each other's text books. Jack had probably as good an understanding of law as was possible without actually attending law school, and Darby had a fairly thorough practical knowledge of medical procedures. And Jack knew the procedure Darby was thinking of.

"There's a doctor in New York," Jack said, "who's had good success with suturing arteries. Stitches, just like with a wound."

Ginny said, "Can such a thing be done?"

Jack nodded.

Granny said, "But that doctor's in New York. Don't do us a lot of good out here."

"I've seen it done," Jack said. "One of my professors took some of us to New York to see it done a few times."

"Can you do it?" Aunt Ginny asked.

Jack said, "I've only seen it done."

Granny said, "Might be his only hope."

"I say we ask him. It's his leg."

Granny nodded.

They went out to the parlor. Temperance was sitting with Carter.

Jack explained the situation to him. Carter said, "How sure are you that you can do this?"

"I'm not sure at all. I was only a medical

student. That's a far cry from being an actual doctor."

"So, if I understand this right, if you try to stitch this artery together and you fail, I lose my leg. If you don't try, then I still lose my leg."

Jack nodded. "I think that about sums it up."

"Then I think I want you to give it a try."

"Then let's get going now. The longer we keep that tourniquet on, the more damage that's going to happen to your leg." Jack looked to Granny. "I want you to be on hand."

She said, "Oh, I ain't gonna miss this for the world."

He said to Darby, "And I want you to assist. I've talked to you enough about it, and you've read the same text books I have."

Darby nodded.

By the time Hunter arrived with Emily and Nina Harding, Carter had already been rendered unconscious with some ether Granny kept on hand, and surgery had commenced. Most everyone had been kicked out of the house. Aunt Ginny and Temperance were waiting in the kitchen, in case they were needed.

Bree explained the situation to Emily and Nina.

Nina said, with little alarm in her voice, "Jack's operating on Father?"

Bree nodded. "It'll be all right. I'd put my money on Jack any day. After all, he's a McCabe."

Kerosene lamps were standing on the coffee table and floor lamps had been dragged over. Jack and Darby had both washed their hands in whiskey.

"Once we're done," Jack said, "presuming this works, we're going to have to wash that wound out with whiskey. Maybe we can put Pa's Scotch to good use. I'm not going to go through all of this just to see the old bastard die of infection."

He looked to Granny and said, "Pardon my language."

"Don't 'pologize to me. We all know about the grief he's caused you. News travels around here. You can't sneeze on one side of the valley without the folks at the other end knowing about it before you put the handkerchief away."

Jack pried the wound open using a couple butter knives from the kitchen. He found the bone. He pushed muscle aside. He saw a fragment of bullet and with a pair of tweezers pulled it out. He then found the artery.

Jack said, "That's the posterior tibial artery."

He could see some torn material at the side of it.

"Darby," he said, "let off on that tourniquet

just a bit. I want to see it bleed. It'll show me where the rip is."

Darby did. The arteries immediately under the tourniquet were a bit flattened, but within a few seconds they began to inflate with blood. Jack watched as the posterior tibial artery filled with blood and began to leak out through the tear at the side.

"It's not a very big tear," he said. "This could be doable."

Granny said, "Have you ever worked with stitches before?"

He nodded. "Only on scrapes and cuts and such. This will be the first time working with something like this. I'll have to move slowly."

"You take your time, child."

He said, "All right, Darby. Tighten that tourniquet again."

Granny then dabbed at some loose blood with a towel, cleaning out the wound.

Jack said, "Let's try the needle and thread. And let's hope my hand is steady."

They waited outside. The Brewsters and the Fords. Hunter was there, and Fred. And Nina and her mother. They all milled about, chatting. And waiting. Some had a mug of coffee or a cup of tea prepared by Aunt Ginny and the girls.

Emily was talking with Mildred Brewster and Elizabeth Ford. Jessica was standing with them. But Ginny noticed Nina was by herself, standing over by the corral. Ginny walked over.

The breeze was picking up, but it was unusually warm for this time of year. The sky was mostly clear, and the light of a three-quarter moon was giving the grass a silvery shine.

"How are you doing?" Ginny said.

Nina shrugged her shoulders. "I don't know. My father is in there, and might lose his leg. I feel I should be afraid. I should be crying my eyes out. And yet I stand here, staring off at the sky. I guess I just sort of feel kind of numb all over."

Ginny nodded. "It's a natural reaction to times like this. Last summer, at about this time, Jack's father was lying upstairs in even worse shape than your father's in now. We didn't know if he was going to live or die. And I felt exactly the way you describe. Numb."

"Why did Father have to do that? Why did he have to go into town?"

"Because of who he is. And because of what he is."

Nina looked at her curiously.

Ginny said, "He's a man of the gun. And he's a man of honor. That combination can be a maddening one, and a frightening one, because when trouble happens, they will always take up the gun to defend people. To defend justice. To defend their home or their town. It's what they do. Just like with Jack. He could have simply turned the outlaw in his jail over to the others, and possibly saved the town and prevented violence. But he couldn't do that. He had to stand against those outlaws, because that's what men like Jack do. And men like your father.

"I will admit, I was wrong about your father. When I first met him, I thought he was trouble. He's a complicated man and it takes some time to understand him, apparently. But I'm coming to think he's a good man."

"But they embrace violence. They bring violence onto themselves. In my father's case, he rode out to meet it. And it wasn't even his fight."

Ginny drew a long breath. How to explain this? "The McCabes are men of the gun. It's probably always been that way with them. Johnny's great-grandfather, who Johnny is named after, was a trailblazer and a scout who pioneered the mountains of Pennsylvania, back when that part of the world was still a frontier. He fought Indians, and he fought alongside Indians. As the story goes, when a girl about your age from one of the first settlements in that area was captured by a band of Indian warriors from an enemy tribe, it was Johnny's great-grandfather who chased after her and brought her home safely."

Nina found herself saying, "Like Jack did with me. Coming to rescue me. It wasn't even something he had to consider. There was simply no question that he was going to come for me."

"That's because he's a McCabe."

"What happened to the girl? The one captured by Indians?"

"Johnny's great-grandfather — John McCabe — married her. They settled in a remote stretch of the Pennsylvania mountains and produced sons. And here the family is now, his descendants, living not much differently than the first John McCabe.

"I don't know if there were McCabes back in the age of knights and chivalry, but if there were, you could almost bet the farm they were carrying swords and were ready to defend the family, or the town, or the kingdom. Such is their way. They fight, and they fight well. But they never conquer. Such is the stuff of legend, and you're in the presence of these men now. Even Bree has this running in her blood, which is why I didn't try to stop her when she rode out to help look for you when you were lost in the mountains. And apparently your father isn't much different.

"This land is place for people like that. Civilization would be too tame for someone like Jack. It would also hem him in too much. Choke the spirit out of him. I am so amazed at myself that I didn't see this in him sooner. They are drawn to open land like this, and the women they marry must be here with them. Like with the original John McCabe, and the woman he married."

"But don't these men attract violence? Didn't this Two-Finger Walker come to town because of Jack and his father? Jack's presence on the trail from Cheyenne is why those men were following us, and why they captured me."

"Did you ever hear the story of how Johnny's father died? Jack's grandfather?"

Nina shook her head.

Ginny let her gaze trail off toward the ridges. They were visible in the moonlight. She said, "He was shot by a man who had robbed a store. But he wasn't shot in Montana or Texas or New Mexico Territory. He was shot outside of a small farming town in central Pennsylvania."

This made Nina's eyes widen a little.

"Johnny had just returned home from spending a couple of years out west with the Texas Rangers. His two brothers had come home too, and they were with their father cutting firewood. The robber simply happened upon them and fired one shot that caught their father and killed him. You see, violence is not relegated to any one specific area. The west, or anywhere else. It's something that has dogged the human race from the very beginning and isn't showing any signs of letting up soon. Living back east doesn't protect you from it. Staying away from men like Jack McCabe won't keep away the violence.

"You came with your family willingly to the west. And now here you are. And here Jack is. The man who, without a second thought, rode out into the night to save you from those outlaws. And with a bullet wound in his shoulder. And then he stood fearlessly to defend the town against Walker and those outlaws.

"If I may be so bold, who else would you rather be the father of your children?"

Ginny looked at her. Nina looked back. Ginny didn't quite fix her with the Gaze, but she did look firmly. And the girl looked firmly back, and didn't flinch.

Ginny nodded. The girl would do. She had passed muster. The only question was, would she see the point Ginny was trying to make?

The kitchen door opened. All eyes were suddenly on the doorway, as Darby Yates stepped out. From the corral, Ginny and Nina could see Emily rushing over followed by everyone else to hear the news.

"Come, child," Ginny said to Nina, reaching a hand out to her.

Nina took the hand, and they started for the house.

■ ■ ■ ■

It was three hours later when Carter woke up. Jack was sitting on the coffee table, a glass of Kentucky whiskey in his hand. What little was left from the bottle he and Darby had mostly emptied the night Darby arrived in town.

"Oh, my head hurts," Carter said.

"It's a side effect of the ether. We had to keep gassing you to keep you from waking up."

"My leg?"

Jack said, "Can you feel your foot?"

Carter thought about that. He wiggled his toes. "Yeah. I guess I can."

"Things went quite well, considering. The shin bone's broken, and it's going to be splinted up and you won't be doing a lot of work around the house. I suppose I could help out, as long as you don't aggravate me too much."

"No promises there."

"The tear in the artery wasn't very big. I got it sewn back together with two stitches. We found both fragments of the bullet. All in all, I'd say you were quite lucky."

"What about infection?" Carter shifted a bit on the sofa and winced with the effort.

"Hey, don't move around. You have to lie still for a while. Once we're sure the stitches

681

are going to hold, then Granny Tate is going to splint your leg up good and solid. But until then, you have to lie still. And I don't think you have to worry about infection. We washed that wound out really thoroughly with whiskey. The best infection prevention I've ever seen."

He nodded. "I remember on the trail."

"I wanted to wait until you woke up to do it, but Granny thought it best not to wait."

"I bet you did."

Jack shook his head, and took a sip of whiskey, and found himself grinning.

"What?" Carter said.

"I was just realizing something. Aunt Ginny said no education is wasted. I think I see her point, now. If I hadn't spent those years back east in school, you wouldn't have your leg now."

"Women have this way of being right all the time."

"They do seem to, don't they?"

"Confounding habit."

Jack chuckled and took another sip of whiskey.

Carter said, "What about my wife? And Nina? Where are they?"

"They're outside. Darby gave 'em the news, and there was lots of hugging. They've already been in here to see you, but you were too busy being unconscious to notice."

"I can be that way sometimes."

"Emily is going to stay the night. Bree's headed back to your farm with Nina. Bree's going to stay with her."

"That's quite a sister you have."

"Yeah. But don't tell her that. She'd be insufferable."

Carter chuckled. "Did Nina talk to you?"

"Just enough to say thank you. That's about all."

He shook his head. "She'll come around. I just hope it's before you're all gray haired."

49

September rolled into October and autumn settled into the mountains. Each morning now greeted Jack with a layer of silvery frost. The oaks and maples that stood in places along the valley floor, such as around the small lake, had burst into reds and yellows, and then dropped their leaves and now stood skeletal and gray.

Jack pulled on his jacket and stepped from his office to head over to Hunter's.

The morning sky was gray and overcast, with a wind coming down from the mountains. Felt like snow, Jack thought.

He glanced to a small hill that rose behind the hotel. On that hill now stood a cabin, and smoke was rising from a stone chimney. Jessica and Darby were awake, he figured.

They had been married three weeks earlier. They had told Jack she was with child, but he doubted anyone other than he and Granny Tate knew. As far as the rest of the community would be aware, they had conceived almost directly after their marriage and the child was Darby's.

"Besides," Darby said. "In a very real way, I am the father. It's not who begats you, it's who raises you. And I'm gonna raise this child like it was mine."

Jack couldn't have put it better himself.

He figured within a short while Darby would make his way down the hill to join him at Hunter's for breakfast. Darby still wore a tin star on his shirt and was taking his duties seriously as a deputy marshal. This little community had seemed to awaken something inside him, and he had a peace within that Jack had never seen in him before. He was sure Jessica had something to do with it, too.

Darby had taken a stage down to Bozeman and the bank there, and returned with a pocket full of cash. He not only furnished his and Jessica's cabin comfortably, but he bought a second desk for the jail and a good rifle rack, and three more rifles from Franklin's to fill the rack with. He also paid for a new iron stove, and the old one was hauled out to stand beside the office. *That way,* Darby said, *if we want coffee during the summer, we light up the stove outside so we don't have to heat up the office.*

The jail cell in back of their little marshal's office was now empty. A couple of weeks ago, Dan Bodine had ridden in with a couple of deputies to pick up the prisoners.

Walker said to Jack, "You ain't heard the last of me. That I promise."

Dan Bodine said, "I wouldn't worry about Two-Finger Walker. He's wanted in three states and two territories. If one doesn't hang him, the other will."

As Jack walked toward Hunter's, he took a glance about the town. Smoke was drifting from the stove pipe in the side of Franklin's store, and likewise at the hotel.

This little town was where Jack belonged, he knew. He was home. For the first time in many years, he felt like he truly had a place in the world.

Two horses were tethered in front of Hunter's and both bore the Circle M brand. Josh and Dusty, he figured. They rode into town a couple of times a week now for coffee with him and Hunter and Darby. And at least once a week Jack would ride out to the ranch for coffee with them.

As he stepped up on the boardwalk, he heard the sound of a wagon approaching, from the direction of town that meant it was coming from down in the valley.

It was Carter and Nina. His leg was wrapped in a heavy looking wooden splint, but he had kept the leg. He was in a coat and his floppy hat was pulled down tight, and Nina was in a coat and scarf. On the seat between Carter and Nina was a pair of wooden crutches, the ones she had used the summer before when she had sprained her ankle.

Carter turned the team toward Jack and reined it in beside him.

"Howdy, Marshal," he said. "Turnin' off kind of cold this mornin'."

Jack nodded. "Tends to do that this time of year." Jack touched the brim of his hat and said, "Nina."

"Jack," she said.

To Carter, Jack said, "How's the leg?"

"Still there. In no small part due to you."

Jack shrugged. "Well, it's not like I had anything else to do that day."

"Yeah, and I was just layin' around on your sofa, in everyone's way."

Nina gave a sharp huff, and held out both hands in a stopping motion. "Will you two just stop it? How can you joke about a thing like that?"

Carter said, "We are what we are, Sweetie."

She shook her head but said nothing.

He said, "I'm here to see Granny Tate. She wants to check the circulation in my foot. And I'm here to pick up some supplies at Franklin's. I talked Nina into coming with me."

Jack said, "It's mighty good to see you again, Nina."

Carter said, a little impatiently, "Will you get down from this wagon and go talk to the boy?"

"Father, we have to get you to Granny Tate's."

"I can get there myself. I'm a big boy. Been gettin' myself around for a long time."

"Will you at least listen to reason?"

"Never have. Don't see the point in doin' so now. Get down from the wagon."

She shook her head with resignation and climbed down. Jack offered his hand which she took.

Carter turned the team and headed off toward the Freemans' cabin.

Jack said, "Was it entirely his idea to come along?"

"Mostly." She said. "Well, not really. I came along partly to keep him out of trouble."

"A hard thing to do."

"Tell me about it. But I have to confess, I was hoping I might see you."

He said, "Would you like to take a walk with me?"

She looked at him and smiled. "I think I'd like that very much."

ABOUT THE AUTHOR

Brad Dennison was born in rural New England and grew up reading Louis L'Amour, Luke Short, A.B. Guthrie, Jr., and even Edgar Rice Burroughs. Brad fell in love with the Old West at a very young age. It began with movies and old TV series like *Gunsmoke* and *Bonanza,* and later expanded to western novels. This led to his study of western history. The pioneers, the Indians, the cattlemen, the gunfighters. His interest in history is not so much about wars and great leaders, but the people who lived on the land. And that's what he writes about. The people and what it might have felt like to be there. His first western, *The Long Trail,* was recently released in large-print paperback by Wheeler Publishing. He is a member of the Western Writers of America.

The employees of Thorndike Press hope you have enjoyed this Large Print book. All our Thorndike, Wheeler, and Kennebec Large Print titles are designed for easy reading, and all our books are made to last. Other Thorndike Press Large Print books are available at your library, through selected bookstores, or directly from us.

For information about titles, please call:
(800) 223-1244

or visit our Web site at:

http://gale.cengage.com/thorndike

To share your comments, please write:

Publisher
Thorndike Press
10 Water St., Suite 310
Waterville, ME 04901

MAY   2016